NB
–
Newton
is not ourfu[illegible]
character

D1375113

GANGLAND SOHO

– Marlborough Street
court 1795

– Judge sportingly refused
to convict girl for
soliciting unless she
had contraceptives
in her handbag.

Clubs began in 1912 p43

50-50 club. Gargoyle
in 1925.

Blue Film ref p46

Monkey Benneworth – jaw
broken ± 1926 but a
serious "name"

Also by James Morton

Conned: Scams, Frauds and Swindles

Lola Montez

Gangland

Gangland Bosses

East End Gangland

Caravan Club 6 WKS 500 members
Jack Rudolph Neave
IRON Foot Jack P56

GANGLAND SOHO

P57 Fish & chips

JAMES MORTON

P58 Gangs of 50 pickpockets
working football
crowds

P59 → Sabini Bros
wrecking slot machines
thus... protection merchants
There was plenty of work
for Tomas, racecourse P61
work,
Dog track,
WW1 — White City

PIATKUS

Demanding money with
menaces from bookies

PIATKUS

First published in Great Britain in 2008 by Piatkus Books
This paperback edition published in 2008 by Piatkus Books

Copyright © 2008 by James Morton

The moral right of the author has been asserted

All rights reserved
No part of this publication may be reproduced, stored in a retrieval system, or transmitted in any form or by any means, without the prior permission in writing of the publisher, nor be otherwise circulated in any form of binding or cover other than that in which it is published and without a similar condition including this condition being imposed on the subsequent purchaser

A CIP catalogue record for this book
is available from the British Library

ISBN 978-0-7499-2881-0

Typeset in Scala by
Action Publishing Technology Ltd, Gloucester
Printed and bound in Great Britain by
CPI Mackays, Chatham ME5 8TD

Papers used by Piatkus are natural, renewable and recyclable products made from wood grown in sustainable forests and certified in accordance with the rules of the Forest Stewardship Council.

Piatkus Books
An imprint of
Little, Brown Book Group
100 Victoria Embankment
London EC4Y 0DY

An Hachette Livre UK Company
www.hachettelivre.co.uk

www.piatkus.co.uk

P 70 One eared
Alfred Skurry

For Dock Bateson, with love

For about 10 years... up to 1926 the French actually controlled prostitution in London
p 79

Giuseppe Messina p 79
Chain of Brothels in Alexandria

The "badger game" p 82

p 84 10 strong gang of blackmailers
& 40 strong gang of young men
(groomed & kitted out) placed in
restaurants, hotels, bars to
solicit wealthy looking me.
"Brother" or priest then
asks for £500 to send
spoiled son to OZ

P90 Admitting what sin she could avoid & do more

Ellison was hosted as the best / better than Detectives Jack Slipper + Nipper Read together p 117

Background to Soho / London prostitution p 123
Messinas £10 000 / week on prostitutes

60's & 70's Clubs in London spring up like mushrooms p 153/4
Good names

[illegible] p158

Telegraph 3/12/08 - says "Re-offending rate (re-incarceration rate) Nationally in UK is 67%"

Contents

p165 1960s clubland

"1000 purple hearts could be sold in 30 mins"

p167 Krays ...

p169 Gambling legalised 1960s

Acknowledgements

My thanks are due to Jeremy Beadle, J.P. Bean, Bill Bridges, Alan Brooke, Paul Daniel, Louis and Elizabeth Diamond, Ronnie and Kitty Diamond, Denise Dwyer, Frank Fraser, Adrian Gatton, Hazel and Tony Gee, Jonathan Goodman, Jeffrey and Shirley Gordon, Mike Hallinan, Dea Langmead, Loretta Lay, Barbara Levy, Paul Lincoln, Brian McDonald, who generously shared with me his research on the gangs of the 1900s, Ian Muir, Gerry Parker, Anita Price, Nipper and Pat Read, John Rigby, Neil Rose, Heather Shore, Matthew Spicer and Edda Tasiemka, as well as many others on both sides of the fence who prefer not to be named. My thanks are also due to the staff of the British Library, the Newspaper Library at Colindale and the National Archives at Kew.

As is always the case, the book could not have even been begun and certainly not finished without the continued support and help of Dock Bateson.

Introduction

The first court in which I ever appeared was Marlborough Street Magistrates' Court, defending a young woman who had looted the perfume department of John Lewis. I need not have bothered. It was a waste of her money. In the 1960s £25 was the tariff for a first offence of shoplifting, whether the offender was represented or not.

As the years went on a number of my clients either lived or, more often, had clubs in Soho and fell foul of the licensing laws, which they mostly simply ignored. As a result, I appeared on a regular basis in front of the formidable magistrates who sat there.

In my earliest days, the incumbents were the ex-naval officer Leo Gradwell and Edward Robey, the barrister son of the great comedian George. They shared a room above their respective courts and did not get on well. It was said that the second to leave the room turned the photograph of the other's wife and children to the wall. Of them Frank Milton, later the chief magistrate, paraphrased a little rhyme, converting it to:

Oh to live in Soho
The land of the ponce and the sod,
Where Robey speaks only to Gradwell
And Gradwell speaks only to God.

In those days cases of indecency between men in the various Soho cottages were not treated with any sympathy. In his upper-class drawl, John Maude, who later sat at the Old Bailey, asked a police constable, who had spread-eagled himself on the roof of a lavatory the better to keep observation on what went on in the cubicles below, 'Officer, are you happy in your work?' On another occasion a magistrate hearing an indecency case I was defending – and he must have heard a couple a day, every day of the year – was told that when the policeman had flashed his torch he had seen Smith with Jones's penis in his mouth. The magistrate pushed back his chair and exclaimed, 'God, how disgusting!' It was easy to see it was not going to be one of my more successful days.

He was not the Marlborough Street magistrate who had a penchant for the ladies who appeared before him. This one took rooms in what might politely, if inaccurately, be called an hotel off Shaftesbury Avenue and persuaded his wife that when he was sitting he had to remain within the boundaries of his jurisdiction 24 hours a day.

It was yet another who was the stipendiary in a case in which I appeared for a youth. His mother came to court with her erring child and I told her who was sitting. 'He chucked my case last week,' she said. 'What for?' I asked adding, 'He's not a bad old stick.' 'Tomming,' she replied, adding in her turn, 'Nah, he's a punter.' He generously would refuse to convict a girl of soliciting unless contraceptives were found in her handbag.

In the 1980s, tiring of life as a defence lawyer, I decided to apply to become a stipendiary myself. My problem was that I had to supply references, preferably from a High Court or at least an Old Bailey judge or two. Instead of them the only person of any fame I could manage was an old TV wrestler and Soho frequenter for whom I once acted in a bastardy case. 'Jim,' he'd said at the time, 'I wouldn't mind having indigestion if I'd bit the apple.' He clearly wouldn't do and it was only when I saw the 'punter-stipe' leaving the Venus Rooms, a striptease club in Old Compton Street, that, so to speak, I seized the afternoon to ask for a reference. That it came to nothing is another link in the long chain of events leading to this book.

Marlborough Street court first opened for business in 1795 and closed its doors to become a grand hotel in 2002. Its jurisdiction was

Soho and part of the West End. Soho is said to be named after the hunting call 'so-hoe!' and people settled there after the Great Fire of London had moved thousands from the City. Although its boundaries are generally regarded as Oxford Street to the north, Coventry Street and Leicester Square to the south, Regent Street to the west and Charing Cross Road to the east. North Soho was what has become Fitzrovia. And so my boundaries have extended to the Euston Road in the north, Tottenham Court Road in the east and Great Portland Street in the west. Of course the denizens did not stay within the Square Mile so to speak. Often they flitted across the Charing Cross Road or into Regent Street and from time to time even further afield. I have followed them on some of their missions.

While the Marlborough Street court may never have seen the Krays in its dock, over the years there were some famous names, including Oscar Wilde and Mick Jagger, through its doors. As always, profit is the keyword in a book on the underworld and so many of the more celebrated domestic murderers who graced the court can barely have a mention. Nevertheless, there are some who deserve recognition.

In 1725 Catherine Hayes was burned at the stake for the murder of her husband John, who had a chandlery business on Tottenham Court Road and Tyburn Road, which would become Oxford Street. She was expecting to receive £1,500 on his death and persuaded Billings, her son by a previous lover, and a lodger to help her. After the unfortunate John Hayes had been butchered while drunk, his head was dumped in the Thames. Once it washed up, neighbours identified him and on 9 May 1726 Catherine went to Tyburn, drawn on a sledge where, unfortunately, the hangman Richard Arnet failed to strangle her before the flames spread and she was roasted alive. Thackeray's story *Catherine* is based on her career.

In 1761, the year when the madam Charlotte Hayes opened her 'nunnery' in Marlborough Street, one of the more celebrated murders of the eighteenth century took place in Leicester Square. In March that year the Swiss miniaturist painter, Theodore Gardelle, fell in love with his comely landlady Anne King. His passion was unrequited and early one morning he tried to rape her. She beat him off and was in the process of giving him a sound thrashing when he picked up a poker and knocked her to the ground. He believed he had killed her and, thinking the best thing would be to dispose of the body, decided to dismember it. There were no other lodgers and he sacked the maidservant before he began his work, which took him five days. Some parts were burned, some hidden in the attic or outhouses and some put in the outside privy. The neighbours became suspicious of the smell and smoke and called the constables. He was hanged by Thomas Turlis on 4 April that year on the corner of Panton Street and Haymarket.

On Christmas Day 1836, Hannah Brown of 45 Riding House Street became the victim of her potential husband, James Greenacre, who had a shop in what is now between 19 and 20 Tottenham Court Road and was trying to perfect an early form of washing machine. She disappeared after visiting a friend in Windmill Street. Greenacre killed her because he discovered she did not have the fortune he was expecting to acquire on the marriage.

On 30 September 1843, a German, Peter Keim, was stabbed to death in Marshall Street by a one-time friend, Wilhelm Steltynor, who seems to have tried to castrate him. The inquest jury sitting at the York Minster, Dean Street, was told that, when questioned by a constable, Steltynor had said somewhat enigmatically, 'I meant to run it into Mr Keim and had it not been for the leather inside of his trousers, I should have ripped it all out.' He was sentenced to death but he was reprieved after the German ambassador intervened.

One of the most famous of Soho murders occurred in late October 1917. On 2 November the torso and arms of a woman were found wrapped in a meat sack and sheet in Regent Square, Bloomsbury. Nearby in a separate parcel were her legs. The dead woman, 32 year old Émilienne Gérard, was traced through a laundry mark on the sheet to 50 Munster Square near Regent's Park. On the mantelpiece was a portrait of a Soho butcher, Louis Voisin, and in the flat was a £50 IOU. When he was seen by Detective Inspector Wensley, Voisin was asked to write down 'Bloody Belgium' and he spelled it 'Blodie Belgian', exactly the spelling on a piece of paper found with the torso.

In the basement of 101 Charlotte Street, where Voisin lived, was a cask in which Émilienne's hands and head were found. His explanation was that she had told him she was going to France and asked him to look after her cat. When he went round he found her head and hands on a table and panicked. However, from the amount of blood in the cellar at Charlotte Street it was clear she had been killed there. She had been beaten about the head and there were signs of strangulation.

The prosecution's version of events was that Voisin had two mistresses and they met for the first time when Émilienne came uninvited to shelter from an air raid. Voisin was in bed with Berthe Roche; the women fought and Émilienne was struck a number of blows to the head.

Although it was likely that it was Berthe who hit Émilienne – Voisin was far too strong to have done so little damage to her skull – he took the full blame at the trial. Instead of waiting for an interpreter, Mr Justice Darling passed the death sentence in French and Voisin was hanged on 2 March. Roche died two years into a seven-year sentence as an accessory after the fact.[1]

One of Soho's more entertaining murder cases was the 1936 killing of Douglas Bose by Douglas Burton. Bose had been living with, and treating badly, the one-time Augustus John model, Sylvia Gough, blackening her eye. When she appeared at their shared haunt, the Fitzroy Tavern, the 21-year-old Burton offered her the use of his flat. Later at a party he beat Bose to death with a hammer. His defence was that he had been driven insane by his unrequited love for another Fitzrovia habitué Betty May, known as Tiger Woman, who in her early life appeared in Paris cabarets. The defence succeeded. Old Bailey juries of the time never liked sending the middle-classes to the gallows, and Burton spent a relatively short time in a mental institution. One of the Tiger Woman's more popular numbers was 'The Raggle-Taggle Gypsies', which she later sang with enthusiasm and without a skirt in Wally's, a basement club in Fitzroy Street.

One unsolved nineteenth-century murder was definitely for profit. Robert Westwood, who invented and patented the eight-day watch, was not a fortunate man. In 1822 he had been tied to a bed and robbed by William Redding, who had previously been convicted of capital crimes and had been transported. Redding, who was thought to have been involved in the murder of Mary Donatty in Bedford Row the same year, was hanged.

Then on 7 June 1839, Westwood was attacked and killed in his rooms in Upper Rupert Street, which were set on fire. His throat was cut and some 80 watches valued at around £2,000 were missing. He was not a well-liked man. On one occasion when a sea captain returned a watch to him he snatched it from the man and stamped on it. On another he held a pistol to a customer's head. He had also made numerous appearances at Marlborough Street court charged with minor assaults. Consequently, there were a number of possible suspects for his murder. Indeed, on the inquest jury was a man who had worked for Westwood and was reputed to have quarrelled bitterly with him. However, when he said he would give £50 of his own money for the arrest of the criminal, any thought of his involvement was wiped away. One neighbour, Nicholas Carron, a paper hanger in the traditional rather than criminal sense of the word, fled to America shortly after the murder and disappeared without trace.[2]

On 6 December 1894 Marius Martin, a French-born night porter at the Café Royal in Regent Street, was found beaten to death in neighbouring Glasshouse Street. The motive may well have been robbery, but there was also the suggestion that he was deeply unpopular because he had been reporting other staff for taking home leftover food. No one was ever charged.

In the decade before the court closed, there was a great escape from the cells by a bank robber, David Martin. A transvestite, who rather gave the game away, signalling his modus operandi by robbing banks dressed as a woman, Martin was also an expert lock picker. Charged with shooting at a policeman, on Christmas Eve 1982 he escaped from the cells at Marlborough Street and was off. He was not recaptured until the following March, when he was caught in a tunnel at Belsize Park underground station. In the meantime, a television producer, Stephen Waldorf, who had no direct connection with Martin, was shot by police who mistook him for the fugitive. He survived. Martin later committed suicide in prison after a row about which television programme the inmates should watch.[3]

1

Early Whores and their Pimps

From the time of the arrest of a 'lewd woman' in Soho Fields for breach of the peace in 1641, Soho has become synonymous with sex. It was certainly its home when, in around 1750, the madam Jane Goadby is credited with introducing the luxurious French-style brothel to London. After a visit to Paris she opened a house in Berwick Street, where the girls were decked out in lace and silk and underwent a weekly medical examination. Goadby had a long run as a madam. In 1779 the *Nocturnal Revels* commented that she was still 'laying in good stocks of clean goods, warranted proof for the races and watering places during the coming summer'.

One of the girls in her establishment, Elizabeth Armistead, married the Whig leader Charles James Fox at the age of 45. She lived to be 91 and among her earlier lovers had been the Prince of Wales, later George IV.

In 1760 another Soho madam, Charlotte Hayes took up with an Irish con man Dennis O'Kelly, who later became a colonel of militia. Born in 1720, he came to England in 1744 and for a time worked as a sedan carrier and a billiards marker. Both he and Charlotte Hayes spent time in the Fleet debtors' prison and were released in 1760 on the death of George II. The next year she opened a protestant 'nunnery' in Great Marlborough Street. O'Kelly was now a racing man and it was through his turf connections that he introduced the Dukes of Richmond and Chandos to the house.

In 1770, with some of their money, O'Kelly bought a half share in the five-year-old racehorse Eclipse and then paid 1,750 guineas to buy the animal outright. It was a sound investment. The unbeaten Eclipse was never even really extended. He won over £25,000 and sired three Derby winners, two of which were owned by O'Kelly. His progeny earned an enormous £160,000. Eclipse was still covering 50 mares a year when he died in 1790.

Charlotte Hayes wasted much of the money she earned, and in 1770 and again in 1776 she was back in a debtors' prison. O'Kelly died a rich man in 1788 leaving her £400 a year and a parrot that could recite the 104th Psalm. It was not sufficient and she was yet again in the debtors' prison in 1798, after which she retired to Canons, a country estate in Edgware, where Eclipse had been buried eight years earlier.

Seventeen sixty-one was indeed a vintage year. It was then that the beautiful Italian-born Theresa de Cornelys, who had for a time been the lover of the great Italian adventurer Jacques Casanova – by whom she may have had a daughter – took a lease on Carlisle House in Soho Square. There, for the next 20 years, she gave a series of subscription balls, in reality little short of orgies; 12 balls and suppers were for the nobility and another 12 for the middle classes. Entrance was 2 guineas a head. There was also an annual fancy-dress ball. One of the regular attendees was the Belgian clockmaker Joseph Merlin, who also invented roller skates and wore them during one party when, apparently playing the violin, he lost control and slid the length of the floor crashing into Mrs C's expensive mirrors.[1]

In June 1763, when Casanova arrived from Paris bringing with him Cornelys' son Joseph by the dancer Pompeati, he was less than pleased to find that his former mistress had become too grand for him. He had been hoping to resume his position with her but instead was obliged to take rooms in Greek Street. His time in London signalled the beginning of his end as a great lover. He became re-enamoured of Marianne Charpillon, whom he had previously met in Paris and who, along with her mother and sisters, was now working as a prostitute. She led him a merry dance, taking his money and never surrendering the favours over which he had become besotted.

On 27 November she had him brought before the blind magistrate

Sir John Fielding, who bound him over to be of good behaviour in the sum of 40 guineas. Casanova had his revenge. Parrots must have been common currency in London at the time. He purchased one and, after teaching it to say in French, 'The Charpillon is a greater whore than her mother', sold the bird at a public house for 50 guineas. An attempt to sue him failed when Charpillon discovered she would need two witnesses to say that he had trained it.

Casanova lasted only a few more months in London. Over a short time, Charpillon and her family had taken him for over 12,000 guineas. After he won 520 guineas from a Baron Stenau, who gave him a forged bill of exchange in settlement, he was summoned to make it good or face proceedings for which the penalty on conviction was hanging. In the second week of March 1764, suffering from a venereal disease contracted from the baron's mistress, he fled to Brussels and then to Germany.[2]

But by the 1770s Soho was losing its cachet as an area for high-class prostitution. The madams such as Hayes, Goadby and Sarah Prendergast moved their houses nearer to St James's and were setting up in George Court. The adventuress Theresa de Cornyles was now in decline. Her nemeses were her competitors. In 1772 she went bankrupt trying to take trade back from William Almanack's premises in St James and the new magnificent Pantheon in Oxford Street. She died, worn out and ruined, in a debtors' prison. With her decline came that of Soho as the place for what we might now call the B-list celebs to be seen.

In the first half of the nineteenth century, Soho recovered its fair share of prime London brothels. Possibly because of the cold but more likely because of their school days, Englishmen have often had a penchant for flagellation. The White House at 21 Soho Square, run by Thomas Hooper, was an upper-class brothel where discipline was the speciality and was said to have had George IV as a patron. A Mrs James, who had been a maid in the family of Lord Clanricarde, ran one at 7 Carlisle Street, retiring to Notting Hill to live in luxury on the profits, but the best flagellation brothel in London was said to be that of Mrs Theresa Berkley at 28 Charlotte Street, where the speciality was the eponymous Berkley Horse.

The device, made in 1828, was an extending frame that, according to Henry Spencer Ashbee, could 'bring the body to any angle that might be desirable'. She was also reputed to have kept a more eclectic collection of instruments of torture than any other dominatrix in London. They included birch rods, which she kept in water so they remained pliant, a dozen cats-o'-nine-tails, nettles, and battledores made of thick sole leather with inch-long nails, as well as a prickly evergreen known as butcher's bush.

Mrs Berkley was reputed to have made £10,000 in eight years, and, when she died in 1836, her missionary brother, who had spent 30 years in Australia, renounced his claim to her estate. Her executor presented the Horse to the Society of Arts at the Adelphi, while the Crown took the remainder of her fortune.[3]

Street prostitutes, if sufficiently beautiful, could graduate. It was in New Compton Street that Harry Angelo saw Emma Hamilton, later Nelson's Gift to the Nation, leaning against a post on the corner. That evening he bought her some biscuits and arranged to meet her again. He did not keep the appointment and the next time he saw her she had graduated to living at Mrs Kelly's in Arlington Street.

It was on 19 May 1853 that William Ewart Gladstone, then Chancellor of the Exchequer, committed one of the indiscretions that have linked his name to the prostitution of the time. Opinion is divided as to whether he saved prostitutes or merely saved them until later, but that evening he met a girl in Long Acre and brought her back to her lodgings in King Street. Unfortunately, he was seen by a young man who thought that, if he did not share the knowledge with the general public, Gladstone would get him a job at the Inland Revenue. The Chancellor was made of sterner stuff and the man received a year's hard labour, later halved thanks to Gladstone's intervention.

Throughout the nineteenth century Regent Street was known as the haunt of prostitutes. In 1894 a man complained to *The Times* that, unless he was in company with his daughter, he could not walk down the street without being accosted.[4] And it was a reputation that continued into the twentieth century. Shaftesbury Avenue and the Charing Cross Road were constructed in the late 1880s and, with the disappearance of King Street, Hog Lane and the Newport Market, divided Soho into two parts cut off from mainstream London. Now prostitutes, minded by their bullies, were on every corner; there were restaurants that were façades for brothels and then as now massage parlours to which young women were recruited as 'nurses'. Leicester Square hotels were slow to clear prostitutes from their lounges and Shaftesbury Avenue was soon known as The Front. With prostitutes soliciting from the steps, the fountain in Piccadilly Circus of a cherub shooting an arrow – originally called the Angel of Christian Charity, commemorating the work of the reforming Lord Shaftesbury 50 years earlier – was informally renamed Eros.

The vice trade was pushing up the rents in Soho and, while some brothels were neat and indeed respectable, others were simply places where the visitors were robbed on the staircase before they ever got near the girls' rooms.

When W. Hall, a lay preacher, was sent to work at St Anne's Church, Dean Street, in 1891 he was warned that anyone who took a stand against the vice trade was likely to meet an untimely death. Indeed, in the letterbox one morning there was a postcard with a sketch of him turning a corner. A man behind him was stabbing him and he was due to fall into a coffin. There was a skull-and-crossbones motif and beneath the coffin were the words 'Spy, villain, this much good for you. Revenge'.

He survived, but it was a particularly rough time. Nevertheless, from 1892, efforts were made to clear away some of the brothels, and there was help from the Charing Cross Vigilance Society.

Then, on 1 May 1905, came one of the early-twentieth-century Metropolitan Police scandals, when a French woman, Eva D'Angeley, was arrested for 'riotous and indecent' behaviour in Regent Street. The charge was dismissed after a Mr D'Angeley told the stipendiary that he was married to the lady and that she was merely waiting for him. Better still Sub-Divisional Inspector MacKay told the court he believed them to be a respectable married couple. So amid allegations of corruption, police harassment and bribery, a Royal Commission was established into methods and discipline in the force.

The D'Angeley case was one of 19 selected for examination by the Commissioners and now rather different facts began to emerge. Reporting to the Commission, MacKay claimed that Greek Street 'is one of the very worst streets I have to deal with. In fact it is the worst street in the West End of London.' He had made further enquiries into Mrs D'Angeley and her husband and now realised he had been overgenerous towards the pair. They had retreated to Paris with such speed that they had forgotten to pack their trunks as well as forgetting to pay the rent on their lodgings. Unsurprisingly, offers by the Commission to pay their fares back to London were ignored. The case throws up all sorts of questions about MacKay. How could an experienced officer not recognise a French pimp? Why did he not ask for a short adjournment to make proper enquiries? But, as is so often the case, much of the report was a whitewash. The Commission found that, 'The Metropolitan Police is entitled to the confidence of all classes of the community.'

One of the abiding myths of Soho has been that, in the early years of the twentieth century, it was a home from home for the white slaver, something fuelled by the good Pastor Hall and others of St Anne's Church. Mothers fretted that their daughters who ventured into the fringes of Soho would fall foul of the white slaver and, in a restaurant or café, would meet up with what appeared to be a respectable woman, feel the prick of a needle and wake up on a cargo boat to Cairo. A slightly less horrifying version was that the girl would be taken to a strange house in a strange neighbourhood, where she would be detained for a day or two and ill-treated by villainous men before being turned out in the depths of night to make her ruined way home.

Percy Savage, a former superintendent of the CID who had worked the Soho patch, cast doubt on what amounted to this urban myth, saying he had never been able to find the slightest corroboration for these melodramatic kidnappings:

> Of one fact only have I succeeded in assuring myself, and it is that some girls rely on a somewhat vivid but limited imagination in order to excuse their voluntary absence from home when confronted by anxious and loving parents or matter-of-fact and incredulous employers.[5]

Statistics are difficult to obtain and there is little doubt that young Jewish women fleeing the European pogroms were met on the docks in the East End and placed in lodgings that were little better than brothels. But was there a wholesale shipment of these girls to Cairo and Buenos Aires? The research of Sol Cohen of the Jewish Association for the Protection of Girls and Women claimed that in 1900 there were 125 such cases and in 1902 the number had almost doubled. He accepted, however, that many of the women had been prostitutes before coming to England and that in most cases there was no coercion.

The findings differed from those accumulated four years later for a Metropolitan Police report that found that such cases were few and far between. They thought there were probably only half a dozen cases and, even so, these were French and Belgian girls – which made things all right, of course.[6]

Over the next six years, vigilance committees, allied to a variety of religious and social agendas, continued to pressure the police, claiming that white slavers were kidnapping virtuous girls and so 'reaping huge harvests of gold'. They had some support from the journalist George Sims, who, writing of Soho, thought that there were dozens of gambling dens run by foreigners who farmed out the streets to the 'unfortunate alien women' upon whom they lived. There was, he said, a well-organised syndicate that loitered in milliners' and dress shops specifically to recruit English girls.[7]

Indeed, there was generally an antiforeign feeling, with one newspaper in 1896 describing the denizens of Soho as speaking in 'a sort of mongrel, bestial dialect more fit for the lips of gorillas and chimpanzees . . . a sort of reeking hotch-potch of obscene and quite meaningless expression'.[8]

There is no doubt, however, that at least two well-organised and successful gangs operated in Soho in the first decade of the twentieth century. In 1910 Vera Wilson, a prostitute working in Wardour Street and the Leicester Square area, was kept under observation, and her French pimp Charles Peneau was arrested and charged with living off her immoral earnings. After the first remand hearing the wily solicitor Arthur Newton negotiated with Wontner's, the prosecuting solicitors, for a noncustodial sentence to be imposed on the basis that Peneau was a boy of 19 from a good family, who were horrified by what had happened to him. The solicitors and magistrate agreed, but they were fooled. Young and from a good family Peneau may have been but, as Wilson later told the police in a fit of pique, he was a close associate of a ring of white slavers that included Altar or Aldo Cellis, Alexander Berard and two Spaniards operating the Paris end, Damiani and Casalta.

Cellis, who was possibly Swiss-born or possibly Italian, had convictions in Australia. Along with a Frenchman, Alexander Nicolini, he had been recruiting Belgian girls, telling them they would be going to Wellington in New Zealand and Buenos Aires. On 30 November 1910, defended by Newton, Cellis and Berard pleaded guilty to conspiracy to procure women and received six months with hard labour to be followed by deportation. Two of the women 'rescued', Mireille Laparra – who had been recruited at the Gare d'Austerlitz in Paris – and Marguerite Bescançon, were not pleased to be taken back to the Continent. According to a letter from the National Vigilance Association, which escorted them, the girls spent the crossing to Calais flirting with any men who came within eye contact.[9]

The second ring was rather more long-lasting, wider in scope and, when it came to it, much more dangerous, at least for its members. Indeed, this was the first time that 'Red Max' Kessel came to police notice in a career that would continue until his death a quarter of a century later.[10]

The investigations into this gang also began in 1910 with Marguerite Leroy, otherwise know as Antoinette Poulain, being given a sentence of a month for being a common prostitute along with another month for assaulting a client. Even before the assault she had been under observation and was seen handing money over to two men in cafés, restaurants and pubs in Soho, including the Admiral Duncan in Old Compton Street. Enquiries were made and it was found a gang of traffickers was operating from 40a Wells Street. At first the men were identified only as Max (who was Kessel) and Leon, whose name was Brieux and who had been running girls, including Vera Wilson, out of the Café Henry in Bloomsbury.[11] For the time being enquiries lapsed.

On 17 October 1912 a small White Slave Traffic Squad, with a total strength of 14, was formed. On 7 November the next year John Curry, the detective inspector in charge, reported:

> I have to say that there has been an utter absence of evidence to justify these alarming statements, the effect of which was to cause a large shoal of complaints and allegations [many contained in anonymous letters] to be received by the police, against persons of all classes.

There was no case of an innocent girl being kidnapped. 'Mostly [they are] Jewesses of Russian or Polish origin [who] go to Argentina and Brazil.'[12]

The strength of the squad was duly run down.

One good thing had been the Criminal Law Amendment Act 1912, which provided the police with power to arrest on suspicion without a warrant, increased penalties and, at Quarter Sessions, allowed the judge to impose a flogging. As a result, said *The Times*, a number of foreign pimps had fled abroad.[13]

One of the first women potentially to fall foul of the Amendment was Queenie Gerald, described as an actress, who was charged that between 15 December 1912 and 13 June 1913 she unlawfully lived on earnings of prostitution. When the police raided her at Abingdon House, Piccadilly Circus, they were admitted by a woman dressed as a nurse. Gerald was found to have £201 on her together with a quantity of jewellery and gold. Three girls between the ages of 17 and 19 worked for her, dividing their earnings equally. In the end she did rather well. She received three months in the Second Division with the deputy chairman at Quarter Sessions saying there was no suggestion of any cruelty by her, nor had she corrupted the girls. The newspapers were outraged, as was the Ladies' National Association, which wanted to see a more severe sentence. Questions were asked in Parliament and MPs suggested she had been dealt with leniently because of names found in her black book, which had been suppressed.[14]

On her release she immediately set up in Maddox Street and advertised in the *Pelican*:

> Anturic bath salts; effective in the cause of rheumatism. To be obtained from Gaynor, first floor, 9 Maddox Street, Regent Street W. Telephone 4658, Mayfair.

The police kept watch on the premises but she had learned her lesson and there was never again evidence she was using the premises as a brothel. She would, however, resurface time and again over the next fifteen years.[15]

2

A Crooked Lawyer and his American Clients

With improved sailing time between New York and Liverpool, from the mid-1870s some of the great late-nineteenth-century American criminals were coming over to work and play in London, particularly if they found things a little warm at home. They included the so-called Emperor of Crime, Adam Worth, also known as Harry Raymond, who stole Gainsborough's painting of the Duchess of Devonshire and slept with the canvas under his bed for the next quarter of a century; Annie Gleason, who was posing as the daughter of General Ulysses S. Grant; as well as the redoubtable Chicago May Sharpe (or Churchill) and Sophie Lyons, another talented thief and blackmailer.[1]

Chicago May Sharpe, born in Ireland and whose first husband until his death had been part of the Dalton–Doolin outlaw gang, together with her friends worked the hotels and restaurants in and around Shaftesbury Avenue and Leicester Square, including the Alhambra – famous for decades for its ballet girls – which stood on the site of the present-day Odeon, picking up men, relieving them of their wallets and, when the opportunity arose, indulging in a spot of blackmail. What they needed was a reliable lawyer to help them out when things went sour. And the man they turned to was Arthur John Edward Newton of Great Marlborough Street.

Sharpe thought reasonably well of Newton: 'He was a smart man, charged good-sized fees and knew the ropes . . . He represented both big and little criminals and fixed his fees according to his clients' ability to pay.'[2]

The wonder was that Newton was still on the rolls of those allowed to practise as a solicitor. He had already been around the block a few times and had received a short prison sentence to go with it. Rather better educated than some solicitors of the time, he qualified in 1884. His father had been an actuary and manager of the Legal and General Assurance Society and Newton went to a preparatory school and then Cheltenham College, where he excelled at football, before he served articles with the fashionable firm Frere Foster in Lincoln's Inn Fields.

He then opened offices opposite Great Marlborough Street Police Court and within a matter of a few years his was one of the biggest criminal law practices in London.

A cartoon by the fashionable Spy in the magazine *Vanity Fair* showed Newton in a double-breasted waistcoat and wing collar looking rather like Clarke Gable as Rhett Butler, and the adulatory article by Jehu Junior that accompanied it had Newton as 'not eloquent but he is lucid; and though he is strong yet he is courteous. He can swim; he had more than once been found guilty of giving a conjuring entertainment. He has the great advantage of good appearance.' As for his imprisonment, '. . . and then he once got himself into trouble by too zealous defence of an undeserving client'.

The 'undeserving client' was Lord Arthur Somerset and the case the Cleveland Street Brothel Scandal of 1886, which stemmed from the arrest of certain boys who worked in the post office at St Martin's-le-Grand and supplemented their income by male prostitution.[3] It was thought, at first, that one of the boys had stolen money from the Receiver General's Department and Charles Swinscow was asked how he could have as much as 18 shillings (90p) in his possession. Pressed for an explanation, he said it was from going with men at 19 Cleveland Street. He had, he said, been persuaded by Henry Newlove first to 'behave indecently' with him and then to go to the male brothel in Cleveland Street run by Charles Hammond which catered for the nobility. Another boy, the attractively named Thickbroom, was also involved.

When questioned Newlove said that a visitor to the brothel was Lord Arthur Somerset, a major in the Blues and extra equerry to the Prince of Wales. Somerset approached Newton to act for him and the lawyer's part in the affair was to try to get potential witnesses against his client out of the country.

Early on in the inquiry, when it became apparent that it would be a far-ranging one, Newton went to see the Assistant Director of Public Prosecutions, Hamilton Cuffe, to warn him that if Somerset were to be prosecuted another name would appear. It would be that of Prince Albert Victor, known as Eddy, the eldest son of the Prince of Wales and grandson of Queen Victoria. It may be that Newton was exercising a spot of blackmail on behalf of his client – throughout his career there were suggestions that he was never averse to this. There may have been nothing sinister in Newton's approach, but it was sufficient for Cuffe to inform the Director, Sir Augustus Stephenson, and so on up the chain to Lord Salisbury, the Prime Minister.

Even though he had offered substantial terms – £50 cash, a new suit of clothes and £1 a week to run for three years as well as their passage to Australia – Newton failed in the attempt to spirit the boys away. What he was able to do was to warn Somerset that a warrant for his arrest was imminent. His Lordship left for France the next day. He died at Hyères on 26 May 1926.

As for the boys, Newlove received four months with hard labour in the House of Correction and Swinscow and Thickbroom were dismissed from the post office. Hammond fled to Seattle.

Summonses were issued against Newton, his clerk Frederick Taylorson, and a translator, Adolphe de Gallo. There was a general feeling among the public and the police that people in high places had been allowed to get away with things. Newton was to be the sacrificial lamb and, it must be said, he acted as such. Submissions that there was no case to answer failed at the police court when the three were committed for trial. All this cost money and now Newton was looking around for help. Lord Arthur's father, the Duke of Beaufort, contributed £1,000 (he had been asked for £3,100). Others did likewise.

At this stage it is probable that few thought anything serious would happen to Newton. De Gallo had already gone from the proceedings when the Grand Jury refused to indict him. Taylorson, meanwhile, was causing trouble. He refused to listen to the advice of his and Newton's counsel, the great and formidable Sir Charles Russell QC, and plead guilty.

The trial opened on 16 May 1890 in the Queen's Bench Division. With Taylorson still remaining adamant that he would plead not guilty, the charges against him were dropped, which shows that sometimes, at least, the client has the better judgement.

This left Newton to face Mr Justice Cave, a man with considerable experience in bankruptcy but little in criminal law. Russell had persuaded the prosecution to drop five of the charges in return for a plea of guilty to the sixth, a general count of perverting the course of justice. It was all intended to be a low-key affair. He had been told that 'a persuasive rather than a hostile attitude towards the authorities would result in the matter not being too deeply gone into'.[4] His mitigation was therefore that a young man had acted overzealously to prevent his client being subject to blackmail. There were still few at that moment who thought that anything more severe than a bind-over would be forthcoming. They were wrong.

When Cave passed sentence on 20 May he made it quite clear that he did not think Newton had been acting from these altruistic motives:

> Your offence has been committed for the purpose of securing the absence of these persons from England in the interests of wealthy clients, and to impose a fine, therefore, would only in all probability result in their paying the fine for you. I must, therefore, pass a sentence of imprisonment.[5]

Newton was sent to prison for six weeks. His brother lawyers thought he was being badly treated and 250 firms, including the great Lewis and Lewis, signed a petition to this effect. On his release he tried once more to tap the Duke of Beaufort and was again disappointed, something about which Newton felt extremely bitter. All was not bad news, however. He had already learned that the Law Society was not disposed to take any action against him. His brother solicitors' hard work on his behalf in his absence paid off.

Nor had the quality of his work suffered by his absence. In 1894 he took over the placing of a reward for the Duchess of Marlborough's jewels, which had been stolen at Waterloo Station. The next year he acted for Alfred Taylor, the co-defendant of Oscar Wilde, and three years later for the disreputable Count Esterhazy in a successful libel action against the *Observer*, when he was awarded £500.

By the turn of the century Newton had one of the biggest criminal practices in London. His clients ranged from the louche to the criminal; from the music-hall star Marie Lloyd through Dukes and Duchesses to chorus girls and adventuresses; from actors to the talented but dishonest American jockey, Tod Sloan; and mostly he did what he could for all of them. He had the reputation as a great fixer with the ability to charge an astounding £100 for a telephone call that removed the wart from a client's back.

Newton first acted for Chicago May Sharpe in 1900, when she quarrelled with Julia Barrington, who had run a brothel in New York and had brought over four girls to work in London. The fault was entirely that of Sharpe, who enticed one of Barrington's girls to go to work with her. Barrington retaliated by denouncing Sharpe to the detective Jack Stevens, known – because of his swarthy skin rather than his religion – as Jew Boy. Sharpe then pulled the woman out of a cab and tore off her wig. A few days later there was a fight involving Grace Fowler, another of Barrington's girls, outside the public library in Trafalgar Square, which ended up with Sharpe being accused of stealing a $500 earring. The case was thrown out but Sharpe noted that, when Newton learned she had a criminal record, he upped his fee.[6] It did not stop her from sending him a steady stream of American clients, many of whom had been caught too near other people's safes.

In 1907 when she and Charles Smith shot and wounded her former lover, the talented safebreaker Eddie Guerin, near Russell Square underground station, it was again to Newton that she turned for her defence. The reason for the shooting was a longstanding quarrel over a robbery in Paris. Guerin believed, rightly, that she had shopped him, as a result of which he had been sent to Devil's Island, from which he had escaped, killing his fellow escapers (which he admitted) and eating them (which he did not). Newton also could seemingly be used as a conduit pipe for messages. In a letter intercepted by the authorities at Holloway Prison she wrote to her current boyfriend, Baby Thompson, 'You can hear all from Arthur Newton'.[7]

It was not one of Newton's more successful cases. Smith and Sharpe appeared in front of Lord Darling claiming that Guerin, who lost two toes in the incident, was shooting at them and they were acting in self-defence, but the jury convicted them without leaving the box. Smith received life imprisonment and Chicago May a mere 15 years. After serving 10, she was deported to America.

Guerin stayed in London, where he was part of a team who were unsuccessfully trying to remove a parcel of jewels from a French dealer, Frederick Goldschmidt, who was in town in June and July 1909 to try to sell them.[8] There were a number of teams on the lookout and it was really only a question of who could actually get to the jeweller. First past the post was the former lightweight jockey Harry Grimshaw at the Café Monico in Shaftesbury Avenue.

Goldschmidt stayed at De Keyser's hotel on the Embankment and it became clear that the only time he ever put his case down in public was when he washed his hands. On 9 July he went to the lavatory in the Café Monico, put his bag beside him and, as he reached out for the soap, was pushed off balance and the bag was snatched by the small but extremely quick Grimshaw. As Goldschmidt chased after him, his passage was blocked by another member of the team, John Higgins. The jewels, worth some £60,000, were never found. Had the pair struck the previous day, the haul would have been nearer £160,000.

Within a matter of hours, the police obtained a search warrant of the noted receiver Kemmy Grizzard's home in Dalston and found him at dinner with his guests, three potential buyers. Grizzard and his company sat at the dinner table while the police searched the house, but nothing was found. After they had gone, Grizzard drank his now cold pea soup and at the bottom of the bowl was a diamond necklace from the haul, which was then cleaned and sold.

Higgins, defended by Newton, received 15 months' and Grimshaw three years' penal servitude to be followed by five years' preventive detention. It was thought that altogether six men were involved in the snatch and the police had their eyes on two great Australian thieves and confidence tricksters, Walter Macdonald and Daniel Delaney, but no more arrests were made.[9]

The diminutive Annie Gleason first appeared at London Sessions for an attempted theft from Christie's in 1905 when she received three years. In January 1909 she married an American, Theodore Albert Gillespie, who was one half of a comic duo, Ferguson and Mack, and they lived together at 34 Little Newport Street. It was a bigamous marriage because her real husband, Mickey Gleason, was serving a sentence in Munich. Two years later she received five years for theft, again at London Sessions. Gillespie visited her in the cells and died of a broken heart (she said) within a month.

But her real downfall came when, on 23 April 1915, she was back at the Old Bailey along with another American, Charlie Allen. This time it was not simply switching fake for genuine jewellery but robbery with violence of a jeweller Wladyslaw Gutowski from Percy Street, when they stole some £1,600 worth of gems. As Mrs Ferguson, she had been working with some Russians thieves. She told the jeweller that she was being kept in style by an English milord who wanted to buy her some valuable diamonds. She had already dealt with Gutowski, buying a small diamond ring from him for £27 as part of the come-on. Now she was staying at the Savoy Mansions, where some years later the actress Billie Carleton would kill herself on the night of the Victory Ball.

On 10 February, Gutowski dutifully appeared for the appointment, bringing some £20,000 of jewellery with him. He was sandbagged and then chloroformed by one of the Russians posing as a page. Allen was the lookout man. When the police searched the flat, they found a lady's silk handkerchief in a drawer and Gleason was traced through the laundry mark. None of the gems were recovered.

At least in court she and Allen were given their due when they were described as 'two of the most dangerous thieves in the world' and she was 'looked upon as one of the most successful American thieves we have here today'. Allen received 12 years and 12 strokes of the cat. Gleason was sentenced to ten years and, as she left the dock, 'looked reproachfully' at Mr Justice Lawrence.[10] Allen died in prison. She was released on licence on 27 January 1923 and died 12 years later in Chicago.[11]

A look through the Metropolitan Police files and reports in *The Times* shows the number of serious cases in which Newton appeared. He featured for the defence in most of the major murder trials of the decade but in 1911 he was suspended by the Law Society for his conduct in the case of the dentist Harvey Hawley Crippen, accused of poisoning his wife, the music-hall actress, Belle Elmore.

By the time of the Crippen trial Newton was 50, with a taste for the finest Havana cigars and a penchant for wearing dove-grey gloves, which he ordered by the gross from a glove maker in Jermyn Street. Asked about the gloves he commented, 'But in our profession it is so difficult to keep one's hands clean.'

According to W.E. Henchy, his managing clerk, Newton had angled for Crippen as a high-profile money spinner, which would enable him to pay off his racing debts. A heavy gambler relying largely and foolishly on the tips given to him by Tod Sloan, he was also a serious money borrower.

Crippen thought he was to receive £500 for his memoirs from the *New York American*. Newton had also obtained £1,000 for Crippen to undertake a two-month lecture tour of the States in the event of an acquittal. Newton invested some of Crippen's money, which the man earmarked for his mistress, Ethel Le Neve, in the Charing Cross Bank, but, sadly, the bank failed on the day he stood trial. It owed £2,500,000 to depositors and had failed through a fraudulent land speculation in Canada.

What really upset the Law Society, however, was the deal Newton made over the sale of Crippen's confession. It was then common practice in a sensational murder, when there was no legal aid available except representation under the Poor Persons' Defence Act, for a newspaper to pay the defence costs. The *quid pro quo* was that the defendant would give an exclusive story to the funding paper with, in the event of a conviction, a death-cell confession to be published usually on the Sunday after his execution. Newton simply fabricated the confession. On 12 July 1911 he was suspended from practice for 12 months.

All was not well at the Marlborough Street court in the years before World War One. The Metropolitan Police Commissioner received a series of complaints that his detectives were shaking down the Soho gaming club and brothel owners in return for which they were either left alone or were warned of imminent raids. The clerks at the court were also suspected of leaking documents to the club owners and there was more than a little thought that solicitors were doing the same. One solicitor disappeared completely and a second was caught in a raid on a particularly low-class gambling den. This left a couple of other firms and the temporarily restored Mr Newton, but now his mind was on bigger things.

In 1913, along with a Berkeley Bennett, he was charged with conspiracy to defraud a young and rich pigeon, Hans Thorsch, in another fraudulent Canadian land deal. Bennett falsely represented himself as a close relation of Gordon Bennett, the millionaire proprietor of the *New York Herald.* Newton banked the cheques. A third conspirator, Count Festetics, who was certainly Hungarian, but probably not a count and who most likely devised the operation, was never found, but the trio cleared around £9,500 profit from the unfortunate Austrian.

Pleas that his practice would fail and that his wife would be left penniless went unheeded, particularly after the officer in the case pointed out that Newton had been living with a mistress for some years He received three years' penal servitude and Bennett half that.[12]

This time, the Law Society did strike him off the rolls and the firm passed to his son, but it did not remain long in business. After his release, Newton became a private detective and also a marriage broker, negotiating settlements between those who were rich but had no social status and those who had but were penniless. His prison sentence in no way diminished him in the public eye. Until his death he wrote several series of articles about his most famous cases. He could also be relied on to help out in the dodgy divorces that were so much a feature of the 1920s, supplying girls to be the 'woman named' in a petition.

Game to the last, shortly before his death on 3 October 1930, living at 71a Ebury Street, Chelsea, Newton was fined for his involvement in a gambling club in the West End. He was then seventy.

3

The Great War

For a time immediately after the Great War broke out, the authorities were keen to promote the belief that what were then described as the industrial classes, and London criminals in particular, were behaving well. In September 1914 Robert Wallace KC, sitting at the County of London Sessions, said that, 'the spirit of restraint which has come over the people is perfectly marvellous'. *The Times* commented in the December, 'The criminals, we are assured by those who know them, are too patriotic to take advantage of the nation's need . . .'

Perhaps a little carried away, a London magistrate told *The Times* that month:

> The criminal is a patriot. There is a genuine feeling of public spirit to be noticed today among those whom we call the criminal classes. Not only the graver forms of crime – those attended by violence, for example – but the most casual type of offence is less common than in the time of peace. The same moral improvement in the criminal was noticed – though not in so marked a degree – during the South African War. The criminal, like the honest citizen, is impressed by the war conditions which make it every man's duty to give as little trouble as possible.[1]

It may have been Chartres Biron who spoke to *The Times* because he later wrote in his memoirs:

> The war had a curious effect on the work of the London police courts. It almost disappeared. This was partly due, no doubt, to high wages and abundance of employment. The early closing of public houses undoubtedly helped; but the criminals, to do them justice, stood by their country.[2]

That may have been the view of the magistrates and *The Times*. At ground level, however, police officers took a different one. In his memoirs, George Cornish, the senior detective officer at Tottenham Court Road, wrote that because of the heavy workload involving rounding up enemy aliens in and around Charlotte Street which housed the prewar German colony, 'Crime, too, increased owing to our depleted staff and the general unrest and excitement.'[3]

They were right to keep an eye on the quarter. In 1916 the Spanish-born spy Adolpho, who claimed to be a Spanish journalist on a Madrid paper, was arrested in Whitfield Street. Put on trial, in the July he received 10 years' penal servitude.

Certainly, not all the industrial classes behaved creditably. Desertions began almost immediately. On 12 August 1914 one of the earliest, Donald Lesbini, shot and killed Alice Storey, who worked at a cheap shooting gallery in Tottenham Court Road. Lesbini, of Greek origin, had taken offence when she called him Ikey. He was convicted and sentenced to death but was reprieved. In prison his mental stability deteriorated and in 1931 he was sent to Broadmoor.

One concern of the authorities was the amount of alcohol being consumed, particularly by female munitions workers. A survey of four London public houses for one hour one Saturday evening showed that 1,483 men and 1,946 women consumed alcohol. In January 1915 David Lloyd George claimed that, 'Britain is fighting Germans, Austrians and Drink and as far as I can see the greatest of these foes is Drink.'

In April that year King George V, setting an example to the nation, said that until the war was over there would be no alcohol drunk in the royal household. Six months later a No Treating Order prohibited people buying alcoholic drinks for others. Pubs now shut three hours earlier at 9.30 pm. Taxes on whisky were increased. By the end of the war, a bottle of whisky which had cost 4 shillings (20p) in 1914 now cost £1. Naturally, as a result, whisky was stolen by the vanload and duly sold on to publicans.

It was also desirable to keep serving officers away from gambling clubs. In April 1915 the Court of Criminal Appeal upheld a sentence of four months on James Gibson, who had been running *chemin de fer* games in the West End. The danger, thought the court, was that officers who had lost were encouraged to find other players in the hope that their debts might be wiped off. Later in the war, the authorities began to stamp on women-only gambling dens catering for wives whose husbands had been in a good financial position before they joined the services.

As the war dragged on, officers, particularly in uniform, had to be kept out of London brothels. In January 1917 a man called Brewis from St Helens visited Queenie Gerald, who had now elevated herself to the aristocracy and was the Hon. Geraldine Gaynor, and complained he was made drunk and drugged. 'In the morning he discovered he had damaged the bed upon which he had slept during the night.' She wrote demanding first £25 and then £68 for damage to the bed, carpets, bedclothes and dressing table. He went to his solicitors and they contacted the police.

Police enquiries showed that military officers in uniform had also visited her at Maddox Street and it was thought there might be a case for prosecuting her under Section 13 of the Defence of the Realm Act, but in the end no action was taken.[4]

Cocaine was now introduced to London in bulk by Canadian soldiers. Although there was heavy traffic between Amsterdam and German cities and Paris from about 1911, it had not been a serious problem before the war. Generally it was sold in small bottles under another name.[5] The maximum penalty was £5 and at first the only prohibition on its sale was to the troops. However, in the six months from the beginning of January 1916, with a box costing 3d (1¼p) selling for 2/6d (12½p), there were more and more instances of women addicts. There was also some evidence that women were taking flowers and chocolates to soldiers in hospital, meeting them on their discharge, giving them cocaine and then stealing their arrears of pay: 'Cocaine has dangers for women apart from its ruinous effect on the nervous system. It is fatal to self-discipline and therefore a predisposing cause of moral as well as physical destruction.'[6]

Finally a prohibition order against selling cocaine and opium not on prescription came into force in July 1916.

That year a letter to Inspector Kerry at Marlborough Street named, or at least identified, ten men involved in selling cocaine in and around Shaftesbury Avenue. They included the 26-year-old one-legged Willie Johnson, who lived with a prostitute in New Compton Street. The letter informed the police that Johnson, the porter at the Ambassadors Café de Paris, across the road from the Ambassadors Theatre, had his drugs bought for him by an Alfy Benjamin from a chemist in Lisle Street. At the time there was only one chemist in the street – Wooldridge & Co. at number 26. Other distributors were a 'Swiss man' and 'four Jewish boys' who frequented a sandwich shop at 89 Shaftesbury Avenue. The police reported that it was patronised chiefly by 'prostitutes and Continental undesirables', as was the Ambassadors café.[7]

One night the police watched Johnson approach two women on the corner of West Street and Litchfield Street and, while trying to escape the officers, he dropped 11 boxes of cocaine. His was the first recorded London drug bust. Since the police had not seen him actually try to sell drugs, he was acquitted.[8]

In July 1916 a gang of dealers was trapped by Gilbert Smith, a Canadian military police officer who, posing as an ordinary soldier, bought half-crown (12½p) boxes from a collection of Soho denizens and foreigners, who received two to three months apiece. The foreigners, including Georges Wagnière, the Swiss man referred to in the letter, were then deported. Frederick Freemuller, a 19-year-old butcher, and Mark Cohen, who lived in Tottenham Street, also received three months.[9]

The previous year, in December 1915, Captain Ernest Schiff had denounced Jack May, who ran Murray's Club in Beak Street, writing to the Attorney General, Sir John Simon:

> A very bad fellow, Jack May, is the proprietor of Murray's Club in Beak Street – a quite amusing place. But for vice or money or both he induces girls to smoke opium in some foul place. He is an American, and does a good deal of harm.[10]

May, whose real name was Gerald Walter, also owned the sister club Murray's Riverside in Maidenhead. At the time, police investigations found no evidence that he was corrupting young women or that he was the same May who had been named by a Chinese man caught two years earlier, but for the next five years May would continually be named as a dope dealer.

Not that Schiff was all he might to be. He probably denounced May because they were treading on each other's toes and he wanted to stamp first. In fact, Ernest Schiff was a thoroughly sinister piece of work. Born of naturalised Austrian parents, he was educated at Eton. Although he had been commissioned in the Royal Sussex Regiment, he seems to have generally supported Germany during World War One – he kept his fingernails cut in the pointed German style. He was regarded as a cool, clever gambler who employed a stable of girls from Soho and the West End to give him gossip from which, along with blackmail and pimping, he relied for his income. It was rare a dope party was held in Soho that he failed to attend.

His end came when in March 1919 he went to Cornwall and tried to persuade the daughter of a tin miner, Albert Nicholls, to return to work for him on the London streets. He had gone there with a Selina Moxon, allegedly his housekeeper but in reality one of his mistresses. They had stayed at the Tinner's Arms in Zennor, where Nicholls's daughter worked, and had then gone to live at the Grey House, Carbis Bay.

When Nicholls found out what had happened he went after Schiff and knocked him down, breaking three ribs and his nose. He died three days later. Nicholls was charged with murder and committed for trial on a manslaughter charge. The officer in the case, Sergeant Matthews, told the jury he thought Nicholls was absolutely justified in what he had done and 'would not be a father if he did not go and see him [Schiff]'. Nicholls gave evidence that he knew Schiff carried a knuckleduster and had boasted he carried a gun.

Mr Justice Lush, summing up to the jury, told them people could not take the law into their own hands, but they were having none of these high-flown sentiments and acquitted Nicholls without leaving the box.[11]

Jack May did rather better than Schiff, although at the 1920 inquest of the actress Billie Carleton he was sufficiently worried about being named as the first to supply her with drugs to instruct the very fashionable and expensive Sir Edward Marshall-Hall KC to make a denial on his behalf.

Abortionists flourished despite the heavy sentences that were handed down and the probability of facing a murder charge if the girl died. Generally, however, the abortionists were convicted only of manslaughter. The courts were at pains to point out that every woman who went to an abortionist was just as liable to prosecution. In September 1916 a judge at the Old Bailey, sentencing an abortionist to four years' penal servitude, bound over a number of women to come up for judgment in a year's time. This was, he said, a warning to the public generally. In future the women themselves would be dealt with severely.

That year there was a marked increase in juvenile crime, something that was attributed to the bad influence of the cinema. On 29 September Montagu Sharpe KC, chairman of Middlesex Sessions, told a Grand Jury,

> 'At places of entertainment where exciting episodes are shown the final scenes are not revealed to the audience – the birching and punishment which inevitably comes as a result of juvenile adventures.'

Fraudsmen flourished. A new market for 'wounded' soldiers and officers as well as for those organising bogus charitable collections began as early as November 1914. By April 1915 the courts were warning the public against giving money to beggars in khaki.

That month, a deserter, Joseph Orchard, hobbled on crutches around Victoria Station to such effect that a lady hired a bath chair for him to be taken to the zoo for a day's outing; a man bought him another set of crutches and a barrister paid for him to go to a soldier's home for a week. He was arrested after being thrown out by the staff. The same week Lancelot Dickinson Chapman, a deserter from the Royal Field Artillery, wearing a VC and claiming to be the sole survivor of 'L' Battery at Mons, received ten months' imprisonment for a variety of frauds, including taking 5 guineas from Gaumont Graphics in Soho to film him as a returned hero.

Naturally, the old con tricks were still in use, including the so-called Irish fortune. In 1916 two conmen were sent to prison at the Guildhall. They had a copy of a newspaper with what purported to be an item in the stop press:

> £60,000 FOR CHARITY
>
> The celebrated will case of *O'Connor v O'Connor* was concluded today.
>
> A lucky Irishman inherits £300,000 of which £60,000 has to be distributed by gentlemen of independent means knowing personally the needs and wants of the people receiving the money the distributor receiving 10 per cent without incurring any responsibility, strange to say all charitable organisations and religious societies are excluded from participation. His Lordship also commended the highly practical idea of personal distribution by respectable gentlemen.

The con was a simple one. A suitable-looking punter was persuaded that he was the ideal person to be part of the distribution process. At the very worst he would receive £6,000 and the criminally inclined might actually keep the whole haul. Naturally, he had to put up security to be part of the team and in return he would get a briefcase full of newspaper. It was a trick which ran until well after World War Two.

By the end of the war there were worries that the armed forces were under attack from syphilis and gonorrhoea, not all, of course, contracted in Soho. In August 1918 there were 1,207 patients with gonorrhoea being treated at the Canadian Hospital, Etchinghill, Lyminge, along with 861 for syphilis and another 244 who were being treated for both. It was claimed that 264 cases of syphilis were contracted from amateurs and 584 from professionals, with gonorrhoea contracted from 386 and 1,078 respectively. Eight cases had been contracted from actresses; one from a bus conductress. It was considered that prosecutions could be brought against infected women who could be forced into 'lock hospitals' for treatment under an Order in Council of 9 May 1918 made under the Defence of the Realm Act, but this was considered to be fraught with difficulties.[12]

Now, with the horrors and deprivations of the war behind them, the Bright Young Things would wholeheartedly embrace cocaine and nightclubs; racecourse gangs would flourish and the face of crime would change irrevocably. Soho would once more assume its rightful position in the underworld.

4

Some Dope Dealers

> It is not so many years ago, less than ten to be precise, that the thought of a West End nightclub haunted by negroes and Chinamen peddling poisonous drugs to stupid women would have aroused a thrill of horror in the land, with the irresistible demand that such a place should immediately be swept out of existence. Today it happens that some pleasure sated girl dies from an overdose of cocaine or morphine, supplied to her by some black or yellow parasite, and people merely shrug their shoulders.
>
> **S. T. FELSTEAD, *The Underworld of London*, 1923, pp. 1–2.**

One of the first and certainly the best known of the major Chinese drug dealers was Chan Nan, known as Brilliant Chang, a stocky figure scarcely five feet tall with patent-leather shoes and a fur-collared melton cloth coat. He described himself as a general merchant and an Admiralty contractor and was described by the *Daily Express* as 'the unemotional yellow man, his narrow slit eyes blank, his face a mask. He had a Chinese wife and three yellow children'.[1]

Chang, apparently the son of a well-to-do businessman, was sent to England in 1913 to pursue a commercial career or study medicine – accounts vary. Instead he opened a restaurant in Regent Street and started drug trafficking on the side from his private suite. In a short time he was looked on as the leader of drug traffickers in the West

End. White women fascinated him and he also trafficked in them. Those who attracted him would receive a preprinted note via a waiter inviting them to join him. Curiously, although the recipients could not possibly think they had suddenly induced an irresistible urge in Mr Chang to write to them, he had a high success rate. From there it was often a short step to drugs and degradation.

In 1917 after men in Birmingham were arrested with correspondence showing Chang was a leading dealer, although there was a period of police surveillance, nothing came of it. Shortly after World War One he was almost certainly the supplier of the drugs that led to two well-publicised deaths. After the Victory Ball, held at the Albert Hall in aid of the Nation's Fund for Nurses, Billie Carleton, the pretty young actress who had been addicted to drugs for a number of years, collapsed and died. Born in 1886, the illegitimate daughter of a chorus singer Margaret Stewart, she was described as 'a frail beauty and delicate . . . all of that perishable, moth like substance that does not last long in the wear and tear of this rough and ready world'.[2]

In fact she was a tough young woman who had been one of Cochrane's young ladies and appeared with Gertrude Lawrence and Bea Lillie in the revue *Some* at the Vaudeville Theatre in 1916. Along with the sinister Reggie De Veulle, she took parties to Limehouse, where she was supplied drugs by a Chinese man, Lau Ping You, and his Scottish wife Ada, who had a house at the eastern end of Limehouse Causeway under the railway bridge that led to the Isle of Dogs.

De Veulle, described as having an 'effeminate face and mincing little smile', had designed Billie Carleton's gown for the ball. The son of a former British vice consul at Le Mans, he had been part of a scheme to blackmail William Cronshaw, a well-known homosexual of the time. The charges were dropped when Cronshaw declined to go ahead with the prosecution.

The inquest showed that Billie Carleton had died from cocaine poisoning and was addicted to opium smoking. It was common knowledge that Chang had been a close friend but, although de Veulle was charged with manslaughter, nothing was ever proved against Chang. De Veulle, prosecuted by Sir Richard Muir, was fortunate to be acquitted of the manslaughter charge but he received eight months' hard labour for supplying drugs to Billie. Ada Lau Ping received five months also for supplying while her husband was altogether more fortunate. Liable for deportation, he appeared in front of one of the few magistrates who thought that a little smoking was no worse than a glass or two of whisky and was fined £10.[3]

Also attending the Carleton inquest was Sui Fong, later described as the Yellow Snake of the Underworld when he, Yong Yu and Long Chenk all received three months at Marlborough Street and were recommended for deportation. Fong's wife was described as an 'Austrian Jewess' and Yong Yu had married an English girl. Fong had come over at the turn of the century as a steward on a liner and had been linked with one of the most spectacular gambling dens where, after the gaming had finished, orgies took place. He was also a marriage broker between the Chinese and English girls.

Then, on 6 March 1922, a dancing instructor, Freda Kempton, was found dead, also from an overdose of cocaine.[4] She was to have married a Manchester businessman on the Monday after her death and a friend recalled that she had promised to give up dancing after her fiancé had sent her money for clothes for the wedding. This time Chang did feature. He had met Freda and her friend Rose Heinberg in the New Court Club off the Tottenham Court Road the night before. The next day Freda had suffered from a splitting headache and had gone into convulsions. At the inquest Chang faced a hostile series of questions. The story from Rose Heinberg was that Freda had asked him if anyone died from sniffing cocaine and he had replied that the only way to kill oneself was to put it in water. 'She was a friend of mine, but I know nothing about the cocaine,' he told the coroner. He had given her money but not drugs. 'It is all a mystery to me.' The *Empire News* was ecstatic:

> There was no mistaking the thrill that passed through the court room as the Chinaman in his matter of fact fashion referred to the bedroom incident and went on to speak of the present of £5 which he gave to the erring girl on that occasion.[5]

The coroner ruled that there was not sufficient evidence to link Chang with the death of Freda Kempton but not before he had taken the opportunity of delivering a little homily: '[It is] disgraceful that such a dangerous drug as cocaine should be handed about London helping to ruin the bodies and souls of inexperienced girls.'

The jury recorded a verdict of 'suicide during temporary insanity'. The *News of the World* reported, 'When the jury returned the verdict, Chang smiled broadly and quickly left the court. As he passed out several well-dressed girls patted his shoulder while one ran her fingers through his hair.'[6]

In the flurry of unwelcome publicity after Freda Kempton's death, there were claims that two girls had disappeared from the Tottenham Court Road and, when they were found, their clothes had been 'almost torn from their backs in wild frenzy produced by Chang's opium pipe'. For a time vigilantes patrolled clubs and drinking dens belonging to Chinese and black proprietors.

Chang's premises at 107 Regent Street were frequently raided and following one in west London, which netted six Chinese, four of the men were found to be waiters at his restaurant. Eventually, he sold his restaurant and, to the annoyance of the formidable nightclub queen Kate Meyrick, who had her own club at number 43 and who certainly did not want any more police attention, became a partner in the Palm Court Club in Gerrard Street. He then moved to live and conduct his operations at 13 Limehouse Causeway. The premises were almost derelict with an unoccupied shop on the ground floor and he let out the second floor to Chinese seamen. It was the middle floor that Chang used for himself that excited the public. The great bed was a 'divan of luxury'. Silver dragons were everywhere, as was costly furniture all acquired, so the press and police said, through drug dealing. 'This man would only sell drugs to a white girl if she gave herself to him as well as paying.'

The method of dealing from there was simple. Couriers such as Violet Payne, who had a number of aliases and was euphemistically described as a failed actress, bought the drugs in Limehouse and took a taxi to Soho and the West End to sell them on.

Chang was arrested on 23 February 1924. The police had been keeping watch on the Commercial Tavern public house in Pennyfields and a nearby Chinese restaurant. Violet Payne had been seen to flit from one to the other and when stopped she was found to be once more in possession of drugs. When pressure was put on her, she mentioned his name. A small packet containing cocaine was found under a loose board in Chang's kitchen cupboard. Since he did not wish to alienate the Old Bailey jury and, more particularly, the judge, he ran the defence that it had been put there without his knowledge rather than that the police had planted it. The jury did not leave the box before convicting and he was sentenced to 14 months in the Second Division and recommended for deportation. During his imprisonment he continued to be something of a thorn in the flesh of the authorities because, although he could write in English perfectly well, he insisted on writing in Chinese. Since none of the warders could read Mandarin to censor his letters, they had to be sent to the Home Office for translation.

He was deported in April 1925, taken by cab to the Royal Albert Docks, where his family had reserved him a suite on the boat. While in prison, he had been sent numerous letters from women friends and he was now allowed these but not to speak for long with the well-wishers. He left to calls of 'Come back soon, Chang.' During his six-year reign in England it is estimated that trafficking drugs made him over £1 million, most of which he had sent back home.

The British authorities were convinced that with the compulsory retirement of Chang they had struck a major blow against cocaine and opium dealing and, if statistics do not lie, they were correct. Between 1921 and 1923 there were 65 cocaine prosecutions a year. The figure had dropped to five between 1927 and 1929. Over the same periods the opium prosecutions had declined from 148 to 36.

Almost immediately after the conviction of Chang, down went one of his successors. Ah Wong had been his factotum when Chang was running the West End and after his master and mentor had been driven to the East End he took over. It was thought at the time of his conviction in June that year he was making £100 a week.

Not all the drug traffickers were Chinese: according to the *Empire News*, 'The negro rolled, struck, kicked and bit like a savage. He looked like a beast of prey and almost foamed at the mouth . . . the raving maniacal nigger was braceleted.'[7]

This dispassionate account was of the arrest of Jack Kelson after he had bought cocaine from a Chinese café on Limehouse Causeway. At the time he was almost certainly operating for his employer, Eddie

Manning. Kelson, who was regarded in the trade as one of the safest runners between Limehouse and the West End, like Manning also dabbled in the white-slave trade. In October 1926 he received three years for trafficking.

Eddie Manning is often regarded as a successor to the Chang dynasty but in reality he was a contemporary. He was one of a group of dealers in the West End known as the Big Four. A great deal of effort was made by Scotland Yard to prove he was American and so could be deported, but it was eventually agreed he was born in Jamaica, was therefore a Commonwealth citizen and could *not* be deported. His real name was McManning and he came to England in around 1914, working as a labourer until 1916, when he was discharged for ill health. He was then a jazz drummer, and an actor in small-time touring reviews, at the same time running prostitutes and selling drugs from his flat in Lisle Street. The other three in the quartet were Alexander Iassonides, his wife Zenovia and his nephew Leonidas. Unfortunately for the partnership, Manning became fascinated by Madame Iassonides, known as the 'Dope Queen' and by all accounts a striking woman, who, much to the fury of her husband, eventually went to live with him.

In September 1920, Manning received a sentence of 16 months for shooting at three men in a fracas at Cambridge Circus on 11 July that year. If, which is doubtful, the witnesses can be relied on, Manning had been in Mrs Fox's Restaurant in Little Newport Street. The eponymous Elizabeth Fox was a sort of Godmother to the underworld and for the previous 20 years her restaurant had been a home from home for out-of-work actresses, prostitutes and criminals. Always good for advice and, better still, a handout, she was sorely missed when she went to America, where she died from cancer.

Things had been peaceful that afternoon until a pimp, 'Yankee Frank' Miller, who had just been acquitted at the Old Bailey of burglary, tried to blag a pound from Manning and hit Molly O'Brien and threw a lighted cigar in her face when she interfered. Manning chased after and shot at him and his companions.[8] More likely the quarrel was over the division of drug profits.

It was Manning's first conviction and Mr Justice Greer took the view he had been more sinned against than sinning, saying how much he regretted having to sentence a man of respectable character but that foreigners had to be taught that guns could not be discharged on London streets. Even then the police were not totally fooled. There was much more in the matter than met the eye, said the officer in the case. It may be that the men had been turned on Manning by the jealous Iassonides. Certainly that was suggested later.

At the time Manning was living with a prostitute, Doreen Taylor, and some 15 pawn tickets were found when her premises were searched. This should not be taken as a sign that he was impoverished. Pawning stolen goods with no intention of redeeming them was a standard way of realising the profits. Provided he kept proper books and did not have too many stolen items in his shop at any one time, it also offered a promising defence to the pawnbroker if he was charged with receiving.

On his release Manning went to live with Madame Iassonides and now cocaine injections at 10 shillings (50p) each and lessons in how to take the drug were available at the Berwick Street cellar café owned by the pair. On the side Manning ran prostitutes and also illegal and crooked roulette parties, as well as 'dope orgies [at his flat in Lisson Street] at which scenes of the wildest debauchery were witnessed'.[9]

He also came to notice over the deaths of Freda Kempton and Maud Davis, who died in Lumber Court, St Martin's Lane. He was again in the spotlight in January 1922, when a former army officer, Eric Goodwin, died from a drug overdose at Manning's new flat in Hallam Street, Marylebone. Manning gave evidence at the inquest to the effect that he had never known Goodwin take drugs, but he was now well in the frame.

A successful police raid on Madame Iassonides's flat at 33 Regents Park Road in April 1922 resulted in her receiving six months and deportation. She was followed in quick succession by Leonidas in the September and the estranged Alexander the following March, when cocaine was found in a violin case. Alexander had survived one arrest when drugs were found beneath the stair carpet of the Soho café run by his nephew. On that occasion a tame doctor, Percy Edmonds, appeared to give evidence, saying that Alexander was a kind man whom he could not conceive of being involved in drugs. Perhaps generously, the magistrate said it would be unsafe to convict.[10]

In March 1923 the police kept the Montmartre café, in Chapel Street, Soho, which had already been the scene of dozens of arrests, under observation. No meals were ever served nor were male customers. It was used solely for the sale of cocaine to women. A policewoman followed a woman wearing a fur coat into the café, and Jack Rosa, a Maltese, said, 'I will give you twenty packets for the [fur] coat.' The woman held up two fingers, to indicate the number of packets she required, and the policewoman one, and they were taken to the basement for the transaction. This time there was no helpful doctor to give evidence and the court was told that Alexander Iassonides, who had once been a steward on a liner between London and Egypt, was regarded as one of the most sinister figures in the Continental dope ring. Each received six months and Iassonides followed his wife and nephew into exile.[11]

Manning had also received six months for the Regents Park raid on Madame Iassonides, but, since he was British, he could not be deported. After their release and deportation, she and her nephew retreated to Paris, from where she maintained a steady correspondence with Manning.

Just before the downfall of Kelson, Manning received three years' penal servitude for possession of opium but he continued to survive, if not to flourish, for some years more. In 1927 he was fined for harbouring prostitutes and given six months for possessing cocaine. Then in 1929 he received what would be his final sentence. By now he had also been chased out of the drug-dealing world and was into receiving. Property worth £2,000, the result of a number of burglaries, was found at his flat. He was sentenced to another three years' penal servitude and died in E2 Ward, Parkhurst, on the Isle of Wight, apparently from the ravages of syphilis. One of his great fears was of owls and, when dying, he heard one hoot. 'His body shook and his eyes rolled in abject terror,' wrote a fellow prisoner poetically.[12]

One of Manning's close friends in the early 1920s was the jazz musician Sidney Bechet, who played in the orchestra at the Hammersmith Palais and also in Rectors in the Tottenham Court Road. It was a club in which the licensing authorities took a close interest and was described by an enquiry agent as where 'rich male customers are fleeced by wily hostesses'.

After his stint there on 2 September 1922, Bechet and a friend met Ruby Gordon and Pauline Lampe, who claimed they were dancers – Bechet said Gordon was a prostitute whom he had frequented before – in the early hours at the Breakfast Room café in Percy Street and took them back to Bechet's rooms. It was there, claimed Gordon, that both men assaulted her. She said Bechet had pushed her on a bed and tried to strip her. Bechet said the quarrel had arisen when he would not take drugs from her. Both received 14 days, upheld on appeal, and Bechet was deported. He was not allowed to return to England until 1931. Perhaps, given his relationship with Manning, his version of the story does not stand up.[13]

Club

5

The Club Scene

The first London nightclub was founded in 1912 by Frida Strindberg, the year her husband August, the Swedish playwright, died. The Cabinet Club, always known as the Golden Calf, in the basement of a cloth seller's in Heddon Street off Regent Street, was intended to recreate the cabarets of Vienna. Despite being patronised by the likes of the sculptor Jacob Epstein and the writer Wyndham Lewis, described by Ernest Hemingway as 'having the eyes of an unsuccessful rapist', it was not a financial success. It closed two years later after a police raid and, fined £160 with two months in default of payment for selling liquor without a licence, the disillusioned Mrs Strindberg sailed for New York. But, succeeded by the Harlequin Club in Greek Street and a host of others, it lit the way.

By the 1920s there were more than 50 cabarets and dance clubs in Soho and the West End and, with their more or less complete disregard for the licensing laws, they were a constant problem for the authorities. There were clubs for all tastes, such as the actor Ivor Novello's 50–50 club, said to be named after his sexuality, and the Gargoyle in Meard Street, which opened in 1925 with part of its décor by Matisse. Some were basement dives; some required the patrons to wear dinner jackets; some, of course, were far better than others.

Throughout the middle of the 1920s *John Bull* and other newspapers conducted a campaign against the clubs and cafés in Soho where there was prostitution and drug dealing. Complaints included whisky 'of vilest quality sold at half a crown [12½p] a nip'; champagne bought outside at 7/6d. (37½p) and sold inside at 3–8 guineas a magnum; dancing hostesses who gave lessons at a guinea for 20 minutes; a shilling (5p) to retrieve a coat and doors barred 'against a police raid'. Dolls to be given as presents to the dancing partners were sold for two guineas each.[1]

It is impossible, however, from the tenor of the articles not to think that their real targets were foreigners, particularly black men who lived with or off white women. A good example of the attitude comes from the con man Netley Lucas, who worked the rackets in and around Leicester Square, Soho and the Strand. After a spell in Borstal and imprisonment in Canada he took up writing and produced a number of highly successful books. In *London and its Criminals* he took his readers on a tour of London's criminal haunts, which included a café, 'a sink of iniquity off Wardour Street', where, to his apparent horror, the races mixed.[2]

Even in forgiving and cosmopolitan Soho, black men were not generally welcomed in public houses where they might meet white women. On his visit here after World War One the jazz musician Sidney Bechet drank in the Bell in Little Tichfield Street, one of the few that did welcome black men, where the landlady, Mary Rose Kildare, was the wife of the black saxophonist Daniel Kildare. In June 1920 Kildare killed his now estranged wife, as well as a barmaid, and then shot himself.

In 1924 a club run by Carletto Pedotti and Jean Louis Creachadec at 11 Denman Street was described as 'one of the worst of its kind in or near the West End, a rendezvous for undesirables, among whom were aliens of both sexes'.[3] Another target was David Cutler who ran the Shaftesbury Social Club in Great Earl Street. *John Bull* claimed it was not a club at all but a haunt of thieves and undesirable women. 'Formerly the Grape Vine Club run by Cutler who is Russian and served doped drinks'.[4]

There was also the Radio Club at 55 Old Compton Street, 'one room rented at £8 a month where hundreds crowded in to drink after hours and most names given to the police were false'. Next door were the Movie Club, the Havinoo, the Oak Club and the Premier Club.[5]

John Bull had some quick success in denouncing Francisco Sequi

Canals, a Spaniard who, along with his wife Grace, ran the Black Cat Café in Old Compton Street. Canals was deported but not before he had written to the editor complaining of inaccuracies in their article.[6] The trouble was that, as soon as one club lost its licence and closed its doors, very often another opened the same day on the same premises.

Earlier that year, on 10 April 1926, *John Bull*'s principal target was James Kitten's café in Great White Lion Street, Seven Dials, known as 'The Black Man's Café'. Headed A TERRIBLE NEGRO HAUNT. THE KITTEN AND HIS 'MICE': CAFÉ THAT MUST BE CLOSED, the article went on to regale its readers with stories of women who 'have become the degraded creatures solely through continual association with the coloured scoundrels who frequent the establishment'. There had been fights and stabbings, and arrests in the café for drug dealing, but 'one of the most sickening sights witnessed every day in this place is the spectacle of white women shamelessly consorting with black men'. It followed another, more general, article, DOUBLE DYED DOPE DEMONS: DENS WHERE BRITISH GIRLS CONSORT WITH COLOURED MEN.

Kitten, a man from Sierra Leone who had been a chef at the Savoy before purchasing the café, took umbrage and so became one in a long line of villains from Darby Sabini through to 'Mad' Frankie Fraser who wrongly decided to take on a newspaper. He sued Odhams Press and, for his sins, the action was heard by Mr Justice Avory, never notably sympathetic to foreigners. Nor was Kitten helped when the defendants instructed Norman Birkett, one of the top silks of the day. In turn he was represented by the more modestly priced E.H. Coumbe and Lapipo Solanke.

The tone of the case was set early in Kitten's evidence when he said that some of the customers brought in their wives, and Avory intervened to say to Birkett, 'You have not asked if it is the same wife each time.' (Laughter.) There was more laughter when he spoke of a Prince Monolulu visiting the café with his wife.

Birkett: 'He's a racing tipster, isn't he? He's not a prince really.'

Kitten: 'Oh, no. That is what we call him.'[7]

Much of the evidence for the defence came from a Sergeant George Goddard, who had been keeping observation on the premises. The jury hardly retired before finding against Kitten. He was made bankrupt when he failed to pay the costs awarded against him. When he applied for his discharge it was refused on the grounds he was the cause of his own misfortune, by bringing a frivolous action.[8]

Apart from the clubs *John Bull* campaigned against the blue-film industry, which it claimed was growing up. From 1920 it maintained cinemas in and around Wardour Street were showing blue films after the regular shows had ended. One of the more notorious was a two-reeler called *The Fall*, which starred 'Cissie' as the Goblin Queen and a Colonel Andrews. Another was *The Burglar's Surprise*, of which the paper thought 'no dreadful detail of horrible indecency being omitted, many being emphasised by "close-up" pictures'. The rental fee was a substantial £80 a night. Army officers were said to be targets who were prepared to pay up to £5 for a showing. Tickets could be bought from 'gay' women who sold them from a public house near the Palace Theatre. There were also suggestions that Queenie Gerald was showing them at her parties.

The police were adamant that there was no such thing as a blue-film racket. True there had been such films shown during the war and once upon a time these things were made in Germany, but not now, in London, in the 1920s.[9]

Up the social scale from Kitten's café came clubs such as the Shim Sham, run by Jack Isow and the entertainer Ike Hatch, which, according to police files, was frequented by prostitutes, thieves, ponces and lesbians, 'coloured men and women and other very undesirable persons all of whom frequented these premises in order to satisfy their various vices'. One of the thieves was the daredevil safebreaker Eddie Chapman, who favoured the club as well as the Nest in Kingley Street. Isow himself was described as 'an Alien with a very nasty record'.[10]

Then there was the Falstaff in Oxford Street, owned by Con Collins and described by the burglar Mark Benney who worked as a cashier there as

> at that time at its widest and wildest. All the thieves and prostitutes of London came there to spend their money, and they demanded licence . . . Women for ten shillings [50p] a bet walked naked through the rooms. Men walked openly from group to group vending stolen articles. And on the dance floor men lifted the skirts of

> girls as they passed and smacked their bare buttocks to the uproarious mirth of the onlookers.[11]

It closed after fights involving the Sabini race gang.

Then there was the succession of clubs run by Freddie Ford, also known as Roberts, who had 'the appearance and manner of a Guards Brigade Colonel, with a big military moustache, ruddy complexion, oxen shoulders and straight back'.[12] The detective Robert Fabian, 'Fabian of the Yard', suggested that his greatest claim to fame had been the way he simply flouted the licensing laws. 'Fines are part of my business expenses,' Ford is said to have remarked. But the reality was that, in his time, he was a major criminal and his Ham Club in Ham Yard, later known as New Avenue and later still the Havinoo, was the downfall of many an unsuspecting person. Possibly because of his association with the Falstaff, Benney thought the Havinoo Club was positively quiet and respectable.

Ford, whose criminal career had more or less run the gamut of offences, claimed to have sold Peter the Painter a blowpipe used in the 1911 Houndsditch robbery, which led to the siege of Sidney Street. He was sentenced to five years' penal servitude at the Old Bailey in 1912 for wounding. In 1921, along with his longtime partner Hyman Kurasch, he was acquitted of passing forged notes to a man named Boxer. It was a form of the old green-goods swindle. The mark would be sold a small number of genuine notes on the basis that they were forged and no one could tell the difference. He would then be sold a substantial quantity of what would turn out to be blanks.

Three years later, in 1924, Ford was again acquitted, this time of manslaughter. He was, it was alleged, driving a taxi while drunk. His passenger, William Taylor, had been thrown out of the vehicle and killed. By 1926 Ford and his clubs were again in trouble. Patrons of his Soho drinkers were sent at the weekend to the Cursitor Street Club just off Chancery Lane, where black-tie parties were held. He was given three months' imprisonment for licensing offences at that club in March and in the May he was explaining to a jury that magistrates were biased and would not listen to his defence that he was running a genuine club, the New Avenue. It did him no good and he received a month's imprisonment followed by a four-month sentence over the

Havinoo Club, which had opened on the same premises the day after the New Avenue closed.

Quite how genuine the New Avenue Club was is open to question. Certainly, Ford's criminal career did not save him from protection demands. In January 1924 two Sabini men, George West and James Ford, wrecked it. West had a long record, beginning in 1898, when he served two months for larceny, interrupted only by a career in the ring when he boxed as Dai Thomas. In October 1922, he had been acquitted of the attempted murder of a Billy Kimber man, Fred Gilbert, after a shooting in Mornington Crescent. This time he received nine months and Ford six.

In February 1927, by which time the Havinoo was known as the Musicians and Artists Club, Ford went to prison for receiving, along with a man named Chandler. The club was now described by an Inspector Wesley as being patronised almost exclusively by thieves – male and female. If, by mistake, a genuine patron stumbled into the club it was rare that he left with his money.[13] Finally, Ford served 10 years for safebreaking.

In the 1920s and 1930s the really rather dismal Ham Yard off Windmill Street was a particularly sought-after spot by nightclub and bottle-party proprietors. Apart from Ford's clubs, at one time or another the proprietors of the Dilly Club – frequented by 'men and women of the worst character' – the Panton, Joker, Last, National Theatre, Blue Lantern, Lido, Mandarin, Melton, Hollywood, Skyscraper, Mother Hubbard, Top Hat and the Stage, an outpost of the club of the same name in Wardour Street, had all appeared in court.

Further up the scale were the nightclubs run by the celebrated Kate Meyrick and her daughters. She was by no means a conventional Irish beauty. A stern rather dumpy little woman, Kate Meyrick is said to have run her flagship the 43 Club in Gerrard Street (where centuries earlier Dryden had lived) with a rod of iron, expelling Darby Sabini's men, Billy Kimber's Elephant Boys (from the Elephant and Castle) and rowdy Oxbridge undergraduates with the same aplomb. Fabian recalls her saying, 'Fun is fun but vulgarity is vulgarity. Out you go, my boy.' But it was not always so. In May 1932 she was fined after a police raid. The police evidence included hearing 'a disgusting song' that had been applauded, and of the solicitation by a prostitute, 'Are you on your own, dear?' The street was full of clubs. A few doors along from the 43 was a black club, the Big Apple. Next door to that was Hell, run by Geoffrey Dayell and patronised by Sam Henry, who, like Ernest Hoey, made his fortune from the bottle party.[14]

Sad-eyed, drab and dowdy, she would sit behind her desk in the narrow entrance hall collecting the £1 entrance fee. But she was an astute businesswoman, even though she did not take up her career until her forties. From the profits she educated her children well. One son went to Harrow, the daughters to Roedean.

The daughter of a doctor, Kate Meyrick was born in Dublin in 1875. Both her parents died young and she was brought up by a grandmother, first in Lancashire and then back in Ireland. She married a doctor, Ferdinand Richard Holmes Merrick, and for a time they lived in Brighton.

One version of events is that she had left Merrick in 1918, alleging cruelty and his failure to support their eight children under 21. The plucky independent woman was a role that appealed to her and to the newspaper readers. 'I admit I was first and foremost a business woman, but I was also thrown on the world with eight children to be given a decent start in life, and very little means wherewith to do it.'[15] After her death, Merrick produced his version of life with Kate:

> I think there were two kinks in her mind which made her take up the night life. One was a mad craze to earn a great deal of money for herself. The other was to lead an independent life. She had been a militant suffragette in the old days. She believed in a woman doing everything for herself, and that is why she wanted to make a bit of money independently of me.[16]

In 1919 she was in London nursing her daughter May during the influenza epidemic when she answered an advertisement placed by George Dalton Murray, 'Fifty pounds wanted for partnership to run tea dances.' And her career was born. In April 1919 they set up Dalton's Club in Leicester Square as 'a rendezvous for members of the theatrical and variety professions and their friends'. Other proprietors were a Mrs Hooker and one of Mrs Meyrick's daughters. The friends seem to have been an eclectic mix. Between 22

September and 5 October that year, according to Sergeant George Goddard – who, along with his long-term junior and ultimate nemesis Wilkin, was keeping observation undercover – 292 prostitutes were seen to leave the club. 'I was so cleverly disguised, if I might say so, that my own colleagues failed to recognise me,' he told the court. It was the beginning of undercover officers in top hat and white tie. Herbert Muskett, the senior partner of the solicitors Wontner's, who regularly prosecuted in club cases, thought Dalton's 'an absolute sink of iniquity'. 'We are trying to keep Belcher out and other dope fiends,' Mrs Meyrick plaintively told the police.[17]

On 28 January 1920 she and Dalton were each fined £50 with 25 guineas costs. She was sentenced to 26 days' imprisonment in default of payment. Dalton did not pay his fine and disappeared for a time. In turn she claimed she had lost £500 over the venture. It was the first of many clubs and many convictions.

Ma Meyrick, as she was called, then moved from Dalton's to Brett's Dance Hall in a basement in the Charing Cross Road with a female band and with dance instructresses, who included Freda Kempton. Ma claimed some of her hostesses earned up to £80 a week and married aristocrats, but they were the fortunate ones. In 1922 the club was prosecuted when an undercover surveillance officer saw a man pull down the top of a woman's dress. There was also an allegation that a woman had been sitting with her legs crossed so exposing her knee.[18]

By then, however, Ma had moved on to, among others, the Silver Slipper, the Cat Burglar's, the Bunch of Keys, the Manhattan and Proctors, which became her most famous club, the 43. The premises of the 43 had a back exit through a courtyard beyond the outside lavatories which led to another yard to a shop – kept unlocked as an escape route for police raids – and into the sanctuary of Newport Market. The escape route may have saved the faces of some of London's politicians and aristocracy who loved to mix with the underworld, but over the years Kate Meyrick went to prison five times.

From 1924, when the Conservatives were re-elected, the strait-laced, reactionary Home Secretary, Sir William Joynson-Hicks, believing that clubs were undermining social barriers, was keen to stamp on them. In July that year the 43 was raided by Goddard and, after another raid in the December, Ma was sentenced to six months by Sir Chartres Biron who thought she was 'a lady of good appearance and charming manners and conducted her various clubs with more decorum than many, but with also a fine contempt for the law'.[19]

She seems still to have been pulling the strings from her cell and the next year her son Henry and her Girton-educated daughter Dorothy Evelyn were merely fined for a similar offence in relation to the same club.[20]

On 10 March 1926, Dorothy Evelyn, known as Polly, married the 19-year-old Lord de Clifford, whom she had met at the Gaiety Club. He was fined £50 in June for giving the false age of 22 and inaccurate details of his parents. For a time she managed the Manhattan Club in Denman Street, which was being looked after by Mrs Meyrick's 25-year-old daughter-in-law Irene when it was raided in the May. Irene was fined £150. 'It is the most bogus of all bogus clubs I have had to bring to the notice of a court,' said Herbert Muskett pompously.[21]

By the summer of 1928 Mrs Meyrick was living in Regents Park. The family got up for breakfast at 5 pm and lunched before going to the various clubs at 11 pm. There was reputed to be a rich backer behind Mrs Meyrick – possibly the financier Alfred Lowenstein – who paid her a high salary and gave her a substantial share of the profits.

At the beginning of June the marriage of Ethel Isobel Merrick, known as May, to the 14th Earl of Kinnoull was announced. 'Our future plans are not yet decided but I think I can say for certain that we shall disassociate ourselves from the nightclub business,' said the Earl of Kinnoull. It was not to be. The very next day the Richmond Club, also at 43 Gerrard Street, was registered. Ma had let the premises to Kinnoull and within weeks he was well entrenched in the family business. He and May were now also running a club in Maidenhead. She had previously been running the Silver Slipper.[22]

The wedding took place on 6 June in a twice-postponed ceremony at Marylebone Register Office. None of his family appeared and Ernest Hoey, who invented the bottle party and ran a wine merchants in Warwick Street and Rupert Street, was his best man. The divorced Kinnoull had had something of a chequered love life. In 1920 he had tried to marry Mrs Trewartha Surle, a South African widow, but the marriage had been stopped because he was underage. Nevertheless, his marriage to May survived.

On 22 June 1928 Mrs Meyrick received six months for selling intoxicants illegally and for selling without a licence and out of hours on 18, 19, 21, 22 and 23 May. The 43 had now become the Cecil Club and had 20 dance hostesses. Her daughters, the 19-year-old Kathleen Lady de Clifford and the Countess of Kinnoull, were in court. In mitigation Norman Birkett argued that she had not been convicted for the previous three and a half years, but the reason for that would become apparent over the next few months.[23]

Now the clouds were gathering over Mrs Meyrick and her clubs and it was no longer simply a question of 'victimless' licensing offences accompanied by relatively modest prison sentences. She was in the sights of those in high places. On 3 March 1928 the Home Secretary Joynson-Hicks wrote to the Police Commissioner Sir William Horwood suggesting that the club was

> A place of most intense mischief and immorality, even going to the extent of doped women and drunken men . . . I want you to please put the matter in the hands of your most experienced men and whatever the cost will be, find out the truth about this Club.[24]

There had been allegations reaching Scotland Yard since 1926. One letter dated 10 February that year, signed 'Ex-waiter', read, 'So is the notorious Mrs Meyrick reaping her golden harvest. Apparently it is a matter of heavy bribes to the inspectors. Otherwise they would not allow the scandal to go on.'

There were also suggestions that cocaine was available at the 43. A letter in July 1928 read,

> Are you aware that Mrs Meyrick the wickedest woman in London who has two nightclubs in London is opening a third in Regent Street and openly laughs at the police as shown by the fact that she pays Sergeant Goddard a few hundreds a week? The barman at the 43 is rolling in money. One waiter has land in Italy worth £2,000. They get it by robbing visitors by overcharging.

Goddard was asked to investigate and duly reported that all was quiet on the West End front, adding, 'It is regrettable that persons who make such insidious and lying attacks cannot be traced.'[25]

It was during her sentence for the Cecil Club that the Commissioner for Police also received what were known as the 'Liberty's' letters, purporting to be from a man who worked at the store, and who maintained that George Goddard had interests in brothels and clubs. The writer also claimed Goddard was taking money from other clubs as protection against their being raided. They included Alexander's Club in Greek Street, run by Alexander Engelman, complete with 'crooks, prostitutes and all classes of ill repute', and Molinari's, a brothel over a laundry run by a Dutchman at 14 Old Compton Street 'of years standing'. Bribes came from Murrays in Beak Street as well as the Haymarket Social Club, which the writer thought was one of the worst places in the West End.

Despite hours of work, the police were never able to discover who the writer was and rather took the view that he did not work for Liberty's at all. Whoever he was, he also had good information regarding the Goddard household finances: 'Goddard resides in his own freehold residence in Streatham, and he also owns a beautiful Chrysler motor car. His brother-in-law is also in business provided by money supplied by Goddard.'

It was all correct. In fact the businesses were pawnbrokers. What was more, as the police delved into Goddard's finances, they discovered that this £6-15s-a-week officer had £500 in a Selfridges deposit box and £12,000 in an account in Pall Mall. From where had the money come?

Goddard certainly could not have come by this money honestly and it was now believed he had acquired his considerable fortune by gifts from Mrs Meyrick in return for tip-offs over raids. Some of the notes could be traced back to her. The police also found he had been involved with a Mrs Gadda, who kept a brothel at 56 Greek Street and who changed money for Goddard. He had recommended no action be taken against the premises.

A month after her release in November 1928, into the dock went Goddard, Kate Meyrick and her manager Luigi Rebuffi, all charged under the Prevention of Corruption Act. Mrs Gadda had sensibly left England.

Corruption was something Goddard denied throughout the trial, maintaining he was no more than a successful gambler – £7,000 had come from winnings on the turf – and an investor in a music-publishing business, which had netted him another £5,000. Ever the astute businessman, he had invested money in a scheme to sell rock – edible rather than audible – at the Wembley Exhibition of 1924 and then he had dabbled on the foreign-exchange market. These ventures had produced £4,000 and £2,000 respectively. He had, he said, reported irregularities in the running of the Meyrick clubs. Indeed he had but, for his £100 a week, he had also reported that the difficulties in bringing a successful prosecution were almost insurmountable.

He was done for by the evidence that a secret observation had been kept by senior officers without letting him know, so that in turn he could not tip off the nightclub queen. Unfortunately, they appeared in front of Mr Justice Avory, the so-called hanging judge, who sentenced her and Rebuffi to 15 months' hard labour. Goddard was sentenced to only three months more and ordered to pay a fine of £2,000.

On his release he was back in court, this time as plaintiff. After his conviction the Commissioner of Police had, somewhat prematurely, confiscated all his money, claiming it to be the property of the Crown. In fact, Goddard had been convicted of taking only some £900 in bribes and an order was made that a substantial part of the money be returned to him. He retired to the country and lived off his investments, founding Chessington Zoo.[26]

Kate Meyrick was released from Holloway prison at 8 am on 27 January 1930. A crowd, many of whom were in evening dress, gathered from dawn onwards to see her and, as she emerged through the prison gates, there were cheers and she was presented with big bouquets of lilies and carnations.[27] When Muskett had told the magistrates that fines did absolutely no good and prison seemed to have little effect, he was right. She returned to the West End, opening fresh clubs and served two more sentences, both following raids on the 43. In 1932, faced with yet another prosecution, she promised to stop operating.[28] She was by then in very poor health, brought on in part by the unhealthy working conditions in her clubs over the past decade and also the poor conditions in Holloway Prison.

One journalist, R.C. Corder, thought her eyes were 'tragic', adding,

'The eyes of her haunt you. She talks with her lips and listens with her eyes.' The magistrate agreed to bind her over in return for a promise she would not open any more clubs. She was also fined £50 with 60 guineas costs and rather generously he allowed her time to pay. She had been running the Bunch of Keys – the 43 under another name – with her daughter Nancy and had avoided the police by using the Newport Place escape route.[29]

On 19 January 1933, Kate Meyrick died after a bout of pneumonia at the age of 56, at the home of her son-in-law, Lord Kinnoull. At the time of her death the 43 was known as the 43 Dancing and was being run by her daughters. Dance bands throughout the West End observed a two minutes' silence in her memory. The newspapers were mixed in their tributes. The *Evening News* thought her to have been 'a resolute, forceful little woman. There was little of which she was not reckless in her ambition to win fortune and position for her family.' The *Daily Mail* took a sterner attitude – but, then, it was publishing her husband's view of life – describing her as 'a strange product of the unbalanced post-war years' and adding that the chief vice had been 'young men squandering money on tired and jaded women'.[30]

In its heyday the Silver Slipper was showing £500-a-week profit and on Boat Race night 1927 the 43 alone took £600. She had been advised in her investments by the Belgian-born magnate Sir Alfred Lowenstein and at one time was worth in the region of £500,000; but, after his death on 4 July 1928, the shares in his company collapsed.[31] She subsequently made a series of poor investments and her fortune diminished. She died leaving an estate of just under £800.

On 3 May 1939 her daughter, Irene, married the Earl of Craven in what could be described as odd circumstances. On the previous evening the earl, who was later described in court as suffering from the first stages of alcohol poisoning, had been drinking before he met Irene in the Gaiety Club, one of her nightclubs. Marriage was apparently discussed and the next morning they married at St Peter's Church, Pimlico, after Irene had obtained a licence. They parted the same day and, rather unchivalrously, almost immediately he petitioned for an annulment on the grounds that, through alcohol poisoning, he was incapable of giving his consent. He claimed that his wife and her sisters had effectively kept him apart from his own family

– who would have prevented such a rash act – until it was all too late. In evidence the vicar said he thought he was behaving oddly. As a wedding ring he produced a signet ring and he thought the earl was in a dream, but he gave his responses and signed the register correctly, albeit shakily. The next year his petition was dismissed, and that of Irene for a restoration of conjugal rights – if indeed there had been any to restore in the first place – was granted.[32]

The next year Irene was fined £125. Her club, the Melodies Bar at 20 Shepherds Market, was struck off and the premises disqualified for 12 months. The police had received complaints from the RAF and a visiting police officer found the members' book in disarray, drunks and, worse, effeminate people, one of whom powdered his face and another invited the inspector home.[33]

In 1934, a sentence of 20 months' hard labour was handed out to a *soi-disant* phrenologist, escapologist and strongman, and now proprietor of the Caravan Club, Jack Rudolph Neave, known as 'Iron Foot Jack' because of a shortened leg and the iron frame he wore to support it. The basement club – financed by the burglar Billy Reynolds, who received 12 months – opened on 14 July 1934 in Endell Street and was described by the trial judge as a 'vile den of iniquity that was likely to corrupt, in fact, did corrupt the youth of London'. Neave had also run the Jamset and the Cosmopolitan before he opened the Caravan, for which he paid a rent of £300 a week. Within six weeks the club had nearly 500 members.

Following complaints from the residents, police had kept watch for some nights with one officer suffering the indignity of having to dance with another man. The first raid was aborted because the inspector in charge feared there had been a tip-off but when it eventually took place the evidence was that on one night there were some 40 men and 26 women in the club. Thirty-nine of the men were said to be of the 'importuning type' and 18 women were 'of the prostitute class'. On the night of the raid it was packed to the gunnels with 77 men and 26 women, of whom 76 were discharged and 27 sent for trial. 'He's got hold of my titties,' said one man. 'Fancy being found in a pouf's brothel,' said a Jean Williams. Perhaps more importantly the police found a small arsenal of weapons including a dummy revolver, two air pistols and ammunition, knuckledusters and bludgeons.

Neave remained in Soho. During the 1950s he was said to have run a derelict restaurant in Greek Street. There was an enormous menu in French from which everything except '*poisson et pommes frites*' was deleted. If by mischance there were any customers, Neave explained that the chef was ill but the fish, which he himself would cook, was exceptional. He then sent a boy to the local fish-and-chip shop.[34]

Another club fell foul of surveillance in November 1936, when Billie's Club at 6 Little Denmark Street was raided. The police had been keeping it under observation for several nights during which the usual 'degrading' scenes had taken place. Of the 50 or so people in the club, most were of the 'nancy boy' type. For the cabaret, a man in evening dress sang in falsetto. Men danced with each other and called themselves and their friends by girls' names. Some of the men wore rouge and powder. One had a hand inside the top of his partner's trousers and another asked for a drink of 'whisky and sodder'. When an officer asked what that was the barmaid told him, 'It's what they come here for.' Another undercover police officer, asked to dance by a man, pleaded cartilage trouble. By today's standards it all seems incredibly innocuous. Nevertheless it was sufficient to earn Billie Joyce 15 months.[35]

Fish 'n chips
all else deleted.

6

The Gangs Are All Here

Even before the Great War there were plenty of small businesses in Soho able, if not willing, to offer up protection money to home-grown talent. Many of the businesses, cafés and restaurants were owned by Continentals, who had suffered at the hands of the police in their own countries and so were easy prey for the locals. In a three-year period from July 1897 the police raided 37 foreign-owned premises in Soho. Twenty were being used for gaming and the remainder for prostitution. There were also the street bookmakers, who congregated at the corner of Tottenham Court Road and Oxford Street, to be protected by the likes of Billy Kimber, originally from Birmingham.[1]

Soho has never had a resident gang in the way that other gangs, such as the Krays and the Richardsons, have owned their own territory. Prior to World War One three disparate gangs fought over the area – the Elephant Boys from the Elephant and Castle, the Hoxton Boys, also known as the Titanics, and a team from Kings Cross led by Michael Macausland.

The Titanics came from Nile Street, Hoxton, and were said to have been named after the liner because they were so smart. This cannot be correct because the first reference to them is in 1902, well before the liner was launched. They were said to be up to 50-strong and were talented pickpockets working football crowds, the music halls, theatres and the underground – in fact anywhere crowds congregated. Inroads were made into the gang after arrests at a north London football match followed by a series of raids by the police. One man who rose to be a senior member was Alf White, who would, after the war, join the up-and-coming Sabinis.

The Elephant Boys, said to bite the heads off rats, were regarded as the most ferocious of the gangs. Indeed it has been said that without their help it was impossible to have absolute control over Soho. While the Sabinis reigned supreme for a time, generally the Elephant Boys' participation continued until well after World War Two.

The post-World War Two gang leader, Billy Hill – who could rightly be called Boss of Soho if not Boss of Britain's Underworld, the slightly more grandiose title bestowed on him by the hero-worshipping journalist Duncan Webb and his publishers – thought Soho was a wonderful place in the 1920s:

> Society thought they were slumming when they rolled from Curzon Street to Gerrard Street in their then modern Rolls Royces. The bottle party was all the rage too. Every cellar in Soho was occupied and packed. Cafés and restaurants, run mostly by aliens from the Continent, flourished. Speilers turned over more ready cash than did the Riviera casinos. Every club, speiler, many small cafés, had slot machines operating in them. These slot machines, adjusted properly, would earn a fortune in one night's play. A fortune for the owners. Not the proprietor in whose premises they were installed. The owners never got their fortunes however. Darby Sabini and his boys managed to 'win' too often on those machines. And if they were not paid up in hard cash the machines were wrecked along with the premises.[2]

And, according to Hill, there were the public houses and more streetwalkers than ever before – girls who, in addition to their trade, had a useful sideline in steering mugs into the afternoon drinking clubs and the nighttime spielers (sometimes spelled 'speilers'), or illegal gambling clubs.

Reaping the benefits of the Soho cash cow were the Sabini brothers led by Darby:

> From all these sources of immense wealth the Sabinis were drawing

revenue. Bottle parties, clubs, public-houses, cafés, even ordinary shops, had to pay protection money to the Sabini extortionists. None dared refuse. If they did the Sabinis gave information to the police which compelled the law to act for some broken petty regulation. Individuals connected with the premises were attacked in the streets. Proprietors of businesses finished up in hospital; the streets Up West were literally paved with gold for the Sabinis.[3]

Hill had his information from the once notorious Eddie Guerin, now very much on the slide and little more than a hotel sneak thief, yet a man who was friendly with Hill's sister Maggie, leader of a band of women shoplifters known as the Forty Thieves.

But who were these Sabinis? Although they operated principally from Saffron Hill, Clerkenwell, and were sometimes known as the Italians or the Raddies, the family exercised considerable influence over the Soho underworld of the 1920s and 1930s. Over two decades they dominated street and racecourse crime until the brothers, along with their formidable friend Pasqualino Papa, known as Bert Marsh, were interned as enemy aliens at the beginning of World War Two, appropriately enough at Ascot racecourse.

Just how many Sabinis there were and exactly which was which is difficult to unravel. The leader was undoubtedly Darby, but from time to time, when it suited him, he was known as Fred or Charles, the names of two elder brothers.

In all, there were six of them, beginning with Frederick, born in 1881, who, according to police files, traded as a bookmaker, Bob Wilson, at the Harringay Greyhound Stadium and took no part in the other brothers' affairs. Next came Charles, who was two years younger and was a list supplier working for the bookmaker Joe Levy in what the police thought was a protection racket. He owned shares in West Ham Stadium and was believed to be 'slightly mentally deranged'. Certainly by 1940 he had spent some time in mental hospitals. Then came Joseph, who on paper was the villain of the family. He had served in World War One in the Royal Welsh Fusiliers and then the Cheshire Regiment before being wounded in France. Invalided out, he was granted a 12-shillings-a-week (60p) pension. On 12 October 1922 he received three years' penal servitude for his part in the shooting of

Fred Gilbert in Mornington Crescent in part of the racecourse war of the time. The police thought, however, that after that he had split from his brothers and there was no evidence that he was operating behind the scenes. He traded as Harry Lake at Harringay dog track.

George Sabini was the youngest of the brothers – there was a disabled sister – who had no convictions and worked at both Harringay and White City. He was not regarded as being any part of the gang but it was noted that his name alone would provide him with protection. It was Ullano, better known as Darby, and Harry, known as Harryboy, who provided what was euphemistically called protection and what, in reality, was demanding money with menaces from the bookmakers.[4]

Darby Sabini was born in 1889. His Italian father died when he was two and the family were raised by their Irish mother. He left school at the age of 13 and boxed professionally from 1909. He first won a novice competition in February that year and at one time it was thought he could, in the words of Marlon Brando, 'have been a contender'. It is said that while still in his teens he had knocked out the fancied middleweight, Fred Sutton, in the first round. He boxed intermittently over a seven-year period, continuing until his last bout, when he lost over 16 rounds at the National Sporting Club in 1917. Unfortunately, he did not like the training required and instead became a strong-arm man for the Anglo-Italian Dai Sullivan's promotions at the Hoxton Baths.[5]

Later, he was employed by George Harris, a leading bookmaker of the time, again as a strong-arm man. Less than average height, Sabini always wore a flat cap and a shirt with no collar. He also wore a dark-brown suit with a high buttoned waistcoat and a black silk stock (cravat). He had selected this outfit when he was 20 and wore it for the rest of his life, indoors, outdoors, and so, it is said, sometimes in bed, where he slept with a loaded revolver under his pillow.

Harryboy was educated at St Peter's Roman Catholic School in Clerkenwell and then went to work for an optician. During World War One he worked in a munitions factory. He then became a bookmaker's clerk, working first for Gus Hall and later for Walter Beresford. When the latter died he became a commission agent. By 1940 he was a wealthy man with money in bonds for his children's education, bank accounts and a number of properties. His solicitors regarded him as a 'conveyancing client'. He was also a life governor of the Northern Hospital.

After World War One attendance at racecourses boomed, particularly at the Southern tracks, at which trotting was also a popular spectacle. Before the war the Birmingham gangs had established a hold on racecourse protection and now they sought to expand their empire. Under the leadership of Billy Kimber, who described himself as a bookmaker and punter, and the heavy gambler Andrew Townie, they metamorphosed as the Brummagem Boys despite the fact that most of the members came from the Elephant and Castle. Their organised racecourse protection began in around 1910 and for a time Kimber's mob took control of the Southern racecourses such as Newbury, Epsom, Earls Park and Kempton. Later, Kimber's men also had a loose alliance with one of the offshoots of the Hoxton Mob. In fact, Kimber was not a layer but instead controlled the best pitches on the courses, leasing them out on a half-profit but no loss-sharing basis. According to some accounts, Kimber was well regarded and it was looser elements out of his control who terrorised the mainly Jewish bookmakers in the cheaper rings at the Southern courses. The bookmakers themselves seem to have accepted the imposition fairly philosophically.

In some versions of the legend, the meteoric rise of Darby Sabini can be traced back to a fight in 1920 he had with Thomas Cooper 'Monkey' Benneworth, a leader of the Elephant Boys, when Benneworth deliberately tore the dress of an Italian girl serving behind the bar of the Griffin public house in Saffron Hill. Benneworth was knocked out and humiliated by Sabini. When his broken jaw had mended he returned with members of the Elephant Boys and in turn they were driven out of Little Italy by Sabini with the help of young Italians who looked on him as their leader. Now, with them behind him, he saw the opportunity to muscle in on some of the smaller gangs who were providing protection around the racetracks. Although the big gangs such as the Broad Mob from Camden Town, the mainly Jewish Aldgate Mob, and the Hoxton Mob could boast a membership of up to 60, they would be spread thinly because they were obliged to operate at several tracks a day. The Sabinis moved in in force.

Throughout the early 1920s there was a long series of battles between the Sabinis and Kimber and his men until, after interventions by Walter Beresford, the Sabinis and Kimber agreed to divide the racecourses between them and the racecourse wars died down. Now, with the Sabinis controlling the South, where there were more meetings, and Kimber and his friends the rest, the bookmakers were firmly in their hands.[6]

Meanwhile, from the 1920s onwards, the Sabinis had been branching out, taking interests in the Soho drinking and gambling clubs, and installing and running slot machines, and one of their principal hangouts was the Admiral Duncan in Old Compton Street. They were also extending their protection to criminals. If a burglary took place, the Sabinis, just as did the Krays years later, would send round for their share.

Darby Sabini may have finally made his peace with 'that fine fellow Billy Kimber', as a former police officer Tom Divall once described him, but for some time he had been under threat from other sources inside his own organisation. Some of the troops decided to seek a higher percentage of the takings. The four Cortesi brothers (Augustus, George, Paul and Enrico, also known as the Frenchies) were deputed to act as shop stewards to put the case. Almost immediately afterwards part of the Jewish element in the gang, to become known as the Yiddishers, also formed a breakaway group. In true business fashion, the Sabinis negotiated. The Cortesis would be given a greater percentage; the Yiddishers were given permission to lean on one, but only one, of the bookmakers under protection.[7]

However, peace did not last long. The Yiddishers began to side with the Cortesis and, with defections among the troops to the Frenchies, the Sabini position was substantially weakened. Then on 19 November 1922, just before midnight, Darby and Harryboy Sabini were trapped in the Fratellanza Club in Great Bath Street, Clerkenwell. Darby was punched and hit with bottles while Harry was shot in the stomach by Augustus and Enrico (Harry) Cortesi. Darby suffered a greater indignity. As he told the police court, his false teeth were broken as a result of the blows from the bottles. He was also able to confirm his respectability:

I am a quiet peaceable man. I never begin a fight. I've only once been

> attacked. I've never attacked anyone. I do a little bit of work as a commission agent sometimes for myself and sometimes for someone else. I'm always honest. The last day's work I did was two years' ago. I live by my brains.

He had only once carried a revolver and that was the time he was attacked at Greenford Park trotting track. Indeed he turned out his pockets in confirmation that he was not carrying a gun.[8]

The Cortesi brothers, who lived only five doors from the Fratellanza Club, were arrested the same night and, at the Old Bailey on 18 January 1923, Augustus and Enrico each received a sentence of three years' penal servitude. George and Paul Cortesi were found not guilty, as was Alexander Tomasso, known as Sandy Rice. A rather sour note on the Home Office file reads, 'It is a pity that the Cortesis were not charged with the murder of the Sabinis.'

Meanwhile, anonymous letters to the police detailed a series of incidents for which the Sabinis were said to be responsible. The principal correspondent was 'Tommy Atkins', who said he had been victimised and, if the police cared to contact him by putting an advertisement in the *Daily Express*, he would reveal all. Meanwhile, he alleged that Edward Emmanuel and a Girchan Harris were financing the Sabinis and that they had a number of members of the Flying Squad in their pay as well. The police inserted the advertisement suggesting a meeting, which was declined by 'Atkins', who, nevertheless, did supply details of some 12 incidents, including an attack by James Ford and George Langham, also known as Angelo Giancoli, on bookmaker John Thomas Phillips in Brighton. He also reported the story that the brother of George Moore had been killed and that the *Evening News* racing correspondent JMD had been attacked at Newmarket. There was a suggestion that Billy Westbury had been injured so badly that he was now 'mentally insane'.

The police could find no trace of the death of Moore's brother and reported that poor Billy Westbury had suffered only 'minor injuries'. It was correct, however, that JMD had indeed been attacked.

Without their leaders, the Cortesi faction had folded, but 1925 was apparently a vintage year for gang fighting in London. The list of incidents is formidable. According to the newspapers, on 15 February there was a razor slashing in Aldgate High Street and another slashing took place at Euston Station on 24 April. On 21 May ten armed men raided a club in Maiden Lane looking for the Sabinis or their men. Later that night shots were fired in the Harrow Road. On 30 July, three men were wounded in a club in Brighton. There was an incident when men fought on Hampstead Heath on 3 August. Five days later a man was attacked in the Marshalsea Road in the Borough and on 16 August, 24 men fought in Shaftesbury Avenue. Four days after that there was a pitched battle when 50 men fought with razors on the corner of Aldgate and Middlesex Street.

The story that Darby Sabini broke his jaw may, or may not, have been true but Monkey Benneworth remained an implacable foe. His list of convictions do not give him true credit for the mayhem he caused. He was first before the courts in July 1917, when he received probation at the County of London Sessions for theft. Then he got eight months at the Old Bailey in January 1922 for receiving. He was at the Epsom Derby meeting in 1924 when he collected another three months from the magistrates for being a suspected person. On 3 June 1925 he was bound over in the sum of £100 to be of good behaviour for his part in the hunt for the Sabinis in Maiden Lane. The gang's information was sadly astray that night because they broke up a tailor's shop in the belief it was a Sabini-owned club.

Nineteen twenty-five was something of a vintage year for Benneworth. He was back in court on 1 September for throwing a typewriter through the window of a barber's shop in Waterloo. For that he forfeited his £100 and, undeterred, with three others he attacked the Valli brothers and broke up the Union Club in Frith Street on 27 September. As was often the case, witnesses were far too afraid to identify him and he walked free.[9]

The police, asked for their comments, were dismissive, saying that the fight at Middlesex Street had been a minor incident and the one in Shaftesbury Avenue was total invention. They accepted the Maiden Lane incident and that Monkey Benneworth had been involved which, since he had appeared in court, he clearly had. As for the Hampstead Heath fight, there was no evidence that race gangs were involved. And as for allegations that Flying Squad officers were standing by watching some of the incidents, this was totally incorrect. Indeed the newspapers should be ashamed of themselves for such irresponsible reporting. However, in the House of Commons, the Home Secretary, William Joynson-Hicks, vowed to stamp out the race gangs.

That year Darby Sabini lost another battle when, following a series of unfavourable articles, he sued D.C. Thomson, the proprietors of the offending *Topical Times*, for libel. On the day of the action he failed to appear and costs of £775 were awarded against him. He did not pay and bankruptcy proceedings were commenced.[10]

After that, Sabini – tired perhaps of trying to keep the peace between the Jewish elements in his gang and the White family, led by the patriarch Alf – rather drew in his horns. He retired to the calmer shores of Brighton, leaving behind him Harryboy as the *de facto* leader of the clan. In October 1929, Darby was fined £5 for assaulting bookmaker David Isaacs. After an incident at Hove Greyhound Stadium, he had attacked him first in the Ship Hotel and then in a billiard saloon. When Isaacs was asked why he had not brought witnesses, he replied, 'How can I get witnesses against a man like this, when everyone goes in fear of their life of him?'

Two years earlier, in 1927, the so-called Battle of Ham Yard had taken place, with factions led by Wal McDonald of the Elephant Boys and Harry Sabini, which resulted in Sabini being cut across the cheek.

'Until 1927,' wrote the author Peter Cheyney, 'the Hackney Gang [the Sabinis] was supreme in the West End. Then came the battle of Ham Yard when the gang suffered a severe reversal in terms both of blood spilled and prestige lost.[11]

After that things died down, possibly because another leading Elephant Boy, Bert McDonald, Wal's brother, left for America along with Billy Kimber.[12]

Things flared up again on 25 January 1930, when the old villain and another opponent of the family, Jack 'Dodger' Mullins, who was now out of prison and exercising his muscle, led a team looking for Sabini men in Soho. They found one, Angelo Costognetti in the Argus Club in Greek Street. Costognetti was unmercifully beaten and thrown on the fire while Edith Milburn, who tried to protect him, was also given a beating. On 5 May, Mullins and the Steadman brothers, Charles and George, were acquitted.[13]

The fight on 6 February 1930 in the Admiral Duncan in Old

Compton Street may have had its origins at Sandown Park when a Sabini man, Sid Baxter, demanded £10 from another Elephant Boy Jim McDonald. McDonald knocked him down and as a result was a target for reprisals, particularly when Baxter enlisted the support of the ex-boxer George Sewell, who liked to be known as the 'Cobblestone Kid' and was the father of the well-known character actor of the same name. In turn, Billy Kimber asked the Phillips brothers, John and Arthur, to help McDonald. Working on the principle that blessed is he who gets his blow in first, the brothers and four other men then attacked Sewell, cutting his throat with a piece of broken glass. For their pains they received long sentences. Sewell temporarily retired to be with Darby Sabini in Brighton.[14]

In June the next year the Elephant Boys went on another rampage, breaking up Cypriot and Greek cafés in Rathbone Place and extending their activities down into Windmill Street and the café of Zacharias Panagi. It was not something that the Sabinis could treat lightly and again reprisals were swift.

And, just as swiftly as they had arisen, so did the street fights die away. It was not until the middle 1930s, by which time Harryboy Sabini had expanded their territory into greyhound racing, that they again came under another serious threat. This time it was from Alf White, whose extended family – including his son Harry and their friends – had been getting stronger over the years and were now set to challenge their former allies.

Frank Fraser, who as a boy carried a bucket for the Sabinis at the racecourses, may not have thought too much of Harry White's ability on the cobbles, but there is no doubt he undertook his fair share of interwar protection.

In January 1931 White could be found along with the Russian-born Eddie Fleischer, or Fletcher, in a fight outside the Phoenix Club in Little Denmark Street. The manager Casimir Raczynski, who wrestled as Carl Reginski, and a man called Fred Roche had been attacked as they left the club, and White and Fleischer were accused of malicious wounding. Raczynski had his throat badly cut. The matter, as did so many of these affairs, blew over. When the case came up for committal, Roche said he had made a mistake while still suffering from the effects of the attack. Now he was sure that, whoever hit him, it was neither White nor Fleischer. The one independent witness, Thomas Jeacock, who had identified the pair, was pleased to tell the court that Roche assured him he had made a mistake. In such ways are things sorted out.[15] Running parallel with that case was one concerning Raczynski's brother, who was accused of taking an iron bar to a customer and a waitress in the Phoenix. Again, the witnesses failed to come up to scratch. Indeed, they failed to come to court.

Like Darby Sabini before him, Alf White maintained a low profile so far as the courts were concerned. Then, in April 1935, the police received a series of letters complaining he was one of the worst racecourse pests and blackmailers ever to set foot on a racecourse. And, worse, he had the police in his pay. It may have stirred the authorities into action, because in the July he and his sons William and Alfred Jr each received 12 months' hard labour for assaulting John McCarthy Defferary, the licensee of the Yorkshire Stingo in the Marylebone Road, at the Wharncliffe Rooms on 17 April that year. The fight had been at a dance in aid of St Mary's Hospital and Defferary lost the sight of his left eye. There was a suggestion that Carrie White, Alf's daughter, had been given £12 taken from the victim.[16]

It was after the Battle of Lewes racecourse in 1936 and two serious outbreaks – in the second of which a Kings Cross man, Michael Macausland, died – that an accommodation was reached. On the night of 12 March 1938 Macausland was attacked outside his home in Kings Cross when two cars drew up, and up to eight men, allegedly including two white men; Eddie Raimo and Jock Wyatt, slashed him and John Phillips, who went to protect him. The case against Raimo and Wyatt collapsed when the prosecution offered no evidence at the Old Bailey at the end of May. The 24-year-old Macausland died in the July – from a kidney disease, said a pathologist, but Macausland's wife of seven weeks said he had never been the same after the attack. 'It was murder – it was no natural death,' called out a man after the inquest verdict of natural causes. 'Let the jury see his clothes. Look at the cuts on his face.'[17]

The death of Macausland followed an affray in Soho in February the previous year in which his brother had been involved. Eddie Raimo and Jock Wyatt would both go on to be key men in the history of London crime. Raimo, a man who modelled himself on George

Raft, wearing a black shirt with a white tie, maintained his allegiance to White for over a decade, and Wyatt who linked up with Billy Hill, turned his undoubted talents to safebreaking for which he received 12 years in 1950.

Now it was agreed the Sabinis should have the West End and the Whites the Kings Cross area. They became known as the King's Cross Gang and Alf White would hold court in the Bell Public House or Hennekeys in the Pentonville Road, exercising strict discipline among his followers. 'No bad language was allowed,' says John Vaughan, a former police officer from King's Cross. 'First time you were warned. The next time – out.' It had been the same with Darby Sabini: women were to be treated properly and Italian youths could not drink before they were twenty. His had been a reasonably benevolent dictatorship.

But towards the middle of the 1930s a new face had arrived in Soho from the East End, where he claimed he had protected Jewish people against the Fascist leader Oswald Mosley. He may well have protected them but it was at a price he set. The man was John Comer, born Jacob Comacho, and far better known as Jack Spot; either (he said) because he was always on hand if you were in a spot or (probably more likely if more prosaically) because of a mole on his face. Spot always maintained, with no evidence to back it whatsoever, that he had been taught his trade by the American Sam Clynes, who had been a member of the New York based Murder Incorporated and came to England in the 1930s. Clynes died in prison at the end of World War Two and Spot, so he said, arranged his funeral.

Well before then, however, Spot had been involved in an incident that was held against him for the next 20 years, when he is said to have given evidence against Jimmy Wooder. Once again it is difficult to disentangle myth from reality. Wooder ran an Islington-based protection team and Spot's friend Itchky Simmons was the victim. As the doorman of the New Moulin Club, owned by the one-time world champion boxer from the East End, Ted 'Kid' Lewis – who at one time, misguidedly, was a Mosley man – he was attacked by Wooder and given a kicking. Then in December 1936 he took another beating from him and three others, this time in Fox's, a billiard hall in Dean Street. It is now that Spot is said to have given evidence on his behalf. The case was a curious one and also involved 'Kid' Lewis as well as the boxing promoter Jack Solomons. Simmons was said to be Lewis's minder, which was a bit odd because, of all people, Lewis should have been able to deal with any trouble himself. In his memoirs Lewis suggests Simmons was simply the doorman.

At the end of the case, the recorder, Sir Holam Gregory, had some strong words to say:

> We have had to listen to an unpleasant case which arises out of an affray in one of those horrible and vile places that exist in the West End under the title of a club.
>
> Those places exist and do untold harm to the community. Young men are still being corrupted there; fights are taking place nightly.[18]

Gerry Parker, Spot's onetime henchman, has the story that Wooder and others later gave Spot a bad beating with the butts of cues in another Soho billiard saloon when he was again trying to help Simmons. Later, Spot learned that Wooder drank in Whitechapel at a club, Pancho's. He caught up with him in the lavatory and cut him from ear to ear.[19]

What is certain is that in 1938 Spot received six months for an assault on poor Simmons in a club in the City – it was a matter of protection and his self-publicising story that he received his sentence for helping break up a Fascist march is so much rubbish. It was while Spot was serving his six-month sentence in 1939 that he came to the notice of the one-eared – the other had been bitten off in a fight – Arthur Skurry from West Ham and earned this very hard man's approval. Spot told Parker that the incident that gained him recognition stemmed from Antonio 'Babe' Mancini and his dislike of Jews, which manifested in his habit of spitting in their prison food. Mancini was a long-term Sabini man who served a number of short sentences mainly resulting from thefts and fights at racecourses.[20] Spot at first refused to eat the food that Mancini had fouled. Mancini had also been appointed the prison barber and Spot was sent to him. When he found Mancini was the one to cut his hair, fighting broke out and Mancini came off badly.

'Skurry was a diddicoy. He saw Jack do up "Babe" Mancini and that's when he said he didn't realise Jews could fight. Skurry was like the King of Upton Park,' says Parker. Unlike a great number of Spot stories, this one cannot be disproved. Mancini was certainly in prison at the time, serving a sentence of one year's hard labour imposed at Folkestone Quarter Sessions for stealing a wallet at the racecourse.

In any event, Spot must have impressed Skurry, for over the years he forged an alliance with the Upton Park gypsies, who generally 'protected' small market stallholders. Fighters they may have been but they were not smart and, effectively, the Upton Park Mob – with luminaries such as Skurry, Teddy Machin, Porky Bennett and Jackie Reynolds – became Spot's boys after World War Two ended.

At the beginning of the war there was one last protection-related death. On 13 November 1939 Charles 'Chick' Lawrence from Hoxton was found dead in Stepney with severe head injuries. The police believed he had been badly beaten and his body dumped in the area, one that he did not normally frequent. A name associated with the killing has long been that of Albert Dimeo, known as Dimes, Bert Marsh's long-serving friend.

7

The Roaring Twenties and Thirties

By the 1920s prostitution in Soho was firmly in the hands of the French and their leader, Juan Antonio Castanar. Lithe, dark and handsome, he was an accomplished tango dancer who at one time had had a £50-a-week contract with the great Pavlova. He then opened a school for dance in Frith Street, using it as a front for what was known as 'white-birding' – selling women to dance troupes abroad at £50 a girl. Dance academies were popular at the time, charging up to £50 to teach girls to dance but, except for the very talented, there would be no job available except in clubs, where they would effectively be prostitutes.[1] There is a story that during Castanar's time in Soho he was paid a visit by Darby Sabini at his dance school, then in Archer Street, to retrieve the daughter of an Italian whom he was trying to lure into prostitution. Castanar is said to have handed the girl back without demur. Given Sabini's reputation it is possibly even a true story but there are other stories that Sabini then had Castanar's premises torched.[2]

The reverse side of Castanar's business was to arrange marriages of convenience for foreign women – generally prostitutes wishing to acquire a British passport – to threadbare Englishmen. It was a trade that had been going on from the turn of the century. Generally, the women, often infected and unable to get a certificate to work in France, would come over on a cheap-day-return ticket. Once in England they would be met at the port and brought to London, where they would go through a marriage of convenience and be whisked away to a flat.

One of the leading marriage experts on this side of the Channel was Archibald King, who in 1924 received three years' penal servitude for bigamy. Helping out by scouring the Soho labour exchange for other suitably derelict Englishmen was George Venier who spent much of his time in Old Compton Street and at the Black Cat Café, that source of annoyance to the magazine *John Bull.* Others in the team included a former jockey, Myles Fogler, Joseph Rizzo, Rene Janssens and Alfredo Sauvaget, known as Freddo, one of a number fancied for the murder of the French gangster, Martial LeChevalier, whose jugular was slashed at the corner of Air Street and Berwick Street shortly before midnight on 27 June.[3]

Castanar's great rival was Casimir Micheletti, an Algerian known as the Assassin because of his ability with a stiletto. Micheletti, who gave his occupation as a furrier, was described as an extremely good-looking young man with dark hair, mild of manner and soft of voice, who could fight with the savagery of a tiger.[4] Both ran strings of prostitutes; each loathed the other and when Castanar was slashed across the face at the 43 Club in Old Compton Street, although no charges were ever brought, it was common knowledge that Micheletti was the attacker. He was also another of the suspects in LeChevalier's murder.[5]

LeChevalier, well known in Soho, was one of around a dozen Frenchmen involved in the passport and white-slaving rackets of the time. Two months earlier he had arranged a marriage for Helen Chantenne to a John Burns and was now living off the girl's earnings. LeChevalier had quarrelled with a man known as 'the Algerian' in the Gordon Billiard Saloon in Frith Street. Witnesses also suggested that LeChevalier had double-crossed Freddo Sauvaget over the passport racket and that night he was attacked by four men. Although an alert was put out to arrest Sauvaget at the ports, he was never found.

The Sabini name could often be relied on to produce terror in the community even when the family had nothing to do with things. In early October 1925 Giovanni Periglione, Georges Modebodze and Wilfred Cooper were charged with demanding money with menaces from a cook, Gaston Reynaud. Periglione and Reynaud, who had lodged together in Old Compton Street, had quarrelled and fought. Later Cooper told Reynaud that Periglione was going to cut him but for £100 he would put him under the protection of the Sabini gang, of which he was 'chief', something that must have come as a surprise to both Darby and Harryboy.[6] Cooper received four years' imprisonment and wrote to the police to say he could provide information about the killer of LeChevalier. He was interviewed but his story was discounted.

Micheletti was a more or less innocent witness in another murder trial. On 5 April 1926 yet another Frenchman, Emile Berthier, shot and killed a motorcar dealer, Charles Ballada, in the Union Club in Frith Street, which had been wrecked the previous year by Monkey Benneworth. The club had a wooden bar along one side, tables and chairs, a couple of fruit machines and some crude murals on the walls. When the police arrived they found Ballada sprawled in a corner, shot in the stomach.

Berthier described himself as a wine merchant and indeed he had a business in Tooley Street, but he was also known to be a prostitutes' bully; and, although Ballada – described as an acrobat – had no convictions, he also lived with a prostitute and thief.

According to the evidence of a Juan Gabaron, known as L'Espagnol, Berthier believed Ballada owed him money and went up to him saying, 'My friends, I respect them, but those who owe me money including my partners will have to pay me, otherwise I am going to settle with them. I shall do them an injury.' Ballada replied, 'You must not talk like that. You must do things not talk about them.' Berthier then shot him with an automatic pistol.

A member of the club promptly hit Berthier over the head with a billiard cue but he escaped, stopping only to have his wounds cleaned, before he caught the train to Newhaven, where he was arrested about to board the packet for Dieppe.

Berthier had earlier written a letter, which was produced at the trial:

> I know the [*sic*] Micheletti wants to kill me because I do not give him any more money. You must admit I have given him enough. See, actually that makes £1,500 all the money I owe and he is asking for more. While he is away for a month I warn you that if he continues

to ask me for money I shall do my best to kill him. He has killed two or three others and this man is an assassin.

That was the story according to the evidence, but another version is that Micheletti had swindled Berthier of £2,000 and Ballada, who closely resembled the Algerian, was shot by mistake. On the other hand the detective Robert Fabian believed a feud between Ballada and Berthier had originated in Paris. At the Old Bailey Micheletti gave evidence to the effect that he was terrified of Berthier. Ballada was, he said, his friend.

The jury took only minutes to find Berthier, whose father had committed suicide by throwing himself off a building at the Lyons exhibition in 1904, guilty but insane. He was later repatriated to France.[7]

In April 1929, both Micheletti and Castanar were deported from England, but within a few weeks Castanar managed to smuggle himself back for a short period before he was once more thrown out, this time permanently. He made his way to Paris and earned a modest living as a tango dancer and running a small stable of girls. In February 1930 he and Micheletti met in a café in Paris and later that night Castanar shot his rival dead. At his trial he blamed the killing on a mysterious man known to both of them as Le Marseillais. It was he who had shot Micheletti, put the gun in Castanar's hand and ran away. The story did him no good. Castanar was not believed and was sent to Devil's Island.

The years 1935 and 1936 saw an outbreak of murders of prostitutes and a pimp in Soho. The killing of the girls began in November 1935 when Josephine Martin, known as 'French Fiffi' – the French and other foreign girls were generally known in Soho as 'Fiffis' – was strangled with her own silk stockings in her flat above the Globe Club in Archer Street. In fact, she was Russian-born and had married a waiter, Henry Martin, to gain citizenship. She was well regarded in the block as quiet and respectable but she was known to have acted as an agent for the dope dealer and white slaver Emil Allard, known as Max Kessel. A name in the frame was that of her brother Albert Mechanik, who had once run the Polyglot Club in Rupert Street, to whom she gave money on a regular basis. His argument was that, since she was his sole source of income, there was no reason for him to kill her.[8] There was no evidence against him and he was never charged.

Then, on 24 January 1936, Allard's body was found under a hedge near St Albans in Hertfordshire. He had been shot a number of times. Allard had been in and out of London since 1913 selling women to Latin American brothels and arranging marriages for foreign prostitutes. Although he lived in James Street off Oxford Street, he was killed at 36 Little Newport Street in a flat leased by George Lacroix. Also known as Roger or Marcel Vernon, Lacroix, sent to Devil's Island for robbery in 1924, was one of seven to escape in 1927 – indeed, one of the relatively few to make a successful escape from the penal colony. Lacroix lived with Suzanne Bertrand, who had 'married' an Englishman called Naylor and so obtained her passport to work the Soho streets.

The officer in the case, the slightly dubious Chief Inspector 'Nutty' Sharpe,[9] traced the car used to dump the body to a garage in Soho Square owned by another Frenchman, Pierre Alexandre. Through him he found Suzanne Bertrand's maid, Marcelle Aubin, who had been sent to order the car and it was on to Little Newport Street, where he found pieces of glass on the pavement that matched those found in the car. In his dying struggle, Allard had broken the flat window.

But by then both Lacroix and Bertrand were long gone back to France. An application for their extradition was declined and they stood trial in Paris in April 1937. It was then that at least some of the story came out. The killing had, it seems, been personal rather than business. Lacroix had been in partnership with Allard, marrying off the women. They had first met in Montreal, where they were in the white-slave trade together. They both fancied Suzanne Bertrand, who had been with Lacroix since he left his wife in 1933.

There was some peripheral evidence that explained rather more. Georges Hainnaux, known as Jo Le Terroir, told the tribunal that Allard had confessed to killing a white slaver, Bouchier, in Montreal in 1930, who was the so-called Le Marseillais, said by Micheletti to be the one who killed his rival Castanar. Lacroix was sentenced to 10 years, to be followed by 20 years' banishment, and Suzanne Bertrand was acquitted. Le Terroir took the view that the killings of Bouchier, LeChevalier, Micheletti and Allard had all been part of a long, drawn-out struggle for the control of prostitution and the white-slave racket in Soho and on the Continent.

Hainnaux was certainly correct about the killing of the white slaver. Henri Bouclier, known as Old Martigues, the slang name for a man from Marseilles, was shot and his body dumped at Laval-sur-la-Lac on 1 July 1930. It is probable that both Allard and Lacroix were involved in the killing.[10]

In April 1936, five months after the death of Allard, Marie Jeanet Cotton was strangled in Lexington Street. Born in France, she had married a Louis Cousins. A woman of some means who acted from time to time as a moneylender, she had been living with an Italian café owner and it was in his house that her body was found. No charges were ever brought.

The same month Constance Hind (or Bird) was strangled in her flat in Old Compton Street, this time with a piece of wire. Next, on 16 August 1937, Elsie Torchon, who adopted a French accent and was known as French Paulette or French Marie but who came from Croydon and worked in Wardour Street, was found strangled with her scarf in Bath Row, Euston. The police and newspapers were keen to play down any suggestion that the deaths of these three women were any spillover from the death of Allard, instead preferring to promote a 'Jack the Strangler' who had killed the women after quarrels over terms and conditions.

Certainly they were correct regarding the death of Torchon. This was solved by fingerprints and had nothing to do with the earlier deaths. In fact her killer was extremely fortunate not to hang. Two months earlier he had been sentenced to 10 years for manslaughter after strangling another prostitute, Catherine Chamberlain, against the wall of Fenham Barracks in Newcastle. Now he was identified from a fingerprint on the metal rim of Elsie Torchon's handbag. To avoid any possible prejudice he was tried at the Old Bailey under a different name. He claimed he had accidentally strangled her when he pushed her and she fell. Again, the jury acquitted him of murder. Sentencing him to 16 years for her manslaughter, Mr Justice Atkinson commented, 'It is well for you that the jury did not know of your history'.[11]

Not all the control of prostitutes was in French hands – a survey found that 98 per cent of girls walked the streets, some earning only £1 a night – but that was where the real money was.[12]

There were of course the independents, and among them Luis Hubert and Lucile Longuet, who in late October 1923 were arrested in a New Oxford Street flat equipped with handcuffs, whips, birches and indecent photographs. Although she was alleged to have sold a girl for £50, the pair were dealt with only under the Aliens Act offences and each received six months. Queenie Gerald surfaced from time to time. In 1921 there was a fracas and she was convicted of disorderly behaviour. She was reputed to tour the lower-class nightclubs in Soho recruiting girls who, rather than remain on the streets after midnight, used them to pick up clients. That was the year she featured in the exposé *Sex Slaves in a Piccadilly Flat*, in which she appeared on the cover of the book with a whip and cowering girls, and there were stories of girls who had been badly thrashed at her 'parties'. But there was never again any proof that she was operating a brothel.

Over the years she was denounced by magazines such as *John Bull*, to whom she angrily replied, complaining that the real procuress of the town was Rose Phillips (also known as Heathcote, Gutteridge and Letta, and variously of Great Portland, Berners, Kingley, Orchard, and Panton Streets).

In 1922 Gerald, who walked into restaurants with an ill-tempered parrot in her muff, had moved out of Maddox Street after being sued for the rent and was working from Long Acre. At some time she took up with a former police officer, Robert Gordon Brown, a curious man who after his retirement from the Met became the superintendent of a workhouse. Quite what was their relationship is difficult to divine. She paid the rents on various flats and, although he was in his late sixties, he seems to have been her protector. Certainly on one occasion he rescued her from an angry crowd protesting about her activities. Eventually she threw him out; punches were exchanged and she brought a County Court action for assault. She claimed £50 and was awarded a farthing.[13]

In July 1926 when she was residing at 85 Newman Street off Tottenham Court Road she was involved in a curious incident when she claimed that an ermine stole and muff and a kimono worth around

£1,150 were stolen by men she said she had simply invited in for a drink. There was more to it than that, and it seems that the men, all of whom had prior convictions, thought they could steal from her without her going to the police. They were wrong. She was more than their match. Her cleaning lady – read 'maid' – gave evidence that she kept handcuffs and five whips in the flat and the Hon. Geraldine, as she now was, had no hesitation in saying they were for her protection, nor was she embarrassed in explaining bits of her past. Indeed the judge, Sir Ernest Wild, seems rather to have admired her. John Harris and Victor Lester received four years; the third man, Jonas Price, who claimed to have paid her £5, was sentenced to 18 months' hard labour. She was suitably grateful to the police and wanted to give £5 to a young constable. This generous offer was refused and two senior officers took the trouble to return the money to her, at the same time having a good look round her premises and later posting a warning that no young officers should go there alone.[14]

The deportation of Castanar and Micheletti and the flight of Lacroix effectively signalled the end of the French control of prostitution in Soho. Now the Maltese Messina brothers – Carmelo, Alfredo, Salvatore, Attilio and Eugenio – took over.

The Messinas' father, Giuseppe, came from Linguaglossa in Sicily and in the late 1890s went to Malta, where he worked in a brothel in Valetta. There he married a Maltese girl and his first two sons, Salvatore and Alfredo, were born there. The family then moved to Alexandria in 1905, where he built a chain of brothels. The remaining sons were all born there, and their father ensured they were all well educated. In 1932 Giuseppe Messina was expelled from Egypt. Two years later Eugenio, the third son, born in 1908, came to England. He was able to claim British nationality because his father had sensibly taken Maltese citizenship. With Eugenio was his wife Colette, a French prostitute. It was on her back that Messina founded his London empire.

More girls were recruited from the Continent and as the empire grew he was joined on the management side by his brothers, who all adopted English-sounding names. Eugenio was Edward Marshall, Carmelo was Charles Maitland and Alfredo became Alfred Martin. When they take false names most criminals stick to the same initials but Salvatore and Attilio were exceptions. Salvatore was Arthur Evans and Attilio took the name Raymond Maynard. Properties were bought throughout the West End and the brothers turned their attention to English girls. The technique used was age-old: good-looking girls were given a good time; seduction, possibly with the promise of marriage, followed – and then it became time to pay. If the good life was to continue the price for it was prostitution.

The girls were under the day-to-day charge of the French-born Marthe Watts, who to obtain British citizenship had married Arthur Watts, an alcoholic Englishman brought to Paris for the purpose. Born in 1913, according to her story she had been placed at the age of 15 in a brothel in Le Havre after lying about her age.[15] There followed a career in the brothels of Europe, ending with her marriage to Watts. From her point of view the marriage was a total success. She saw him only when she was charged with brothel keeping in London and he was dragged to court to give evidence that he was indeed her husband and as a result she could not be deported.

In April 1941 she met Eugenio in the Palm Beach Club, Wardour Street. Within a month she became his mistress and a few weeks later she was out working the streets for him. Her loyalty seems to have been remarkable: despite regular and savage beatings – the favourite method seems to have been with an electric-light flex – she stayed with the family, taking charge of the new girls. As a mark of her devotion she had herself tattooed over the left breast, '*L'homme de ma vie. Gino le maltais*' – a tribute she later had removed.

After the introductory period involving fine restaurants, clubs and lavish presents, life with Eugenio Messina was no fun for any of his girls. They were not allowed out on their own; during the war they could not accept American servicemen as clients; they were not allowed to smoke; nor, curiously, were they allowed to wear low-cut dresses or even look at film magazines where the male stars were in any sort of undress. They did not take off their clothes with the customers. Worst of all was the ten-minute rule: clients were allowed to stay only that length of time before the maid knocked on the door. It seems to have resembled the Paris and Miami slaughterhouses where girls never leave the bed and a bell rings after 15 minutes. The other Messina brothers seem to have been more relaxed in their attitudes, particularly over the ten-minute rule.

8

Violence Has Nothing to Do With It

Gangs do not have to wield knives and guns to be antisocial, and, indeed, some of the most dangerous have been those whose members use the pen and the tongue as opposed to the sword.

Those who offer friendship and even love on however fleeting a basis often have the wallet rather than the heart as the object of desire. Those who decide to sample the delights of Soho and are befriended by young men and women they meet there often pay dearly for this temporary and usually unrewarding experience.

Just how many blackmailers have operated in Soho is impossible to say. The homosexual George Ives, who kept a scrapbook of newspaper clippings before World War One, pasted in a couple every year but these were the cases that came to the courts. At the end of the nineteenth century, men such as Freddie Atkins, who picked up men in the Alhambra and took them back to a hotel room where his partner, 'Uncle' James Burton, burst in, were usually never prosecuted.

The end of the 1914–18 war saw the return of girls as decoys. They would pick up young returned officers and tell them about select and private Victory Dances with a five-guinea entrance fee. Once through the door the mark might find a buffet and wine but there would also be crooked card games and with them the opportunity for blackmail or the badger game (in which men are lured into compromising positions with boys or women, only for the boy's or girl's 'father', 'uncle' or 'brother' to burst in and demand compensation).[1] Victims were reluctant to go to the police and so some of the teams ran for years without the inconvenience of a prosecution.

In May 1927 George William Taylor, described as a professional blackmailer, received a sentence of penal servitude for life. He led a gang who latched onto, and leeched from, Captain Richard Dixon, who had been caught in a classic badger trap in Soho. One evening at the Palace Theatre the captain had met Norman Stuart, who described himself as an art dealer but who, apart from his blackmailing activities, played the banjo outside public houses and to theatre queues. A fortnight later he went with him to a room in Shaftesbury Avenue, when in came Stuart's 'brother'. The version according to the captain was that he had arranged to meet Stuart at Knightsbridge Tube station. Stuart suggested the captain leave his bag in his room and the trap was sprung.

Although he denied any indecency, over the next three years the captain was blackmailed to the tune of £10,000. It was only then that he summoned enough courage to go to a solicitor, who went straight to the police. Led by Taylor, the gang had shown great ingenuity in separating the captain from his money, including introducing him to Arthur Brown, who posing as a 'detective' offered to 'deal with the blackmailer'.

Stuart may have played the innocent but he was, nevertheless, an experienced blackmailer. Two months before his arrest, his wife had been sentenced to 18 months for a straight badger-game blackmail when her brother, David Nicholls, received three years. She also posed as Stuart's sister, defending his good name against the captain's allegations. Stuart received 12 years.

Others in the team included Alfred Tanner, said to be Hebrew in profile and mean in expression, who posed as Detective Lynch and netted 15 years. Joseph Maples, the right-hand man, had first been sentenced in 1912 for robbery with violence. He and another man had beaten up and robbed a victim whom they had taken to a room. For the next 15 years he worked the badger game. Described by himself as a pedlar and by the police as a sodomite and 'professional blackmailer', Maples also received 15 years. Frank Leonard, who received 10 years, was in fact Max or Abram Glown, a Russian-born scout for the team, selecting likely boys who passed on the details of possible victims.

It was the clumsiness of the last of the enlisted men, so to speak, that led to the break-up. Arthur Brown was really a well-thought-of burglar and safebreaker known as Newcastle Arthur. He was drawn in because of the immense amount of money to be made and for his sins received eight years' penal servitude. Brown had visiting cards printed in the name of Detective Sergeant Benshaw, appropriately inscribed 'Blackmail a Speciality'. It was when Brown failed to get results that the captain finally went to his lawyers. Blackmailers never quit when they are ahead.

Taylor, who spoke several languages, was said to be the son of a former government official. Known in the underworld as the Sheik, he was probably born in Egypt. He was certainly in Alexandria when he deserted from the army, for which he received a five-year sentence in July 1918.

At one time he ran a café in Sauchiehall Street, Glasgow, and was a known putter-up for safebreakers and swindlers. A great gambler and friend of the French ponces LeChevalier and Ballada, Taylor was also thought to be linked to a poisoning case in the West End. Completely ruthless, he had once shot at his mistress when she declined to become a decoy for the team. For this he received a modest four months. When another victim told him, 'I'll end my life,' Taylor replied, 'Best thing you can do.'[2]

Amazingly, Maples's wife and Taylor's girlfriend wrote to solicitors for the captain, asking that he intercede to have their sentences reduced. It was a course of action that appealed neither to the captain nor his solicitors. The pair also argued that, since the captain was a wealthy man, the loss of a few thousand pounds did not materially harm him and, while some blackmail continues for the life of the victim, they had been operating on the captain for only a matter of three and a half years. Unsurprisingly, it was not an argument well received by the Court of Appeal. At least Newcastle Arthur Brown had the decency not to appeal.[3]

Sentencing Taylor and his crew, the Lord Chief Justice had taken the opportunity to advise anyone caught in such a position to go to his solicitor or the police. They could also be sure to be able to rely on the discretion of the press.

It was all very well for the Lord Chief to be so positive. In fact, as a general rule, the authorities and courts were by no means sympathetic to men who found themselves paying money after a homosexual relationship. Thirty years later, when the Wolfenden Committee on Homosexual Offences and Prostitution reported in 1957, it quoted the case of a man A, aged 49, who met B (35) in a cinema. They went to A's flat, committed buggery and did so for the next seven years. B then began demanding money and over a three-month period obtained some £40. A complained to the police and as part of a pathetic little statement to the police he wrote, 'I sent the money because I thought from his letters that if I did not do so he would tell the people at the shop and where I live that I had had sexual intercourse with him.'

The Director of Public Prosecutions recommended that no action be taken over the blackmail but that both be charged with buggery. Each was charged with two specimen counts. Neither asked for matters to be taken into consideration; neither had previous convictions. Each received nine months' imprisonment.

Back in January 1933 the one-time West End actor, the lank-haired Harry Raymond, received five years for blackmail. In his heyday he had appeared in the West End in the stage version of Edgar Wallace's racing thriller, *The Calendar*, but those days were long gone. On his release on licence in October 1936 he took the lease of the Philary, a café in Lisle Street, from where he led what was described the next year at the Old Bailey as a 12-strong 'gang of blackmailers and sodomites'. Additionally, up to 40 young men were groomed and kitted out by Raymond before being placed in hotels, restaurants and cinemas to solicit wealthy-looking men. Part of the training was in patience and it was only after a series of theatre visits and late-night suppers that there was the obligatory visit to the hotel room or flat. And there the boy, now in tears, would say he would be obliged to tell his parents or, worse, his brother, who just happened to be outside.

The gang included one man who, posing as the vicar of an East End parish, sought out the erring military and other gents, suggesting they might like to pay £500 for the expenses of the defiled youth to go to Australia.

In just over a year one senior officer paid £10,000 for his sins to Raymond, whose web spread from Cornwall to the Shetlands. The end came when Mr A from Sussex plucked up the courage to go to the police. Raymond was arrested in a teashop near Victoria Station when Mr A took officers to overhear Raymond say, 'Five thousand pounds. You know I can ruin you unless you pay.' Apart from his team of blackmailers, Raymond was also running foreign prostitutes from his café. This time he received 10 years.[4]

He was still at the game 10 years later, when he pleaded guilty to obtaining money by false pretences while posing as a private detective from the H. Banks Detective Agency, Manchester. This time he received five years. His pleas of not guilty to blackmail were accepted by the prosecution. By then Raymond had founded the Pygmalion Kama Society, which purported to be an Oriental society for people interested in 'the rituals of sex'. Leaflets entitled 'Temple of Lust and Passion' were handed out in the street to men, inviting them to the society's premises just off New Bond Street. Subscriptions were between three and five pounds, but once there the men were trapped into paying money rather than have their loved ones know they had been on the premises. 'One of the most sinister characters ever to lurk in the criminal haunts of Soho,' thought the *News of the World*.[5].

Not all blackmailers worked in such extensive setups. Many were pairs or trios or were husband-and-wife teams. In March 1923 Jerome and Adolphus Cooper received three years and 18 months and 24 and 20 strokes of the birch respectively in another blackmail scam. The judge said he was sorry neither was fit enough to receive the cat. They had taken their victim to a Shaftesbury Avenue flat for a drink and then demanded his money and jewellery.[6]

There were always variations on the game and three years later two Gerrard Street moneylenders, Adolphe Levy and Maurice Herbert, perished along with their 18-year-old secretary, Olive Walton. The pair sent her to see a Mayfair broker, Samuel James, on a spurious piece of business and, half an hour after she returned to Soho, a complaint of indecent assault was made against him, promptly dismissed by the Marlborough Street stipendiary. James must have smelled a rat from the first, saying, 'If it's the Herbert I know I'm not having that from him,' and went straight to the police, who listened in to a meeting when Levy, discussing terms, first agreed to accept £1,000 on his secretary's behalf but, as with all good blackmailers, when it seemed James would pay the sum, upped the ante to £1,500. The pair received three years and the girl was bound over to come up for judgment if she offended again.[7]

Blackmail has been called 'Murder of the Soul',[8] but in 1927 Henry Charles Wiltshire came within an ace of being charged with the murder of his partner, in fact his wife Madeleine, in the badger game. They had their claws in a vicar who had sensibly gone to a genuine private enquiry agent when Madeleine was found dead on 25 April in a flat in Litchfield Street, poisoned after drinking potassium cyanide disguised as tea. Two cups were found in the flat. There was some evidence that Wiltshire had bought the cyanide, which, a witness claimed, he told her was for use in 'coining', that is, making counterfeit coins. He denied this and the coroner, calling him a liar with a cock-and-bull story, said he could not be sure who had supplied the poison, whether it was suicide, a suicide pact or indeed murder. Wiltshire was chased out of the court and into the street, where he was attacked before the police managed to release him. The crowd then caught up with him again and were once more held back as he made his escape.[9]

A far more professional and longer-lasting operation was that of another of the more notorious of Soho's blackmailers of the interwar years, the tiny and eccentric theatrical wig maker and costumier, William Berry 'Willy' Clarkson, who used to wash his own socks and recycle letters sent to him. Clarkson had rooms opposite a notorious public lavatory in Dansey Place, which was known locally as Clarkson's Cottage.[10]

The lawyer William Charles Crocker, who knew Clarkson well, described him thus:

> His hair, dyed a near-chestnut, was curled poetically. The heavy moustache, like the horns of a cow, turned up a little at either end. The beard, modelled on those of the Sikhs, was parted in the middle and brushed wide open. His chubby cheeks were lightly touched with rouge. From his shiny buttoned boots to his ladylike coiffure he was artificiality personified. He cast himself for the part of the artistic simpleton, a businessman, *malgré lui* of whose coy, languishing innocence everybody, *just everybody*, took advantage.[11]

Simpleton he was not. For nearly 50 years most theatre programmes in London had the legend 'Wigs by Clarkson', but, unfortunately, he had two other undesirable professions – blackmailer and insurance fraudsman – to go with his legitimate one. In all, 11 of his business premises burned down.

Clarkson died in suspicious circumstances on 12 October 1934 while investigations into his fire claims were under way. Then began a series of complicated manoeuvres that would lead to the downfall of one of the great criminal lawyers of the day, Edmond O'Connor, and that of a thoroughly evil solicitor's clerk, William C. Hobbs, who had been a helpmate when Clarkson blackmailed the unfortunates he met in his cottage. Between them they produced a forged will in Hobbs's favour.[12]

Clarkson had actually made a homemade will in which he had forgotten to leave the residue of the estate to anyone. Since he had no relations, this meant his estate would be forfeit to the Crown, something that was anathema to Hobbs. At the beginning of 1935 another will under which Hobbs took the residue, apparently made in 1929, was found at O'Connor's offices. O'Connor was by this time in Hobbs's grip: the clerk had guaranteed an overdraft for him. The will was a hopeless effort, leaving amounts of money to people whom Clarkson had not even met by 1929 and misspelling the names of people to whom he had been close or who had worked for him. Crocker set to work to expose Hobbs and four years later had him arrested.

Edmond O'Connor, a Kerryman of immense geniality, had been regarded as one of the great solicitor-advocates and it was said of him that, had he gone to the Bar, he would have been a second Edward Marshall-Hall, the great English barrister and noted orator who died in 1927.[13] In his earlier and, for him, happier days, he had defended just about every worthwhile criminal of the era, including Frederick Guy Browne, who ran a racket in stolen second-hand cars from Great Portland Street, in the celebrated 1927 shooting of PC Gutteridge; a handful of other murderers; the adventuress Josephine O'Dare; the club owner Freddie Ford; and the blackmailer George Taylor.[14]

Deeply in debt to the tune of £14,000, O'Connor had failed to attend his bankruptcy examination and fled to Ireland in June 1936, where he was living in desperately poor circumstances under the name of Moran. All his money had gone on drink and gambling. In fact, he was in such a poor way that, when Chief Inspector Leonard Burt went to Dublin to retrieve him, O'Connor had literally only the suit he stood up in, a razor, shaving stick and a florin (2 shillings, or 10p). When he brought him back to London, Burt personally bought O'Connor a shirt and tie rather than have him appear in such a derelict condition in front of the Marlborough Street magistrate he had known in better times. Hobbs received five years and O'Connor, to include a series of embezzlements from his client account, seven.

It mostly ended happily. The insurance companies reclaimed their money from Clarkson's estate. O'Connor died in Clapham shortly after his release but Hobbs lived until 1945. Long after World War Two Clarkson's Cottage was dismantled and sent to America, where it was rebuilt.

Soho and its surrounds has long been a happy hunting ground for forgers. Back in 1905 the self-styled Australian 'Dr' Talbot Bridgewater of the Progressive Medical Alliance not only carried on his surgical operations – mainly abortions – from 57 Oxford Street, but was helped by a motley crew of criminals including William Shaknell and Lionel Peyton Holmes as well as the attractively named Willy 'Moocher' Wigram, convicted of stealing £1,500 from a Glasgow bank. There is no question that Bridgewater did not look after his friends, for he paid for Moocher's defence. When not at the operating table, Bridgewater's assistants were out on the streets stealing letters and forging cheques – 'scratching', as it was called. Early that year, Bridgewater gave evidence on behalf of Holmes, saying the charge of uttering a forged cheque was a disgrace. The jury twice failed to agree, but Bridgewater might have been advised not to enter the witness box. He, Holmes and Shaknell were on trial at the Old Bailey by the November in which the principal prosecution witness was an old convict, Charles Fisher, seeking to reduce a 10-year sentence for warehouse breaking by peaching on his former friends. After an 11-day trial, Bridgewater received seven years' penal servitude, Shaknell two years less and Holmes a modest 15 months with hard labour.[15]

But the best was yet to come. In the middle 1920s, banks, and the Midland Bank in particular, came under siege from two sources. The first was led by the adventuress Josephine O'Dare, working with the very talented forger William George Davis, who functioned in and around the Tottenham Court Road. O'Dare exotically claimed to have been born in Shanghai but was, in fact, Theresa Agnes Skryne, known as Trixie, the daughter of a farm labourer on the Welsh borders. Davis, who had served with distinction in the Machine Gun Corps, had tired of being a mere soldier and had commissioned himself as Captain Danvers DSO of the Tank Corps, sometimes ennobling himself as well. He had also already served 18 months for forgery and penal servitude for fraud when he met O'Dare, then aged 17, at a charity fundraising event in Hereford, and they soon recognised each other's talents. In Dartmoor in 1923, where he was serving three years for the fraud, he met a John Noonan, who specialised in taking letters from mailboxes by fishing them out with gum attached to a piece of string. On their release Noonan brought any stolen letters from banks and finance houses to Davis, who put them to good use.

O'Dare, a high-spirited filly, spread her wings further, mixing in Soho with Billie Carleton, taking a little cocaine, throwing lavish parties in Mayfair and, to her downfall and that of Davis, becoming the mistress of an elderly Birmingham solicitor, Edwin Docker, who was suffering from delirium tremens. It was decided that Davis would forge his will to leave her £15,000; to friends, Dolita and Adrian Morton, £3,000 each, and himself £2,000. Since the estate amounted to around £20,000, this effectively cut out Docker's two sons, who had been kindly allowed by Davis and O'Dare to inherit the residue. Unfortunately, while he had the handwriting off perfectly, Davis omitted to insert a proper attestation clause and the wheels soon came off. Until they did, O'Dare had been going round the moneylenders borrowing against the strength of her inheritance. Bankruptcy proceedings followed and Davis promptly sold a highly colourful and inaccurate version of her life story to the *Glasgow Weekly Herald*. He received £150; she nothing. And this is what may have turned her against the man she denied was one her lovers, but who certainly had been.

At the Old Bailey in March 1927 O'Dare pleaded guilty to a variety of charges relating to the will and other forgeries and, realising on which side of her bread there might be margarine if not butter, elected to give evidence against Davis, on whom she blamed all her woes, suggesting he had effectively blackmailed her into the forgery racket.

She gave evidence well, admitting what sins she could not avoid, but no more. She had been put back for sentence until after her evidence and expected six months, which meant that, with time served on remand, she would walk out a free woman. She was sadly disabused and received four and a half years penal servitude. When her appeal was heard, Mr Justice Avory was dismissive of the idea that there should be substantial rewards for those who discovered there was 'not honour among thieves'. Is not four years better than ten? he queried.

In June 1927 Davis received 12 years. At least he had the accolade from the police that he was one of the top forgers in the world and 'managed to convey the individuality of the original signature of the counterfeit'. Noonan received three and a half years; Morton received three and his wife half that.

Before she went to prison, O'Dare had left behind her self-serving memoirs with the *Reynolds News*, in which she claimed she had had an affair with Mr 'A', Sir Hari Singh, as well as being pursued by Major George Armstrong, hanged for the poisoning of his wife. Again, all her troubles she blamed on Davis. There were subsequent suggestions that she might be released early – something backed by Wontner & Co., who had acted for the prosecution – but the Home Office would have none of it. After her release she sued *Reynolds News*, claiming that she had never given them permission to publish her story. In fact the dealings had been with her half-brother, who had received the less than munificent sum of £110. Earlier he had also received a sentence for fraud. O'Dare was awarded a farthing damages. She then completely disappeared from view until, in September 1951, living under the name Joan Brookes, she committed suicide taking an overdose of barbiturates.[16]

The second gang of Soho counterfeiters, said to be over 20 strong, was run by an equally impressive forger Owen Jennings (or Jack Seymour), who had also served with distinction in World War One. As a youth he had served four years for possessing housebreaking implements by night and on his release joined the Dorset Regiment. During the war he won the Military Medal and Bar and lost part of his hand, receiving 8 shillings (40p) a week permanent pension. As a result, he was known as 'Three-Fingered Jack'. In April 1923 he served two months for theft but his real triumphs were yet to come.

When he was sentenced in February 1928 it was estimated that he was responsible for 90 per cent of the country's forgeries, and when his home was raided the police found what they described as a forgery factory with hundreds of different pens, inks and erasers. Bank experts thought his efforts were the best they had ever seen. He received six years, to be followed in March 1935 by another five. Described then as 'the most expert forger in Britain', he was still on licence from the 1928 sentence.[17]

Between the wars Australian confidence tricksters ran riot throughout the West End working crooked card games, including a particularly virulent game called Anzac poker, bets on pre-run races and the Irish will fraud (see Chapter 3).

One team was led by Patrick O'Riley, known as 'Australian Paddy', and his second lieutenant Walter Macdonald, known as 'Australian Mac', with as bait 'Blonde' Alice Smith, who had worked on the 1909 Café Monaco jewel theft, and Clara Whiteley, born in Cape Town. In April 1919 Whiteley received nine months for a diamond theft of stones worth £4,000.

She had met the jeweller William Giles in a café in Soho and told him she had an American naval friend who wished to spend a lot of money on her. Giles took her to see a second jeweller in Bond Street, who, after a lengthy lunch, went back to her flat at 115 Great Portland Street, where the naval friend was to meet them to be shown the stones to be made into a ring. The jeweller went into the drawing room and she promptly locked the door on him and decamped. A few days later she was seen at lunch in London and was caught trying to change a cheque. The stones were found marked by four narcissus bulbs buried in a garden in Windsor Road, Dublin.

The next March she was involved in a curious incident when a chorus girl, Mona Crawford, was accused of slashing a woman in the leg with a razor in Leicester Square. Now under the name of Iris

Barclay, Clara claimed she had seen the girl drop the razor and had picked it up. When she was cross-examined she refused to say whether she was indeed Clara or if she had received nine months. She denied having dropped the razor herself but it was thought she had slashed the woman, mistaking her for someone else. Mona was found to have no case to answer.

On 28 July 1920, still under the name Iris Barclay, she received a further 15 months for stealing £8 from an Egyptian medical student. In 1921 the gang planned the theft at Dover railway station of the dressing case of Miss Ruby Wertheimer. They expected to clear £50,000 in jewellery but they abandoned her case when they found it contained only £260. This led to Macdonald's careless arrest for card-sharping, for which he received nine months.[18] From then on, now addicted to drugs, she was in and out of court until in July 1925 she was returned to her parents in South Africa after being found guilty of stealing £105.[19]

For their part, the Australians continued on their merry way. Later, Denny Delaney who before he came to England had served sentences in his home country and South Africa, specialised in smash-and-grab raids, which in the mid-1920s were fast becoming flavour of the year. Delaney introduced a relay system of getaway cars in a robbery and used women as spotters and stalls – the former reconnoitred the premises and the latter diverted the assistants. A charming man, who had his women associates billing and cooing over him – he tended to call them Sweetie-Pie and Ducksy-Wucksy – he worked out of Soho with the London criminal Reggie Roberts. One of their more spectacular robberies was a wage snatch at Euston Station and a second was when Delaney organised a raid on a furrier in the West End. Part of the proceeds was a dummy, which, at a crucial moment in the chase, was thrown into the path of the police car. The driver naturally did not wish to run over what appeared to be a naked woman and swerved to avoid the body, so giving Roberts and Delaney time to escape.[20] Delaney died in harness, collapsing in the street following a heart attack, leaving a successor in a man known, because of his marcelled hair as the Platinum Blond, Charlie Barwick.

9

Soho in World War Two

Immediately after the declaration of war against Italy, there was rioting in Soho. On 9 June 1940 the police raided the Italian Club in Charing Cross Road to make arrests; Greeks fought Italians and restaurant windows were smashed.[1] Italians who had lived in England for decades were promptly arrested and among them were the Sabinis. Darby Sabini was arrested as an enemy alien at Hove Greyhound Stadium on the night of 6 July and Harryboy (alias Harry Handley, Henry Handley and a few other names), partial to highly polished spring-sided boots, eight days after his brother.[2]

By the November, Darby Sabini, now in Brixton Prison, had still not appeared before a tribunal to determine whether the reasons for his detention were justifiable. In Home Office correspondence he was described as being in semi-retirement and was believed to be a man of considerable means. It is apparent that the authorities were using the war to smash the Sabinis by quite wrongly portraying them as enemy aliens. Such evidence as there was showed they spoke little Italian and had few convictions between them. It seems improbable that they could, or would even want to, lead an insurgence. The consensus of opinion is they were arrested not for political reasons but because it was both a convenient way to break up the gang and also a reprisal for the successful gold bullion robbery said to have been organised by Bert Marsh at Croydon aerodrome in 1935.[3]

The police report leading to Harryboy's arrest described him as

> one of the leading lights of a gang of bullies known as the Sabini gang who under the cover of various rackets have by their blackmailing methods levied toll on bookmakers . . . He is a dangerous man of the most violent temperament and has a heavy following and strong command of a gang of bullies of Italian origin in London.

Harryboy appealed against his detention under regulation 18B. The appeal was delayed and so, ill advisedly as it transpired, he applied for a writ of *habeas corpus*. In his affidavit he said he had never been known as Harry Handley – in fact Handley was his mother's maiden name although curiously he was the only legitimate Sabini. The evidence of his arrest was that the police had gone to his house at 44 Highbury Park, Highbury New Barn, north London, on 20 June 1940 and asked Sabini's wife where Harry Handley was. The reply had been 'upstairs'. It was also successfully argued that he could be described as being of 'hostile origin', even though he had an English mother and his father had died when he was a child. His brother George had a daughter in the Auxiliary Territorial Service and a son in the Royal Army Service Corps who had joined up immediately after war had been declared with Italy. So far as he was concerned he would be prepared to enlist at once. The authorities were none too pleased when Harry was released from detention on 18 March 1941. He was, however, promptly rearrested for perjury over his use of the name Handley and on 8 July that year he received a sentence of nine months' imprisonment.[4]

It was the questioning of Darby Sabini which threw some more light, and indeed shade, on his background and his family. His real name, he said, was Frederick Sabini and he accepted he was also known as Frederick Handley. He was born in Clerkenwell in 1888. His mother was indeed English and his father, who had been an asphalter, had come to England from Italy in 1850. He, Darby, had been abroad only twice in his life, when he boxed in France. He had four children. He himself had joined the East Surrey Regiment in 1908 and had wanted to join a defence regiment at the start of the war, but had been refused on the grounds of his health. He was a printer's representative and was a life governor of some 18 hospitals. It later turned out that a donation of £40 or more secured a life governorship in some of them. He agreed he was known as Attavios.

While Darby Sabini was in Brixton, his old adversary Detective Inspector Ted Greeno took the opportunity to blacken his character and those of some of his leading henchmen. Sabini was, 'A gangster and racketeer of the worst type. One who it is most likely enemy agents would choose as a person to create and lead violent internal action against this country.' He was Number 6 in the list of those most likely to assist the enemy. Number 2 was Augustus Cortesi, and, although the name of Number 1 is deleted from the file, it is likely it was his brother Enrico. In third spot came Harry Sabini and then Bert Marsh, Silvio Mazzaro, Alfred White, James Ford, Herbert Wilkins and in 12th place Edward Smith, known as Emmanuel, the financier of the Sabinis. Indeed MI5 reported that there had been plotting between enemy agents and people such as Numbers 3 to 12.

It was while in Brixton that Darby wrote a helpful explanatory letter:

> My real name is Octavious Sabini not Frederick Sabini or Frederick Handley. I used the name of Fred Handley has [*sic*] my boxing name. Darby is my nickname. My friends call me Fred but I am not the same has Frederick Sabini my brother. Signed Octavious Sabini.

Whichever is correct, this left Soho open to Kings Cross-based Alf White and his gang, who had split from the Sabinis, and the Yiddishers, who had been at odds with the Italians for years. One of the Sabini men who remained outside the sweep was Antonio 'Babe' Mancini, the man whom Jack Spot claimed to have attacked in Brixton Prison before the war. It was he who would lead what was left of the group to maintain Italian interests.

Before World War Two, protection had been something of an art form. A fight was started in a club and a certain amount of damage was done. Perhaps a foot went through the skin on the drum, tables were overturned, a few glasses were broken. The next day came a visit from a sympathetic representative of the Sabinis or others who would point out how disruptive such incidents were in frightening off punters and how they could be avoided by payment of a small weekly sum. By 1941, however, the rules of the game had changed. Now it was thought best to inflict the maximum amount of damage possible on a rival's premises. If the club closed for good so much the better. There was one fewer competitor.

On 20 April 1941, 'Fair Hair' Eddie Fleischer, now known as Eddie Fletcher, and Joseph Franks were involved in a fight with Bert Connelly, the doorman of Palm Beach Bottles Parties, a club in the basement of 37 Wardour Street. The premises, all Italian-maintained, also housed the Cosmo on the ground floor and the West End Bridge and Billiards Club on the first. Fletcher was given a beating and banned from the club by the manager Joe Leon, whose real name was Niccolo Cariello.

Ten days later Fletcher returned and Sammy Ledderman, a Soho inhabitant of 30 years – he was a friend of Jack Spot and later gave evidence against the Kray Twins – came to the Palm Beach to tell Mancini, the dinner-jacketed catering manager and doorman for the night, 'They're smashing up the [Bridge and Billiards] Club.'

What had happened was that Fletcher and other members of the Yiddisher Gang, including Moishe Cohen, had been playing pool and cards in the club when in walked Joseph Collette, Harry Capocci and Albert Dimes, then currently AWOL from the Royal Air Force. Fighting broke out, started by Albert Dimes, said the witnesses, who may not have been wholly impartial. The unfortunate Fletcher received another beating and was taken to Charing Cross Hospital, then a matter of minutes away.

At first Mancini seems to have wanted to stay out of trouble but Joe Leon then asked him to go to the door of the Palm Beach and let no one in. He changed out of his evening clothes and went upstairs to see the damage.

As he was on the stairs he heard someone say, 'There's Babe, let's knife him.' Mancini thought the speaker was Fletcher, who claimed he had returned to the club to retrieve his coat. Mancini sensed someone was behind him and went into the club followed by Fletcher, Harry Distleman – known as 'Little Hubby' or 'Scarface', although no prosecution witness would accept that latter sobriquet for him – and another man. Little Hubby had managed the Nest Club in Kingly Street for four years from 1934 but had apparently not worked since, supporting himself, according to his brother 'Big Hubby' Distleman, by successfully betting on the horses and greyhounds.[5]

It was then that fighting broke out yet again, with Albert Dimes being restrained by his elder brother, Victor. Little Hubby Distleman was stabbed. As usual, few of the 40 people in the club saw exactly what happened, but the consensus of such witnesses as were prepared to speak up was that it was Mancini did the stabbing. In fact, Distleman had said to two companions, 'I am terribly hurt. Babe's done it.' It did not have the same evidential strength as a formal dying declaration but it certainly did not help Mancini. There must have been more than a grain of truth in the belief by the police that trouble had been deliberately caused because just at the end of the fight who should arrive but the longtime Sabini man, Thomas Mack.

Mancini had then chased after the unfortunate Fletcher and had almost severed his arm. When he was interviewed, he told Detective Inspector Arthur Thorp, 'I admit I stabbed Fletcher with a long dagger which I found on the floor of the club, but I don't admit doing Distleman. Why should I do him? They threatened me as I came up the stairs and I got panicky.' The next day, however, he said he had the dagger wrapped in a rag with him when he went up the stairs. Mancini had, in fact, known 'Little Hubby' for something in the region of 15 years.[6]

Mancini was unlucky at his trial. The brief to the prosecution suggests that, if he offered a plea to manslaughter, 'Counsel will no doubt consider it, as the witnesses of the assault on Distleman are vague and shaky.' It is not possible to say now whether any such plea was offered, or whether the prosecutor did not accept it. It was argued that, if self-defence was rejected, a death in a gang fight in such circumstances should only be manslaughter and indeed the judge, Mr Justice McNaughten, summed up to that effect. In fact, in a not dissimilar case three months earlier this is exactly what had happened. The jury, however, after a retirement of a bare 55 minutes, convicted Mancini of murder and an appeal met with no success at all. The judge had, if anything, been too favourable in his summing-up, said the Lord Chief Justice. A further appeal to the House of Lords also failed and Mancini became the first London gangster to be hanged for nearly 25 years.[7]

Following the Mancini trial, Dimes, Collette and Capocci were again arraigned, this time before the Recorder of London, Sir Gerald Dodson. One by one the witnesses for the prosecution failed to identify them and the trial collapsed. Capocci was acquitted but Dimes and Collette were bound over in the sum of £5 to come up for judgment in the next three years. 'You were probably expecting prison,' said the recorder, 'and no doubt you deserve it.' Dimes was returned to the RAF where he did not remain for very long.

According to his biography, the fight allowed Billy Howard, another Soho and south London resident – then also currently a deserter – to take control of the clubs at 37 Wardour Street and provide the necessary protection for much of the war.[8]

On 17 June 1943, Darby Sabini, under the name Fred, and who by then had been released from internment, was seemingly convicted of receiving £383 worth of wine and silver that had been stolen by soldiers from the Uckfield house of a retired Sussex magistrate. The jury had rejected his defence that he thought that he was buying goods from a hotel that was being sold out. The recorder, Gilbert Paull, passing sentence, told him in the time-honoured words judges love to use to receivers, 'It is men like you who lay temptation before soldiers. If there were none like you there would be no temptation to steal.' Sabini, who was said to have no previous convictions, received three years' imprisonment. It is now not wholly clear whether it was indeed Darby who was convicted. Before the war he had been convicted of assault and his fingerprints should have been on the police files. It may actually have been his brother Frederick, who also lived in Brighton, or, there again, he may have been using the name Fred, as he had done over the years.

After the war, Harryboy joined his brothers in Brighton. Darby's son had joined the RAF and was killed in action. In the late 1940s Darby functioned as a small-time bookmaker with a pitch on the free course at Ascot. When he died in Hove in 1951 his family and friends were surprised that he apparently had so little money. Yet the man who had been his clerk, Jimmy Napoletano, was stopped leaving the country on his way to Italy with £36,000 in his possession. Sabini's wife returned to live in Gray's Inn Road, Clerkenwell.

During the war the Messina brothers evaded military service simply because they failed to report. Warrants had been issued but they were never served, and the Messinas maintained a low profile as far as the authorities were concerned. Gino Messina, who had worked with his father as a carpenter, built himself a hiding place in the form of a bookcase with a removable bottom shelf in his Lowndes Square flat. Unknown visitors had to be cleared through a series of front men and front women before they were allowed in to see him.

The Messinas may have escaped unharmed, but during the war prosecutions for brothel keeping in England and Wales rose from an average of 198 in the years from 1935 to 1939 to 944 in 1944. Unfortunately, the Metropolitan Police did not publish their figures for the latter years of the war, when, with the increase in American and Colonial troops in the country, the figures generally rose exponentially with a number of brothels specifically catering for the visitors.

There were more problems for the visiting troops from good-time girls than the professionals. Leicester Square was described by Admiral Sir Edward Evans of the London Civil Defence as 'the resort of the worst type of women and girls consorting with men of the British and American forces . . . At night the Square is apparently given over to a vicious debauchery.' The amateurs were nicknamed 'Piccadilly Commandos' and because of the need for economy – and also the mistaken belief that pregnancy could not follow sex in the upright position – intercourse was often conducted against a wall (by both amateurs and professionals). The men were therefore prey to professional girls working with pickpockets at what the underworld had known as the 'buttock and twang' game for two centuries. While they were having sex, the girls' pimps would take the men's wallets from their back pockets. And of course there were the badger and Murphy games (the Murphy game sees a mug sent around the corner for something, but the promised deliverer does not turn up).

There had been a proliferation of drinking clubs patronised by black-marketeers serving bad liquor and where the waiters would expect a tip of 10 shillings (50p). The journalist Lester Powell had a friend who was blind for a week after taking a couple of glasses in one club. At 2 am there would be a cabaret with nude dancers and a male striptease, which was highly regarded by the punters.

There were also afternoon drinking clubs catering for soldiers on leave – Powell said there were hundreds to the north of Leicester Square – with what he described as 'travelling white slaves'. Girls would come in with their 'aunt', who as the afternoon went on would suggest they and the soldiers should go back to her flat. He maintained a number had been dragged into prostitution because their boyfriends had defaulted on black-market deals and they were left to deal with the debt.

One of the Piccadilly Commandos was the cause of a murder at the end of the war. On 4 September 1945, a waiter, Gordon Johnson, was stabbed to death by an American serviceman, Private Thomas Edward Croft, in Mac's Dance Hall at 41 Great Windmill Street, run by Alfred McAlister.

It was all over a girl called Lena, who went by the name Rita. She was more or less engaged to Johnson but she was also sleeping with Croft's friend Joe Devine on a commercial basis. Devine and Croft had been drinking and went to find the girl, whom they discovered dancing with Johnson. Devine and Johnson had a short fight but when that was broken up Croft took a dagger from his boot and stabbed the unfortunate man, who died within minutes.

There was no time wasted by the American authorities in dealing with the case. On 21 September Croft pleaded not guilty but was found guilty and, despite an appeal by the prosecutor for the death penalty, was sentenced to life imprisonment.[9]

Things had become so bad that in August 1942 the *Sunday Pictorial* began a campaign to clean up Piccadilly and surrounding areas.[10] That month a report by Superintendent Cole recorded that the Circus area featured 'a lower type of prostitute, indiscriminate in their choice of client and persistent thieves'. Glasshouse Street had 'a little better class' while Soho had 'the lowest types of all – drabs'. In contrast, Shepherd's Market and Burlington Gardens had prostitutes who were 'rather expensive and using fairly clean premises for their trade'. The girls in Maddox Street, who would include those belonging to the Messinas, were 'French prostitutes, a colony among themselves, clean and businesslike, who though persistent in their soliciting rarely cause trouble'.[11]

The Messina girls may have been clean and businesslike, but they were at risk from a whipping by their owners. Nevertheless, a ponce can have his uses. One is that he provides the working girl with some sort of protection, and is often on hand if the punter causes trouble. Independents are generally more at risk from the punters. In

February 1942, when four women were murdered within a week, one girl was lucky.

The first victim was Evelyn Margaret Hamilton, a 40-year-old chemist's assistant from whom the killer stole £80, who was strangled in an air-raid shelter in Montague Place. Her body was found on the morning of 9 February. The second, Evelyn Oatley, known as Nita Ward, a prostitute, was killed and her body mutilated with a tin-opener the same day in her room in Wardour Street. The third, Margaret Lowe, known as 'Pearl', was killed on Tuesday, 11 February, in what she called her office, a flat in Gosfield Street off Tottenham Court Road. Her body had also been mutilated. Finally, on the Thursday, away from Soho, the body of Doris Jouannet, the wife of a hotel manager who doubled as a part-time prostitute, was found to have been strangled with a stocking and then slashed in her flat in Paddington.

On the Thursday evening another young woman, Greta Hayward, was attacked after she had been persuaded to go for a drink with a man to the Trocadero at Piccadilly Circus. Afterwards, he pushed her into a side street by the Captain's Cabin, near what was Norris Street, and tried to strangle her. She was saved when a passer-by heard her scream. The man ran off, dropping his gas mask with an Air Force number 525987. He then travelled to Paddington, where he picked up another prostitute, Kathleen King, who also broke free from him and this time he dropped his uniform belt.

The mask and belt were traced to 29-year-old Gordon Frederick Cummins, married to the private secretary of a theatrical producer, who claimed to be the illegitimate son of a member of the House of Lords and was known to his mates as the Duke. Now there was a problem. Cummins had an alibi for the time of the murders of the first three women. He claimed another man had taken his mask and belt and he had the man's mask to prove it. His billet passbook showed he was in his barracks and his roommates swore they saw him go to bed. When they awoke in the morning he was still there.

The police traced another girl who had been attacked by a client between the time Doris Jouannet had been murdered and Greta Hayward was attacked near the Captain's Cabin. She had met him outside Oddenino's, then a very popular restaurant in Regent Street, and had taken him back to her flat, where, curiously but fortunately for her, she had kept her boots on. He began to twist a necklace on her neck and she kicked him. He fell off the bed, apologised and gave her what was then the substantial sum of £10. The police traced the notes to Cummins's regiment's pay day.

The alibi was broken when one of his mates told the police that on the Monday he and Cummins had gone out together after lights-out using a fire escape. Cummins had paid for his friend to go home with a girl and had gone with one himself. Chief Inspector Edward Greeno traced her to her flat in Wardour Street. Cummins had come home with her but had suddenly given her £2 and left. While Greeno was interviewing her he saw eyes looking through two holes in a blanket. He tore it down and there was the girl's black ponce. Greeno had seen what Cummins must have seen a few days earlier.

Cummins was a man who kept souvenirs of his victims. A Swan pen belonging to Doris Jouannet was found as well as a green propelling pencil belonging to Evelyn Hamilton. Despite the evidence against him, Cummins pleaded not guilty. He was defended by D.N. Pritt, but it was a hopeless case and the jury retired for just over half an hour before convicting him. Some people, however, were not convinced and a petition was organised claiming Cummins was innocent and there had indeed been a mix-up with the gas masks. He was hanged on 25 June 1942 at Wandsworth.[12]

The next year a career criminal who was rather more fortunate was Harold Loughans. He benefited from a mistake by the pathologist Bernard Spilsbury, who at the time had a reputation with judges and juries for infallibility. On 28 November 1943 Loughans left Warren Street Tube station, which was being used as an air-raid shelter, stole a jeep and drove to Portsmouth. There he was disturbed by the landlady, Rose Robinson, a 63-year-old widow, when he was burgling the John Barleycorn public house. Despite having a deformed right hand – he was missing the ends of his fingers as a result of an accident in a brickyard – he strangled her, drove back to London and was home safely in the shelter by 5 am.

Arrested when found in possession of stolen goods, Loughans made a confession to the murder as well as to a robbery in St Albans. A thread found on a back button in the pub was similar to one from Loughans's coat and fibres on a boot were similar to those on Mrs

Robinson's bed. Loughans, who retracted his confession, called an alibi in which four people said he was in the Warren Street shelter, and the jury disagreed. Spilsbury, called by the defence in the retrial, said he did not believe Loughans could have exerted sufficient pressure to strangle the unfortunate Mrs Robinson and such was his reputation the jury preferred to accept his evidence in preference to that of Professor Keith Simpson. Loughans later served five years for the St Albans robbery and then a further ten years preventive detention. Shortly before he died in 1963 he sold his story to the *People* in which he confessed he had, indeed, strangled Mrs Robinson.[13]

By the end of the war and shortly after, the black market was the thing for the criminal. Frank Fraser, who used Bobby's Club in Rupert Court to find a buyer for his wares, recalled,

> It was risky being in the black market in the sense of getting rid of the gear. The blag was easy enough but then you was at the mercy of other people. At the end of the war when the black market was at its best, if you got hold of any silk stockings then you was your own master. Them, snout and Scotch were winners and you could ask your own price.[14]

One of the most notorious open-air informal black markets was outside the Rainbow Club, fashioned out of Del Monico's and Lyons Corner House on the corner of Shaftesbury Avenue. The club, for American servicemen, opened in November 1942 and from then on watches, cameras, silk stockings and pens were all on offer to the Soho dealers in Berwick Street market. As the number of American troops dwindled from 1.5 million in May 1944 to rather under 25,000, it finally closed its doors on 8 January 1946.

At the time guns were readily available. American weapons and ammunition could be purchased at Rainbow Corner with handguns going for £25. In the final stages of the war, a Luger was priced at £60, but by the autumn of 1944 its price had slumped to half, and in December that year it was said to be a mere 30 shillings (£1.50) or around £60 in today's currency. After VE Day hundreds of revolvers were sold at £5 apiece in Ham Yard.

Polish criminals were major players in the black market, their activities ranging from dealing in stolen whisky to the handbag game, a form of confidence trick. A smartly dressed woman would be seen carrying a new handbag around the West End and Soho clubs. When asked where she had purchased this generally unobtainable item she would say that the man she was with was a manufacturer. Orders were taken, money handed over and neither she nor the handbag was ever seen again.

One black-marketeer who kept a flat in Soho, in addition to a bungalow in Gloucestershire and two other London addresses, was Frank Everitt, a London taxi driver known, possibly ironically, as Honest John. On 18 October 1945 his body was found pushed into a National Fire Service pumping station. He had been shot with a single bullet behind his left ear. His taxi was later found abandoned in Notting Hill.

In November that year a Russian, Reuben Martirosoff, known as Russian Robert, was found in the back seat of his Opel in Chepstow Place, South Kensington, shot through the back of the head. Another black-marketeer, he had been a big gambler in Soho in the Bees Club, in which Albert Dimes's brother, Victor had an interest.

It was not a difficult case for the police. There were fingerprints in the car and within a week a Pole, Marian Grondkowski, was found in the East India Dock Road with Martirosoff's cigarette lighter and wallet. He promptly put up the name of his friend, another Pole, Henryk Malinowski. Each claimed the other had shot Martirosoff and forced him to go along with the robbery. Both were hanged. The file on Everitt was closed.

Soho has long been a magnet for runaways and it was in Maxie's café in Gerrard Street that, at the end of the war, 16-year-old Zoe Progl first met the women who would provide her with a support system during her early days there. She also met the dapper con man, the *soi-disant* Count Alec Kostanda, who wore a monocle and drove a Rolls-Royce.

He claimed to be aged 51 and to have been a major in the Indian Army. But, at his trial for burgling the Spenser Arms in Putney and assaulting a policeman with his own truncheon, the court was told there was no trace of his birth at either Somerset House or in Dublin and he was thought to be an alien.[15] Thirty years later he was still a feature of the Soho club scene.

Soho was also a Mecca for deserters, and Progl took up with a Canadian on the run, John Joseph Gelley, living with him in Newport Place. In May 1946 Gelley robbed a clergyman with violence at a West End hotel and received four years. On 14 November that year he and Kostanda escaped from Wormwood Scrubs. Gelley returned to Progl, who was by then living in Frith Street in a flat used as a safe house by deserters. In February 1947 they were raided and she was sent to Borstal for forging post office books. The gang had been infiltrated by a policewoman posing as a prostitute.[16] At the end of Gelley's sentence he was deported, but for her it was the beginning of a spectacular career of burglaries and prison escapes lasting nearly 20 years.

Other Sohoites came and went during the war. Jack Spot was called up. According to Spot's memoirs he was an active soldier in an anti-aircraft regiment waiting for a chance to get at the Germans. Disappointed that he never received a commission, Spot raged on about how demeaning and wasteful it was for a man of his ability being obliged, for three years, to shine his boots and buttons, having to suffer from a sergeant's temper and taking orders from 'pasty-faced little runts with officers' pips'. He implies the hostilities would have been over a great deal sooner had he been in charge of the war effort.

Spot was always keen to see anti-Semitism among his colleagues; fight followed fight and he gained a reputation as a troublemaker. Eventually, following a short time with the marines, he was sent to see a psychiatrist, who recommended him for a medical discharge in 1943. From then on he commuted between London and Leeds, where he worked in the black market.

Before the war, the man who would come to rule over Soho in the early 1950s, Billy Hill, had become the master of the smash-and-grab raid. Now, in 1940, with the blackout in force and a complete boon and blessing to criminals, a series of daring raids took place. Frank Fraser recalls,

> You could nick a car, take the back seats out, take it to the West End, do a job, and the chances of getting caught were just about nil. I'll never forget one in Hanover Square. It was a high class gentleman's tailor, a very high class one at that. We had on wardens' helmets with the letters A.R.P. on them and armbands. We smashed the windows in with the car and when people came looking, asked them to stand back, saying, 'Control, please stand back'. People were helping to load the car up.[17]

The police were convinced that Hill was behind, if not an active participant in, most of those early raids. On 1 February 1940 Ciro's Pearls in Bond Street lost almost its entire stock. The windows had been covered with screens, which provided protection from view as the burglars, who had forced the metal grille and front door, ransacked everything. The next month Hill was arrested after a midmorning raid on Carringtons, the jewellers, in Regent Street. Some £6,000 worth of rings, which in today's terms would be worth around £250,000, were stolen. Hill was placed on an identification parade but not picked out.

He was arrested again after a car mounted the pavement in Wardour Street on 21 May. At first passers-by thought the car had been out of control but a man in the passenger seat stood up and, leaning out of the sunshine roof, robbed the shop through the broken display window. Another robbery was at Phillips in New Bond Street, when jewellery worth £11,000 went. This time the second car, which had been stolen, had the engaging new number plate: MUG 999. Hill survived yet another identification parade.

His luck ran out on 26 June 1940, when he and two longstanding friends, Harry Bryan, nominally an Islington bookmaker, and 'Square Georgie' Ball, were arrested in a failed robbery on Hemmings & Co. in Conduit Street.[18] A PC Higgs threw his truncheon through the windscreen and, with the crowd joining in, Bryan and Ball were arrested. Hill fled into Bruton Street but by now the crowd and two more policemen were after him. He managed to get onto a roof and, despite the old trick of saying to a policemen who climbed after him, 'He's in there,' in almost pantomime tradition the watching crowd shouted, 'That's him.' Bryan and Ball drew three years apiece but Hill managed to negotiate a charge of conspiracy, which carried a maximum of two years. For him it was off to Chelmsford, where he worked as the prison barber.

A one-month sentence at Marylebone for being a suspected person followed Hill's release and then, in the terms of the trade, it all came on top when he was given information about a potential armed robbery. On 15 July 1942 a postmaster in Islington was to be the target during the lunch hour. The old Alf White man, Jock Wyatt, and Teddy Hughes went with him, Wyatt as lookout. The robbery went well until a lorry driver rammed their getaway car. Hughes and Hill were caught in the car and Wyatt, instead of sauntering away, tried to run and was also arrested.

In those days it was possible to exchange some of a sentence for strokes of the cat and Hill and the others asked Sir Gerald Dodson, the Recorder of London, if this could be done. Unfortunately, Hughes had a weak heart and it was not thought he could stand the punishment. It was a question of 12 strokes or none for all and so Wyatt and Hill received four years and Hughes a year less. For Hill now it was off to Dartmoor.

On his release he saw the war as one great opportunity – 'that big, wide, handsome and oh, so highly profitable black market walked into our ever open arms'.[19]

Ever the organiser, Hill set to with unmatched enthusiasm. Writing of the black market he would recall, 'It was the most fantastic side of civil life in war time. Make no mistake. It cost Britain millions of pounds. I did not merely make use of the black market. I fed it.'

And one way in which he fed it was the theft of bedsheets from a services depot in the southwest of England. Lorry load after lorry load was taken. He estimated that thousands of pairs were stolen each week and sold at £1 a pair. He also raided a warehouse full of fur coats, which were sold at £6 each. Whisky went for £500 a barrel, the same price as a barrel of sausage skins. He was, he said, clearing around £300 to £400 a week, a fantastic sum for the time.

By late 1945 there were estimated to be around 20,000 deserters and criminals on the run. There was also a spate of serious robberies and on 4 December came the kidnapping of the manageress of a jeweller's in Mayfair. The keys to the premises were taken from her and jewellery valued at £18,000 was stolen. In the first 11 months of 1945 indictable crime was up 26.5 per cent on 1944 and 35.7 per cent on 1938.[20]

As a direct result, on 14 December 1945, 2,000 policemen invaded Soho, checking pubs, dance halls, clubs and cafés for deserters. There had been two previous raids, which had not been notable successes. Nor was this a spectacular achievement: 500 were taken to police stations and 75 detained, but, of the 15,161 people who were questioned, only 32 deserters were caught and another 21 people arrested. Three men were found with stolen furs in a car on Westminster Bridge. Apart from that the crimes were not the most sensational. Two were for housebreaking, four for larceny, nine for unlawful possession and one for criminal damage in Leicester Square. Set against this modest success, that night a safe was stolen in High Holborn, another firm robbed both the YMCA and premises in Harrow and a Clapham postmaster had his keys stolen.[21] As befitted his growing reputation Hill was thought to have been a planner rather than participant in many of these operations and certainly in the kidnapping of the shop manageress.

On VE Night the Messina girls naturally did that bit extra for the family. Marthe Watts recalled that, although she stayed out until 6 am to try to total half a century of customers, she remained stuck on 49.[22]

10

After the War was Over, Didn't We Have Such Fun!

By the end of the war there was a well-established pecking order in Soho and, to mix metaphors, wearing the crown, if somewhat uneasily and by sufferance, was the White family, who still had control of drinking clubs and spielers. Then there was the loose alliance of Billy Hill and the Italians, now released from internment, together with Jack Spot, who had assembled a miscellaneous combination of men, including Arthur Skurry and his gypsies from West Ham.

Hill was interested in Soho and the cornucopia of treats the area offered. Spot wanted the racecourse pitches and protection money. With horseracing up and running again, the Whites also controlled the allocation of the bookmakers' pitches at point-to-points and on the free course at tracks such as Epsom and Brighton. Bookmakers were required to pay for their pitch as a donation to the local hunt, but how much of that reached the stirrup cup is another matter.

The trouble was that the Whites, now run by Alf's son Harry, were not sufficiently hard men to keep control of what was a dangerous game. Frank Fraser recalls the family thus:

> If you had a crooked copper they were the ideal men to handle it. If anyone was in trouble and could get a bit of help they were the ones to go to, but as for leaders they didn't really have the style. All in all they were a weak mob and they were ripe for taking.[1]

A former Flying Squad officer who knew Harry White well describes him like this:

> Really he was a most gregarious fellow. He was very 'hail fellow well met' and Cockney in the manner in which Americans expect. He was always smartly dressed, a very heavy smoker and drinker and a nuisance when he had over imbibed.[2]

The family's serious and rapid decline began with their ousting from control of Yarmouth racecourse in October 1946, when Spot slashed the White man Eddie Raimo. Moey Levy, a Jewish bookmaker who had once been part of a powerful family in the Aldgate area, had been warned off his pitch at Yarmouth by the Whites and he now appealed to Spot for help to deal with the situation. Spot travelled to the course with his team, where Raimo was in charge of the White operation. Since his appearances in court before the war, Raimo had glassed Billy Hill in a public house in Clerkenwell. Now, faced with Spot, he was cut and simply backed down. It was a bad sign for the Whites.

There were further troubles when, in January 1947, Johnny Warren, part of what could be described as their extended family, followed Spot into the lavatory of a public house in Soho and made the mistake of mocking him over the fact he was drinking only lemonade. He compounded this by making what Spot considered to be an anti-Jewish remark, suggesting, 'Here was another Sheeney trying to take over.' Later, Spot would say he knew the consequences of what would happen if he dealt with Warren and at first simply asked him what he wanted. Aggravatingly, Warren replied, 'Any time'. And, recounted Spot, 'Bump! Down into the piss he went. I thought I shouldn't have done it and I went out. I don't know what happened but in a minute a mob comes looking for me.'

Spot was fortunate. He was joined by Teddy Machin, Georgie Wood and Hymie Rosen. They went to the Nut House, a club in Sackville Street, where Harry White and four or five others – including Billy Goller – were drinking. Accounts vary as to what happened next. Spot's version was,

> Harry had seven of the toughest of his boys with him when I led my

> pals into the room. There wasn't any politeness this time. They knew what I'd come for. And I sailed right in. At the first smack I took at them Harry scarpered. You couldn't see the seat of his trousers for dust.

Over the years Spot's account of the fight varied and the incidents were telescoped or expanded to suit the teller. Whether this particular incident occurred immediately after the Warren episode or whether it was the culmination of several minor run-ins, one thing is certain and that is there was a near-fatal fight. Quite who was there is unclear but there was certainly Billy Goller, who had his throat cut and nearly died, Harry White and a racehorse trainer Tim Sullivan. With Spot were Johnny Carter and, some say, Monkey Benneworth.[3]

That night Spot's patron, the club owner and man about town Abe Kosky, was dining with a senior officer from Savile Row police station when the news came through that Goller had been badly injured. Spot had almost ignored his own maxim, 'You must never cut below the line here, 'cause, if you do, you cut the jugular – and the hangman is waiting for you . . .', and Goller received the last rites. Spot was packed off to Southend to a club at the end of the airport runway managed by Jackie Reynolds on behalf of the Upton Park gypsy, Benny Swan, a Spot man through and through. When he recovered, Goller was given £300 and matters quietened down temporarily but, so far as Soho was concerned, the Whites had lost considerable face. Spot had become a man to be seriously reckoned with in the hierarchy. For some time afterwards Goller wore a scarf around his neck to hide the stitching.

Accounts mark the end of the Whites as coming in the week of 9 July that year. There had been talk of a gang fight at Harringay Arena on the night of the Joe Baksi–Bruce Woodcock contest, but Detective Chief Superintendent Peter Beveridge had put a stop to it. Now, according to both Hill and Spot – although their versions differ as to who plays the more heroic part – the Whites were ousted in a single night of violence. In Spot's version Harry White simply vanished, while Hill's account, written by his amanuensis Duncan Webb, who could always tell a good story, has one White roasted over a fire. Whichever, if either, is the correct version, the Whites reign was over:

> 'It's allright,' I said to Benny the Kid [Spot]. 'We won't need shooters in this town anymore. Get 'em off the boys and get rid of them.' They collected the shooters and the bombs and the machine gun and destroyed them. They were actually thrown down a manhole.[4]

In Spot's version Beveridge called at his flat in Aldgate and asked him to come to the police station. Spot was quite pleased to comply, because upstairs there were James and George Wood, who had a quantity of arms in pillow cases in their room and the last thing Spot needed was a search. At the station Beveridge explained the facts of life to him.[5]

The stories that Hill and Spot had a thousand men behind them when they saw off the Whites are, of course, complete exaggeration and many doubt that the clearout was even approximately on the scale Spot and Hill portray in their respective memoirs. Beveridge's own are silent on the point. Indeed, Spot's version, which has him chasing down two White men – one of whom he beats and the other he lets go – is probably indicative of the actual scale of the enterprise.

Whichever is correct, for the next eight years Spot and Hill ran Soho in an increasingly uneasy partnership with, at first, Spot the senior partner. The reason for this was that in August 1947 Billy Hill was wanted on what he claimed was a trumped-up fur-robbery charge and fled to South Africa. He returned a few weeks later and in October gave himself up. The next month he received three years' imprisonment, to be met on his release at the prison gates by Spot.

In general, however, this was Spot's peak. He and Hill were working together but often also in separate fields. Spot was regarded as the man to be seen over any racecourse problems and he was used as a debt-collecting agency by men in Leeds, Manchester and Birmingham who had been swindled by the smarter operators in London. His fee was 50 per cent of the money recovered – the standard tariff for such an operation.[6]

Hill had a hand in any pie that produced money:

> Visitors and strangers must have found the West End a rather dull place with no running gang-fights and feuds . . . The truth was that we cleared all the cheap racketeers out. There was no longer any

> blacking of club owners and restaurant keepers. In fact so peaceful did it all become that there was no gravy left for the small timers.[7]

So far as prostitution and the Messina brothers were concerned, on the face of it neither Hill nor Spot was interested. Under the surface, however, the Messinas paid a tax to them in the form of a fee for using Soho premises.

What were the pair like?

Reporter Michael Jacobson thought, 'Spotty, whom I knew very well, was nothing more than a paid thug. He had no initiative of his own. He was never a gang leader. Hill was.'[8]

Australian Paul Lincoln, who wrestled as Doctor Death and who opened the Two 'I's' Coffee bar in Old Compton Street, was in London as a young man:

> I was only 20 when I came to Soho, straight out of the Bush. I was naïve and my friends were frightening me with all the tales of these gangsters. What a disappointment. When I met the King of Gangsters Jack Spot he looked like an extra out of *Guys and Dolls*.[9]

Man about Soho Daniel Farson did not like Hill: 'I decided that his unpleasant reputation was confirmed by his face, which had the sallow complexion of underdone pork; his eyes were piggy too.'[10]

Others spoke well of Hill in particular. The clerk of one of the firms of solicitors he used recalled,

> He reigned almost with the blessing of the police. He was a very likeable bloke, always paid his bills. If you overlooked his reputation you'd never have dreamed who he was. While he was in control there was a peaceful scene. He kept discipline.

Others believe the peaceful reign was simply that Spot and Hill paid off the police. 'All top men, they work with the law to a certain degree,' recalls one Northern hard man. In the end, his inability to do so was perhaps Spot's biggest failing. An even less charitable view of Hill comes from the daredevil safebreaker, Eddie Chapman, who had been released from prison during the war for work in German territory and was one of his Hill's former friends: 'He kept control with the razor. People were paid a pound a stitch, so if you put twenty stitches in a man you got a score. You used to look in the evening papers next day to see how much you'd earned.'[11]

There were a few relatively minor continuing problems to be dealt with such as who had the lucrative concessions for the photographers and the bird-food vendors in Trafalgar Square, particularly at the time of the Festival of Britain, which Hill wanted for his brother Archie. And this again brought another serious and independent player into view – Billy Howard.

In his biography it is suggested that the right to the concessions would be decided by a bare-knuckle fight with Howard taking on all comers and the last man standing to be the winner. It is difficult to see how Howard would have agreed to conditions such as these, particularly as he was not by any means a young man. Nevertheless, he continued to knock down or retire his opponents until, at the end, he came to face Tony Mella, a man with no great ability in the professional ring, but who was one of the best street fighters of his era. Mella duly won and the concession was claimed by Hill, who had backed him. Howard was not pleased and explained the rules of the game to him. Hill climbed down, agreeing that Howard would benefit from the pot over the period of the Festival.[12] It is certain the fight took place, but other versions have Howard beating Mella.

In theory, another problem for Hill to deal with was Robert Emmett, known as Jimmy or Flash Jimmy. Earlier, Emmett had taken against Archie Hill and the old villain Dodger Mullins, both of whom he cut badly with a razor. Reprisals were required and when Hill heard that Emmett was in the Paramount Dance Hall in Tottenham Court Road he took Teddy Hughes, known as Odd Legs because of his limp, and two others to deal with him. In turn Emmett was badly slashed.

In the end the 37-year-old Emmett, who had something in the region of 20 previous convictions, including three for wounding, dealt with himself. He had quarrelled with a Charlie Cozens and on 16 November 1950, on the lookout for the man, found him in Rupert Street. He chased after him and fired a number of shots, hitting his coat and trousers. He was arrested in the East End after a matter of hours and on 12 December received 10 years' preventive detention at the Old Bailey. The seriousness of the crime was that the shooting took place outside the Café de Paris, a nightclub in which Princess Elizabeth was at the time eating a filet of sole and drinking champagne. She was not told of the incident.[13] After his release, in the 1960s Emmett had a club in Wardour Street, which was a fashionable place for villains and negotiators, such as Frankie Holpert, to meet with the police. He later went to the Canary Islands, where he died.

One thing in which Spot had a hand that went seriously wrong was the London Airport Robbery on 28 July 1948, which was to have been the first major postwar robbery at Heathrow Airport – then called Heath Row. The robbers included the cream of the Upton Park Mob and therefore Spot's men, the Wood brothers, Franny Daniels and Teddy Machin. Spot has generally, but not necessarily correctly, been given the credit for planning the robbery. It took place while Hill was still serving his three-year sentence and, although there have been stories that he advised from his cell, given conditions in prison at the time, these really are fanciful.

The target was to be the bonded warehouse, which contained nearly £250,000 worth of goods, including diamonds, and was due to receive £1 million in gold the next day. The job had been meticulously laid out with inside help. Dummy parcels were sent from Ireland and Franny Daniels checked they had arrived when, as an authorised driver, he was allowed in the customs sheds. Then a warehouseman reported he had been offered a bribe and the Flying Squad was called in.

The plan had been to drug the guards at the warehouse and at first the raid seemed to go according to plan. The messenger with the tea was intercepted, and barbitone was dropped in the jug. But the guards had been switched and replaced by members of the Squad. The tea was put on one side and the three 'guards' lay on the floor seemingly asleep. The members of the gang entered, hit one of the detectives with an iron bar to ensure he was unconscious and then took the keys from his pocket. At that moment other members of the Squad attacked the robbers, five of whom escaped. Teddy Machin fell into a ditch, was knocked unconscious and as a result was overlooked in the search. Franny Daniels held onto the underside of a van and, instead of being able to drop himself off at the first set of traffic lights as he had hoped, was carried to Harlesden Police Station, from where he made his way home. Scorched by the exhaust, he wore the burn on his shoulder for the rest of his life. The great burglar Billy Benstead also escaped. The next day a patched-up collection of the remainder went into the dock.

Teddy Hughes received 12 years' penal servitude, Sammy Ross a year fewer and Alfred Roome of Ilford received ten years. The very respected Jimmy Wood of Manor Park collected nine and his brother George eight.

When the Wood brothers came out of prison they transferred their allegiance to Billy Hill. Billy Benstead had already moved. As for Spot, who sometimes claimed responsibility for the robbery, sometimes not, the police could never prove that he was the organiser but his interests were disrupted, and, under pressure, his gambling club in St Botolph's Row in the city was closed.

Was Spot really the organiser? Many doubt it. Despite his claims of organisational ability, his detractors do not think he had the brains to plan such a coup. There is no doubt many of his associates were involved and that Spot knew of the robbery. Most likely the organiser was Spot's patron and wartime black-marketeer Abe Kosky. The plan was certainly hatched at Botolph's club, which Spot ran for him. Kosky had sufficient funds and it was said of him that he could not even lie straight in bed. Spot's gradual decline can almost be traced from the failure of the raid.

On the other hand, Billy Hill went from strength to strength. On 21 May 1952 came the first really successful major postwar robbery. The Eastcastle Street Great Mailbag Robbery was undoubtedly a Billy Hill production – devised, arranged and orchestrated by him. A post office worker who had been steadily losing in one of Hill's Soho spielers came to his notice and was approached for useful information. It was supplied in return for the cancellation of his gaming debts, and Hill went to work.

The robbery was carried out with immaculate precision. A mail van was kept under observation and followed every night for months on its journey from Paddington Station to the City. Rehearsals took place in the suburbs under the pretext of shooting a film. Cars were stolen specifically for the raid. On the night of the robbery, once the van left

Paddington a call was made to the West End flat where Hill had lodged his men.

Because of roadworks near Oxford Street, there was a diversion and, as the van turned into Eastcastle Street, one of the stolen cars blocked the driver's path. Six men then attacked the three post office workers and looted the vehicle. The van was driven to Augustus Street in the City, where the cash was transferred into boxes on a fruit lorry belonging to Jack Gyp, who was minded by Sonny Sullivan, another of Hill's men. Eighteen out of 31 bags were taken. At first it was thought that £44,000 in old notes had been stolen but the full damage became known later in the week. The total was in the region of £287,000.

From the word go, Hill was seriously suspected of the robbery but, despite intense police activity for over a year – headed by Superintendent Bob Lee, then second in command of the Flying Squad – there were no charges.

According to Hill, the night before the robbery, nine men – all of whom had been selected and warned of the raid the week before – were collected and taken to a flat in the West End, where they were locked in before being fully briefed on the operation. Hill set a precedent on the necessity for keeping a tight hold on his men. It was one that was ignored by Bert Wickstead when he tried to arrest the Maltese pornographers in Soho, only to find they had been tipped off. Hill's precautions were adopted by Nipper Read when he came to arrest the Krays in 1969.

Just who was on the raid will never be fully established. It is highly likely that the brothers Slip and Sonny Sullivan were both participants, although Sonny Sullivan later denied Slip's involvement.[14] The housebreaker and all-rounder George 'Taters' Chatham was certainly there. Chatham, a degenerate gambler as well as being one of the most talented cat burglars of that and many another generation, was said to have received £15,000 for his efforts.

'He was a good snooker player but not as good as he thought,' recalls one Soho frequenter. 'He used to play at the Red Fox in Hammersmith and these hustlers were coming in and taking his money off him.'

Chatham gambled his share away within a matter of weeks in one of Hill's clubs and then had the misfortune to be found trying to blow

Hill's safe in an attempt to recoup his losses. Stan Davis, who put up bookmakers' pitches at the races, recalls that Chatham approached him at the next Epsom meeting trying to borrow £25 from him. 'He lost that and on the way home he hit the Epsom post office. I bought the stamps and savings stamps off him.'

Hill found, as did Spot after the airport robbery, that the police took reprisals. They may not have been able to pin the Eastcastle Street raid on him but they were able to raid his spielers on an almost nightly basis. Eventually, he handed them over to others. He was now also having domestic troubles. His wife, Aggie, was on his back trying to persuade him that with the money from the robbery he could actually become legitimate. He maintained that he owed a loyalty to the men with whom he had worked over the years. According to his autobiography, he was still providing money for the wives of the men such as the Wood brothers and Teddy Hughes, who had gone down over the airport robbery. However some of his earnings he invested in a legitimate toy business. He also claimed to have given Spot £15,000 from the raid, later regarding his generosity as one of his most misplaced gestures.

Another problem was that the previous year Hill had also become emotionally involved with 'Gypsy' Phyllis May Blanche Riley, who had had something of a chequered early career and was then working behind the bar in one of his clubs. She had, by some accounts, run away from home in east London and had joined the Upton Park gypsies, from where she had taken her sobriquet. She had also been on the game, minded by a Maltese pimp known as Tulip, who took her from Hyde Park to Mayfair, where she was then run by a pimp, Johnny Belan – 'Belgian Johnny' – with whom she remained until Hill fell for her charms and fiery temperament. Frank Fraser remembers her: 'She was a cracker, really good looking and real fire.'

Another Spot man, Gerry Parker, describes her as 'not pretty but a good-looking woman with jet-black hair and high cheekbones. She had a mouth on her but she was a fine-looking woman.' Author Brian McDonald recalls her, too: 'Gypsy? I think she attacked Hill once. She gave him a few good clouts one day and people had a good laugh. Billy Hill – and Bobby Ramsey as well – was keen to go with brasses.'[15]

In the September of 1951 Belan had made further overtures to

Gypsy, who was offended, and so, in turn, was Hill. Ever handy with his knife, he cut the Belgian on the face and neck. Some hours later Hill telephoned Spot to beg him to go to Charing Cross Hospital, then near the station, to see if he could straighten things out. Spot was obliged – at some personal expense – to try to persuade the man not to name names. Spot would later claim that Belan had told him how much Hill hated him (Spot).

For the moment, however, the faithful Aggie was left with the New Cabinet Club and the gift of a poodle, Chico. Hill went to Tangier with Gypsy and then toured North Africa. 'I ate food I had never heard of, met people who were actually kind as well as educated, who were friendly although they were loaded with gelt.' With a senior Moroccan police officer as his partner, he acquired Churchills, 'the second best club in Tangier'.

Hill maintained the reason for his return home was that the pull of London was too much for him. Aggie was still there running the club and so was Spot, but another scenario is that in Churchills one night the quick-tempered Gypsy hit a well-connected woman, cutting her face with the diamond ring she wore, and they were asked to leave.

Domestically, there were, however, other problems with Gypsy. Now Queen of the Underworld, she was unhappy to be reminded of her past. When in September 1953 she was approached by a pimp she persuaded Slip Sullivan, a man who over the years suffered greatly at the hands of knives and women, to have him thrown out of a Paddington club known as French Henry's. In turn the pimp was protected by the tearaway and all-time Soho loser, Tommy Smithson. Sullivan took a bad beating at his hands – Hill says his throat was cut – and reprisals were required to maintain the status quo.[16]

When it came to it, Tommy Smithson, in his own chequered and largely unsuccessful career, suffered at just about everyone's hands. An ex-fairground fighter with a penchant for silk shirts and underwear, a man of immense courage and little stability or ability, Smithson was known as Mr Loser. Born in Liverpool in 1920 and brought to the East End two years later, he served in the Merchant Navy until his discharge in the 1950s. Back in Shoreditch he found things had changed. Maltese immigrants had assumed control of clubs and cafés and Smithson decided to set up his own protection racket devoted to these Maltese businessmen as well as working a spinner with Tony Mella around the dog tracks.[17]

Acting as minder and as a croupier, initially Smithson protected George Caruana, said to resemble Tony Curtis, whose gambling clubs included one in Batty Street, Stepney. At the time Caruana and the other Maltese were keen to avoid trouble and Smithson soon extended his interests to a share of the takings in the clubs. A shilling in the pound from the dice games earned him up to £100 an evening. With his profits he was able to buy into a series of drinking clubs in Soho.

Now, after cutting Sullivan, Smithson went into hiding, only to be given up by the Maltese he had been protecting. Told there was a peace offer on the table, Smithson was asked – ordered is perhaps a better word – to attend a meeting at the Black Cat cigarette factory in Camden Town. He took with him the Paddington club owner Dave Barry and at least one gun, a Luger. Arrayed against him were Hill, Spot, Sonny Sullivan and the long-serving Spot man Moishe Goldstein, known as Blueball, because of the colour of one of his testicles. Spot explained to Smithson that they were simply there to talk and he, Smithson, handed over the gun. Just as Spot was putting it away, Hill suddenly slashed the unprepared Smithson. The slashes on his face were in the form of the sides of the letter V down each cheek meeting at his chin; it was a Hill trademark. In his book he wrote:

> Early in life I decided that the best stroke for chivving was the V for Victory sign, or a cross on the cheek. They remember that, and whenever you saw anyone wearing one you knew that it was Billy Hill who had done it.[18]

Another version of the Smithson slashing is that Spot held the unfortunate man while Hill went to work. Whichever is correct Smithson was also slashed over his face, arms, legs and chest. Barry ran away and Hill, realising how badly Smithson was injured, turned white. This could have been a hanging matter. Smithson was then thrown over a wall into Regent's Park and it was left to Spot to send Moishe Blueball to call an ambulance and drive Hill back to his flat.

Fortunately for everyone, Smithson survived and 47 stitches were put in his face. Nor did he talk to the police. His reward for honouring the code of silence was a party, the sobriquet 'Scarface' and £500 or £1,000, with which he bought a share in another drinking club in Old Compton Street. According to some accounts it was Spot who paid the compensation. The club was quickly closed by the police and Smithson bought another, this time a spieler. This too was closed down and Smithson took up receiving as an occupation. But then word began to spread that he was a police informer and he received a further 27 stitches. But the original slashing by Hill had, in effect, been the last joint enterprise of the now rival Bosses of London's Underworld.

Almost all gang leaders whether in London, New York, Melbourne or Macau have come a cropper when they have raised their heads into public view, and for a time Spot observed the rule that his should stay firmly below the parapet. True, he was on good terms with the *People*'s columnist Arthur Helliwell, who wrote regularly on a Sunday about both him and Hill without naming them in his column 'Follow me Around'. Indeed it is Spot to whom Helliwell is referring in this piece. Note the 'in' references:

> In the last five years I have often spotlighted the Big Shot's activities. He walked into my office with two bodyguards and announced his intention of 'quitting the shady side of the street'.
>
> No one knows who the next Big Shot will be but '– gambling dens, racetracks etc. will be decidedly unhealthy spots'.[19]

It is curious, however, how little was generally known of Spot in Fleet Street even as late as 1953. A note to the *Daily Mirror* news desk in September that year read:

> Comer is known as Jack Sprott. He is thought – almost certainly – to be the brains behind the London Airport bullion attempt in 1948 and the £250,000 mailvan theft last year. Comer frequents most of the Soho betting clubs and does a lot of pavement betting in Gt Windmill Street, outside Jack Solomons's gym. I think there is a tie-up somewhere between Comer and Solomons. Comer is invariably attended by a bevy of smoothly dressed 'gorillas' and I have seen him in company of a very attractive dark-haired woman.[20]

The writer was correct about the dark-haired woman, who was his wife Rita; wrong about the mail van; only possibly right about the airport; and certainly correct about Spot's connections with Solomons.[21]

11

Goodbye to the Messinas

By 1946, with the Messina brothers' weekly earnings now at £10,000, the girls were taking £100 a night and being paid £50 a week. Even if takings dropped after the war the business was still a worthwhile target for other ponces.

The beats of independent prostitutes were jealously guarded and sales of them were well organised. In the mid-1940s the buyer paid the vendor a percentage of her earnings for an agreed number of months in return for the seller ensuring that there was no trouble from girls on neighbouring beats. In Soho, two men working for the Public Morality Council reported that one midnight they were approached by 35 women in a 100-yard strip. Seven were still working at 4 am.

Although most of Soho prostitution was still controlled by the brothers, other low-grade pimps were moving in on their territory, hanging out in clubs such as the billiards club at 3 Carlisle Street, where, on 15 June 1948, Amabile Ricca 'Ricky the Malt', poetically, if probably inaccurately, described by the *News of the World* as 'the worst Maltese in Britain', was shot and stabbed to death. Francis Xavier Farrugia and his brother Joseph were charged with his murder. In the end Joseph received five years for manslaughter and Francis, who had thrown away the weapons, six months. Regarded as a fearsome bully of whom the Ferrugias and other Maltese were terrified, Ricca had a conviction in 1932 in Malta for discharging a firearm as a result of which a death occurred. Shortly before his death he had also served 18 months for malicious wounding in London.[1]

In March the previous year Carmelo Vassallo and four other Maltese had endeavoured to muscle in on the Messina enterprise, demanding protection money of £1 a girl a day. Retribution in all forms was swift. At a meeting in Winchester Court, South Kensington, Eugenio Messina took off two of Vassallo's fingertips. But it was not sufficient for the girls. Marthe Watts and two others, now apparently thoroughly frightened by these other marauding Maltese and what might happen if they gave in to their demands, went to the police. Some might think the girls had been put up to this by their masters.

Carmelo Vassallo and the four others stood in the Old Bailey in April 1947 charged with demanding money with menaces. All the prosecution witnesses staunchly denied they were 'Messina girls'. One of them, Janine Gilson, admitted knowing the Messinas for three years but denied she had ever spoken to them. 'I know them as diamond merchants and I know them as very wealthy people', she told the jury.

This sort of rubbish could not possibly be swallowed by any sensible jury but there was backup evidence. The police had been on watch in Burlington Gardens, off Piccadilly, when the five Maltese drew up and one shouted out to the girls, 'It's better for you to give us the money, otherwise I will cut your face!' In the car the police found a hammer wrapped in newspaper, a knife and a life preserver. At the men's flat there were a knuckleduster and an automatic pistol with six rounds of ammunition. Convicted of demanding money with menaces, Vassallo and two others received four years' penal servitude.

Eugenio Messina, who had had no takers for his offer of the enormous sum of £25,000 to anyone who could smuggle him out of the country before his trial, received three years for Vassallo's fingertips. The brothers were now known figures and questions were asked in Parliament. In view of what had emerged at the trials, where Marthe and the other girls had loyally lied, denying their involvement with the brothers, would the Home Secretary appoint a commission to inquire into organised vice in London? No, replied Mr Chuter Ede: 'Any inquiry would not help the police because their difficulties arise from the fact that, although they may have good reason to suspect such activities, they are sometimes unable to obtain evidence upon which criminal proceedings could be based.'

Then as now.

But John Foster, MP for Norwich, who was putting the questions, was not satisfied. What about an examination of the Messinas' bank accounts? Was Mr Ede aware they were popularly supposed to be making half a million a year, that they had no fewer than 20 girls working for them and that they owned a West End estate agency? But Mr Ede was having none of it and the remaining brothers continued to flourish.

All, that is, except Carmelo – Marthe Watts's favourite. Conscious of the privations his brother Eugenio was suffering, he tried to bribe a prison officer at Wandsworth Prison, for which he received two months plus a £50 fine. On his and Eugenio's release they were given £700 by the girls, who had conscientiously been putting their money in the safe for them – watched, it has to be said, by two of the other brothers. On Eugenio's release he bought himself a Rolls-Royce. But, for the purposes of the courts, the Messinas went underground. There was no question now of having knife fights with the Maltese opposition. According to Marthe Watts complainants were simply framed:

> I am sure, from some of the remarks passed by some magistrates, that they did not believe there was such a thing as the Messina Gang. They certainly did not when Sally Wright was charged with assaulting Rabina Dickson Torrance with a knife. Sally Wright pleaded that Torrance was a Messina woman, that the whole charge had been framed by the Messina Gang, and that she was innocent.
>
> She was by no means the first person who had not been believed after pleading that she had been victimised by the Messina Gang. It seems that when anyone upset the Messinas all they had to do was enlist the aid of the Courts, apparently with police assistance, and that someone was conveniently imprisoned, and incidentally discredited for life.[2]

The thwarted takeover did, however, spell the very beginning of the end of the Messinas' reign. Now Billy Hill's biographer and unpaid press agent Duncan Webb began his campaign against the brothers.

One of the many supporting actors in Billy Hill's cast of players, and one who was used both to improve the gang leader's own image and damage that of Jack Spot, was the very curious reporter from the *People*, Thomas Duncan Webb. In fact, Webb did not like the title 'crime reporter', preferring 'crime investigator'. He began his career with the *South London Press* in the 1930s and then served in the war in West Africa before he was invalided out in 1944, after which he went to the *Daily Express* working under the legendary editor Arthur Christiansen. From there it was a move to the sister paper the *Evening Standard*.

Webb had, without doubt, a dark side. He overstepped the role of investigative journalist and became a confidant and effectively a tool of Billy Hill, meeting and eating with him and his associates in Peter Mario's restaurant at the Leicester Square end of Gerrard Street.[3] He was actually present when a decision was made to frame Jack Spot over the slashing of the Glasgow hard man Victor Russo, but he claimed he could not have heard what went on because he was behind a curtain.[4]

Shortly after his discharge from the army in 1944, he had managed to acquire a conviction at Plymouth Magistrates' Court for communicating the movements of His Majesty's ships. He had telephoned the *Daily Express* and spoken so loudly that he had been overheard. He was fined £50 on 26 August that year.

That may have been a relatively young reporter's excessive zeal but his next appearance in the dock was altogether more curious. This time he appeared at Marlborough Street on charges of grievous bodily harm and impersonating a police officer. He had, so the court was told by a prostitute, Jean Crewes, agreed to have intercourse with her for £2. They had what she quaintly described as 'connections' and he went to the bathroom to 'cleanse himself'. It was after that he refused to leave the flat. She said she would call the police and he then left with her. In the street she borrowed two pennies from an actor, Herbert Gardner Wadham, to make a call to the police. They walked back to her flat, where Webb showed Wadham his press card, masking it so it appeared to be a warrant card. He seems to have arrested Wadham and then hit him in the face. As they marched along Tottenham Court

Road Wadham approached a temporary reserve policeman and asked for help. At the police station Webb denied ever having seen Wadham. The grievous-bodily-harm charge was reduced to one of common assault and he was bound over in the sum of two guineas under the Prosecution of Offences Act. The charge of impersonating a police officer was dismissed.[5]

He was sacked after his conviction and moved to the *People*, a broadsheet in name but a tabloid in spirit, making his name with the case of John George Haigh, the so-called acid bath murderer. Webb really was a disciple of the gutter press. Haigh had a wife living in a bigamous marriage in Cornwall. The week after Haigh's execution Webb arranged a remarriage for the woman, with himself as best man. Naturally, it was featured in the *People*.

In September 1950 he published his exposé of the Messinas under the banner headline, ARREST THESE FOUR MEN and beginning:

> On the night of 30 June 1950 I performed one of the most distasteful duties I have ever carried out in my career as a crime reporter – something I never want to do again. I went to the West End of London and picked up a woman of the streets.

Crewes, Wadham and Marlborough Street had conveniently been forgotten.

The paper backed the report with photographs both of the Messina girls and of the flats from where they operated. According to the writer Robert Murphy, on the day after the story was published all the brothers came looking for him and found him with Hill in the Brunswick Arms, Bloomsbury. The Messinas were effectively frozen out by the stares of the locals.[6] The story may well be apocryphal because there is no mention of the incident by Webb in the next issue of the *People*, although the week after he relates how he and a woman companion were knocked about by men and a woman in Long Acre. The men shouted, 'The Messinas are pals of mine. It's about time you journalists were done proper.'[7] Late that month there was also an attempt by the faithful Marthe Watts to have him charged with demanding money from her with menaces. Webb had had a photograph taken of her in Mayfair and she alleged he wanted £50 not to publish it. She said she had only £7, which Webb claimed was not enough. The Metropolitan Police Solicitors Department thought there would have to be a great deal more backup evidence to bring a case.[8]

Now Eugenio and Carmelo loaded up the yellow Rolls-Royce and left for France via Dover. Though they returned using false passports they were never again seen openly in this country. The next to go was Salvatore. Attilio and Alfredo remained.

Attilio had been living near Marlow with Robina Torrance, who had brought the false charges of assault against Sally Wright when the girl had tried to leave the family. His work in clearing things up completed, he too headed for France, leaving behind only Alfredo, living with Hermione Hindin, who worked as Barbara. On 19 March 1951, Alfredo was arrested at his Wembley home and charged with living on immoral earnings and trying to bribe a police officer. He had offered Superintendent Mahon, one of the arresting officers, £200.

At his trial at the Old Bailey he gave his employment as that of diamond merchant. No, he did not know that Hermione was in fact Barbara. No, he did not know she had more than 100 convictions for soliciting. When she went out in the evening, he thought it was to see a relative. It was a great shock to him to learn she was a common prostitute. He had brought his personal fortune, some £30,000, to Britain at the beginning of the war and had dealt in diamonds. He had both diabetes and high blood pressure, which was why he did not really work. What on earth was this vice ring organised by his brothers? Alfredo received two years' imprisonment, concurrent on each of the charges, and a £500 fine. In fact, Barbara worked in the next-door flat to Alfredo's real wife, a Spanish woman, who worked under the name Marcelle.

For the moment it seemed the hold of the Messina brothers – one in prison and four abroad – had been broken. In celebration of his success, Webb, a devout Roman Catholic, put an advertisement in *The Times* offering thanks to St Jude.

On the face of it, after their convictions and flight in 1950, the remains of the Messina empire was looked after by their cousin Anthony Micallef. Then, with the Coronation coming up in 1953, there was a sudden surge of foreign prostitutes in Soho and Mayfair. Spurious marriages – which would prevent any deportation of the women

– were arranged by a London solicitor, or at any rate the police thought so. Now Webb set himself the task of finding out who was behind Micallef and he discovered it was the seedy Antonio 'Tony' Rossi, born in Corsica, who liked to be known as the Lion of Montmartre, fronting for the brothers. In turn Webb dubbed him 'The Jackal of Soho'.

In practice, the ever-faithful Marthe Watts took over control of the increasingly young girls whom Eugenio was sending over from the Continent, often after picking them up at tea dances. Each girl kept her own accounts and it seems that, such was the mixture of loyalty and fear, they never tried to skim for themselves. Every thousand pounds earned meant a bonus trip to see Eugenio in Paris. The money, however, went over by courier.

But now Attilio was back making trips to England. Alfredo's solicitors at his trial had been Webb, Justice & Co., and Superintendent Mahon began to follow the firm's clerk, Watson, as he made trips to Europe. In October 1951 Watson went to his home in Chalfont St Giles for a short time, left and got into another car, which drove off towards Amersham.

The car was stopped by Mahon and inside, with Watson, was Attilio. He was charged with living off the immoral earnings of Robina Torrance and received six months' imprisonment, the maximum sentence.

Certainly this should now have been the end for the brothers, but it was not to be so. Eugenio, Carmelo and Alfredo controlled matters from Paris until November 1953, when Eugenio was kidnapped and released only on payment of £2,000. In some disarray, the brothers moved their headquarters to Lausanne. In the meantime, Attilio had completed his short stretch and, under the name Raymond Maynard, had again set up a light housekeeping arrangement with Robina Torrance in Bourne End. Deportation papers were served on Attilio in 1953 but the Italian authorities declined to have him and, once the *People* had traced him to The Hideaway, his appropriately named cottage, he moved to south London, reporting daily to the police as an Italian national.

But Eugenio had surfaced again, obtaining a British passport under the name Alexander Miller and buying 39 Curzon Street in Mayfair from a Mrs Augustine Johans, who continued to manage it as a brothel. In September she was fined £25 but in the raid the police found £14,000 in a safe. As a result, the premises were taken over by Hermione Hindin and Mrs Johans moved elsewhere.

On 31 August 1955 Carmelo and Eugenio were arrested in the Horse's Neck at Knokke-le-Zoute and charged with being in possession of firearms and false passports and procuring women for prostitution. It was only then that the extent of their current British empire became apparent. Title deeds to four central London properties were found in a safe box together with long reports from Marthe Watts and Mrs Johans. One, by Watts, showed that one girl, a former nurse working as Therese, had earned £2,400 in six weeks. Eugenio had gone through his prospective-fiancé routine before marrying her off to a stray Englishman. Eugenio received seven years' imprisonment and Carmelo was deemed to have served his sentence. He had been in custody on remand for 10 months and was released. He disappeared, but not for long. At the end of 1956 appeals were heard in the Belgian case. Carmelo had his sentence doubled *in absentia* while Eugenio had seven months knocked off. But where was Carmelo?

In October 1958 he was found sitting in a car in Knightsbridge and arrested as an illegal immigrant. He received a six-month sentence and was deported at the end. He died in the autumn in Sicily. But now where was Attilio?

He was working hard, or rather Edna Kallman, initially seduced by promises of marriage and the good life, was. She had been under his control for ten years, put out to work under the tutelage of Robina Torrance. Attilio knocked her about continually until, in sheer terror of a further beating, she managed to bring herself to return to her parents in Derby and they called the police. Edna Kallman had earned between £50 and £150 a week over those 10 years and had been allowed to keep only £7 a week for herself. On 9 April 1959 he was sentenced to four years' imprisonment and on his release went to Italy. Salvatore lived in Switzerland while Alfredo, who could claim British citizenship, died in Brentford in 1963.

That really should have marked the end of the Messinas as an active force in prostitution in Soho and the West End but in the late sixties Eugenio and Carmelo were still paying the rent and rates of premises in Mayfair.

Eugenio Messina went to Italy, where he lived in San Remo. On 12 March 1970 he married Maria Theresa Vervaere – who had worked out of Curzon Street under the name Mary Smith – and died the same day. When his brothers arrived, they found that his safe had been emptied. Vervaere-Smith now wanted her share of the Eugenio fortune. She did, however, have serious problems. She had married a former Shanghai policeman, William George Smith, in August 1954 and he was still alive. She claimed that Smith had married a Russian woman and so her marriage to him was bigamous. As an alternative she claimed she had not understood that the ceremony at Paddington Register Office was, in fact, a marriage to Smith. Unfortunately for her, it turned out he had obtained a divorce from the Russian in Nevada in 1946 and the judge ruled that she knew full well the significance of her marriage and she therefore had no claim to Eugenio's fortune.

According to her biography, Marthe Watts married and settled down. Robina Torrance, who had a son by Attilio, also settled down, running an antiques shop in Henley-on-Thames and later marrying a local man. She died in August 1992.[9]

There are plenty of solicitors who have become too close to their underworld clients for their own good, and in 1955 one of the first postwar solicitors to find himself in serious difficulties was Ben Cantor. He had been one of the solicitors who acted for the Messina brothers and was then acting for Joseph Grech, another Maltese, who was sent to prison for three years for a housebreaking offence. From his cell, Grech unloaded a series of legal bombs.

He had, he said, given a Morris Page around £150 to hand to Detective Sergeant Robertson, who had been in charge of the case. There was to have been a further £150 to Robertson on an acquittal. He also alleged that Robertson had coached Ben Cantor about the questions to be put at the trial. When Robertson, Page and Cantor appeared at the Old Bailey, charged with conspiracy to pervert the course of justice, Grech unloaded some more bombs. His conviction, he said, had been brought about by perjured evidence of other officers acting on the instructions of an Inspector Reuben Jacobs, attached to West End Central.

Jacobs, he said, had asked him for £2,000 so that none of his flats or brothels would be raided. After negotiations the terms were set at £500 down and £30 a week. Cantor had, said Grech, been the bagman taking £100 to give to Jacobs. According to Grech, Cantor came back saying, 'He wants £500.'

When he came to give evidence, Cantor was in difficulties over his relationship with Tony Micallef, who had been accepted as a surety by Robertson. Could any honest solicitor have genuinely put him forward as a suitable person? The jury thought not and Cantor received two years' imprisonment, as did Robertson; the intermediary, Morris Page, went down for 15 months. After his release Grech claimed he was a marked man and an attempt had been made in January 1957 to run him down in Seymour Place. Cantor, who was thought to have been involved in the arranged-marriage racket, faded away.

In November 1955 the *Daily Mail* revealed that Detective Superintendent Bert Hannam had lodged a report with the Commissioner, Sir John Nott-Bower, revealing 'a vast amount of bribery and corruption among certain uniformed officers attached to West End Station'.[10] According to Hannam's report, the corruption involved 'club proprietors, prostitutes, gaming-house owners, brothel-keepers and men living on immoral earnings'. It appeared that Hannam had interviewed no fewer than 40 men serving prison sentences arising from West End vice.

The extent of corruption can be gauged by the fact that it was found that some uniformed patrolmen in the vice-ridden streets of Soho were receiving up to £60 a week in bribes.

Hannam found, so the article said, that 'evidence was "cooked" by police officers to benefit accused people. Details of previous convictions were suppressed in many cases so that men standing on charges were fined nominal sums instead of going to prison.' The article continued,

> Gaming houses, where [the card games] faro and *chemin de fer* were being played quite openly, were tipped off at a fee when a raid was to take place. Proprietors were warned to get 'mugs' in on a certain

day, so that the regular customers could escape arrest. Brothel-keepers were told that certain evidence could be adjusted for a price. Huge sums of money changed hands. The 'adjustment' was for an officer to say in evidence that upon the raid taking place he found a number of fully clothed women on the premises, whereas, in fact, they were nude. That gave the premises an air of respectability – and halved the fine.

> The hundreds of prostitutes who infest the West End streets are included in the bribery racket.
>
> One officer is pointed out by them to be the richest policeman in the Force.
>
> Most of these unfortunate girls appear on a special 'roster' due for appearance at a magistrates' court on a certain day for the usual £2 fine for soliciting. If the day does not happen to suit the woman, a 'fee' is paid for postponement.

The Commissioner acted swiftly. Summoning effectively the whole of 'C' Division at West End Central, he climbed onto a table and gave his men a pep-talk:

> I wish to tell you how much I deplore the imputations which have recently been made in the press which reflect on the reputation of the whole force and, in particular, all of 'C' Division.
>
> In one of today's papers reference has been made to certain statements regarding the officers of 'C' Division in a report submitted to me by Detective-Superintendent Herbert Hannam.
>
> I want it to be known that there is no truth whatever in this, and that none of the subjects referred to in that report have been so much as mentioned in any report submitted to me by the Superintendent.

There was something of what now would be called a damage-limitation exercise from the authorities. In a statement to the press,

Nott-Bower went on to deny that 450 men might be transferred from Central London.

Certain confidential papers had gone missing but, 'Neither is there truth in reports that "top secret" or even "secret" papers have been missed from Scotland Yard. Those that were found in a house have no security importance whatever.'

In December 1955 it was revealed that the wardrobe locker of a detective sergeant who had been assisting Detective Superintendent Stephen Glander had been forced. Papers had been disturbed but nothing was taken. An inquiry that involved a number of officers in submitting their fingerprints for comparison at first seemed to have come to nothing. But then, in January 1956, a detective sergeant employed in the Central Records Office of Scotland Yard was charged with stealing a file and communicating it to the man to whom it referred.

The next month Inspector Reuben Jacobs was dismissed from the force. A disciplinary board had found him guilty of assisting a prostitute to obtain premises, failing to account for a prisoner's property and failing to disclose in court a man's previous conviction. Jacobs took it hard and applied to the Divisional Court to quash the conviction on the grounds that by reason of his mental health at the time he was unfit to prepare his defence, to cross-examine witnesses, to give evidence on his own behalf and call his witnesses. The application was rejected. Jacobs had also been in a case in which he deliberately falsified his notebook so that a suspect was provided with a cast-iron alibi. Later, when he went to Kent and applied for a licence to run a public house, the chief constable himself appeared to oppose the application.

There were certainly leaks. The veteran solicitor Jeffrey Gordon, who as a young man worked for Leonard Gost of Allen & Son – who advised the Westminster Council on whether sufficient evidence had been accumulated to prosecute – remembers, 'Suspicion fell on the staff that they were the ones who had tipped off the brothel owners but my principal was the only one to see the papers which came from the police and were kept locked away.'[11]

'We had our own inside tap,' said safebreaker Eddie Chapman. 'One of the Assistant Commissioners was having it off with a bird on the strength and she used to tell us everything he told her in bed'[12]

ack Spot, Rita and her sister (centre) at the Hideaway Club in 1955.

Spot's lurid version of Soho in the 1950s.

Carl Reginsky, slashed by the Whites. Note the scar under his chin.

Paul Lincoln as Doctor Death. Along with fellow Aussie Ray Hunter, Lincoln established the Two 'I's coffee bar in Old Compton Street. He thought Jack Spot looked like an extra from *Guys and Dolls*.

Heavyweight champion Bert Assirati, strongman for Peter Rachman and doorman of La Discotheque.

George Tremlett 'Fuzzy Ball Kaye'. Club owner, friend of the Krays and slasher of Tony Mella.

etective Sergeant Harry Challenor: self-
ppointed scourge of Soho.

Jimmy Humprheys, nemesis of the Porn Squad.

below Kenneth Drury of the Porn Squad on his way to court.

etective Sergeant George Goddard, too close
friend of the nightclub queen Mrs Meyrick.

Tommy Smithson, club owner, enforcer and all-round loser.

below Phillip Ellul, who was convicted of the murder of Tommy Smithson on 25 June 1956.

Frank Misfud; a gangland king of the 1960s.

below Tommy Smithson's funeral.

ɔho club owners Ronnie and Reggie Kray – The Twins.

lly Hill's book launch at Gennaro's (now the Groucho Club). Among the guests are (from right) ɔbby Warren, Tommy Falco, Bert Rossi (smoking), Billy Hill (in bow tie), Ruby Sparks and Frank aser. It is possibly the journalist Hannen Swaffer who is playing the piano.

Two of the Messina brothers – Kings of Soho vice in the 1940s.

The Italians in the 1920s: Enrico Cortesi is sitting wearing the boater, Derby Sabini is standing his left shoulder.

arren Street car dealer, financier
ıd pimp Stanley Setty, murdered
' Donald Hume.

Albert Dimes and his wife celebrate his acquittal over the 'fight that never was'.

ırmer world light-heavyweight
ıxing champion and Charing
oss Road Nitespot owner Freddie
ills has an ice-cream licked. He
ıs found shot dead outside his
ıb on 25 July 1965.

ght Hill attends the funeral of his
nchman Billy Blythe.

left A young Frank Fraser, club owner a
enforcer for Billy Hill and the Richards
brothers takes a holiday in Paris.

A spiv is caught selling nylons.

below The Rainbow Club for US Servic
men at Piccadilly Circus. From here P
goods were passed on to the spivs.

Perhaps if the authorities had not been so keen on presenting a whiter than white picture the troubles of 20 years later would have been avoided.

12

Out, Damned Spot!

The beginning of 1953 was not a good time for Jack Spot. In the January when the police raided the Vienna Club, a spieler in Crawford Place, Marylebone, they found a dice game being played on the billiard table. It was all pretty low-key. Seven shillings (35p) was found in a box and when the men were searched they had £7. 9s. (£7.45) between them. On 12 January at Marylebone court Spot was bound over in the sum of £10 not to frequent a common gaming house for two years. He was back at Marylebone two months later when on 7 March he was fined £20 and Sonny Sullivan a fiver more for being in the same club.[1]

Spot was now on the slide. The Jockey Club was helping the big-credit bookmakers prepare for the legalisation of off-course betting and smaller bookmakers and their protectors were being squeezed. Spot's team was disintegrating. Slowly he was losing both his gang and his reputation. The word was out in the underworld that he was a grass. 'We'd had his sheet pulled from the Yard,' said Eddie Chapman, 'and there it was for all to see.'[2] He was not being helped by mass defections of his troops to Hill and, worse, this one-time hard man was becoming something of a figure of fun. Married to the stunningly beautiful Rita, he found that domesticity did not suit him, and he was being openly mocked that when the baby cried he had to go home to look after it. Then there were troubles over the bookmaking pitches.

The same month, Spot was arrested by Detective Sergeant Sid Careless for possessing an offensive weapon under the Prevention of

Crime Act, which had just come into force. He had received a telephone call that someone had a 'nice fur coat for sale – very cheap' and went to meet him at Piccadilly Circus.

Spot would recall,

> Me, like a mug, I go and meet him. He gives me the fur coat and I paid him and walked away. Then out of a car come four detectives. One of them was known as Careless – he couldn't care less is right. And I'm taken to the station. They bring a knuckleduster round and they say, 'You're charged with carrying an offensive weapon.' It was all the work of that cunt Sparks who was the right hand man of another bastard – Greeno – biggest thieves the world's ever known.[3]

Spot was taken to the station and charged with both offences, the work, he would claim, of Billy Hill acting in conjunction with Herbert Sparks and Ted Greeno, both one-time heads of the Flying Squad. He was certainly right to regard them with suspicion. Greeno was far too close to criminals for his own good and Sparks's career was, by the end, in ruins.[4]

Curiously, the receiving charge was dropped but, as for the offensive weapon, there was no point in those days in Spot's alleging it had been planted. That was a quick route to a conviction and imprisonment for defaming gallant officers.

Spot appeared at Bow Street and pleaded guilty to possessing the knuckleduster. In mitigation it was argued that, working as a commission agent in Camden Town with of all people Alf White, he carried up to £400 in cash, and so needed a knuckleduster for his protection. He had bought it in a store in Holborn about a fortnight previously. He was fined a modest £20.[5]

On 21 October 1954 Spot committed a serious blunder, forgetting the cardinal rule that then prevailed that, however tiresome a journalist might be, he should not be touched. Duncan Webb was ghostwriting Billy Hill's autobiography in serial form at the time and was at a hotel in Kingston on Thames when he received a message to telephone a man called Nadel. He did so and found it was Spot, who had previously threatened to break Webb's jaw. Now he said he had to see him right away and it was over the articles.

At 10.30 that night Webb met him on the steps of the Dominion, then a cinema, in Tottenham Court Road. Spot greeted him by saying, 'Come on, it's bad.' He took him into an alleyway, where he knocked him down and Webb broke his wrist as he fell.

Spot's version was slightly different and in some respects bears scrutiny. He said the meeting had been in the Horseshoe, Tottenham Court Road. Webb had told him that Spot was no longer the Guvnor and that Hill had taken over. Then he had made the dangerous remark, 'How did Hitler miss you?' 'So I took him round the back of the Dominion and we had a nice talk and I gave him a right hook which I shouldn't have done.'

Spot was initially charged with grievous bodily harm. He may have lost much of his power in the West End but he still had some contacts, and Webb was straightened with £600. The blow that knocked him down had, on reflection, not been with a knuckleduster but had been more of a push. On 18 November 1954 at Clerkenwell court Spot now pleaded guilty to a charge of actual bodily harm and was fined £50 with 20 guineas' costs.

Webb may have been straightened so far as the criminal action was concerned but he also brought a civil action for damages. On 5 March 1956 he was awarded £732, a tidy little sum for the time, which would have enabled him to buy a part-occupied house in Tottenham if he had so wished and had received the money, which he never did.[6]

On the other hand, Hill had been thriving. Another robbery produced a second major triumph for him. In another meticulously planned job on 21 September 1954, his team attacked a bullion lorry in Lincoln's Inn Fields, clearing £45,000.[7] Less than a fortnight earlier he had announced his retirement. 'I've made my pile so I'm quitting.' Aged 43, he was now sitting peacefully in the sun in the South of France spouting pabulum to the ever-faithful Webb. The spielers were bringing in a good sum each week; everybody was behaving themselves. If there was any trouble he would be told in his daily telephone call and would catch the next plane back.[8]

Spot must have wished he was in Hill's place. Now he was having trouble over the allocation of the bookmakers' pitches. At Brighton one day Spot ordered that the usual allocation of the pitches be altered. Stan Davis, who put them up, complied and, when he had done so,

'Albert [Dimes] saw what we had done and he went raving mad. He gave me a kicking and Tommy Falco had to pull him off me.'[9] Spot saw himself as under threat and asked the up-and-coming Kray Twins to mind him on the free course at the Epsom Spring meeting. But his days were numbered.

The effective end of Spot's reign came on 11 August 1955. He was in the Galahad when he was told that 'Big Albert' Dimes wanted to see him. This must have been the crowning insult. His temper up, he went to find Dimes and caught up with him on the corner of Frith Street.

Spot had now ventured into Italian, and so foreign, territory. It was here that a good deal of street bookmaking was conducted. Spot went after Dimes with a knife and Dimes ran away. Now came Spot's big mistake: he chased after him. Apart from the fact there would have been no court case if he had let him run, his status in Soho would have soared. Dimes's flight was watched by other Italians and it would have been a tremendous feather in Spot's cap to be able to say that the great Albert had fled from him. Instead he went after him and now they fought almost to the death on the street and inside a grocery shop, where, ironically, Bertha Hyams, a large Jewish lady fruiterer, broke up the fight by banging Spot with a brass weighing pan.

'If she hadn't intervened Spot would have done him,' says a bystander who never gave evidence. 'Once she hit him, Albert got the knife away and did him.' Dimes got away with Bert Marsh in a taxi. Spot picked himself off the pavement, staggered into a nearby barber's shop, said, 'Fix me up' and fainted.

Dimes went to the Charing Cross Hospital and Spot to the nearby Middlesex. Spot had been stabbed over the left eye and in the left cheek as well as the neck and ear. He had four stab wounds in the left arm and two in the chest, one of which had penetrated his lung. Dimes had his forehead cut to the bone, requiring 20 stitches, and had received a wound in the thigh and one in the stomach.

For the moment, the press coverage was all of Spot. Flowers and telegrams of good wishes were sent to the hospital. Breath was held until the great man had something to say to his waiting public. 'There ain't gonna be no war,' he said, and the *Sunday Chronicle* for one breathed a sigh of relief. 'The pronouncement was passed along the grapevine. The effect was an immediate lessening of tension in Soho.'[10]

Once the news of the fight broke there was a flurry of activity. Gerry Parker remembers that he was in Sussex at the time:

> Sonny [Schack] was now more or less in charge and he'd sit in Lyons Corner House in Coventry Street and keep saying, 'We've got to declare war.' It didn't help. Things were very tight with Old Bill at the time. They were determined to clear things up one way or the other. Even if they weren't, who was going to fight on Jack's side? There was no general, no captains.

Spot claimed he was discharging himself from hospital because Rita had been threatened. For his defence he instructed the solicitor Bernie Perkoff, whose father had run the Windmill public house in the East End, which Spot had used and which before the war had once been wrecked by the Sabinis on the rampage.

The way Reggie Seaton, later to become chairman of the Inner London Quarter Sessions, put the case for the Crown was that Spot had started the attack, and that Dimes had at sometime in the struggle wrestled the knife from him and had struck back, going far beyond the limits of self-defence.

There was clearly a case to answer, said the magistrate. Spot and Dimes were committed for trial at the Old Bailey. Spot was committed in custody but Dimes was given bail. Although, as Parker recalls, Spot would say of his prison experience he was 'in for a haircut and a shave and he'd laugh about it', Spot did not like prison. Isolated and in some despair, on 30 August he was found in his cell at Brixton with his wrists slashed, and was moved to a special cell.[11]

The trials that followed were genuinely sensational. At first Mr Justice Glyn-Jones refused an application for separate trials. This, on the face of it, was reasonable. The defendants were charged with making an affray. One of the tenets of prosecuting is to have as many people in the dock as possible, so, with luck, they will run what is known as a cutthroat defence and blame each other, which will result in convictions for all. Unfortunately, he had what would be described, in the world of Spot and Dimes, as 'a touch of the seconds', or second thoughts. The next day he asked counsel for Spot, Rose Heilbron QC, who was later to become the second woman High Court judge, and G.D. 'Khaki' Roberts, regarded as the best cross-examiner at the Nuremberg war crimes trials, who appeared for Dimes, what they had to say about making an affray in a public place.

Roberts argued that the reactions of a man fighting for his life could never be described as making an affray. Seaton then tried to argue that the affray was in the greengrocery shop itself, where the fight had ended. If, he argued, it was a public place, then Dimes's conduct after he had taken the knife from Spot was capable of being an affray. It was not a view accepted by the judge, who withdrew the count of affray against both Spot and Dimes from the jury, saying that, if they wished, they could acquit Dimes on the charge of wounding Spot. 'It is not for Dimes to prove that he was acting in self-defence. It is for the prosecution to prove that he was not.'

The jury did not agree, and Glyn-Jones discharged them saying, 'A joint trial without the first charge would not be lawful.' The separate trial of Spot was fixed to take place 48 hours later.

It began on 22 September 1955 at the Old Bailey. Now Reggie Seaton and E.J.P Cussen appeared for the Crown with Rose Heilbron QC and Sebag Shaw defending. Heilbron, the first woman to have been appointed Queen's Counsel, had the advantage from Spot's point of view of being Jewish, as was Sebag Shaw, who also later became a judge, but who in the meantime could be found in spielers throughout the West End.

The first of the eyewitnesses was the bookmaker Sebastian Buonacore, known as Vesta, who had been a street bookmaker working in Frith Street for something like 14 years, with Bert Marsh as his partner. He accepted he was friendly – but not *that* friendly – with Dimes and had known him 20 years. In fact he didn't really know if Dimes went racing at all. Wasn't all this a quarrel about rival betting pitches? No, not in the least. Didn't Marsh and he employ Dimes? Utter nonsense. He certainly didn't employ Dimes as a paid servant and he couldn't even remember getting him to put money on a horse for him. Wasn't it true Spot had said, 'I'm not going to stand for it. I've been going racing for the last 20 years,' and Dimes had replied, 'You needn't go any more, because you haven't got any more pitches'? Not that Buonacore knew.

Spot's defence was that Dimes was the first one to shove him before Spot pushed him into the road and Dimes charged back at him, pushing him into a pile of boxes at the Continental Fruit Store. Then Dimes produced a knife and slashed at Spot. But Buonacore would not be shifted. Spot was the man who had the knife. He hadn't seen either of them use it.

Bert Marsh was not about when he was called first time around but, despite the recorder rather hopefully suggesting he added nothing to the previous evidence, Heilbron wanted him nevertheless. The quarrel over betting pitches, originated by Dimes and Marsh, was the crux of her case. When he did give evidence Marsh said he thought he was a good friend of Dimes and a friend of Spot. It was a fairy tale that he resented Spot's monopoly of racecourse pitches. He had not told him so at Epsom. He had never had a bad word with him in his life. So far as he was concerned, he hadn't seen Dimes with a knife.

Spot told the court that he lived at 12F Hyde Park Mansions and was a bookmaker, mainly at point-to-point meetings and tracks in the South where there were free enclosures. He bought the ground for the day and charged the bookmakers. He'd been doing it for 20 years and Bert Marsh, Vesta and Italian Albert were very jealous. Dimes was a strong-arm man for Marsh.

It had started in August at the Epsom meeting. Marsh had told him, 'You've been going racing a long time, and you have all the best pitches. I think it's about time you were finished.' He said he had taken no notice but later he received a note.

The reason he had gone to Frith Street was that he wanted to make clear why Marsh wanted him to leave. He had asked 'What's this all about? And Dimes had replied, 'This is your final warning. I don't want you to go racing no more.'

He then accepted that he pushed Dimes, who then drew a knife and stabbed him. In fact, it was he who had managed to wrest the knife from Dimes and stabbed him in self-defence.

Then came the clincher in the form of a surprise witness, the 8-year-old Reverend Bazil Claude Hudson Andrews of Inverness Terrace, Bayswater, who had held an appointment at Kensal Green for 39 years.

Andrews, shabby, admittedly, but undeniably a gent with an upper-class accent, was something, in this world of cockney, Italian and middle-European voices, to which the white middle-class jury could relate. Indeed, in the days before the country lost a large proportion of its faith in religion generally and the Church of England in particular, the evidence of the clergy was highly regarded by the courts. Rogue vicars were the rarity rather than the norm.

Andrews had, it seems, read newspaper reports of the trial and realised something was seriously wrong. It had astonished him because, quite by chance, he had been in Frith Street at the time and it was the darker man (Dimes) who had attacked the fairer man (Spot) – although many would have thought the fairer man was indeed Dimes. He had deliberated for some time about involving himself and it had preyed on his mind. 'Ultimately I decided I had better do something.'

According to the reporter Arthur Tietjen, five minutes into Andrews's evidence a detective in the court leaned over to him and commented, 'Arthur, the old villain's bent.'[12]

But the jury did not see him in that light. It was enough to tilt things in favour of Spot, who leaped up and down in triumph in the dock, his hands raised like those of a successful boxer, and was first admonished and then discharged by the Recorder.

It was, of course, a field day for the newspapers. Allen Andrews wrote of Spot,

> There is not a tearaway gangster in town now who would give a throw of the dice in a spieler – or illegal gambling joint – for his chances in the future. Mobsters maintain he is NOT a crook in the sense of being a criminal who is a master of his craft.[13]

The taunt was out that, unlike a real crook such as Billy Hill, 'Jack Spot had never tasted porridge.' A week later the Home Secretary announced that the situation of control of bookmakers must never be allowed to reoccur.[14] Harry White was also smartly out of the stalls with the story of Spot's threats and attacks on him back in 1947, along with a cowardly attack on the elderly bookmaker Newcastle Fred at Pontefract races.[15]

The *Daily Sketch* had, however, beaten everyone to the line. Not only had it got the Parson under wraps but, in a great example of a journalistic each-way bet, it had editorials blazing, 'The threat is that if the gangster Spot is again put on trial and sent to prison the underworld will "blow the top off" about the police and their methods in the West End.'[16]

The *Sketch* also had Jack Spot giving his story, something they justified with, 'When the facts are known the public will realise why at the moment the *Sketch* is giving publicity to Jack Spot's own life story.' Over the next few issues it railed at the police and the Director of Public Prosecutions, asking why nothing was being done about Soho's gangland.

Duncan Webb was also up and running. According to him Spot had been tried by his own gang and found wanting. Only Blueball and Schack were remaining staunch. The Woods brothers and the others had seen the light. Billy Hill 'by sheer force of personality had kept the peace in the underworld and seen fair play'. Spot was nothing but a tinpot tyrant.[17] Next, as the unofficial press agent for Billy Hill, with the help of Albert Dimes, Webb did not even have to dig very deep in the soil to find out about Andrews. In fact, a flip through *The Times*'s index would have shown that, back in the 1920s, he had been made bankrupt when, he said, he had gone to the moneylenders on behalf of a friend who promptly defaulted. That may have seemed bad luck, but there was something about a wine merchant's account as well. Far from being a respectable old gent, the reverend was also keen on the horses and didn't pay his debts.

For a time Andrews tried to brazen things out. Protected by the naïve or opportunist – depending upon how you look at it – but certainly pro-Spot *Daily Sketch*, he set out his stall:

> I am fully aware that cowardly people who dare not come forward into the light of day are suggesting that I am a fraudulent witness and that I hoodwinked Mr Comer's legal advisers.
>
> I would recall to you that when I gave evidence last week I gave it on my solemn oath, and I need not remind you that I am a clerk in Holy Orders also. I therefore wish to affirm in the most solemn terms that what I said in the witness-box was the whole truth and nothing but

> the truth. Any financial difficulties due to my change of address and my harmless flutters in the sporting world are temporary ones, due to my age and inexperience.

That same day the prosecution conceded that given the acquittal of Spot and the subsequent revelations it would not be safe to proceed against Dimes. The newspapers were overjoyed. Here was 'the fight that never was'. Dimes weighed in with an account of the state of Soho in the *People*, in which he recalled that Spot had pleaded, 'Don't cut me Albert. Please don't cut me.'[18]

The *Sketch* turned the parson over soon enough: 'I am beginning to remember things which had slipped my memory. I shall be able to tell the police all about them. It is strange how one's memory fades.'

As the days went by and with the Director of Public Prosecutions apparently dragging his heels, the Spot articles grew smaller. Soon, Spot, Dimes and the parson, who had knocked the runaway spies Burgess and Maclean out of the headlines, were themselves replaced on the front pages by the love affair between Princess Margaret and Group Captain Peter Townsend.

The wheels of the law were, however, grinding and the story now emerged that before the trial Andrews had been in Spot's old haunt, the Cumberland Hotel, looking for someone to touch for his breakfast, when he had met Peter MacDonough, another friend of Spot, who had rented the parson a room a year earlier. MacDonough told him he could earn some money if he cared to say six words – presumably, 'It was Dimes who attacked Spot.' Andrews leaped like a trout at a mayfly and was taken to Hyde Park Mansions, vetted by Rita and then taken to see Perkoff. For this service he would receive £65, and, if Spot were to be acquitted, he would 'never want'. There was some corroboration of Andrews's new story from the doorman of the Cumberland Hotel, who placed him with MacDonough, and from another person, who had seen him at Hyde Park Mansions. There were also the obligatory 1950s and 1960s 'verbals,' or fabricated oral responses purportedly from suspects to bolster the police case. Arrests followed but it was a thin case.

Into the dock with Rita went MacDonough, Moishe Goldstein and Bernard Schack. They could not say they had not been warned. As if the arrest of Rita Comer had not been sufficient, the ever-useful Hubby Distleman had already told Schack, 'If I was you, Sonny, I would get a ship and get out of the country.' In Holloway awaiting her trial, Rita lost two stone in weight despite a daily diet of 'roast chicken, duckling, rare delicacies, fruit and flowers', which Spot had delivered to her.[19]

In theory it should not have been difficult to destroy Andrews as a prosecution witness, but theory and practice are two completely different things. The difficulty for defending counsel was that here was a sanctimonious old sinner who was playing the age, deafness, memory, sympathy and repentance cards with some skill:

> It was very wicked of me. I was very hard up and I was tempted and I fell. It is rather humiliating for me to have to tell you. I was desperately hungry. I had had what is called Continental breakfasts and nothing in between. I was very poor and hungry and I should not have yielded but I did. Thank God, I have asked to be forgiven!

Even the experienced silks could do nothing with him and to add to the discomfort of the defence Andrews announced his life was in danger.

Everyone gave evidence. So far as the 45-year-old MacDonough was concerned, he suffered from ill health and could not even attend chapel because of the steps he would have to climb, certainly not those at Hyde Park Mansions, to which he had never been. He certainly had not mentioned the possibility of earning £25 to Andrews. Indeed, apart from seeing him in the Cumberland Hotel, he had not seen him until four days after the trial. Goldstein and Schack had acted only out of the goodness of their hearts. Goldstein said that although he suffered from a Jewish persecution complex he was a respectable East Ender whose sole interest was in his family. He was a bookmaker who had known Spot for 28 years and when he was arrested he went to see Rita. 'There was not a soul who could help her because she has two babies.' Schack had been similarly minded. He had known Spot since he was a boy. 'I had heard most of his friends had deserted him. They were fair-weather friends.' He had always believed Andrews's story. Indeed he would take an oath on his children on it. Goldstein had first seen Andrews at Mr Perkoff's office. The next day he had been to see Rita and had found the kindly old gentleman there. He had been surprised but reassured when Andrews told him, 'I have come to cheer the good lady up.' Not a single word had been uttered by him or anyone else about perjured evidence.

Andrews's few weeks of fame soon passed, and he faded into obscurity.

Goldstein as the ringleader received two years and MacDonough and Schack a year apiece. Rita Comer, as the downtrodden wife fighting valiantly for her husband, was fined £50. The betting had been 4–1 on an acquittal. Spot had been in tears when he heard of his wife's conviction but was now quite happy with British justice. Unsurprisingly, Schack's wife was not so happy. Now Spot comforted the wife of his fallen soldier. 'I'm so sorry, dear.' She said two words in reply and hurried off. As Spot left with his wife – 'Love, let's go' – people outside the Old Bailey shouted, 'Good luck, Rita.'[20]

The crowd outside the Bailey may have been supportive but the case marked the end of Spot as any sort of a figure in Soho. Ronnie Diamond, who had clubs in the area at the time, recalled:

> There was a big nightclub in Windmill Street and Jack went in with us one night. We must have been twenty-five handed. It was all 'Hello Jack, glad to see you making it back up.' We didn't pay for a thing but afterwards Jack got a message saying, 'Don't come back.'

Spot would have done well to leave things well alone but instead he arranged for a young man, Joey Cannon from Paddington, to shoot at Hill and Dimes. The plan came to nothing but, as a reprisal on 2 May 1956, Frank Fraser was instructed to lead a team, who slashed Spot as he returned to his flat at Hyde Park Mansions. Spot would not name his attackers, but his wife Rita did, and Fraser and Bobby Warren received seven years apiece. Bert Rossi, who Fraser claims was not there, as he does Warren, received five.

In turn, he was set up by Hill over the slashing – in June 1956 – of Victor Russo, who refused to go along with the frame-up. Instead, Tommy Falco took his place. Spot was quite rightly acquitted. He then set up the Highball and another club in Notting Hill. These were firebombed and smashed up and he dropped out of the underworld. He went to Ireland before returning to work in a meat-packing factory. Rita left him and Spot died more or less penniless on 12 March 1995.[21]

On the other hand, Hill, Dimes and Bert Marsh continued to prosper. Hill now seemed impervious to the dangers of having Webb so close to the action. His brother Archie once told Fraser, 'If Bill ever gets nicked, his downfall could be Duncan Webb. The law ever got into Duncan, he wouldn't stand up.' Fortunately for everyone, it never happened. Duncan was not questioned, so avoiding the possibility that he might cave in and tell all.

Hill was, however, now well on the way to being a media celebrity. His autobiography, ghosted by Webb, was launched at a party held at Gennaro's restaurant in Romilly Street, now the site of the Groucho Club. It was attended by such luminaries as Frannie Daniels, Battles Rossi, Frank Fraser and Albert Dimes. Also in attendance were Webb and Hannen Swaffer, the 'Pope of Fleet Street', as well as the louche Birmingham businessman Sir Bernard Docker and his wife. Henry Sherek, the theatrical impresario, was one of the partygoers to wear a policeman's helmet. Swaffer gave a speech, 'I have no doubt that if I had come from the same environment as Billy Hill I could easily have become what he was. Don't kid yourselves. We all could.'

Fake telegrams were read out. 'Sorry I can't be here, I'm in a Spot.' 'Have a topping time. Britain's No. 1 hangman.' Lady Docker, initially said to be nervous about the occasion, had asked for police protection. Instead she was provided with a minder, Ted Bushell. Afterwards, she was quoted in the *Daily Mirror* as saying, 'I didn't know Mr Hill before, but now I think he's a charming person.' She then claimed she had been misled into attending the party and issued proceedings against both Webb and Odhams Press, alleging fraudulent misrepresentation. She had been photographed being kissed by Hill as Sir Bernard stood smiling beside her.[22]

In 1959, when her jewels, valued at £150,000, were stolen, she summoned Hill to her flat to ask if he could retrieve them. The meeting lasted four hours and ended in mutual admiration. 'I promised her I would not leave a stone unturned until I got those jewels back for her. She knows I am a respectable man now.' 'Billy once gave me a flower from his buttonhole at a party – I'll never forget that. Oh, it's so rare that I come up against a gentleman like Billy Hill and I mean a gentleman,' she simpered.[23]

If Fraser is correct, Billy had given her more than a flower, or perhaps she was speaking in euphemisms:

> . . . when Albert and I were wandering about looking for Bill [at the launch party] we opened a door and there was Hilly giving her Ladyship one. Albert gave her a slap; he thought it was disrespectful because her husband was at the party. I just burst out laughing.[24]

Overall the party did not go down well in the newspapers, which generally adopted a holier-than-thou attitude, and there were righteously disapproving comments. Journalists had forced themselves to go and drink the champagne on behalf of their readers. William Hickey in the *Daily Express* wondered whether he was being priggish and thought it was, 'all so stupid . . .They are not heroic characters. They are sad, little men who have lost their way.' Simon Ward wrote in the *Daily Sketch*, 'It was the most insolent gesture the Underworld has ever made.'[25] Two ex-police were actually present and enquiries were made as to whether action could be taken to forfeit pensions. It was discovered they were not on pensions and so it could not.

Albert Dimes remained an almost unseen Godfather, keeping out of the public eye and surfacing on only rare but sometimes quite unfortunate occasions, one of them being when he was mentioned unfavourably in a murder trial in Brighton. In 1956, the year after the fight, he was awarded £666 for a back injury sustained when the cab in which he was travelling was involved in an accident with a van. He was, he said, working as a commission agent, earning about £10 a week. He was fortunate enough not to have paid tax since 1951. A little later in a separate case he agreed to pay arrears of National Insurance contributions of £135. In June that year he was named in the House of Commons by the MP Anthony Greenwood, who called him a 'squalid, cowardly, small-time hoodlum'.

Dimes had this curious trait of getting himself into no-win situations. In January 1963 his name came up in the trial of a former apprentice jockey Lipman Leonard 'Darkie' Steward, charged with conspiracy to dope racehorses. At the end of the trial Dimes had a barrister appear in court to express his innocence about horse doping. It cut no ice.

Dimes last swam into public view in early 1968, when he was at the Tavistock Hotel in Bloomsbury to discuss money owed by a Max Fine to a 'Mr Corallo', described in a subsequent libel hearing as an 'American gangster'.[26] He also met Angelo Bruno of the Philadelphia family – of whom it was said he was the secret and trusted representative – when Bruno came to London between 27 November and 3 December 1966 as part of a gambling junket organised by a New York gaming club. Another of the card players on the trip was the celebrated Meyer Lansky, now accepted as one of the great Mafia financiers. Dimes visited Bruno in Philadelphia the next year to discuss the installation of gaming machines in various clubs.[27]

Dimes also went to America in 1968 and American couriers met him in London shortly before his death.[28] He had, by then, acquired a degree of respectability, obtaining a licence to open a betting shop almost opposite Ronnie Scott's jazz club in Frith Street. When Scott moved to the premises, Dimes had sent round a magnum of champagne.

He died at his home in Beckenham and was buried at St Edmund's Roman Catholic Church on 20 November 1971. His funeral was well attended with 200 mourners including the actor and gangland hanger-on Stanley Baker, to whom Dimes had given technical advice for the film *Robbery*. The imprisoned Krays sent a £20 wreath with the inscription, 'To a fine gentleman' – a gesture that annoyed Dimes's friends on the grounds that it brought shame to the family. The wreath was destroyed. At the service the priest spoke of how proud Dimes had been that he could recite the Creed in Latin.[29]

Dimes's death ended his unbroken 40 years' involvement with Soho, its clubs and frequenters. But was Dimes the true Godfather of the Italians or was there someone else standing behind and over him and even Hill? As the years have passed more and more people agree that, when it came to it the Guvnor, if not of Hill, but of the Italians was the redoubtable Bert Marsh. A Soho denizen recalls, 'Bert ran a betting shop in Frith Street and had an off-licence in Old Compton Street and an interest in at least six books. He was a quiet man, a very,

very dapper man. He was the Guvnor all right. He died back in Italy, a very rich man.'[30]

A former Flying Squad officer recalls, 'He was something of a mystery. I met him in the early sixties in Clerkenwell when I was going out with an Italian girl. He was a very pleasant man, very courteous. People respected him, something I didn't understand then. I was later told that he was the Mafia's top man in this country and a man to be friends with.'[31]

A Kray friend, Stan Davis, who knew them all, thought, 'He was the Daddy.'

It is interesting how legends arise. Bert Marsh did not die in Italy. He died in London on 3 October 1976 after visiting his model daughter in Hampstead. He did not die a rich man. His estate amounted to £1,503. He is another of whom it was said that when the news of his death was heard a party was arranged, this time in Little Italy.

By the end, things did not go well with Hill, either. He ran clubs, dabbled in antiques, cheated at cards. He also took up with a young African woman, Diana, who was determined to become a singer but who sadly had a history of mental problems. She had a son by the thief Johnny Dobbs and the boy was adored by Hill. Unfortunately, he could never bring himself to break completely with Gypsy (see Chapter 10), with whom he had latterly been running a club in Surrey.

It was not a relationship that could last and, after a number of unsuccessful attempts, Diana committed suicide. Hill ended his days at his flat in Moscow Road being cared for by Percy Horne, an old friend from Borstal. A heavy smoker, he died on New Year's Eve 1983.

Hill is buried in an East End cemetery and ironically his occupation on his death certificate is given as 'demolition'.[32] He left no will, nor were any letters of administration taken out, but he is reputed to have left his substantial fortune, which he had brought back from Switzerland, to Gypsy with instructions to bring up Diana's son, which she did. Over the years she has steadfastly refused to give any interviews. He also left a letter for Frank Fraser saying that he had given £50,000 to Dimes to look after for Fraser while he was in prison, but that Dimes had squandered it.

13

Postwar Clubbing

Reading the books by old retired policemen and crime reporters, it is sometimes difficult to know how much licence has been taken. So many gave their villains impenetrable nicknames or wrote 'whom I'll call Jim' that often the stories cannot be confirmed and may just be a piece of artistic imagination to spice things up. One that, at first sight, looks like that is Stanley Firmin's character, 'the Spider of Soho.' Firmin was a *Daily Telegraph* crime correspondent and knew his way around London but, infuriatingly, his 1953 book *Men in the Shadows* is full of master criminals such as the safebreaker, 'known only to the police and the underworld as Santro', and so on.

His 'Spider of Soho' is a master blackmailer, then in his eighties, never arrested, who, from rooms over shop premises, approached by a 'dingy uncarpeted hallway and a bare and unlighted flight of stairs', weaves his evil web of blackmail, in particular over a country gent who quite by chance walks into a nightclub after he has been to town on business. There he meets a woman, whose 'poise spoke of breeding. Her blonde hair was dressed in the style of the moment and she was expensively and exquisitely gowned.' She has been stood up by a man and they have a drink and dance, and meet again. Little does our dupe know that the whole thing is being organised by the Spider from his office and that the girl is a prostitute just off the streets. 'There were wild nights . . . nights studded with sheer depravity in which he was later assured he had taken his full part.' There were gifts of jewellery and money and then she, advised by the Spider, suggested they go into business. After a couple of years the man was ruined and the woman, claiming she was tired of him, simply walked away.

It all might be said to be a splendid piece of Sax Rohmer exotica but in 1950 Eva Holder was convicted of defrauding Peter Haig Thomas. The former Cambridge rowing coach had married into the aristocracy but at the age of 68 had fallen in love with this temptress some 30 years his junior. He had handed over £35,000. He met her while she was soliciting in Soho and paid her £2. 10s. (£2.50) along with 5s. (25p) for the maid. From then on it appears to have been love on his part and, in an effort to keep her off the streets, over a period of a year he parted with the money on the basis that she was investing it in property in Soho or interests in clubs. He set her up in a flat in Lisle Street and intended to take her with him to Kenya but, because of her convictions for soliciting dating back to December 1929, this was impossible.

Curiously, despite these numerous convictions, she had none at all for dishonesty and none for soliciting after he met her. She claimed the money was a series of gifts and that she had left him because she could not put up with him any more. Unfortunately, the jury and certainly the judge, finding it unbelievable that anyone would part with this sort of money, were against her. She received two years' imprisonment.[1] Was this the case that Firmin factionalised?

Billy Hill, newly out of prison, promptly leased the New Cabinet Club from Holder and from that moment, for him at least, it was onwards and upwards. Others involved in the club were not always so fortunate. When Hill became involved with Gypsy Riley and left the club to his wife Aggie, she, in turn, put the management in the hands of Selwyn 'Jimmy' Cooney, killed by Jimmy Nash, of the celebrated Nash family, in the Pen Club shooting in Stepney on 7 February 1960. The police thought it was a matter of protection but they had also fallen out over the payment of repairs for the nightclub hostess 'Blonde' Vicky James's car.

In the 1960s and 1970s, clubs sprang up like mushrooms, changing hands as well as names, sometimes by the minute. There were nightclubs with hostesses – Murray's Cabaret Club in Beak Street was still going strong into its fifth decade. Christine Keeler and Mandy

Rice-Davies, who would feature so prominently in the Stephen Ward vice trial, both worked there in the early 1960s, earning £8. 6s (£8.30) a week.

One girl recalled,

> There was a great many rules attached to employment at the club. It was the worst crime to be late and a girl were fined for this as well as for having laddered stockings, for not wearing silver shoes. There were also fines for having bruises.

> With the fines a girl might end with less than eight shillings [40p] a week but there were additional perks.

> We were allowed to sit out when we weren't working, for a hostess fee which we were allowed to keep. I could earn £30 a week.[2]

There were special clubs for policemen, for villains, for artists, for theatricals – such as the Kismet, a disgusting cellar in the Charing Cross Road, which was known as 'Death in the Afternoon'; for employed and resting actors; for those in the entertainment industry – such as the Candy Box; for journalists; for lesbians – such as the Careless Stork in Denman Street and the Festival in Dean Street; for homosexuals – such as the Duce and the Alphabet in D'Arblay Street; and the Mazurka in Denman Street, run by an ex-Windmill girl, was for the 'Faces', as the underworld likes to call itself. Some were simply drinkers, perhaps with a fruit machine supplied by Frankie Fraser's Atlantic Machines. Others such as the Bees ('bees and honey' means money in rhyming slang), run by Sammy Samuels and patronised by Billy Hill, were spielers offering card games such as faro and poker to the punters. Jack Spot made the Modernnaires club in Old Compton Street a base for his operations, dividing his Soho time between that club and the Galahad, a drinker in Charlotte Street. 'I don't ever recall seeing dice played. It wasn't a big club but in a sense it was one of Spot's headquarters. It was always regarded as being his club,' recalls one frequenter. Charlie Chester's Casino in Archer Street was minded by Frank Fraser and Eddie Richardson and, when they went to prison, by Jackie Hayes, the son of the old East End hard man, Timmy.

Some, such as the Roaring '20s in Carnaby Street were predominantly for a black clientele.[3] There was also the African Club in Greek Street, and the Coloured Colonial Social Club at 5 Gerrard Street where on 17 August 1945 there was extended fighting between black and white American service personnel. When the whites thought themselves outnumbered they went to the Rainbow Club to collect reinforcements.

Some were specifically where the police could meet villains to arrange such matters as bail, the suppression of evidence and payments for services received. Commander Kenneth Drury used to meet pornographer Jimmy Humphreys in the Hogarth Club. Perhaps the most popular of these was the Premier. One former Flying Squad officer recalls:

> Then there were clubs like the Premier where a lot of business was done with Old Bill. In those days the police took their money like they was receiving their wages. They didn't seem to care who knew because it went right to the top, into the Commissioner's office.
>
> That barrister who'd been a copper himself, Bill Hemming, he was always there of an evening with his girlfriend. Tommy Plumley, a great fixer, was another. Don't ever underestimate the Premier when Dave Hatter had it. You got very senior officers in there, not just DIs. Dennis Hawkins used to go and so did Hooter [Ernie Millen], head of the Flying Squad. Not half.[4]

A former club owner recalls:

> In the sixties you could just walk into a Post Office and get a club licence for two and six [12½p]. I had the Top Hat in Piccadilly; it was a drinker for journalists. And I also took over the Spotlight in Wardour Street. I just pulled a gun on the geezer who was running it and said, 'Now I am.' It was a drinker and a spieler, a straight dice game. I just took a percentage of what they won, and I had it about nine months before the coppers shut me down.[5]

Possibly he was unlucky and had upset senior officers. Club owners generally accepted an informal tax by the police. The entertainer Jeremy Beadle, whose mother and stepfather ran the New Hogarth, a drinking club in D'Arblay Street in the 1960s, recalls, 'On a Wednesday someone from West End Central would drop in for a drink and an envelope. It was all very civilised.'[6]

One of the most celebrated clubs in Soho was the Colony Room at 41 Dean Street. Its success was that the clientele were not pigeonholed as they were in other drinking clubs. It was run by Birmingham-born Muriel Belcher, whose parents had managed the Alexandra Theatre. Belcher, described by the writer and jazz singer George Melly as 'a benevolent witch' and by another member as a 'handsome Jewish dyke', for a time was a 'Queen's Moll' at Le Jardin des Gourmets in Dean Street patronised by Noël Coward and his lover Graham Payne.

Over the years she ran a number of clubs including the Music Box in Leicester Place during World War Two. On 15 August 1951 she was fined for licensing offences at the Miramar Bar Club. At the time she was working for the pimp Maurice Cooney but she had by then also opened the Colony Room, named after her lifelong companion Carmel, who came from the Colonies. It was up a flight of stairs, at the bottom of which was an array of dustbins, and had lime-green walls.

The painter Francis Bacon, whom she called 'Daughter', was given £10 a week and free drink to act as 'hostess' and to introduce his friends. And in they came, among them George Melly, the ex-Borstal boy turned writer Frank Norman, Daniel Farson, Jeffrey Bernard and his brother Bruce, the MP Tom Driberg and the actor Trevor Howard. She often gave the male members girls' names. 'Cunt' was her favourite term of opprobrium while 'cunty' was one of endearment. Favourites were called 'Mary'. At closing time she would call out, 'Fuck off, everyone, fuck off, you, fuck off, Francis, fuck off!' until everyone had gone.

Solicitor and Soho habitué Louis Diamond, recalled, 'Everyone went there. Louche, sleazy doesn't begin to describe it. It was the best club I've ever been in. She [Belcher] wanted to buy my wife Vera off me. She said, "You're not a rich man." I said, "Ask Vera."'[7]

One publisher disagrees: 'In the early seventies I was taken there by Farson and spent the afternoon drinking too much with him. I thought it was ghastly. She was so rude.[8]

When Muriel Belcher died in 1979 she left the club to Ian Board, who had been a commis waiter at Le Jardin and was known to the members as Iris. 'He had the most enormous pickled nose, purple and mottled,' recalls one habitué. When he died in 1994 the reins passed to the long-serving barman Michael Wojas.

Daniel Farson thought the Caves de France, to be 'True Bohemia'. It was next door to the Colony and for a time Secundo, the younger brother of the boxer and wrestler Primo Carnera, was the barman. On the other hand, the American writer Elaine Dundy thought it 'A sort of coal-hole in the heart of Soho that is open every afternoon, a dead-ended subterranean tunnel ... an atmosphere almost solid with failure.'

That and cigarette smoke. Farson thought the inhabitants were by no means failures. They included the writer Enid Bagnold, as well as Nina Hamnett, who had been expelled from the Colony for wetting herself while on one of the fake leopardskin stools there. She had been a companion of Augustus John, who was also a former member, and had been a model for Gaudier-Brezeska. In 1947 she was taken to court by her landlady for urinating in the kitchen sink, something the magistrate, who dismissed the charge, did not think physically possible.

Another of the clientele, Sandy Fawkes, had an adventurous life. As a baby she was found in the Grand Union Canal. She became a journalist and author, married the jazz clarinettist and cartoonist Wally Fawkes and then, in 1974, went to America for a short-lived stint on the *National Enquirer*. It was there she met Daryl Golden in a bar in Atlanta and they set off to tour Florida together. Unknown to Fawkes, Golden was, in fact, Paul John Knowles, who had been released from Raiford prison in the state in May that year and who is known to have killed at least 18 people – he claimed the number was 35. The car in which they were travelling had been stolen from a man who had disappeared four months earlier and Knowles was wearing the clothes of another victim. Two days before he picked up Fawkes, he had killed two people, raping one, a 15-year-old girl.

On 16 November, days after they separated, Knowles was arrested at a police road block and the next day he was shot dead by an FBI agent as he slipped his handcuffs and tried to escape. Fawkes was extensively questioned and later would say, in a reference to the film *In the Heat of the Night*, that the police in Macon, Georgia, make 'Rod Steiger look like a fairy'.[9]

The Colony and the Caves may have catered for the louche artiste and passing criminal but the Artistes & Repertoire, known as the A&R – in a building almost opposite the Astoria in the Charing Cross Road and overlooking what had been Freddie Mills's Chinese restaurant and later Nitespot – definitely catered for the criminal fraternity. At one time it was owned by the footballer Malcolm Allison, who was helped out by the former Scots and Arsenal star Jimmy Logie. In its heyday in the 1960s the A&R was owned by Mickey Regan and Ronnie Knight, then the husband of Barbara Windsor, with Regan's brother Brian on the door. It was the drinker of choice for some of the musicians from Tin Pan Alley as well as actors such as Kenneth Williams, Ian Hendry and Ronnie Fraser. It also became a home from home for some of London's prime villains, including the balding, insignificant-looking Jimmy Essex, one of the few men acquitted twice of murder.

Marilyn Wisbey, daughter of Tommy, the Great Train Robber recalled,

> I would say it was the best afternoon drinker especially on Mondays and Fridays. There were more piss-artists and reps (as in salesmen) in there than any other club I know. Singers and musicians would be allowed to get up and play. You would have the hoisters selling their wares; one day in fact I bought a beautiful top-of-the-range set of Chef knives; it was only £80. Then there would be all different firms popping in and out and also madams.[10]

When he sold the club, Knight apparently received £80,000 for his stake, a sum that he invested in Soho peepshows, where, as the journalist Duncan Campbell wrote, '. . . young women took off their clothes and did improbable things with rubber snakes for the entertainment of lonely men who shovelled coins into the slot machine that kept the peep-hole open.'

At the end of the show the men were allowed to buy a £5 disposable camera and take pictures of the girls. Mickey Regan was said to be disgusted by the concept and would not invest his share in the enterprise.

Knight doused any revulsion he may have had with the knowledge that he was taking £3,000 a week.[11]

The A&R itself became something like the boots in *All Quiet on the Western Front*, passing from one owner and one misfortune to the next. After Ronnie Knight disposed of his interest, James Fraser, nephew of 'Mad' Frank Fraser, took over, and in turn Georgie Stokes bought the club. James Fraser was killed in 2004 in a street accident while on holiday in Florida.

Unfortunately, Stokes forgot to renew the licence and the authorities closed it down. Stokes himself was later arrested over smuggling £600,000 of cocaine into Britain in champagne bottles and received a 12-year sentence. In 1989 he began proceedings to allow him to father a child while in prison, claiming it was 'his fundamental right'.[12] In the event, he did not need to wait for the result of his case because in 1991 he escaped from Maidstone Prison and was found in Trinidad seven years later. For years afterwards the premises remained empty.

One man who was a reasonably healthy, if relatively short-term, influence on the finances of both Jack Spot and Billy Hill was the old-time villain Freddy Ford. In his 80s, Ford was now a rich man who owned a number of hotels in Kings Cross, mainly used by the street walkers of the area. He had had the bright idea of making the women take suitcases along with their clients into the hotels, so providing the manager with an instant defence to allowing the premises to be used for the purposes of prostitution. For a time he also worked as an estate agent, living in Newport Place, and renting out flats to prostitutes, turning over more than £400 a week. By then he had racked up nearly 50 convictions.

Now Ford decided that he wished to have the best spieler in London and to have someone run it for him. Premises were found back in Ham Yard and Spot and Hill took over. Naturally, Ford did not see the share of the profits he expected and, after a series of raids, the club was closed.[13]

It was at the All Nighters Club in Wardour Street that Lucky Gordon and Johnny Edgecombe, both from Notting Hill, fought over Christine Keeler in the early hours of 28 October 1962. According to Keeler, Gordon was obsessed with her and, never taking no for an answer, on one occasion had raped her repeatedly. She maintained that she hoped Edgecombe, as another black man, would talk sense into Gordon, but, when Gordon 'decided to go for' Keeler, Edgecombe turned on him and Gordon was badly slashed about the face. Keeler failed to appear to give evidence at Edgecombe's trial in March 1963 and later herself went to prison for perjury. After the fight, Keeler went to live with Edgecombe in Brentford, where he was hiding. In early December she left him and returned to Wimpole Mews to visit Mandy Rice-Davies. Around 1 pm, Edgecombe arrived in a minicab and when the girls refused to let him in he shot at the lock on the front door and also in the vague direction of the girls, who were leaning out of the window. He then took the cab back to Brentford, where he was arrested. Edgecombe was acquitted over the Gordon slashing but was given seven years for the shooting incident.[14]

Before then, however, Keeler claimed she had been attacked again by Lucky Gordon on 18 April. On 7 June 1963 he was found guilty and sentenced to three years for actual bodily harm. The conviction of Gordon was quashed on 30 July 1963 – it was considered unsafe.

The Log Cabin, also in Wardour Street, was another home from home for the criminal fraternity. Former East End hard man Mickey Bailey recalled,

> It held around 30 people, not a lot more, and out of them 30 there'd be thieves of all descriptions, robbers, key men, hoisters, safe blowers, jump-up men. One might be southside and he'd say, 'How you going, anything about?' 'Yeah, I don't know if you'd be interested.' You didn't go down looking for a job as if you was going to the labour exchange, but you might be down there and someone would say, 'You're the very man I want to see.' It was a convenient place for thieves to meet. There was a fellow on the door, Dummy. If you wanted someone got out Dummy would do it for you. There was very few arguments. It was a neutral place to meet.[15]

One former wrestler remembers it rather differently: 'I didn't like the Log Cabin. If you had a row with people there, there was no telling they wouldn't pull a knife or a gun on you.'[16]

He would have been right not to have felt safe in the Rose-N-Dale club in Newport Place, where Michael Barry Porter was shot and killed by Ian Doran after he attacked him with a broken glass on the night of 25 September 1971. Doran fled to Scotland, where he took part in a series of robberies that ended with his receiving a 25-year sentence. Returned to England, Doran received ten years for manslaughter in November 1972.[17] In April 1974 his brother Stephen, who had been fined £50 for impeding Doran's arrest, received life with a minimum of 18 years in Glasgow for his part in a payroll robbery on 21 December 1973, in which a watchman was shot dead.

Not all partnerships between club owners were dissolved happily. One of the Soho club owners of the early 1960s was the halfway decent boxer Tony Mella, who had a few fights at the Mile End Arena. The old villain Buller Ward claimed that a couple of his fights weren't straight and that when he came up against the Southern Area Champion, Mella got a good hiding.

Later he became semi-respectable and began running clubs such as the El Ababi. After Frank Fraser had cut Mella badly in his flat in Old Street he took to employing a minder, Big Alf Melvin, whom he had known through the days of Jack Solomons and his gym in Great Windmill Street. In addition to paying Melvin a wage, he kept promising him a partnership or, at least, a share in the profits. Mella also owned the Bus Stop (formerly the Grill Club), a near-beer cum strip joint in Dean Street (near-beers were shady premises that sold non-alcoholic drinks). The partnership never materialised and there is little doubt that Mella treated the older man badly.

Mella was also heavily involved with gambling machines with interests all over England and there are a number of colourful stories about him. One is that a bayonet was rammed into his backside and left there for several hours. The metal cauterised the wound and it healed. It may be a variation of the one told by the dwarf Royston Smith, who in the 1950s worked with Morton Fraser's Harmonica Gang, wrestled as Fuzzy Kaye, ran with the Krays and who, apart from also running the bilious Kismet Club for a time, had the Midgets Club, exclusively for dwarves, in Gerrard Street, alongside some of Mella's near-beer joints. Seemingly, Mella had been disrespectful to the often spiteful Smith who cut him in the backside in what was known as noughts and crosses. As Frank Fraser colourfully put it, 'I suppose his bum was all he could reach. I don't know if it was true because I never saw it but that was the story.'[18]

Another story is of Mella's death. He had, the story goes, offended a rival organisation and a button man, or contract killer, had been sent from America to carry out the hit. He went to Mella's office and shot him. The gunman then turned and walked calmly down the stairs. Badly injured, Mella managed to take his own gun from his safe, followed the American on to the street, shot him and then died himself.

The truth is more prosaic. During the evening of 28 January 1963, Alf Melvin shot Mella with a Beretta and, as his employer staggered out onto the pavement, turned the gun on himself. That night a detective went into West End Central police station to say, 'There's a party in Soho tonight. Tony Mella's dead.'

At the double inquest some letters by Melvin to his wife were read. 'I came into this world with nothing and I'm going out with nothing,' said one. There was another: 'This bastard Tony Mella has used me in every shape and form. "Sign here. Sign there and everything is down to you". I have been a drunken mug and how he has cashed in on my weakness.'

There was talk that the killing was going to cause disturbances in Soho but all remained peaceful and quiet. Indeed, many sympathised with Melvin and certainly he had a much better-attended funeral than Mella did.

Being a doorman on the clubs could itself be dangerous. Many were recruited by the Lebanese-born Raymond Naccaccian, or Nash, from the YMCA in Tottenham Court Road. The formidable ex-champion wrestler Bert Assirati, one of the doormen for Peter Rachman's La Discotheque above the Latin Quarter in Wardour Street, was stabbed in the arm in the early 1960s. Then, in March 1963, he was told to make himself scarce one evening. That night the relief doorman, ex-guardsman Dennis John Raine, was shot in the leg. He had refused entry to two men earlier in the evening. Above La Discotheque was a room where Nash ran *chemin de fer* and roulette.

Another wrestler, Ian 'Bully Boy' Muir, was shot in both legs when in 1971 he was working as the late-night doorman of the Candy Box in Kingly Street. He also had refused entry to nonmembers and as a result shots were sprayed around the entrance to the club. The likelihood is that Muir was the unfortunate victim of a protection power struggle and an East End hard man, Michael Morris, was arrested but later acquitted. Morris went on to greater things and was finally jailed for 14 years for robbery at the Old Bailey in July 1979.

One Soho doorman who survived without injury, at least to himself, was the ferocious and, in legal circles at least, the famous Norbert 'Fred' Rondel, who also worked at La Discotheque and had his own club, the Apartment, in Rupert Street. Additionally, he worked for Peter Rachman (the landlord notorious for exploiting tenants, whose name gave 'Rachmanism' to the dictionary) and Nash, evicting their unwanted tenants. In 1976 he was accused of conspiracy to rob the Spaghetti House, a restaurant in Knightsbridge in which several of the staff were held in a siege that lasted five days. The allegation by the prosecution was that, after a Lino Termine – who owed him money from gambling and had worked at the restaurant – told him that, every Saturday evening, managers from other branches would come with the week's takings, Rondel set up the robbery that was led by one of his employees. In what would otherwise have been an uncomplicated heist, one of the managers escaped and the remaining men were held hostage. Termine pleaded guilty and received a six-year sentence. Rondel was acquitted, as he was later for blackmailing a club owner in Paddington. He had previously served three years for assault when he was convicted of biting the ear off a tenant whom he was evicting for Rachman. But perhaps his greatest claim to fame is his failed attempt to sue his former barrister for negligence when defending him. The case eventually went to the House of Lords, which finally ruled that a barrister had immunity from such an action. For many years after, Rondel unsuccessfully campaigned to have the decision reversed.[19]

On 11 February 1961 a homemade cocoa-tin bomb was thrown into the Gardenia Club in Wardour Mews, blowing a hole in the door. The manager, Harry Bidney, had refused admission to some men. On the previous Friday the owner of a nearby club had been slashed when he also refused admission. 'A gang of young men are trying to terrorise club owners, but I'm not afraid,' said Bidney. The young men were undoubtedly from an up-and-coming north-London-based crime family.

It was protection of clubs that exercised the mind of Detective Sergeant Harold 'Tanky' Challenor, who had had a fine war record, winning the Military Medal. Based at West End Central police station, he saw himself as operating a one-man scourge of the underworld in the early 1960s – 'Soho sounded like Chicago when Challenor described it'[20] – but was seen by others as operating his own protection racket.

His finest hour, to be followed by his undoing, came with his arrests in September 1962 of Riccardo Pedrini, Joseph Oliva, John Ford, Alan Cheeseman and James Fraser. They were, he claimed, running a protection racket, leaning on the pimp Wilfred Gardiner, then in charge of the Phoenix Club and the Geisha in Old Compton Street. Challenor claimed Oliva had a bottle of turpentine with a piece of rolled-up towel in the neck and a knife in his pocket as he drove along Berwick Street. Fraser was also found to have a knife. Cheeseman and Pedrini were found to have weapons on them, which they said had been planted. Both claimed they had been assaulted. On 6 December all except Fraser were found guilty of conspiracy to demand money with menaces. Fraser was found guilty of possessing the knife. All were jailed and it was not until 1964 that the Court of Appeal quashed their convictions.

By this time there had been other victims of Challenor, including the West Indian cricketer Harold Padmore, whose mistress, Patricia Hawkins, worked in the Boulevard Club, a clip joint in Frith Street, and whom Challenor arrested for obtaining money by false pretences. Padmore went to the police station to ask about her and Challenor promptly arrested him, knocked him about, sang a popular song of the time, 'Bongo, bongo, bongo, I don't want to leave the Congo', and commented to other officers, 'Take that black bastard out of my sight. I wish I was in South Africa. I'd have a nigger for breakfast every morning.' Patricia Hawkins was found not guilty and later Padmore accepted £500 for assault and false imprisonment.

Challenor's downfall came when he moved into political circles, planting bricks on demonstrators – protesting over the death of Lambrakis, a Greek political activist – on 11 July 1963 outside Claridge's hotel during the visit of Queen Fredericka of Greece. One man, Donald Rooum, was able to prove the brick had been planted and, on 4 June 1964, there was Challenor at the Old Bailey along with three junior officers on charges of corruption. In a matter of minutes the jury found Challenor unfit to plead. The medical officer at Brixton prison thought he had been 'abnormal for a very considerable time'. The junior officers received sentences of three years.

A subsequent inquiry was headed by Arthur James QC, always a safe pair of hands. Diagnosing paranoid schizophrenia was extremely difficult and it was no fault of his colleagues that they had failed to notice his antisocial behaviour, such as jumping on the table and singing or indeed walking home to Kent each night. In cases where there was a conflict of evidence between the police and a criminal, that of the former was invariably to be preferred.

Challenor was quickly released from hospital and took work as a solicitors' clerk. As the years went by he never accepted he had planted bricks or fitted up villains, preferring to claim there were 'still blank areas in my memory where "the Brick Case" is concerned'.[21]

Quite apart from the sex-club war in the middle 1960s, there was a separate battle going on over protection in clubs where purple hearts were the drug of choice and 1,000 could be sold in 30 minutes. On 14 June 1964 the *Sunday Mirror* claimed the leading protection gang was known as the Peacemakers, headed by a man who carried a Derringer. It was the usual business: if protection was not paid, the club was wrecked. The following week Raymond Nash was interviewed and admitted he had for a short time carried a gun for his own protection after one of his clubs had been damaged.[22]

The petrol bombings were by no means all protection-inspired. Sometimes it was a disgruntled customer who caused the most damage and loss of life. In April 1966 a man died when he was trapped in a lavatory that had a sticking door, during an arson attack on a club at 23 Lisle Street. Three youths had been thrown out of a club after a row with a hostess over overcharging. The hostesses had barred the door, which the youths then tried to break down. When that failed they set fire to rubbish on the stairs. The hostesses escaped through the windows but the man, who had been drinking, could not get out. Later that night the youths went to the police and received remarkably lenient sentences, ranging from Borstal training to two years' imprisonment.

On 4 February the next year 16 people were injured when a petrol bomb went off in Greek Street. In 1975 a man died in an arson attack on a club in Peter Street and in August 1980 38 people died when a fire broke out at the Rodo's and El Hueco clubs, mainly used by Spaniards and Latin Americans, on the first and second floors of a building in Denmark Place. The prosecution alleged that John 'Punch' Thompson, who was convicted of murder and jailed for life in May 1981, had fired the club as revenge for being overcharged by a barman. Thompson maintained it was a case of mistaken identity.

14

Those Were the Krays

The first real sign that the East End-born Kray Twins Ronnie and Reggie were moving into the West End came in 1956, when they became involved in a drinking club, the Stragglers, in Cambridge Circus. As teenagers, they had been taken by their elder brother Charlie to Bill Kline's gymnasium in Fitzroy Square and at the age of 20 had been involved in a fight in a drinking club in Tottenham Court Road. Reg Kray hit 'an African' over the head with a truncheon until it broke. His twin then stabbed him. The man survived. After an identification parade at which Ron, but not Reg, was picked out, no charges were brought. On their first real venture into gangland society they provided protection for Jack Spot, who felt threatened by the Italians at the 1955 Epsom Spring race meeting. Years later, the Twins claimed they had no time for Spot:

> It wasn't that we liked him. We despised him really. We just turned out with Spotty to show everyone that *we* was the up-and-coming firm and didn't give a fuck for anyone. Old Spotty understood. Whatever else he may have been he wasn't stupid. He knew quite well that though we were there in theory as his friends, we meant to end up taking over from him.[1]

They were now extending their fledgling empire of clubs and billiard saloons in Stoke Newington, Whitechapel and Aldgate westwards. On paper at least, Reggie Kray was a great admirer of Billy Hill, looking on him as his mentor:

> When I was in my early twenties, the man I wanted to emulate most of all was the former gang boss of London's underworld, Billy Hill. The prime reason for my admiration was, that apart from Billy being very physical and violent when necessary, he had a good, quick thinking brain and this trait appealed to me most of all[2] . . .
>
> I like to think, that in some ways I have come close to emulating him; to be honest, I acknowledge that he stands alone and there will never be another Billy Hill.[3]

Ronnie was by no means as keen and others say that, in his declining years, Hill was terrified of the pair.

The Stragglers was run by a docker Billie Jones but before the Twins' involvement the clientele were prone to fighting among themselves, something that reduced the profits. Jones's friend, the ex-boxer Bobby Ramsey, who had taken the rap and served three months in South Africa after Billy Hill slashed the Johannesburg club owner Arnold Neville, mentioned the problem to the Twins. In a matter of days the club was running smoothly and profitably and they had a share.

By the early 1960s with gambling about to be legalised, they now reached an accommodation with the Italians. Soon the Twins started to lean on the wealthy but still up-and-coming property developer Peter Rachman. A fight in the Latin Quarter, where Rachman was holding a party, led to his giving Ronnie Kray a lift back to his home in Valence Road and an agreement to pay £5,000 to avoid trouble in Notting Hill, where Rachman was himself leaning on recalcitrant tenants. Rachman's caving in to the Twins so quickly is difficult to understand. He had working for him three of the most uncompromising men in the business: the retired heavyweight wrestling champion Bert Assirati; another wrestler, Peter Rann; and the completely out-of-control Norbert Rondel, who, although German, had wrestled as the Polish Eagle. Both Assirati and Rondel were, at one time or another, on the door of Rachman's club, La Discotheque, in Wardour Street, which in an earlier life had been the El Condor, run by Diana Dors's boyfriend, the bodybuilder Tommy Yeardsley.

It was in La Discotheque that Reggie Kray grabbed Mandy Rice-Davies by the arm and demanded she serve him a drink. As Mandy recalls, when she refused saying she did not work there, he replied, 'Now you do, get me a drink.' She asked her minder Jimmy to go and deal with this rude man, but when he returned a white-faced Jimmy told her it was Reggie Kray and she should apologise. She refused and Rachman was summoned. Told to apologise, once again she indignantly refused, and it ended with Rachman writing a substantial cheque to pacify Kray.

After Rachman's death on 29 November 1962 following a heart attack, his wife Audrey continued to pay the rent on the premises. The shares in the club were nominally owned by Albert Grew, who had 90 per cent, with the remaining 10 being held by a bodybuilder, Norman Mann, once a contender in the Mr Universe competition. But the real owner was Raymond Nash, who claimed to be only the manager. It was alleged, something Nash always denied, that it and its sister club La Discotheque in Streatham were the centre of the purple hearts trade.[4]

The Twins were also apparently leaning on the painter Francis Bacon. One Soho figure of the time recalls:

> Francis Bacon was tucked up [blackmailed] by the Krays. He went into Wheeler's one day with a black eye and two Kray men came up to the table and said, 'You're here. Don't forget. We told you.' The man with him said, 'What's this about?' One of them said, 'You his wife?' – and the man did [beat up] the pair of them. The waiters loved it.[5]

On the Twins' behalf Jack 'The Hat' McVitie cut a man's throat in a club upstairs from the Log Cabin. One habitué of the Cabin recalls:

> It was up a flight of stairs and in a sort of hut on a flat roof. The Krays either wanted it or wanted money from it but the Scotsman who ran it wasn't having it. I thought it was rather appropriate when I heard Jack got stabbed in the throat by Reggie.[6]

The club that caused the most trouble for the Twins at the time was the Hideaway in Gerrard Street, run by the homosexual Scots baronet Huw Cargill McCowan. The Hideaway had had a chequered career. At one time in the early 1960s, when it was the Bon Soir, it had been owned by Frank Fraser, Albert Dimes and the owner of a nearby fashionable French restaurant. Dimes lost heart and Joe Wilkins – nephew of Bert Wilkins the old Sabini man – took his interest and also lost money. Fraser recalls:

> I don't know why but the club never did well; it was a nice little place with a band and a cabaret and we had a licence to drink until 3 a.m. but it never took off. We realised that the only way you were going to make a profit was on the insurance . . .

Thanks to Joe Wilkins, the club duly went up in smoke and it was Leopold Harris, the fireraiser from the 1930s, now working as an insurance assessor, who ensured that Fraser and the others had a good pay day.[7]

McCowan reopened the premises as the Hideaway on 16 December 1964. Even before the opening night the Krays had demanded 20 per cent of the takings, rising to 50 per cent. In return, the club would be trouble-free, but their kind offer had been rejected by the feisty McCowan. They booked a table for ten on the opening night and failed to appear and on 18 December a fight involving their friend the writer 'Mad' Teddy Smith broke out in the premises. Afterwards, McCowan settled on 20 per cent.

On 10 January 1965 the Twins and Smith were arrested and charged with demanding money with menaces. Leonard 'Nipper' Read, who was investigating the Krays, pinned his hopes not on the evidence of McCowan but on that of the club's manager, Sidney Vaughan, who had initially backed up McCowan's version of events. He was wrong to do so. Vaughan made a statement to a local vicar that he was being paid £40 a week and then claimed the whole thing was a cook-up. At the committal proceedings he was a hostile witness.

The Twins were aided by the extremely clever and extremely dubious solicitor's clerk Manny Fryde – he acted for them in the preparation of their case – who at one time may or may not have qualified as a solicitor in South Africa. The first trial was aborted after Fryde said he had seen a juror speak to a policeman, something the juror denied. The second ended in a disagreement. By the time of the third trial, McCowan's background had been investigated by a private detective. He had alleged blackmail in three previous cases and had been in a mental hospital. The jury acquitted after a retirement of only 10 minutes.[8] Within hours the Krays 'bought' the Hideaway, renaming it the El Morocco, and throwing a lavish party. With their acquisition the Krays effectively now had a licence to roam Soho and the West End.

By the middle 1960s the Krays were taking money off a number of Soho clubs run by the strip club owner Bernie Silver, who had the Gigi and the New Life in Frith Street, and the New Mill in Macclesfield Street off Shaftesbury Avenue. They also had part of the protection money obtained by others from the Astor, the Bagatelle off Regent Street, and the Starlight off Oxford Street.

Apart from isolated acts – a man they believed was going to poison them had his jaw broken in a club in Old Compton Street – the Krays mainly kept their more psychotic behaviour out of Soho. True, once Ronnie went to shoot Frankie Fraser in Isow's in Brewer Street but Fraser never appeared that evening and Isow's doorman, the ex-heavyweight boxer 'Nosher' Powell, took extreme care when he walked the streets at night after he had barred the Twins for not wearing ties.[9]

It was on behalf of Bernie Silver that the pair engaged in their most bizarre enterprise. They agreed to arrange the killing of the Maltese club owner George Caruana, with whom Silver and other club owners had fallen out. Whether Silver actually knew Caruana was to be killed, rather than beaten up, is uncertain. In any event, the fee was £1,000 and there were other rewards such as the prestige that would accrue, particularly as the Twins were then in negotiations with members of the Mafia over the disposal of stolen bonds.

The assassin was to be a Scot, Paul Elvey, who was arrested after a tip-off as he boarded a plane to London from Glasgow. In the days before scanners and body searches, he had managed to take three dozen sticks of dynamite in his luggage. The dynamite was to be placed in Caruana's car to explode when the ignition was turned on. Elvey had also been given a crossbow and told to practise until he was proficient. He would then be told the name of his victim. He was also instructed to kill a man at the Old Bailey by jabbing him in the leg with a poisoned needle protruding from a suitcase made by the ex-speedway rider Francis 'Split' Waterman. Again, at the Old Bailey in those days there was little if any security thought to be necessary. Jurors, counsel, defendants, police, friends and witnesses all mixed happily in the one tearoom in the basement.

When it came to it, Kenneth Barraclough, the stipendiary magistrate who heard the committal proceedings, found the allegations of conspiracy to murder Caruana too confusing and indeed improbable for him to rule there was a case to answer. But by then the damage was done. Witnesses had come forward in the cases of the murders of George Cornell and Jack 'The Hat' McVitie and in 1969 the Twins were sentenced to life imprisonment.

The one unsolved piece of business with which the Krays have continually been rumoured to have been involved was the death of nightclub owner Freddie Mills, for a short time the world light-heavyweight champion and in his day one of the most popular figures in British sport.

On the night of 25 July 1965, this all-round British hero of the 1940s was found dead, shot in the eye, in his car parked in Goslett Yard at the back of his club, Freddie Mills Nitespot [sic], in the Charing Cross Road, which he ran in partnership with the former manager Andy Ho. Almost immediately the questions arose: was it suicide, and, if not, then by whom was he killed, and why? He had apparently borrowed an air rifle to kill himself. Mills's family and the boxing community generally have never been able to accept that this brave man who had appeared perfectly happy on the day of his death would commit suicide.

At the inquest the police who investigated his death, the pathologist Professor Keith Simpson and the coroner Dr Gavin Thurston were all convinced it was indeed suicide. Simpson thought the wounds were caused by 'deliberate self-infliction'. At the time there was no real attempt by his widow Chrissie Mills's lawyer to suggest that he had been murdered. The only real question raised was *why* he killed himself.

Chrissie Mills told the court that Mills had had a pneumonia virus in the previous weeks: 'He had been worried recently but he didn't tell me a lot. My elder daughter was in hospital with peritonitis and I took such a beating that he kept things from me.'

Thurston, who sat without a jury, in arriving at his findings, said, 'He had business worries but always put on a good face towards life, although Mr Ho told me that this cheerfulness could be deceptive.'

Immediately after the inquest, Chrissie Mills, who was not in court to hear the verdict, said she felt there was something, 'oddly lacking somewhere'. She said, 'I was absolutely stunned when I heard the verdict.'[10]

In his will, which Mills had made 12 years earlier, he left all his estate to Chrissie. It amounted to £3,767 19s. 7d (£3,767.98) and, when all debts had been paid, only £387. 6s. 5d. (£387.32) was left. Where had it all gone? There is no doubt that by 1965 he was haemorrhaging money. At one time he had owned a string of properties in south London, but by now they had been sold and he had also taken out a mortgage on his home. He was said to be 'borrowing' £10 or £20 a week from the club.

There is no doubt that the Nitespot had been doing badly. Clubs generally were not doing well that summer, which is a notoriously quiet time in the trade. An effort to boost the takings by having the singer Mandy Rice-Davies, fresh from her involvement in the Stephen Ward case, had not been helped by a typographical error in the advertisement in the *Evening News*, which billed her as 'Mangy Rice-Davies'. Nor was the club by any means at the top end of the market. The writer Dea Langmead recalls being taken there as a young woman:

> I seem to remember some black ties and also suits – no hard and fast rule, apparently – I know I went with a 'suit' – and there were tables and a small dance floor and a live band. There were girls sitting at the bar and cute waitresses and various brawny, muscular men, and a strange air of it not being quite a top class venue. I think I felt a bit shivery and daring in being there at all, as if rubbing shoulders with the underworld, and if it had been a bit pricey I wouldn't have been invited.[11]

Girls in Mills's club received neither pay nor commission on the meals and drink the customers bought. There were, of course, tips and they were instructed to tell the men they expected £6 for sitting with them. They were also expected to get the men to order two bottles of champagne. Afterwards, the men could take them to a local hotel at a cost of between £15 and £20 a night.[12] Some of the girls were also running the corner game – a scam in which some poor mug is sent around a corner to wait for someone who never appears. Just before his death Mills and Ho were fined £50 each for licensing offences at Marlborough Street court.

According to law student Robert Deacon, who worked as a part-time doorman there and knew the Ho family well, one of the reasons the club was doing badly was that Andy Ho was stashing away money taken from the club in cardboard boxes.

Those who believe he killed himself argue that Mills was a man whose life, for a number of reasons, was becoming intolerable. He had been suffering from bad headaches and was seriously worried about his health; he was no longer being used on television and the radio partly because his speech was beginning to slur; he had serious money troubles; he was gambling; he had had an affair with a young girl and this had caused trouble in his marriage; he was almost certainly bisexual and the suicide of his close friend the singer Michael Holliday had taken a serious toll on him; he was being blackmailed. Perm any three.

The underworld believes he killed himself specifically because he was Jack the Stripper, the name given to the murderer of a number of prostitutes between 1964 and 1965 on the towpath in the Hammersmith area, and was about to be arrested. One of the arguments against suicide is that Mills did not leave a note, but nor do a high percentage of suicides. There is, however, a belief among retired Met officers that such a note was found, and then hidden for the sake of Mills's family. Although there is no available evidence whatsoever that Mills was the Stripper, in some versions of the story there is a detailed confession of the killing of the prostitutes.[13]

The homosexual issue was also raised by Mills's biographer Tony Van den Bergh, who suggested there was a possible relationship between Mills and the boxer Don McCorkindale, Chrissie's first husband, as well as talk of a relationship with Michael Holliday. There is also a curious passage in the book by Jack Birtley that after

McCorkindale's son Donny was
claimed that McCorkindale bega
her so much that the marriag
supporters claim there was no wa
but there is little doubt that, pu
show-business mannerisms.[15]

Nosher Powell has the story of
death – told to him by a policeman –

> Freddie would drive over Waterloo B ... Strand and into Wellington Street as a cut to the West End. Whether he had to go to the toilet I don't know but he stopped at a public urinal and he went in. There was a young fellow and Freddie propositioned him. Next, 'You're under arrest.' He was taken to Bow Street, charged with importuning and released. You could accuse him of murder or robbery and he'd hold his head up high but to be charged with being a poofter was more than he could take.[16]

Could he not have gone to a friend in the police to have had the thing sorted out informally? In the mid-1960s there were certainly some very odd senior officers floating around the club scene in the West End. It is a possibility, no more, that any blackmail was coming from a police officer. John Rigby, then with the Flying Squad, confirms that in the 1960s police officers could be and were bought off on a regular basis: 'If someone was caught in a bog nodding and smiling then, provided it wasn't in the book, forty quid could square it. Once there was a charge then there was nothing could be done about getting rid of it completely.'

There were even rumours that Mills had had a relationship with Ronnie Kray. A Kray associate, Bill Ackerman, claimed that he saw them together in the Society, a club in Jermyn Street, and later in other venues. 'They'd always sit side by side and they were just like a man and a woman together.' It was something Kray denied, saying that he would never have sex with a man as opposed to a boy.[17] This gave rise to another Kray story that Ronnie had picked up a rent boy from the meat rack that functioned near Boots at Piccadilly Circus. Unfortunately, during the sexual play that followed, the boy died and

nd buried in a motorway construction.[18]
ard writing about his father, the London gang boss
, has a long story about Mills and Holliday. The gist of the
hat Holliday had indeed had a sexual affair with Mills and,
eing bisexual, had picked up girls for what were described as
ld sadomasochistic acts on them for titillation before Mills and Holliday had sex with each other'. In around 1959 on one occasion things had got out of hand and a girl had died. Mills had disposed of the body and then persuaded Holliday not to go to the police. Given that Holliday was at the peak of his career this was not too difficult. According to Holliday their relationship had then cooled but had revived in the early sixties. Holliday had, he maintained, insisted that now the sadomasochism was merely acted out, but then another girl died and her body was again disposed of by Mills. It was then that Holliday told the pianist Russ Conway and asked for advice. Before it was given Holliday committed suicide. Billy Howard arranged a meeting between Conway and a Metropolitan police officer at a Brighton hotel. He then warned Mills that he seemed to have got himself into 'a bit of serious trouble' and that, 'You are about to get your collar felt, so I'd arrange to have a brief on call.'

This is, of course, a variation of the story in which the police mark Mills's card that he is about to be arrested for the Stripper murders. It is also a story that is at best third-hand and that none of the principals are alive to confirm.[19]

The comedian Bob Monkhouse knew of Mills's moods:

> Freddie had a very dark side. Denis, my partner who committed suicide, felt a tremendous kinship with him and they palled around together. Denis had this unabashed glee and terrible moments of despondent mood exactly the same as Freddie.
>
> Freddie had male companions and he also consorted with a number of ladies on a casual basis. He'd try anything. With some people when they become famous they feel the right to have anything they want. I didn't see him do it but the story was that Freddie Mills was quite capable of whipping it out and saying, 'Wrap a smile round that.' He'd expose himself in front of anybody. He didn't bother to go

> into the gents. I heard he was less interested in penetration, more in a Clinton–Lewinsky type of activity.[20]

Chrissie Mills and Mills's stepson Donnie McCorkindale were convinced that he had been killed as an example by gangsters, who were extorting a fortune in the mid-1960s from club owners, allegedly under the benevolent eye of certain West End policemen. But which set of gangsters? The Krays, the Richardsons, the Triads, independent gangsters?

The author Donald Sutherland, who was himself something of a man about town of the period, had a slightly different take on things:

> In the underworld it was acknowledged that it was not a Billy Hill job and one likely put down to the Chinese Tongs – a deadly secret society which specialised in assassinations and a grudge killing with a motive in the sinister ring of practising homosexuals of which Freddie Mills was part.[21]

From time to time all the theories have had their supporters. In every case except Sutherland's the argument is that Mills was to be a high-profile example designed to ensure that club owners did not backslide in their protection payments.

The newspapers of the period tended to play up gang warfare and protection, promoting contenders for control of Soho. There were, without doubt, serious incidents. In July 1964 there was a fight in Le Kilt Club, a discothèque in Greek Street. Four men had come in with a girl member and had threatened the barman. The *News of the World* reported that recalcitrant club owners were sprayed with petrol while another man would stand by calmly striking matches until the protection money was paid. 'One gangster is reputed to have 400 tearaways on his pay-roll.' It was something of a ludicrous claim. The Krays at their zenith might have managed to muster 50, including part-time hangers on.[22]

The claim that the Richardsons from south London were involved is an interesting one. It is raised by both Tony Van den Berg and Bill Bavin, who wrote biographies of Mills. However, the timing is all wrong. Even at a first desultory glance the vague suggestions that the Richardsons were involved in Mills's death would seem unlikely. For a start, the Richardsons were not in the protection business as the Krays were. They were basically businessmen who ran long firm frauds.

Nor were they ever suggested to have been prominent in the West End club scene although, after his release from prison following the 'Torture Trial', Charlie Richardson ran a club in Charlotte Street. His brother Eddie, along with Frankie Fraser, ran their company Atlantic Machines, which dealt in one-armed bandits from a basement at 27 Windmill Street. It was to Windmill Street that Fraser took the unfortunate Eric Mason one night after a quarrel outside the Astor Club in Mayfair and set about him with an axe before dropping him off at the hospital in the Mile End Road. Mason needed 300 stitches but when he complained to the Krays he was given a derisory £40 as compensation.

A closer look shows Richardson involvement to have been just about impossible. This was because, after a disastrous fight on 9 March 1965 at Mr Smith's nightclub in Catford, when Dickie Hart was killed, most of the Richardson team were locked up. Of the survivors the dangerous and volatile George Cornell was shot dead the next night by Ronnie Kray in the Blind Beggar. True, Charlie Richardson was still at liberty but he had more pressing matters, such as the release of his brother Eddie on his hands. Apart from that, Charlie Richardson was no fool. The high-profile killing of a man like Mills would be foolish beyond measure, particularly while he and his firm were being investigated so closely by the police, and anyway, and more crucially, it was simply not his game.

Another story is that the Krays were regular visitors to the Nitespot and on one occasion Mills had a row with them and told them to go. They went and it was after that that he was killed.[23] A version of the Kray story is one repeated by Chrissie Mills herself, and has a waiter telling her about them – a conversation she immediately repeated to her husband: 'Those two! The Krays. The waiter, the one who never talks as a rule, has just told me that they are the heads of London's underworld, and that they would kill their own mother.'

Mills then patted his wife's hand and went over to the men to repeat in turn what she had said. The two men, who knew Chrissie by name, looked round at her and then turned back to Mills. 'Don't worry Fred,' one of them drawled back with a wide grin. 'We wouldn't hurt you.'[24]

There have been efforts made to portray Mills as some sort of innocent abroad who could recognise neither a gangster nor a prostitute at five feet distance, but they cannot be right. Mills had moved in boxing and West End circles for years and knew both the faces and the mores perfectly well. It was not as if he had merely made an investment in his Chinese restaurant and nightclub. He was a hands-on proprietor. He knew other club owners and went to their clubs.

When Bob Monkhouse was having trouble with Dennis Hamilton, the syphilitic and jealous husband of actress Diana Dors, not only did the boxing promoter Jack Solomons, who had both offices and a gymnasium in Great Windmill Street, mark the comedian's card, but so did Mills, telephoning him to say, 'I saw Hamilton at the Astor pissed as a fart but bloody dangerous. He's round the twist and that, I know, a nutter – but he'd got it in for you. I mean really got it in, no error. So watch your back, all right'[25]

A photograph of Reggie Kray with his wife Frances and other friends in the club shows Mills, a cigarette in his hand, with his arms around two of the men. In truth the club, and before that the restaurant, had always been a home for the Chaps, as underworld types refer to themselves. Gerry Parker, who for a time ran with Jack Spot in the 1950s, remembers, 'The food wasn't bad. Albert [Dimes] liked Chinese and you'd see him there occasionally.'

In support of the protection story is the one that lighted matches were stuffed down the padding of a banquette in the club, which had also been slashed.

After Nipper Read arrested the Krays, first for long firm frauds and then over the murders of Cornell and Jack McVitie, he began to enquire into Mills's death. He later wrote,

> Nothing would have given me more pleasure than being able to show that Freddie had not committed suicide. In those days there was much more of a stigma attached to the act than there is today. Moreover, if I could link the Krays to it, my investigation would have a major boost. It would have been beautiful to have tagged this murder to them.[26]

Read toured the West End speaking with the usual suspects and faces. All he could get was, 'Oh, Guv, you know better than that.' One man had said, 'We don't make examples of other people. If somebody don't pay we break his legs, not somebody else's.'

Read was by now leaning hard on the smaller fry of the Firm who had been collectors, some of whom were considering their positions as to whether it would be preferable to be witnesses or defendants. Again he had no luck. The response, as he says, was always the same:

> Freddie – no way. When the Twins went to Freddie's place they paid. They'd never nip him. They were boxers too. He was their hero. You can bet every time they went there they paid. No danger.

> However I have to look at it on the evidence and, based on that, I am sadly forced to the inescapable conclusion that he did, in fact, take his own life.

At the end of a dramatised television reconstruction of the Mills story, *In Suspicious Circumstances*, the actor Edward Woodward revealed that Jack Birtley, the writer, had received an anonymous letter saying that the killing had been carried out on the instruction of a man known in Soho as the Guvnor, someone known to Mills. The writer had been offered the contract but, since he admired Mills, he had declined it. The writer backed up his credentials by saying that he had undertaken the contract killing of the prostitute known as Black Rita.

At the time there were two men who could claim the title of Guvnor of Soho and it was certainly neither Ronnie nor Reggie Kray. The first was the now ageing Billy Hill, against whom there is no evidence that he was ever seriously into protection. Hill was a thief and an organiser and putter-up of high-class robberies. In any event he had effectively retired. The only other person active at the time generally known as the Guvnor was Billy Howard. As for the killing of Black Rita, this was a case from 18 years earlier. It is curious that the man offered the contract on Mills would not have been able to offer a more recent example of his work.

Even if, which is by no means certain, Mills was paying straightforward protection money it is extremely unlikely he was paying anything nearly as much as the £5,000 paid by the very successful Colony Club. Assuming, though, that he was, it was by no means an impossible sum. It still does not account for the huge loss of his capital at the time and his liquidation of his property investments.

What really does militate against the Krays being the killers, either personally or by proxy, is that over the last 40 years no single person has come forward to say that they know the man who carried out the killing, nor has there been any whisper of who it might be. The identities of the killers in many of the so-called unsolved gang murders of the period have been open secrets. But no name has ever been raised as the trigger puller in the case of Mills.

In 2002 the old Soho figure Bert 'Battles' Rossi, then in his 80s, who had served five years with Fraser for the attack on Jack Spot, may have provided the solution. He knew the Twins during a period in prison and he claimed that after his release, over a period of time, he acted as their unofficial adviser, particularly to Ronnie Kray. Then, in July 1965:

> Ronnie came to me and said that Mills's partner, Andy Ho, wanted him out [of the club] and that there was money in it for them if they got him out. They'd had an approach through Bill Ackerman. I said I didn't think it was a good idea. Freddie wasn't going to take any nonsense from them and he'd have hit them. Then they'd have had to up the ante so to speak and maybe it would have got out of hand.
>
> I knew Freddie and said I would go round and have a chat with him and I went to see him a couple of days later. At first he didn't seem to understand. He said was I saying that he should move out? I said that his partner had gone to people in the East End. I said, 'Your back's to the wall. Give a little or there'll be trouble.' I left him in an uncertain state of mind. He didn't say, 'Go and fuck yourself' but he didn't say he'd agree.
>
> I said to Ronnie, 'Leave it four or five days. Then if he says he'll go you can tell the Chinese it was down to you and you'll earn a few quid. If need be do what you have to do.' But I didn't want any part of it.

> Five, six, seven days later all of a sudden he's dead in the car. I went to Ronnie and asked what he'd done. I might have been seen coming out of the club and there'd be questions asked of me. Ronnie said it was nothing to do with them and I said, 'Are you sure?' And I believed him when he said he hadn't.

Why, despite all their protestations of devotion to boxing in general and Mills in particular, would they even entertain going against him? Rossi's answer was simply that it was business. There was money in it.[27]

The Chinese suggestion had first been mooted by Tony Van den Bergh in 1991 and at the time was dismissed as utter rubbish.[28] He wrote that while he was researching *The Purse*, a documentary on punch-drunkenness, a Smithfield marketeer whom he called Big Den told him that it was common knowledge that 'Mills was killed by a Chinese gang who wanted to take over his club. Everyone in the Market knows that.' The theory was that a Tong organisation wanted a headquarters in Soho.

But why Mills's club? Surely there were any number of restaurants and clubs in Soho from which the Triads could operate. The answer is that in the early 1960s there was not a great Chinese presence in Soho and he did have a Chinese partner. For the purposes of crime the area was still an Italian- and Maltese-dominated one. The great benefit was that the back of Mills's club was in shadows and with its access from both Oxford Street and the Charing Cross Road, drug dealers would have been able to come and go with relative impunity. Mills had, according to the story, rejected several offers and, in the face of his continued resistance, he was killed.

The argument that someone wanted a ready-made place from which to operate is just about sustainable but it may have all been much more simple: no Triads, just the one man. To criminals, members of the general public are expendable. Criminals will turn at the least provocation, for a slight, real or imaginary, and, if money is involved, professed friendships will fly out of the window.

No solution will please everybody, but Rossi's version – that this was the final straw that drove Mills to take his own life – may well be the answer. It does seem likely that Mills had reached the end of his tether. Given the story from Deacon that Ho was loading money into boxes it may well be that Freddie confronted him and in turn Ho looked to the Twins for help. The news from Rossi that the Krays, while they may not have made any overt move, were going to back Ho may well have been the last straw.

If Ho did want the club for himself it did him little good. After Mills's death the club remained closed for a fortnight as a mark of respect and then reopened. If it had been hoped that the notoriety would bring in new punters it was not realised. It closed finally within a week. It is not now possible to trace what happened to Mills's shares in the club, which were no doubt worthless. The company was dissolved on 6 December 1968 and the records have been destroyed. Some years later the premises became a Spanish restaurant.

In 1993 Peter McInnes, Mills's Bournemouth friend, a man who firmly believed Mills had been killed, contacted Andy Ho, who was then living in Surbiton. He spoke with the second Mrs Ho, who indicated that her husband would be pleased to talk to him, as there was something 'he wanted to get off his chest'. They never met. Ho, who was already in poor health, almost immediately suffered a series of strokes.[29]

15

Some Murders

On 14 September 1945, a month after the war ended, Captain John Ritchie of the Canadian Army was killed in a straightforward robbery. Ritchie left the Criterion restaurant, where he had dined with some friends, and at 10 o'clock went into Soho with a fellow Canadian officer. What he did there for the next two hours is unclear but shortly before midnight his body was found in Bouchier Street between Wardour Street and Dean Street by two police officers. They had passed two soldiers walking in the opposite direction and, seconds later, found Ritchie's body, his head in a pool of blood. The two policemen turned and saw the soldiers make a run for it. They gave chase, but the two men split up.

PC Dimsey managed to capture one of the soldiers, Robert Blaine, and they returned to Ritchie's body. Blaine now said that the other man had been the one who had hit him, giving his name as Jack Connolly, whom he had known for three or four weeks, and saying that they drank together, sometimes at the Duke of York, and sometimes at the Alfred's Head.

On the night of the murder, they had left a pub at about 11 o'clock and went to visit a café. On the way there, they passed a pile of bricks. Connolly picked one up, gave it to Blaine and asked him to keep hold of it for him. Blaine claimed he thought they would use it in a break-in, so he put it inside his tunic. Later, as they walked down Bouchier Street, Connolly asked for the brick and used it to batter Ritchie to death.

Bloodstains were found on Blaine's clothing and, when he was searched, police found £5 in cash, together with Ritchie's bankbook and chequebook. Blaine admitted that he had rifled Ritchie's pockets but still maintained that it was Connolly who struck the fatal blows.

Blaine, who had a long record of theft dating from 1938, was found guilty and sentenced to death. His appeal was dismissed on 13 December 1945 and he was executed 16 days later. No trace of Jack Connolly, if that was his name, was ever found and so one of the killers of Captain Ritchie did manage to get away with murder.[1]

Shortly after the war there was a spate of prostitute murders in and around Soho. The first was that of Frances Mizzi, who on 25 February 1946 was found strangled with her own silk stockings in her flat in Poland Street. After she died, her husband was given three months for living off her immoral earnings.

Then, on 10 November that year, a 31-year-old ex-Borstal girl, Margaret Cook, described as an exotic dancer, was shot outside the Blue Lagoon Club in Carnaby Street. She was heard to say to her killer, 'I know you have a gun. Put it away.' The man, wearing a porkpie hat and a Burberry-style raincoat, was chased but disappeared into a crowd near Oxford Circus Tube station. Cook had been told that a new boyfriend carried a gun but she had said, wrongly, that she could take care of herself. The police issued the description of a man whom they wished to see but no charges were ever brought.

On 8 September 1947 Rita Barratt (or Driver, or Green) known, because of her hair, as 'Black Rita', was shot around seven in the evening at her flat in Rupert Street. The striking six-foot-tall woman, whose husband claimed he did not know of her activities, was the daughter of a former police officer who had been stationed at Bow Street. She had been working in Lisle Street in the afternoon, had a meal in a café with another girl at about 5 pm and had then picked up a man. Another girl in the Rupert Street block heard footsteps and then shots. She ran to the first floor, where she found Rita slumped on the floor. There were no real suspects and no arrests were made. Two suggestions were offered for her death. The first was that, given her father's occupation, she was a police informer; the second that she had been made an example of after she had refused to co-operate with the Messina brothers. The police rather took the view that she had been killed by a stranger with an aversion to prostitutes. There was also the story that she was another with a new boyfriend who was said to carry a revolver.

Just over a year later, on 17 September 1948, the good-looking 41-year-old Rachel 'Ginger Rae' Fennick was stabbed to death at her flat in Broadwick Street. At one time she had worked at the Miranda Club in Romilly Street and had been the proprietor of La Roma at 161 Wardour Street. She had married a black American who left her to go to Paris, where he died. Apart from the times when she was quarrelsome in drink – there are notes that she fought other girls – she was generally well regarded as someone who would give money to children and tramps. In the spielers she was known as a good card player. Over the years she had racked up more than 80 convictions for soliciting, brothel keeping and theft.

In the months before her death she had more or less taken up with a man who came to lunch every Sunday and stayed the night. He denied being her ponce but certainly the police thought he fitted that role, if not that of her killer. All the usual suspects were rounded up and questioned, including John Allen, the so-called Mad Parson, who in 1937 had killed a child in Oxfordshire and who, ten years later, had escaped from Broadmoor. He was quickly eliminated.

There were suggestions she also was a police informer and again that she had been killed to silence her as a deterrent to others. Curiously enough, one magazine suggested she had been killed by a left-over member of the prewar Micheletti gang.[2] In his memoirs Robert Higgins, who investigated the case, thought the knife cuts looked like those found on victims on the waterfronts of the Mediterranean. The knife itself was never found.

Then, later that month came the death of 60-year-old Dora Freeman, who was stabbed in her flat in Long Acre, Covent Garden. Despite signs of a terrible fight no neighbours reported hearing anything, possibly because the killer had turned up the volume on her radio. Again there were stories she was a blackmailer and informer. A variation was that she, as well as Cook, Barratt and Fennick, had been killed by the Jack Spot man, Teddy Machin, as a purely business matter.[3]

On 29 April 1947 Alec de Antiquis was killed when he tried to prevent an Elephant Boy (see Chapter 6) escaping after an attempted robbery at Jay's jewellers near what used to be the Scala Theatre in Charlotte Street. The raid itself had been a total failure. While the staff were held at gunpoint, a member pressed the burglar alarm and a director, Ernest Stock, managed to shut the safe. Next, 70-year-old Bertram Keates threw a stool at the robbers and, after a shot was fired at him, the men ran out into the street. Now a lorry was blocking their Vauxhall getaway car and they set off on foot waving their guns.

It was a time when passers-by would 'have a go' to try to stop thieves, and the gang was first chased by Charles Grimshaw. Then 34-year-old father of six de Antiquis tried to block their path by stalling his motorbike and was shot for his pains. As he lay dying he said, 'I tried to stop them. I did my best . . .'

The robbers were Harry 'Harry Boy' Jenkins, Christopher James Geraghty and 17-year-old Terence Peter Rolt. They were traced through a raincoat found in a room in Tottenham Court Road, which had been bought by Jenkins's brother-in-law. Jenkins, known as 'the King of Borstal', had been released only six days before the murder. Another man, William Wilson, who had been on a previous raid in Queensway, West London, named Jenkins and admitted casing the shop but denied being on the robbery.

The first to confess was Geraghty, who named Rolt, who, in turn, named Jenkins. It seems that the bungling of the raid had been the fault of Rolt, who had been told to wait outside but had decided to follow the others in. However, it was Geraghty who had shot de Antiquis. He and Jenkins were hanged on 19 September 1947. Earlier, Jenkins and another brother, Thomas, had been fortunate. On 8 December 1944, in another raid by them on a jeweller's shop, in Birchin Lane in the City, Captain Ralph Binney had tried to stop a getaway car driven by Robert Hedley. Binney was knocked down and trapped under the car, and dragged for over a mile, dying of his injuries. Thomas Jenkins received eight years but Harry Jenkins had not been picked out on an identification parade. After Jenkins was executed, Lawton, the governor of Pentonville Prison, apparently wrote to his mother saying she could not have his clothes since he had been hanged in them but she could, if she wished, have his belt, braces and shoelaces.[4]

After the war one of the great streets in north Soho for buying used cars was Warren Street at the top end of Tottenham Court Road. Frank Fraser recalls,

> They'd have cars in showrooms and parked on the pavement. There could be up to fifty cars and then again some people would just stand on the pavement and pass on the info that there was a car to sell.
>
> Warren Street was mostly for mug punters. Chaps wouldn't buy one. People would come down from as far away as Scotland to buy a car. All polished and shiny with the clock turned back and the insides hanging out.
>
> And if you bought a car and it fell to bits who was you going to complain to? There wasn't these Fair Trading officers and if there was they weren't as powerful as they are now and there certainly wasn't all these television shows and articles in newspapers.[5]

One of the bigger dealers in the street was the Iraqi-born Stanley Setty. His brother Max, with whom he had quarrelled, owned the very fashionable nightclubs, the Orchid Room in Brook Street and then the Blue Angel in Berkeley Street. However, Setty, whose real name was Sulman Seti, would turn his hand to anything that might produce a profit for him. In Manchester in 1928 he served a sentence for obtaining credit by fraud and associated bankruptcy offences. Apart from dealing in cars, he was regarded as a black-market banker, putting up money for jobs and then taking a cut but not handling the merchandise himself. As a sideline, according to the police, he was a small-time pimp. He disappeared on 4 October 1949 and his sister-in-law reported him missing the next day.

On 22 October 1949, parts of Setty's body were found wrapped in parcels near Tillingham on the Essex marshes, where they had been dropped from a light aircraft. It was not difficult to trace the pilot, Brian Donald Hume, who had hired an Auster from a flying club at Elstree and then left the plane at Southend Airport. Hume, married with a three-and-a-half-month-old daughter, was a typical wide boy of the time involved in smuggling and, like Setty, anything else that would turn a profit, and was known to be short of money. Four days later, when interviewed, he said, 'I'm some kind of bastard, aren't I?' He claimed that two men, 'Mac' and Green, came to him to pilot a plane to drop hot plates used for forging clothing coupons out at sea. For a fee of £50 he had dropped the plates and when he returned to his Golders Green flat he found them and a third man, 'Boy', offering him £100 to drop a third package. He cannot have really thought they were plates because he had heard a gurgling noise from this third parcel and indeed he had thought it might even be Setty, of whose disappearance he had heard.

The prosecution's case was that Setty had been killed – stabbed in the chest – at Hume's flat at 623 Finchley Road and on the face of it the evidence against him was strong. There was a good deal of blood in the flat and Hume had taken a carpet to be cleaned on the morning of 5 October and also a knife to be sharpened locally just before the killing. On the other hand, there were no fingerprints of Setty, nor had neighbours heard anything sounding like a quarrel or fight, certainly not the noise of someone dismembering a body. In the days when a jury's verdict had to be unanimous it was sufficient for Hume to get a disagreement. He was retried and this time pleaded guilty to being an accessory after the fact. He expected to receive a shortish sentence and was not at all pleased with his 12 years.

While he was away his wife, Cynthia, a former nightclub hostess, married the journalist Duncan Webb. As Hume was nearing his release, Fraser and others used to tease Webb that Hume would be coming after him. He did not. Instead, on his release in 1958, he sold his story, I KILLED SETTY, to the *Sunday People*, saying he had, in fact, killed him in a quarrel over Setty's kicking Hume's dog.

That year Hume shot a bank cashier in August and another in November. Both survived but Arthur Maag, a taxi driver who tried to prevent him escaping from a bank robbery in Zurich in January 1959, was not so fortunate. Hume was sentenced to life imprisonment and the president of the court announced, 'Life imprisonment for this kind of man means life. He will never be let out of jail – not this one.' It did not. And he was. Hume was returned to England in 1976 and sent to Broadmoor, from where he was later released. He died in a wood in Gloucestershire in July 1998.[6] His decomposed body had to be identified through his fingerprints.

Alfredo 'Italian Tony' Zomparelli, once the gofer of Albert Dimes, was shot dead in the Golden Goose amusement arcade in Old Compton Street on the afternoon of 4 September 1974 while playing the appropriately named Wild Life pinball machine. His death was the direct result of the killing at the Latin Quarter in Wardour Street on 7 May 1970 of David Knight, brother of the more famous Ronnie. Quite why the earlier killing took place is open to some dispute. The police claimed it was a matter of protection, but Ronnie Knight said it was because of a bad beating outside a club at the Angel handed out to David by a Johnny Isaacs. Ronnie had gone to the Latin Quarter to extract an apology from Isaacs, who, fortunately for him, wasn't there when they arrived. Instead, David, Ronnie, their brother John and Billy Hickson were confronted in the cocktail bar by Billy Stayton, once a Richardson associate. Fighting broke out and in the mêlée Zomparelli stabbed David Knight twice in the chest.

Three weeks later, Zomparelli gave himself up to the police, claiming that he had merely been defending himself. In return, he received a four-year sentence for manslaughter. Hickson was given a suspended sentence for affray while the jury could not agree in the cases of Ronnie and John Knight, also on the affray charges.

After his release, Zomparelli ignored suggestions that the matter had not ended with his modest sentence. 'I think you shouldn't be here,' one doorman told him, but he continued leaning on Italian restaurants until one afternoon he was shot by two men wearing dark glasses and moustaches. The police interviewed more than 1,000 people, including Knight, who made no secret of his loathing of Zomparelli nor of his thirst for revenge. However, he had, he said, been in his A&R Club, a claim correctly confirmed by a number of witnesses.

And there the matter rested until, in 1980, Maxie Piggott, also known as George Bradshaw, a man with bottle-bottom glasses and a mariachi moustache, became one of the many supergrasses who saw a full confession as a way to shorten a prison sentence. From a well-respected south London family whose father had a slot-machine business, Bradshaw had served a seven-year sentence for throwing acid and had escaped from Wormwood Scrubs. On 17 January 1980 he received a life sentence after he admitted Zomparelli's murder and more than a hundred armed robberies. His fellow gunman was, he said, Nicky Gerard, son of his friend, the feared London hard man and fish-and-chip shop owner Alfie, with whom Bradshaw had for a time been in partnership. He and Nicky Gerard had stopped at a Soho costumier for their disguises. Their fee, paid by Ronnie Knight, had, claimed Gerard, been £1,000, of which only £250 was paid. Ronnie Knight and Nicky Gerard were duly charged.

By the time Bradshaw came to give evidence, supergrasses had lost the popularity they had enjoyed 10 years earlier. With Barbara Windsor gallantly supporting her now more or less estranged husband, Knight and Gerard were both acquitted. Bradshaw thought the judge to be 'senile' and that he should have listened more closely to the evidence. In a reissue of his book *Black Knight*, well before the so-called *autrefois acquit* rule was amended to allow the prosecution to seek a retrial if new evidence came to light, Knight admitted he had paid for the contract. Tony Zomparelli's son said that when Ronnie Knight died he would open a bottle of champagne.[7]

Another Soho amusement arcade was the scene of a much nastier killing in 1989. Yurev Gomez, who almost burned to death on 3 April at the Leisure Investments arcade, which stood on the corner of Gerrard and Wardour Streets, in fact survived to name his killer. Fellow employees were not so fortunate.

When an employee of the company came to unlock the premises at eight o'clock that morning he noticed a smell of burning overlaid with chemicals. The small office safe had been ransacked and coins were scattered over the floor. The majority of the takings were kept locked in a room secured by a steel door next to the stairs. The employee heard noises and went to unlock the door. There was the relief manager Gomez, his clothing in tatters, his face and body irretrievably burned. 'Victor,' he said. 'It was Victor who did it.' Victor was Victor Castigador, a Filipino who worked as a security guard in the arcade.

Castigador had a grudge against the company and so led the £9,000 robbery raid on the arcade. He ordered the two security guards along with Gomez and cashier Deborah Alvares into a wire cage in the basement. After gathering paper, Castigador fastened the door and threw lighted matches onto the rubbish over which white spirit had been poured.

When the police arrived they found the two security guards dead as well as Yurev and Debbie Alvarez, who were still alive. The guards had been asphyxiated. Two days later the police arrested Castigador at a flat in Bow. He had £480 of the money stolen in his possession. The police later arrested four young accomplices who were all charged with murder.

Castigador had come to England in 1985. He had, he said, been an assassin for the Filipino government but had become burned out and when he met an English woman, Jacqueline Haddon, decided to retire and settle down. His intention when arriving in England had been to marry her, something he did within a week of his arrival on 10 August 1985. At first they lived in Sussex but the marriage was not a success and he moved to London.

Castigador's complaints were against the general manager, Tony Doroudy, who he claimed was promoting people over his head and failing to pay promised bonuses. At one time Castigador had worked at the company's Oxford Street arcade, where he had broken the jaw of a client he thought to be troublesome. Doroudy transferred him to the Gerrard Street premises – by no means a promotion.

The catalyst was Castigador's suspension by Tony Doroudy for failing to turn up for work. Castigador believed he had arranged this with a duty manager but, when he was told to come in to collect his P45, he planned his reprisal.

He was sentenced to life imprisonment with a recommendation that he serve not less than 25 years. One youth was ordered to be detained during Her Majesty's Pleasure. The other received a term of life imprisonment with eight years to run concurrently for the robbery.[8]

16

Bernie Silver Meets the Maltese

One of the more prominent of London's independent ponces in the immediate post-Messina days was Jean Baptiste Hubert, or Belan, known as Belgian Johnny. He had first come to England with the Belgian Free Forces in 1940 and in his own country had convictions for robbery, theft and in 1953 one for poncing, for which he received 12 months.

By the late 1950s Hubert was living in St John's Wood, driving a Jaguar and running a small string of girls, including a Germaine Borelli, who had a flat in Wardour Street and whom he married at Hampstead Register Office in December 1957.

He really came to the notice of the police when a young girl complained about being given a black eye by her Belgian ponce. She later withdrew the complaint but by then the damage was done. Hubert was arrested at the flat in which he was living with the girl shortly after she returned home early one morning. That evening she had earned £40 at a time when the salary of a police inspector in the West End was £75 a month.

In October 1958 Hubert received 15 months' imprisonment at the County of London Sessions along with a further three months for kicking the arresting officer. In prison he was looked after by one of London's leading bank robbers of the time, who also ran a number of Soho clubs and was then serving a sentence. Hubert, involved in a prison tobacco racket, had been cheated by another inmate who told him the tobacco he had ordered had been seized at the gate and he was out of his money:

> Johnny was telling me this and I knew what had happened. I said I'd get it back for him. I told Sammy he'd got to pull it up or he'd be badly hurt. It all come back to Johnny. Then all of a sudden I'm sent to Swansea. Johnny sent me a letter saying he'd pick me up at the gate when I was let out at the end of 1959 and he was as good as his word. He brought me back to London and said I was partners with him. We had the Tavern in Westbourne Grove and a restaurant at the corner of Spring Gardens and Sussex Gardens.

It had been expected by the police that Hubert would be deported at the end of his sentence, but no order was made and he lasted another year after his release before his club, the Betavon Residential Club in Westbourne Grove, began to be raided on a regular basis. In March 1960 he was fined £200 at Marylebone Magistrates' Court and shortly afterwards the Home Secretary made a deportation order.[1]

In the middle of the 1960s Soho had a far uglier face than it has today. Dirty bookshops were everywhere and near-beer joints, clip joints and cinemas showing pornographic films attracted tourists to see and sample the naughty bits of London. In turn they became the victims of the unscrupulous operators of these establishments, who picked them clean.

Prostitution, clubs and near-beer joints were controlled by the Maltese, who had moved up from the East End to take over the territory after the breaking up of the Messina operation and the retirement of Billy Hill and Jack Spot. Over the years there had been a constant struggle to determine power and control and as a result there were spontaneous bursts of violence as one or other faction tried to establish and redefine territories.

At the time the smoothest operator of them all was not Maltese, but Jewish. Bernie Silver was born in Stoke Newington and had been discharged from military service as medically unfit during the war. He had then been in the building trade before working for the Messinas.

Silver's operations can be traced back to the early 1950s, when initially he ran clubs and brothels in the Brick Lane area of the East End.

In 1956 he was arrested and charged with living off immoral earnings. Along with a man called Cooper and acting as an estate agent, he had been carrying on an extension of the Messina trade by letting out rooms and flats to prostitutes at exorbitant rents.

For three months the police had kept observation in special vans with peepholes and periscopes on premises in Romilly Street, watching the girls returning with men to their flats and money changing hands. The rent books provided to the girls showed weekly payments of between £3 and £5, but in fact they were paying £25 or £30 in cash. A surveyor was employed by the police to assess the true rents of the flats. Many were what he described as 'orange-box' flats with no heat, light or water, a truckle bed and two orange boxes for chairs. These he assessed were really worth 3 shillings (15p) a week. Much classier were the £2–3 flats, which were properly furnished with an old-fashioned brass bed, a card table and some linoleum but no chair.

Silver appeared at the Old Bailey in 1956 along with a prostitute, Albertine Falzon, and seven others in front of the eccentric Judge John Maude, who found there was no case for the defendants to answer.

Maude ruled that a landlord or estate agent was in the same position as a shopkeeper, doctor or barrister who received money from a prostitute as a customer or client, and that they were living on these monies as their own earnings, not those of a prostitute. 'It may be that the problem is so grave that Parliament must do something about it – but this is not for me,' he said.[2]

Silver may have had a lucky escape but the lesson was learned both by him and by others. Flat farmers, as they were known, took steps to distance themselves from their prostitute tenants by setting up a network of cut-offs and intermediaries. But rent books still recorded only a fraction of the actual rent and key-money of around £100 changed hands when a girl took over a flat. Albertine Falzon later married Silver. In the 1970s she committed suicide by leaping out of the flat in Peter Street from which she worked.[3]

Other similar deaths in Soho included Frank Holpert – a go-between for both Silver and porn merchant Jimmy Humphreys – who in November 1973 fell to his death from his balcony, and prostitute Odette Weston, who in May 1975 fell to her death when her flat was fire-bombed. Perhaps the most interesting is that of the vice queen

Irene Micallef, who ran a call-girl racket for her estranged husband Victor. At one time a girlfriend of Playboy club's Victor Lowndes, she allegedly jumped from a roof in Paddington on 25 July 1979, when she was about to leave Soho for a new life with a new boyfriend – although there have been suggestions she was pushed. When her body was flown home to Sweden and taken to a local chapel, the coffin was found to contain the body of a 63-year old man named Medcalfe. Her boyfriend went into hiding, believing there was a contract out on him.

Silver had seen the disasters that happened when rivals fell out and had the sense to realise that a rapprochement was necessary between at least some of the operators. In the middle 1960s he formed a liaison with a Maltese, 'Big Frank' Mifsud, a former traffic policeman and a giant of a man who was considered ruthless by lesser lights. A call to visit Big Frank could strike terror into the heart of the recipient of the invitation, who, like as not, could expect a beating handed out not by the great man himself but by an underling.

Together Silver and Mifsud effectively ruled vice in the West End for nearly two decades, moving from Brick Lane to Brewer Street, where they already had a toehold in Soho through the Gigi strip club. Together they then established the Naked City, the Red Mill and the Pigalle. From there they began to buy up properties using a string of nominees.

The arrangement had been worked out so there would be no rivalry and interclub warfare between them. Say A and B ran the Star Club, B and C owned the Spangled Club, C and D the Banner Club and D and A the America Club. If, therefore, premises owned by Silver or Mifsud were attacked the other operators would suffer and there was therefore no incentive for anyone to cause trouble in another club. The operation was policed by Silver and Mifsud's henchmen including Anthony Mangion, Emmanuel Coleiro, Emmanuel Bartolo and Tony and Victor Micallef. They ran what came to be known as the Syndicate, owning 19 out of the 24 Soho strip clubs then operating. It worked after its fashion, but there was always an undercurrent of bad feeling and a belief that violence was never far away.

Near-beer joints, again run by the Maltese under the overall supervision of Mifsud and Silver, and of which there was one or more in every street, yard and alley in Soho, worked very simply. Young, attractive and scantily dressed girls stood outside the premises, which were often on the first floor or in the basement of buildings. Subtly, and sometimes not so subtly, they would lure customers inside with the veiled promise of sex. Once inside, the men were like moths round a flame unable to resist the flattery and spiel of these 'come-on' girls. They would pay exorbitant prices for non-alcoholic drinks such as blackcurrant juice. Each drink came with a cocktail stick and the girl was paid by the number of these sticks she collected during her stint. Their function was only to rip off the customer for as much as he would pay without complaining. There was certainly no requirement by the management that the girls should have sex with the clients, although many did as a side operation. If so, they took the man to a local address or hotel.

In 1964 the Refreshment Houses Act, which required clubs serving any form of refreshment, including soft drinks and sandwiches, to have a licence, gave the police right of entry into premises. And enter they did, causing a certain amount of trouble to the 'clubs', which were closed down on a regular basis by magistrates sitting at Marlborough Street and Bow Street. The result was that many proprietors did not bother to renew their licences and the premises became clip joints, where a version of the corner game was played out. There was now no pretence that drinks would be supplied or that the girl was a hostess. Money was obtained on the implicit understanding that sexual intercourse would follow. Of course, most of the girls had no intention of having sex and so to avoid the predatory punters a delaying tactic was introduced.

Mostly the girl would persuade the punter that the address was some form of club and that her employer forbade her to leave before a certain time. She would then ask the man to wait around the corner to meet her as soon as she was free. Often the man would wait two or three hours before he realised he had been done up like a kipper. Under the clock at Victoria Station was a well-worn favourite; Marble Arch, by Big Ben, Charing Cross, outside the Ritz or the Regent Palace Hotel and Leicester Square were frequently named by the punters who had spent many wasted hours waiting there. The story Nipper Read, then an inspector at West End Central, liked best, even though he found it hardest to believe, was Morden, a station at the very end of the Northern Line. He asked the Dutch seaman why he had gone that far to wait for a girl and was told that he had paid her £100 adding, 'Well, this is where she tells me she is living.'[4]

Another common scam at the time was the 'blue film' racket, another popular version of the corner game. The scenario was usually that of a smooth-talking tout standing outside an open doorway and inviting tourists to see a blue film. As a come-on he might have postcards showing explicit sex scenes 'from the film'. After taking the punters' money he would direct them up to the second floor and then simply move on to another suitable doorway. There were variations. Sometimes the spiv would actually go to the second floor with the punters and ask them to wait while he went into the projection room to check the film. Off he would go down the back stairs. If their luck was really in the punters saw a film made in Scandinavia showing a woman undressing or nudists playing volleyball in long shot.

With the World Cup coming up in July 1966, Read was afraid that both thefts from visitors and more examples of violence would occur over the summer months. Tens of thousands were coming to London and many who would drift into Soho during the evenings would become the victims of the villains who were waiting to fleece them.

He formed a 12-strong squad of officers from West End Central with the very positive mission, first to harass and shut down the clubs and then maintain a blanket policing operation on the West End.

The first job was to visit the clubs and take down the names of the girls present. They were also given the 'warning formula'. In other words, they were told in no uncertain terms that their freedom to fleece the suckers was over. It was also explained to the proprietors, or their frontmen, that they were committing offences of theft or of obtaining money by false pretences and they had better change their lifestyle. They did not listen. The pickings were far too easy and the clubs continued to flourish – for a time, anyway.

Soon, however, the girls found that some of the 'punters' were in fact plain-clothes officers. In June seven girls were arrested for obtaining money by false pretences or straightforward theft. In the week leading up to the World Cup a further 21 arrests were made by the squad, mainly for theft. By the start of the Cup only four of the clip joints remained open.

By the end of the operation on 31 July only one clip joint was still in business and that only on a haphazard basis. During the period, reported crimes dropped by nearly a half while clip-joint complaints had gone down from 205 in the first week to 12 in the last.

The bosses of the police, if not the clubs, were well pleased. Read's report went to the Home Office and commendations were given. It was announced that the squad would be kept on, although, as with everything, gradually it was allowed to run down because of lack of resources. Even so, the crime rate in the West End was stable for some months to come. But then things drifted back to what Soho considered normality.

If Silver and Mifsud thought they had a tight hold on Soho and were immune from outside attack, except by the police, they had a shock when Tony Cauci, a one-time friend of Mifsud, fell out with him over the ownership of the Carnival strip club. At the end of 1966 and in the early part of 1967 there was a series of petrol bomb explosions at the Gigi in Frith Street, the Keyhole Club in Old Compton Street and a gaming club in Greek Street, all of which belonged to the Silver–Mifsud connection in which neither Tony Cauci nor his employee, another Maltese Derek Galea, had a share.

Cauci and Galea's subsequent trial on a charge of conspiracy to cause explosions took place at a time when links between criminals in Soho and the police were rife and there was considerable concern among some officers that the explosives had been planted. Certainly a witness, Harold Stocker, who said that he had seen Galea running from the gaming club shortly after the fire, gave perjured evidence and, on the advice of Mifsud, Galea turned against his employer. After a retrial at the Old Bailey and an ugly scene when the police had to be called to deal with two dozen Maltese who had suddenly arrived in the lobby to hear the jury's verdict, they were convicted and sentenced to lengthy terms of imprisonment. Once more, a fragile peace was restored.

So far as Silver and Mifsud were concerned, it blew apart again in 1973, when Silver was arrested for living off the immoral earnings of prostitutes and Mifsud went on the run. The girls, run by the Syndicate, had been organised on a factory-line basis. One girl would run a flat from 1 until 7 pm, when the next shift took over until the early hours of the morning. Each girl would contribute £180 a week to the Syndicate. Silver had been responsible for the recruitment and placing of the girls and they clocked on and off their shifts on time. Strip clubs provided up to six shows a day with the girls travelling from one to the next. The flats above the strip clubs were owned by Silver, Mifsud and their nominees.

Now Commander Bert Wickstead moved his operations from the East End and was called in to investigate the Soho vice syndicates. His operation ran side by side with one against dirty bookshops and an investigation into the police Porn Squad. One of the first men he wished to interview was George Caruana, who over the years had had three separate attempts made on his life, by any standards a risky one. One plan had been for his car to be blown up and, perhaps sensibly, he left the country to work a double act with his wife in a strip club in Hamburg. It was in Caruana's house that Tommy Smithson had been murdered in 1956. Now, in 1973, Caruana was located and made a statement, but when it came to it he declined to give evidence. His retraction was to be only one of a series of early disappointments for Wickstead.

In fact, Wickstead had considerable misfortune with his witnesses throughout the case. Apart from Caruana's defection another potential witness, Maltese Frank Dyer, was kidnapped in south London, where he had been driven by that longstanding man about Soho, 'Count' Alec Kostanda, and given a beating, with a gun held to his head, to try to make him disclose what he had told the police.

In October 1973, the top men of the Syndicate took off on an extended holiday. An offer of £35,000 had been made on Silver's behalf – and declined – for the Serious Crime Squad to drop the charge against Silver. It seemed as though Wickstead's work might have been in vain. One of the officers in his squad had given the tip-off that raids were due. Wickstead went through the motions of having the warrants he had obtained withdrawn and then leaked a carefully prepared story that his work had been wasted and his investigation abandoned. For the moment he turned his attention to pornographic books.

Three months later the directors of the Syndicate started to filter back and on 30 December Bernie Silver was spotted at the Park Tower

Hotel in London. He was arrested, along with his then girlfriend, Dominique Ferguson, as they finished dinner and was taken to Limehouse Police Station, where Wickstead felt more at home. He could not discount the fact that at West End Central he might run into corrupt officers who could impede his progress.

That morning a raid was organised on the Scheherazade Club in Soho. Wickstead had stepped up on the stage to announce the wholesale arrest. 'What do you think of the cabaret?' called one reveller. 'Not much,' shouted another. The assembled company, including the band, was arrested and taken down to the East End police station. But the sweep did not net Frank Mifsud. He had been living in Dublin but was tipped off with a phone call on the night of the Scheherazade raid. By the time the gardaí went to arrest him, he had gone.

At Silver's vice trial in 1974 no fewer than four police officers, including Commander Frank Davies, one time head of the Flying Squad, gave evidence on his behalf. Another, ex-DC Sandison, said he had no idea that Silver was involved in prostitution. Sandison went on to run the White Horse in Newburgh Street, Soho, known as the Slate Club because Silver and Humphreys used it – unbeknown to Sandison of course – to drop off money to the police. On 19 December, after a 63-day hearing, Silver received six years and was fined £30,000.

Wickstead had also been reinvestigating the murder of Tommy Smithson, and now he had most of the story concerning the small-time hoodlum's death. Smithson's attempts to blackmail Silver to put up money for the defence of his girlfriend Fay Sadler – who had been accused of passing bad cheques – had come at a most unfortunate time when Silver was preparing his move from Brick Lane into Soho and could not afford any hindrance. Nor could he allow himself to be seen as a weak man. Two contract killers, Philip Ellul and Victor Spampinato, were given the contract and executed their one-time friend, but they were never paid.

After the murder they had gone into hiding in Manchester, where they received a message from the Syndicate telling them to give themselves up. A deal had been arranged that they would be charged only with manslaughter and once their sentences had been served need never work again. They were betrayed, and both were put on trial for murder. Spampinato was acquitted and Ellul sentenced to death before being reprieved on the eve of his execution. He served 11 years and on his release came to London to collect his money. Sixpence (2½p) was thrown on the floor and he was told to pick it up. Later he was taken to obtain a passport and then to Heathrow.

Spampinato was found by Wickstead's officers working as a wine-bar tout in Malta. Ellul was traced by the American police and telephoned Wickstead. Yes, he would come and give evidence against Silver on a conspiracy-to-murder charge. Spampinato did give evidence at the committal proceedings at Old Street Magistrates' Court but did not reappear for the trial. When next traced, in Malta, he owned a villa on the seafront at Sliema along with a new car, and was said to be in possession of £30,000. His contract had clearly been honoured at last.

Ellul was given police protection in a flat in Limehouse. He was kept under close observation but complained, saying that his time in the death cell had left its mark on him and he did not like company. The watch was relaxed and later Ellul said he wanted to return to the States, promising to come back for the trial. There is no such thing as protective custody of witnesses in England and so no reason to detain him. He never returned. It is said he was paid £60,000, which would roughly equal the payment made to Spampinato.

On 8 July 1975 Silver was convicted of ordering the murder of Smithson but his conviction was quashed by the Court of Appeal on 18 October 1976. The prosecution had built its case on the evidence of 'disreputable witnesses', said Lord Justice Lawton, adding, 'It is a very long time for anyone, however good their memories, to remember conversations which took place as long ago as that.'[5] There have been suggestions in the underworld that Silver was not the one who ordered the contract.

Others in the Silver vice case had received up to five years and all that remained was the arrest of Big Frank Mifsud. He was found in Switzerland, where he had been living in hiding in a small tent on the Austrian border and returned to London after fighting a losing extradition battle on the grounds of his ill health. He faced the charge of conspiracy to murder Smithson and also suborning Stocker to give false evidence in the Cauci and Galea case.

Wickstead had already seen both Stocker and Cauci. Stocker

admitted he had been promised £100 for his evidence but, in the tradition of bilking their employees, Mifsud had paid him only £15. Cauci, a round little man with a cast in one eye, had been set up in a coffee bar in Wardour Mews on his release from prison. He gave evidence well at Mifsud's trial and a conviction followed. Mifsud was sentenced to five years' imprisonment, only for the Court of Appeal to quash the conviction. He did not remain in England long. He returned to Malta to live on the proceeds of his Swiss bank accounts along with the other members of the Syndicate.

Silver was released on parole in 1978 and went to Malta from where he was deported. He returned to the West End but was never again quite the same force to be reckoned with. Not that Silver had completely relinquished his interests. According to Victor Micallef, Silver still had a 25 per cent interest in the Corniche Cinema in Frith Street, the new Swedish Cinema Club in Brewer Street, the Cinema Blue in Dean Street and five porn shops.[6] In fairness, Micallef was by no means dispassionate about Silver. While Silver was serving his sentence, Micallef had sold a property in Greek Street they owned jointly for some £40,000 less than Silver believed it to be worth. In his place the newspapers had found a 'New King of Soho', Charlie Grech.[7]

Never one door shuts but another opens. By the 1970s, with the introduction of the escort agency, Soho vice had become an even bigger and more sophisticated business. Again, one of the new kings was not a Maltese but Joseph Wilkins, nephew of Bert from the Sabini days. Originally from Stoke Newington, Joseph was now living the life of a country squire in Surrey.

Physically a large man with thinning and greasy black hair, he had started life as a used-car salesman. Following a move to the West End, where for a time he worked as an enforcer, he took an interest in one-armed bandits and nightclubs before, in 1969, he took over Winstons, then a very fashionable club for tired businessmen – free-spending visitors who could be relied on to waste money on indifferent food and expensive drink, watch a decent cabaret and then have the opportunity to sit with a hostess, which is what they had come there for in the first place.

At one time or another, Wilkins had interests in the 800 Club in Leicester Square (formerly the once fashionable 400 Club, home from home for Guards officers out on the town and, in its glory days, frequented by Princess Margaret), the Islet Town Club in Curzon Street and the Crazy Horse Saloon in Marylebone run by John Bloom, the former Rolls Razor washing-machine tycoon. But Wilkins also had a string of failed clubs to his name, including the Australian Visitors Club and the Minstrel Restaurant,[8] part owned by one of television's Black and White Minstrels troupe.

The circumstances of his acquisition of Winstons were shrouded in mist. At a licensing application before the then Chief Metropolitan Magistrate, Sir Robert Blundell, at Bow Street, the former owner, Bruce Brace, maintained that Wilkins had terrorised him into handing over the club. Wilkins agreed that he had paid no money for the 27,000-member club but said that instead of payment he had settled debts of £6,000. The licence was granted but the club soon closed. In November 1970 Wilkins was arrested at his farm and charged, along with his longtime helpmate Wally Birch, with conspiracy to pervert the course of justice over obtaining justices' licences. They were acquitted.

Wilkins's reign in Soho was a relatively short and certainly troubled one. An aggressive man, on one occasion in Winstons club he is said to have pointed a gun at the former world middleweight champion Terry Downes for making what he thought was too much noise. Downes simply turned and took it from him. But this was by no means the least of Wilkins's troubles.

With Birch he was then running the Eve International, Playboy Escort, Glamour International and La Femme escort agencies. Eve had a catalogue of 200 girls who were available as escorts at a fee of £14 a night upwards and the business soon had a turnover of £100,000 a year. For some time there had been rumours that the more drunken punters from the Crazy Horse had found their way to the 800 Club and, following more drink, had been rolled in the alleyways off Leicester Square. Two of the staff of the 800 were arrested. Wilkins was charged with another conspiracy to pervert, this time along with a solicitor and a detective sergeant, for giving false evidence in the case of one of the club staff. All were acquitted, as were the two staff in their separate case.

On 21 March 1972, while awaiting trial for the conspiracy, he and Birch were shot in the Beak Street offices of Eve International. Both survived, although one bullet punctured Wilkins's lung.[9] Later, his then wife, Pearl, blamed the Krays for encouraging her husband's enemies but, as the Twins were in prison at the time, either their influence must have been marginal or they were wielding considerably more power from their cells than the prison authorities would have wished. Certainly in their youth they had quarrelled with Wally Birch and had been charged with grievous bodily harm following a fight with chains outside a dance hall. On this occasion the Krays had been acquitted. But the Krays never really dabbled in commercial sex. More likely is that his attacker had been someone working in the sex industry, possibly a former employee.

Wilkins was sentenced to two years' imprisonment for his part in the conspiracy over the club licences while Birch received nine months. Released from prison, Wilkins returned to the escort-agency business. In November 1975 he was involved in accusations of the theft of a suitcase from currency swindler Ernest Brauch, a friend and acquaintance of the property tycoon Judah Binstock. There had been a clever plot, said Brauch, involving the switching of a suitcase at Heathrow airport so that he was left with an identical but empty case revolving on the baggage carousel. Wilkins and all the other defendants were acquitted. Nevertheless his empire was crumbling and he was said to owe £90,000 in tax. He complained that his former partner John Bloom had put the skids under him over their dealings in clubs.

By now, however, he had been charged with living off immoral earnings, as had his faithful friend Birch, his long-suffering wife Pearl and some of the girls. The evidence showed that the girls were making £400 a week for themselves, let alone for the agency, which had advertised in the Diplomatic Year Book, in what the trial judge called 'a new and sophisticated form of poncing'. A girl charged £40 for 'a quickie' and £100 for 'longer'. Girls who would not have sex rarely obtained bookings, for which the clients were charged between

£13 and £15. The girls then worked out their own additional fees. On 30 March 1976 Judge Charles Lawton QC sentenced Wilkins to three and a half years. Birch received 30 months while Pearl was given a conditional discharge.

After his imprisonment Wilkins turned to a sophisticated long firm fraud and, following his release from a sentence for that misdemeanour, on 17 August 1987 he was caught sunbathing on a boat, the *Danny Boy*, which unfortunately was carrying £1.5 million in cannabis. The arrest angered Scotland Yard, who had been hoping to follow the consignment to the south London gang who had ordered the drugs. Now Wilkins claimed he was an undercover agent for the Spanish police and in court named Frank Fraser as one of the bosses behind the Costa del Sol drugs racket. Wilkins, whose only drink was said to be Dom Perignon champagne, had remarried shortly before he received a 10-year sentence. In September 1990 he was in Ford Open Prison when he absconded. It had been said he was worried about a split with his new wife. He was retrieved and curiously sent to another open prison, Highpoint in East Anglia. In January 1992 he again absconded while on an unaccompanied visit to the dentist. The next month he obtained a passport in the name of John Fay. He claimed he had been given the passport by the British police to investigate a drug-trafficking ring in Spain and also to obtain evidence against John Blackburn Gittings, once a prominent defence lawyer in London, then the attorney general for Gibraltar. Now regarded as unreliable and a grass, Wilkins was badly beaten up in 2000, allegedly on the orders of the north-London-based A Team and Patrick Adams. Although it was well known that he was in Gibraltar and on the Costa del Sol, the authorities never sought to retrieve him. He died there from cancer in August 2003.[10]

Three months after the Wilkins's vice case, another escort agency bit the dust. This time his friend Peter Utal and Josephine Flynn were convicted. Utal received 18 months and she a suspended sentence for exercising control over prostitutes. There was a simple code against the names of the girls. D indicated they would have sex; V meant they would visit punters in hotels or flats. On their books of 65 girls who would act as escorts, only 14 would not have sex with the clients.

By the early 1990s the Soho sex industry had taken something of a knocking. While the entrance fee to strip clubs advertising double acts and men and women in bed was low, and the lure was that of long-legged girls in fishnet tights on the door, as was always the case the punters had little for their money. If nothing else it shows the rise in inflation. 'The price to get in may be only £2,' said Detective Chief Superintendent Roy Ram, 'but at the foot of the stairs another £8 is removed for "membership". No sooner has the punter's bottom touched the seat than he is presented with the menu – £5.50 for a glass of Coke, £8 for an alcohol-free lager.'

In charge of these operations was another Maltese, Jean Agius, heir to the Messinas and the Syndicate, described as 'short and thin with sparse hair, pale and very unhealthy looking. Over a track suit he wore a showy but moth eaten fur coat. It was all slightly sad.'[11]

According to the *Independent*, however, he was reputed to be wealthy with a Rolls-Royce Corniche in London and a Bentley in Malta. In July 1984 he and five others had been acquitted on charges of controlling prostitutes and also conspiracy to defraud credit-card companies by claiming that money paid to the Sloan Escort Agency of Great Windmill Street and the Number Ten club in Old Compton Street was for food and drink. After he left court he told reporters that the police were mounting a vendetta against him.

17

Beautiful Friendships

Until the end of the nineteenth century pornography was sold in shops in and around the Holywell Street in the Aldwych area. It was there that the pornographers flourished selling Rabelais and Zola as well as titles such as *Lady Bumtickler's Revels, The Story of a Dildoe* and the engagingly named *Raped on the Railway: A true story of a Lady who was first ravished and then flagellated on the Scotch Express.*

By the turn of the century the trade had moved to Soho, where Joseph Vachon and Peter Reuter sold books out of Little Newport Street and Shaftesbury Avenue and Oscar Wilde bought his porn, such as *Sins of the Cities of the Plain*, from Charles Hirsch in Coventry Street. In 1900 the Walpole Press, in the form of Harry Nichols and Alice Taylor, operating from Soho Square, fell foul of the authorities over the privately printed *Kalogynomia or the Law of Female Beauty*.

Peter Reuter came to grief rather by accident. To the outsider his premises seemed to be a straightforward second-hand bookshop but he kept the pornography, which he also sold by mail order, well away from the window. An ingenuous Oxford undergraduate bought a book for £5 and when he found it was not the medical treatise he had thought he took it to his tutor. Four hundred books were seized and off Reuter went to the County of London Sessions.[1]

Another figure of a slightly later period was the New Zealander the *soi-disant* Count Geoffrey Wladislaw Vaile Potocki de Montalk, born in

1889, who spent his days drinking in Soho wearing a purple or scarlet cloak made from curtain material. He claimed the Polish throne but his downfall came when in 1931 he decided to publish 100 copies of *Here Lies John Penis,* a parody of Verlaine. The printer reported the matter to the police and the Count appeared before the humourless Sir Ernest Wild at the Old Bailey. It did not endear the Count to the judge that when giving evidence he preferred to take the oath on Apollo rather than the Bible. Wild, who fancied himself as something of a poet, told the jury:

> Are you going to allow a man, just because he calls himself a poet, to deflower the English language by popularising these words? A man may not say he is a poet and be filthy, he has to obey the law just the same as ordinary citizens and the sooner the highbrows learn that, the better for the morality of our country.

The jury agreed and the Court of Criminal Appeal upheld the sentence of six months.[2]

At the end of July 1937, Thomas Swift of the Cambridge Book Shop in Charing Cross Road had his stock of *Sadism and Masochism* by Dr Wilson Streckel destroyed after a police raid. It did not help him that he argued it was a scientific book for medical students. Not if it was sold to the general public, ruled the magistrate. Down with the book went a whole library with titles such as *Sunbathing Stories* and *Spanking Stories,* which Swift did not even try to argue were educational.[3]

At first, after World War Two, porn shops were discreet with an open front section and 'serious' literature kept behind a curtain. Prices for the books, which were generally not illustrated, ranged from £20 upwards. Postcards from Paris did a good trade at 10 for £1. One of the first importers was the Italian Reno Bergano. Another early purveyor was Tom Fletcher, known as the 'Duke of Richmond', who was, because of his looks, described as 'the nearest thing to Errol Flynn'. He made his money and retired to France, where he was killed in a car crash in Aix-en-Provence.

There were also porn films to be made, hired and sold. Writing in 1954, Robert Fabian, 'Fabian of the Yard', suggested that a 16mm film running 200 feet with a title such as *The Blonde Bandit takes her*

Medicine cost in the region of £8. The hire of the film would cost between £3 and £10. Ten years later punters were taken by car to see blue films for £5 a time. The films were said to have been bought for £20-plus, and Ian Spence, who was ferrying the clients from old Compton Street to a basement in Charlotte Street, was making £100 a week.[4] The films were fairly rough and ready and fairly mild. Girls in coffee bars were recruited for nominal wages and the boys were happy to appear for the free sex. Alan Lake, Diana Dors's second husband, was an unpaid but enthusiastic participant. Thirty years later the titles and contents were much more sinister. One film had a 10-year-old boy apparently sawing off the arm of a woman.

Another filmmaker was Mick Muldoon, who operated the appropriately named Climax Films from premises in Great Windmill Street. He employed a minder and actor, the heavily tattooed Jerry Hawley, who thought he might take over the business but instead ended up dead in Epping Forest in May 1969, stabbed 89 times. Curiously, one of Hawley's last appearances on screen was as a rapist in the forest chasing after unsuspecting girls. Muldoon, his wife Sandra and a youth, Kenneth Eighteen, were all charged with his murder. They claimed it was self-defence but the 89 stab wounds counted against them. Muldoon received life imprisonment, Eighteen received three years and Sandra Muldoon was discharged.

Yet another of the earlier pornographers was John Hawkesford, who apparently spent most of his business time in public houses. He employed Ron 'The Dustman' Davey, whose nickname came because he worked in the refuse department of Hammersmith Council. Davey was also a member of a nudist club in Surrey. From little acorns do strong oak trees grow. First, he sold pictures of female members of the club, then 'doubles' and then photos of women wrestling. At first, reproduction was crude with the photos being printed on a Gestetner with up to 200 selling over a weekend in and around Brewer Street in the courts such as St Anne's and Walker's and Green's. It was from there that Ronald Eric Mason – known as John, and not to be confused with the friend of the Krays of the same name – operated.

The entry into the world of pornography of Mason, who had once been a scene shifter at the Globe Theatre and then a wine waiter at the Connaught Rooms, involved his putting up shelves in the Long Shop in Old Compton Street, where his wife worked for Tom Fletcher. Within weeks he had set up business on his own in Walkers Court with, Fletcher claimed, stock appropriated from his shop. There may have been some truth in his complaint. Mason had already served a three-month sentence for stealing curtains from the Globe Theatre and as a consequence was known as 'Carpet'.

By 1955 he was paying the police protection money but it was not wholly well spent. In 1957 he received 12 months for selling obscene literature. He is credited with repulsing a takeover attempt of his property at 4 Gerrard Street by the south-London-based Richardsons, telling them he had enough protection from the police. The cost of the rejection was a firebomb at the premises and the shooting of his dog.[5]

Generally in the middle 1950s the bookshop owners were paying the police up to £100 a week with an additional £25-plus if they were allowed to stay open until 10 pm, when trade was at its highest. By the 1970s, porn bookshops still generally had two rooms. The first had the girlie magazines but behind a screen or curtain they stocked the hard porn and videos. It was soon clear that takings were better if the hard porn was on display in the first room and this also required a payment to the police for permission.

On his release Mason expanded his business and redoubled his efforts to square the police. Shops were bought through companies and installed with managers. Within three years he was taking £750 a week. He was also paying between £300 and £400 a week to a variety of police officers. It was not something that appealed to his tidy mind but it was not until the arrival of Detective Chief Superintendent Bill Moody at West End Central in 1965 that he was able to put things on a more formal basis. After Mason's Gerrard Street shop had been bombed Moody investigated and, although he failed to find a suspect, it was the start of a beautiful friendship.

Moody also wanted his relations with other pornographers put on a more regular basis. He wanted £1,000 from each of the major players and in return they were effectively safe from a serious prosecution. The Obscene Publications Squad was an autonomous one and, although the Director of Public Prosecutions or the Metropolitan Police Solicitors' Department undertook the prosecutions, they got to see only what the senior officers wanted to show them.

Mason's relationship with Moody took things to a different level. Quite apart from paying his dues, he was encouraged to visit Holborn police station where, wearing a CID tie provided by the officer, he would inspect porn confiscated from other dealers, which he would then buy for cash. The material would be delivered to Soho by Moody's junior officers and resold to the losing dealers. By 1968 things were going so well Moody and his wife went on holiday to Mason's flat in Sitges in Spain. Over the years Mason, despite the heavy expenses of keeping the police sweet – £1,000 a month and extra when special favours were required – became a seriously rich man.[6]

Jimmy Humphreys joined the porn game with the help of Bernie Silver. By the 1960s Humphreys had nine convictions, including house and office breaking in 1958, when he received six years. Released in the autumn of 1962, he took the lease of a property in Old Compton Street and opened a club, a home from home for the criminal and the quasi-criminal, including Joey Pyle from the days of the Pen Club murder (see Chapter 13). He also met up again with an old girlfriend, June Gaynor, known as 'Rusty', once a barmaid, now a stripper, whom he married.

On the advice of Detective Sergeant Harold 'Tanky' Challenor, then operating his one-man independent protection racket in Soho, Humphreys moved his club to Macclesfield Street. Humphreys had been paying protection to Challenor as well as providing him with titbits of information of Soho life. Once in Macclesfield Street, Challenor asked for more money and Humphreys paid him over two lots of £25. He also made an official complaint, which came to nothing more than a polite rejection from the Commissioner. Challenor was cleared after a brief investigation. It was, after all, the sort of thing an officer working in the West End would have to put up with.

The Macclesfield Street Club prospered and Rusty Humphreys was a good business woman. She heard of premises in Walker's Court off Brewer Street and suggested Humphreys open another club, the Queen. It was an immediate and enormous success. For a start it was in the heart of Soho. Secondly, it had the enormous advantage of being opposite the biggest and smartest strip club in London, Raymond's Revue Bar. Customers who could not get into the Revue Bar turned to Humphreys's. Within a year, with at first his wife performing in the three shows the club ran daily, he had become relatively rich. A neighbour in the same small court was Bernie Silver, who, with a frontman, Joey Janes, as manager, ran a bookshop.

Now Humphreys moved the Queens to the corner of D'Arblay and Berwick Streets, where for a time one of the strippers was Hanora Mary Russell, who, as Norma Levy, was involved in the Lord Lambton affair, in which the Conservative minister in charge of the Royal Air Force was photographed in bed with two prostitutes. Just before Christmas 1969 he and Rusty met Commander Wally Virgo at the Criterion in Piccadilly. At the dinner Humphreys complained that Bill Moody would not give him a 'licence' to use his Rupert Street property as a bookshop. Word went down the line and within a week Silver told him arrangements had been made for him to meet Moody at another dinner in Mayfair. Over lunch the next day it was arranged that Humphreys would pay £14,000 for the 'licence' and that Silver would have a half-share in the takings. Moody apparently did not want it to look as though he was allowing newcomers into the fold. Humphreys also had to pay Moody £2,000 a month. No doubt he paid for the lunch as well.

This cosy relationship began to fall apart when in 1971 the eccentric Lord Longford, most celebrated for his long championship of the child murderess Myra Hindley, completed a self-financed investigation into pornography in Soho. The newspapers, notably the *News of the World* and the *Sunday People*, now started a crusade to expose the major players and those who were behind the front men in the shops. Up came the names of Silver, Mifsud, Humphreys and John Mason. Over the months the *Sunday People* added the names of Evan Jeffrey 'Big Jeff' Phillips, who had trained as an accountant, the Repton-educated Gerry Citron, who had originally trained for the law but again had sensibly switched professions, Barry Anderson, Thomas Hawksford, Rex Swift and an American, Charles Julian, to its roll of dishonour.[7]

In 1967, Phillips, who five years later had an estate at High Cockett near Reading as well as owning two other houses and two blocks of flats, had started his career making short 8mm black-and-white films and selling them for £15 each. These early efforts had titles such as *Like Mother Like Daughter*, the blurb for which read:

> . . . a young man who is trying to escape from the underworld, a rich and demanding widow and her precocious daughter. They are surrounded by lesbians, queers and various other unsavoury females.

The films, made in flats borrowed from friends, were sold for £100 a copy, but Phillips was soon summoned by a big dealer, who persuaded him to sell exclusively through him at £1,000 a time.

The relationship between Silver and Humphreys, never strong, was tested even further when, with Silver abroad, the handsome Humphreys had a short fling with his mistress Dominique Ferguson. These things can rarely be kept under wraps, particularly in gossip-bound Soho. Silver took umbrage and at Sandown Park races approached a senior detective with a view to having his rival fitted up. In turn Humphreys approached Commander Kenneth Drury, who, the pornbroker said, charged him £1,050 to have the matter sorted out.

Now Humphreys began to court Drury. This was the era of the sporting clubs, which promoted boxing at major London hotels, and, with Silver and Humphreys vying to provide the better table for senior CID officers at Jack Solomons's World Sporting Club at the Grosvenor House, it was generally agreed Humphreys was the winner.

That year Drury and Humphreys went to Cyprus together with their wives. The next year an article by Laurie Manifold, POLICE CHIEF AND THE PORN KING, appeared in the *Sunday People*.[8] 'A freebie,' said Humphreys. 'To try to find the escaped train robber Ronnie Biggs,' lied Drury. Manifold then followed up his article with a visit to see Deputy Assistant Commissioner Chitty, making it clear he was only commenting on what he saw as an inappropriate relationship rather than alleging corruption. Present at the interview was Wally Virgo. Writs were threatened by both Drury and Humphreys but Drury was suspended a week later and resigned before a disciplinary board could be convened. He had already published an article in the rival *News of the World* justifying his relationship with Humphreys and claiming he was a grass, something that incensed the pornographer. In turn Humphreys gave his version, telling of the wines and dinners he had bought Drury. In fact, he wrote, Drury had put on so much weight since meeting Humphreys he had bought him an exercise machine.

It was estimated that 2 million pornographic publications were sold in 1971 with at least 300,000 films available for screening.[9] As for the clubs and shops, now Humphreys had 11 and Mason 10.

The curtain began to fall on the Obscene Publications Squad, known to all as the Dirty Squad, following the attack on Peter 'Pooky' Garfath, one-time lover of Rusty Humphreys, in the Dauphin Club in Marylebone in October 1972. His seriously nasty slashing by up to six men was possibly a warning to stay away from her when she was released from Holloway after serving a short sentence. Garfath named Humphreys as one of his attackers. There is no doubt Humphreys had a bad temper. On one occasion when being pestered in the New Hogarth Club in D'Arblay Street he had picked up a man by his ear. On another occasion he nearly wrecked the club in a fight.

Meanwhile, the new Commissioner Robert Mark gave the responsibility for enforcing the Obscene Publications Act to the uniform branch, led by Ron Hay and John Hoddinott. Humphreys, who always maintained himself innocent of the assault on Garfath, fled to Amsterdam. Silver and Mifsud also left the country.

In January 1973, in a series of raids by the Serious Crime Squad, including one on Humphreys's flat in Dean Street, literally tons of pornographic material and some of Humphreys's personal diaries were seized. The next month Humphreys wrote from abroad claiming he had not attacked Garfath and that as a reprisal over the resignation of Drury he was being framed by certain detectives who frequented the Leigham Court Hotel in Streatham.[10]

In April Rusty Humphreys complained to A10, the branch that investigated police officers, that Jimmy had had corrupt relations with senior officers and that these were backed up by the entries in the seized diaries. The matter was investigated by Gilbert Kelland, head of the CID, who was told that the diaries had not yet been sent to the Assistant Commissioner because of pressure of work. The diaries contained specific details of meetings with more than 20 officers, many at expensive restaurants. In May, Rusty Humphreys gave Kelland an index book listing home and office numbers of a variety of senior detectives.[11]

In July Lionel Gallwey, a one-time employee of 'Big Jeff' Phillips, made a statement to the police and later persuaded him to make one as well. It was another case of *sauve qui peut*. The lavish-spending Phillips, who committed suicide and died almost penniless aged 33, had come unstuck when he stored porn in Walton on Thames and was raided by the local police. A man leaning on the door to tie his shoelaces had fallen through and discovered the stacks of porn. Phillips telephoned his contacts but was told that since it was out of the Met's area nothing could be done. Jailed for 18 months at the Old Bailey in January 1974, he was also fined £5,000 and ordered to forfeit £2,500 bail. He had until the end of 1975 to find the money. He had been a friend of Babs Lord of the dance troupe Pan's People and the actress Mai Britt, neither of whom knew about his business.[12]

Others to roll over included John Mason, and in April 1974 Gerald Citron's solicitor John Blackburn Gittings indicated his client would make a statement. Some 18 tons of pornography, including 45,000 magazines, had been found in a cowshed on land Citron rented in Surrey. As a reward for his efforts he was merely fined £50,000 when the Old Bailey was told he was assisting in a major corruption inquiry. Given six months to pay, he promptly left for America.[13]

It was not until December 1973 that Humphreys was arrested in Amsterdam. He was not happy with his lot, particularly when he received an eight-year sentence on 25 April 1974. It is when criminals believe themselves to have been wronged that they are at their most dangerous, and now Humphreys, in the hope of buying a reduction in his sentence, began to make a series of statements implicating no fewer than 38 detectives.

On 27 February Drury, Virgo, Moody and nine other officers were arrested. In April that year Mason was fined £25,000 for possessing obscene publications. The court was told he was helping police with their enquiries and now the jig was well and truly up. One retired detective superintendent had been a weekly attendant at Mason's offices advising on articles and generally acting as subeditor. He had been paid £10 a week until his death four years earlier, after which the job was taken over by DCI George Fenwick. Mason also claimed his monthly payments to the Squad had risen from £60 in 1953 to £1,000 by 1971.

At the first trial Humphreys would not co-operate and stayed in his cell. Even so, Fenwick, who received 10 years, and four other officers were convicted. Before the second trial of Virgo, Moody and four others, it was put about by the police investigating the Squad that Humphrey's bottle had gone and in any event he was not as important a witness as Mason. This galvanised him into action – and into the witness box. All six were convicted and Virgo received 12 years. During the trial Moody had started meeting with a prosecution witness, Ronald Davey – Ron the Dustman. As a result, the trial judge, Mr Justice Mars-Jones, ordered him to forfeit £1,000 of his £5,000 bail, but since Moody could come up with only £800, he served 28 days.

Humphreys was back sulking by the time the third trial involving Drury and two others began. Now, a journalist from the *Sunday People* was sent to see him to reassure him that there was a full inquiry taking place into the Garfath conviction. This was sufficient to persuade Humphreys to do his bit and Drury was convicted. One officer, who later resigned, was acquitted after Humphreys told the court he was one of the few officers who had never taken, nor indeed wanted, a penny from him. On 7 July 1997, Drury received eight years and the third officer in the case four. The Court of Appeal later reduced Drury's sentence to five years, saying he had not corrupted younger officers. They also quashed the conviction of Virgo, saying that the trial judge had failed to give a proper direction on the corroboration of Humphreys's evidence.[14]

At the end of August, Humphreys received his reward for services to the Crown. He was released by exercise of the Royal Prerogative. He went to Ireland and was involved in greyhounds when in 1982 he disappeared suddenly. A warrant was out for his arrest over the manufacture of amphetamines.

Humphreys fared better as a porn baron than did his right-hand man Terence John Nicholls – the man who had handed in some confidential political papers stolen from the then Prime Minister Harold Wilson to a Sunday newspaper after buying them for £2,000 on 23 January 1974.

Nicholls – who went under the name Nicky Emmett as a tribute to the hard man and club owner Jimmy Emmett, with whom he had been in prison – received 12 months for possessing obscene articles for gain.

In fact, it was Nicholls's ex-wife who brought John Stuart down in the 1984 case. She was under the impression she had bought a house in Orpington but when it turned out Stuart was only renting it to her she went to the police.

In July 1994, Humphreys and his wife were imprisoned for 12 and eight months respectively for living off immoral earnings and aiding and abetting. He was thought to have made over £100,000 in the previous 20 months. The girls had to pay £180 a day plus £30 for gas and electricity as well as to buy lingerie provided by the Humphreys. They were also required to work daily in shifts running for 12 hours. The girls had to pay an additional £50 a day for card boys – those who place cards for prostitutes' services in phone booths – and June Humphreys also acted as the maid to some of them, a service that did not come cheaply.[15]

Back in the 1970s, with the jailing of the officers and that of Bernard Silver, things began to change in the Soho porn trade. The police were no longer there to be paid for protection and some pornographers moved out of the spotlight of Soho into the relative gloom of Islington and other outposts. Others took a more robust attitude, saying, in effect, 'This is what the public wants. I am providing it. Prove it is obscene.' The golden age of making big money from porn in Soho drew to a close.

But anyone who thinks that with the arrival of the Internet the porn trade in Soho has actually come to an end should be swiftly disabused. In the year to May 2006 Westminster City Council seized more than 27,000 DVDs and videos worth nearly £600,000. It was part of a crackdown on unlicensed sex shops, which have often been a front for organised crime. During that year four unlicensed premises were closed and no new ones opened. From a total of 52 unlicensed premises in 2001 the number had declined to 14. There was, however, still a little way to go.

18

Chinatown, My Chinatown

Where the expat Chinese community goes, like Mary's lamb, Triads are sure to follow. For many years, however, there was a general disinclination to accept the existence of the Triad operation in London and the United Kingdom. In 1991 Detective Superintendent James Boocock admitted,

> I was reluctant at first to accept that any Triad groups existed in London. I was anxious that any criminal elements that existed did not have their street credibility, and in consequence their ability to intimidate, enhanced by being labelled Triads, with all the fear that such a term generates.

Not everyone had agreed. Two years earlier it had been suggested that every Chinese restaurant in London had at least one member on its staff.[1]

Until the late 1950s there was no great presence of the Chinese in Soho. As a cabaret song of the time pointed out, it was still a question of always finding a smile in Lisle Street as the prostitutes paraded there. It is an East Ender, Francis McGovern, who spoke a little Cantonese, who is generally credited with giving the Chinese gamblers their start in the area. The story is that he won the Kaleidoscope, a café on the corner of Gerrard and Wardour Streets, in a poker game and allowed the Chinese to use the basement for gambling.

For a time the new arrivals were prey to homegrown talent. On 16 May 1963 John Henry Maguire received four years at the Old Bailey. Two months earlier he had been running a six strong but short-lived protection racket demanding money from Chinese gambling dens in Gerrard Street and robbing waiters. In one case he had used a 17-year-old Irish girl to lure waiters into the back of a van.[2]

But Boocock had soon changed his mind:

> Quite distinct from these street gangs, however there exists a number of very close-knit groups whose criminal empires are networked throughout the United Kingdom and beyond. They are shrewd, ruthless individuals who have no compunction in resorting to extreme violence in order to punish, intimidate or impose their will on vulnerable Chinese businessmen.

For a time the Chinese themselves also employed English talent to protect them. One Soho doorman recalled,

> I collected money from the Chinese. I was minding cash for them. I also worked minding a man who came here to gamble Sunday to Tuesday. I thought he owned a restaurant in Belgium. Then I heard he was a massive drug baron and had been nicked in Germany and got a sentence. Later it was reduced on appeal and when he came out he was shot dead and dropped in a canal in Holland.[3]

Soon, however, Triad gangs – Wo Sing Wo; Wo On Lok, also known as the Sui Fong; 14K (formed in the 1950s and named after 14 Poh Wah Road, Kowloon); and San Yee On, each with a hard core of around 10 members – were systematically working the six streets of Chinatown (Wardour, Gerrard, Macclesfield, Lisle, Newport and the southern side of Shaftesbury Avenue) demanding protection money from restaurant owners and the gambling interests. As an indication of the amount of money involved, by 1990 14K were said to control a multimillion-pound racket of gaming and protection. In the 1990s they were joined by the Tai Huen Chai or the Big Circle.

Triad organisations require the euphemistically named 'tea money' as a tribute, and the traditional chopping, using a 14-inch beef knife, is regarded as the ultimate sanction. If, for example, the restaurant owner does not pay on the first approach a negotiator is sent in. This meeting will be formal with tea and perhaps a meal in the private room of a hotel. However before a chopping takes place a knife wrapped in a Chinese newspaper may be presented as a final warning. If the man remains intractable he may then be killed.

Apart from protection and straightforward blackmail, the Triads offer such services as loan-sharking. Also on offer are credit-card fraud, gambling, video pirating and prostitution as well as smuggled cigarettes and, in the days before the mobile telephone, phone cards. In 2003 police were seizing 20,000 cigarettes a week. Cigarettes selling at £4 or £5 a sleeve – or carton – in China were going for £45 in Newport Place.[4] In the case of the Chinese-operated brothels in Soho and the remainder of the country, the women who staff them are usually Malay or Thai girls brought into the country as secretaries or tourists who work a three-month stint before being returned home. For reasons of safety as well as loyalty, members of each Triad group will use their own brothel, so, for example, 14K members will go only to a 14K-owned brothel.

If there was any doubt that there were serious crime figures, Triads or not, in Soho's Chinese community they were swiftly dispelled in February 1976. It was then that Kay Wong, a restaurant owner from Basildon, was kicked to death in an illegal gambling club in a basement in Gerrard Street as he sat playing mahjong. He suffered 14 broken ribs as well as a ruptured spleen. The kicks were so savage that the toe of one of the attackers' shoes had split and later the police were able to trace a shop in Leeds where a new pair of shoes had been bought and were also able to retrieve the old pair.

The attackers had wanted to know the address of Wong's son, Wong Pun Hai, whom they believed to be a member of the 14K and partly responsible for the murder in December 1975 of one of their relations in Holland. That murder had been because a dealer, Li Kwok Pun, had failed to make a heroin delivery. The 14K had displayed its displeasure by putting eight bullets into the man's chest.

There had been no problems with the Amsterdam police. The body, decomposing quietly in the dunes at Schevingen, was not found until a fortnight after Kay Wong's killing. Fifteen hundred guilders (then

£300) had been left in Pun's pocket, indicating to all who could read the message that it was not a robbery gone wrong. He may also have died because of his involvement in the murder of the so-called Godfather of Amsterdam, Fookie Lang, who was believed to be an informer who had co-operated with the Royal Hong Kong Police in one of their periodic and often unsuccessful blitzes on Triad crime. Lang had been shot dead outside his own restaurant on 3 March 1975. The 14K gang had exacted their revenge and fled to London. In turn they were now the hunted. Kay Wong was unfortunately in the wrong place at the wrong time. His attackers headed north to Leeds, where they split up. Two returned to Amsterdam while one went to Wales. They were charged with murder and appeared at the Old Bailey in November 1976. Convicted of manslaughter, they received terms ranging from 5 to 14 years.

Some days after his father's death, Wong Pun Hai went to Vine Street police station with the dual purpose of claiming his father's body and clearing his own name of the death of Li Kwok. In turn he was arrested and put on trial for murder in Amsterdam with two others. All were acquitted.[5]

Until recently the Wo Sing Wo were undoubtedly seen as the most powerful of the London Triad operations, a position they established in August 1977 with a ruthless attack on their then principal opponents, Sui Fong. It came in the Kam Tong restaurant in Queensway, the most important London base of the Triads after Chinatown. Three customers were slashed with traditional swords and another, who ran into the street, was chased by a man carrying a meat cleaver. In those few seconds Wo Sing Wo established a control they have been reluctant to relinquish. Sui Fong were effectively banished to operations in West London.

That year, on 11 January 1977, with one of those splendid passages of hyperbole that judges love to use when they can see the next day's morning papers in their crystal balls, Old Bailey judge Michael Argyle had this to say to Roedean-educated Shing May Wong, when sentencing her for conspiracy to deal in drugs:

> When your tiny shadow fell on Gerrard Street, metaphorically the whole street was darkened and you and your confederates walked

> through the valley of the shadow of death. When you drove to the West End of London it was to become spreaders of crime, disease, corruption and even death.

He was rewarded. The *Daily Mail* dutifully reported, 'At that her serenity was gone, she sobbed.'[6]

Hers was a curious story. The reason she gave for becoming involved in the drug world was to avenge her father, apparently a bullion dealer who had been kicked to death in Singapore by a gang of nine youths who lured him to a deserted spot when he was carrying 100 gold bars. Six of the youths were hanged but for May Wong that was not sufficient. She told the court she believed he had been murdered on Triad orders and so decided to infiltrate the group.

She abandoned her beauty salon and boutique business and became a bar hostess in Singapore. Here she met Li Mah, the man who was to become her lover and who also received 14 years' imprisonment.

He, it was said, had fallen foul of the Triads when he owed them money and had agreed to work for them after his family was threatened. When he was sent to Britain to peddle drugs, May Wong left her husband and came with him. May Wong's third partner was Molly Yeow, a beauty consultant whom Argyle described as 'chief of staff'. In turn, she received ten years.

Their first assignment was to sell low-grade heroin and when they proved themselves they were issued with two pounds in weight of good-quality smack, then worth £92,000 on the London streets at £15 a fix.

Over the next six months she and Li Mah brought in £500,000 and in two years her gang brought in £20 million. They were promoted, replacing a restaurateur Chin Keong Yong, known as Mervyn, who had become an addict himself and had started stealing from the Triads.

It was during a search of Molly Yeow's home in Montpellier Grove, Kentish Town, that the police discovered May's address to be in St Mary's Avenue, Finchley. May was away in Singapore but she had left behind two little red books setting out in neat columns the names of retailers, stocks of heroin and the price paid for supplies. To lure her back the police gave out that Li Mah and Molly Yeow had been seriously injured in a car crash. May returned and was promptly arrested.

As with most communities, the problem the police have is in persuading victims to come to court. In 1985 when a Sheffield businessman Chan Wai Chau went to a traditional Chinese wedding in Gerrard Street all went well until seven men arrived. One walked up to Chan and kicked him, so identifying him as the target for the others. Three then stood guard while Chan was badly beaten and hit with meat cleavers. No one tried to intervene, nor indeed could anyone remember seeing anything at all. For a time it was thought Chan would die and he told the police that both he and the other men were members of the Wo Sing Wo and had been involved in a quarrel over the rights to the lucrative Hong Kong soap-opera video market.

By the time the case came up for hearing in 1987, Chan, who had had one of his legs and a thumb amputated, could remember nothing. Nor could he make any identification of his attackers. Nevertheless, they were, perhaps surprisingly, convicted and received, just as surprisingly, modest sentences. By 1991 all but one were back on the streets of their home towns. The year after Chan's case another Chinese businessman involved in the video industry was attacked with cleavers in Shaftesbury Avenue. He had earlier brought a lawsuit against a man he alleged was pirating his videos.[7] After a number of arrests were made in a very serious case in 1990, the victim left Britain and simply disappeared. No evidence was offered.

By June 1991 the situation in London had deteriorated substantially, with the intimidation of Chinese restaurant owners rising to such an extent that the chairman of London's Chinatown Association called for the government to proscribe the Triad gangs.

Then, in 1992, the police must have thought they had a major breakthrough after Lam Ying-kit was shot in a Soho restaurant. Lam had made the mistake of coming from Hong Kong to try to take over a share of control of London Triad crime from the regrouping Sui Fong. The benefits were the revenue from prostitution, loan-sharking, pirated videos and extortion. The dangers were many and the reprisals were swift. George Wai He Cheung, born in Leicester and known as Specky because of his poor eyesight, was nominated as the unlikely hit man. He had joined the Sui Fong after receiving help when he was involved unfavourably with another Triad group.

Probably he was not a good choice. A complete outsider, he spoke better English than Cantonese. Suffering from bad acne, he had a poor track record attracting women; he could not get a job and his only friend seems to have been his dog, Rambo. All he craved was love and respect, he later told the jury at the Old Bailey.

The attempted execution went horribly wrong for both Lam and Cheung. After several failed attempts on Lam, in September 1991 Cheung went up behind the man and shot him. It was a botched effort. Although seriously injured, Lam struggled with Cheung and forced him to drop the weapon. Cheung escaped to a waiting car but within a matter of hours was arrested in a roundup of known Triads. He quickly rolled over and was given a five-year sentence.

Held in a special security unit and with a £100,000 contract said to be on his head, Cheung told the court of his initiation ceremony, how he became the bodyguard of a senior Triad figure, had slashed a man with a double-bladed knife and had been involved in extortion and drug trafficking. The defence was simple. Cheung in giving evidence was trying to obtain a lighter sentence, and, out of spite following a row over a girl, he had also named one man, who had been a stuntman for the Hong Kong actor Jackie Chan. Everyone was acquitted.[8] The police still had a long way to go in making a successful infiltration of the Soho triads.

It was feared the Triad problem would get worse as 1997 approached and Hong Kong reverted to China. The Chinese Intelligence Unit based in the West End had no doubt that Triads resident in the United Kingdom were arranging for other gang members to join them here.

The authorities were correct in fearing there might be an increasing problem. The so-called Snakeheads from mainland China arrived to challenge the long established gangs. They included former soldiers from the People's Liberation Army and took up people smuggling, kidnapping and torture with enthusiasm.

There were also signs of an increasing Vietnamese criminal presence in the area. In May 1999 three Vietnamese were jailed for life following a random murder in Lisle Street. The victim had been asked,

'Do you follow anyone?' meaning to which Triad group did he belong? The trio had already stabbed a man outside the Hippodrome.[9]

Indeed the Hippodrome, which was promoting 'Monday Night is Chinese Night', fell foul of the Triads when warring gangs of the 14K and the WS (Wo Shin Wo) with up to 100 youths involved fought each other. The promotion night was dropped in 2003 but there were objections to a renewal of the licence for the premises. After a series of conditions were agreed, including the use of security cameras to record the faces of clubgoers, it was granted.[10]

Approaching 50 at the time of her arrest, the diminutive Jing Ping Chen, known as 'Sister Ping', is credited with having smuggled more than 200,000 men and women into Britain.[11] Hers was a well-oiled machine with safe houses, cars, a dozen or more on the payroll and overheads of £35,000 a month. Set against this, it is thought one senior member of her organisation earned £300,000 in two months. Her boyfriend, head of the 14K in Rotterdam, was there to provide muscle in the event of any difficulties.

Ping's empire unravelled after the deaths of 58 Chinese whose bodies were found in an airtight lorry in Dover during a heat wave in June 2000. In June 2003 she received three years in prison in Holland and was fined £8,000 but was cleared of any specific involvement in the Dover case.

Things were seen to be changing and the game becoming a great deal rougher when in April 2002 a small arsenal of guns, ammunition and fighting sticks were found in premises in Gerrard Street and Gerrard Place. The searches followed a fight between rival Triad gangs in a Soho bar the previous weekend.

Then on 3 June 2003 Chinese-born You Yi He, thought to be a member of the 14K, was shot and killed in the BRB bar in Gerrard Street. The gunman, wearing a red shirt and said to be of Chinese appearance with long hair, shot him from a distance of 10–15 feet and then simply walked out of the bar. Various scenarios were written about the murder. One was that it was part of a battle for the control of Sister Ping's human trafficking empire.[12] The second was that it was over unpaid gambling debts owed by You Yi He or, more likely, it was that he was owed money he had been illegally lending to gamblers in a casino in Leicester Square favoured by Southeast Asian groups.

His death eliminated the necessity to repay the loan.[13] One thing is clear, however: it was the first time a gun had been used successfully in a Chinese Soho killing.

It is thought that more than 70 per cent of Soho Chinese businesses still pay extortion money to the Triads.

19

Farewell, Old Compton Street

The last 20 years have seen a dramatic change in the structural and social fabric of Soho. Many of the old faces have died or retired but one who has staggered on is Oscar Owide, a one-time friend of 'Count' Kostanda and once dubbed 'Britain's biggest pimp'. Born in Whitechapel in 1931, he opened his first nightclub in Ilford before moving to the West End, where he bought into a number of properties in Swallow Street. In the 1970s he opened Chaplins as a hostess bar. Nearby was the Stork Club, which had some 40 hostesses at the bar. Talking to punters was a modest £45 and one girl told an undercover reporter:

> After the club closes we are allowed to leave with you. We do everything – lesbian sex, spanking, anything. It's a minimum of £500 for a couple of hours. And there are a few girls here who can sort out some coke so we can party all night.[1]

In 1989 Owide received 12 months with nine suspended for a VAT fraud and, although he now owned properties in Spain, on his release he was by no means ready to retire. In 1994 he acquired a lease on the once proud Windmill Theatre, where, from 1932, there had been non-stop revues and the girls posed naked except for a few strategically placed stars.[2] He turned it into a lap-dancing club and approached Peter Stringfellow to go into partnership but the deal was never struck.

In March 2000 he was banned from running a company for seven years. In 2001 he tried to establish the Stork Rooms along with Piers Adam, the club owner, and Marco Pierre White, the restaurateur, but again the deal failed. He was fined again in January 2004; this time it was £200,000 on charges under the Companies Acts.[3]

Just as the area around Times Square in New York has changed almost beyond recognition in the last ten years, much of Soho has been regenerated and become gentrified. The Wardour Street end of Old Compton Street has become an almost exclusively gay area. The Admiral Duncan, once the home from home of the French bullies, the Sabinis and the Whites has become Soho's gay flagship. This has resulted, in part, from the Tory-controlled Westminster City Council decision at the beginning of the 1980s to evict the porn barons.

In June 1977 there were only four strip clubs in Soho; the other apparent clubs were merely fronts where bookings took place before the punters were herded down the street to the shop. In the mid-sixties they had been taken by car but either economy had set in or it was to be part of their ritual humiliation. As the council began to shut down the unlicensed establishments, ten years later the sex industry was down to three clubs and two soft-porn cinemas. It was also a time when gay business became acceptable. With Soho being cleaned up, the pink pound gained in value and the dramatically hetero image of Soho began to change.[4]

When, at a porn trial in 1996, it was revealed there was £30,000 in the defendant's freezer, £19,000 in a carrier bag and £28,000 in a safe, the gangs realised what they were missing by way of profits in the area. The next year an East London family acquired a block of property as well as flats in Berwick Street. Rents went up by £250 a week. One man refused to pay and an employee was slashed around the backside.

At the end of the twentieth century the Home Office lifted its ban on hard-core porn and those who had invested in property in the area benefited enormously. Paul Raymond, who had opened Raymond's Revue Bar 40 years earlier, had for many years operated a policy of buying freeholds and was then estimated to be worth between £300 million and £600 million. Others who had moved in included David Sullivan and Ralph and David Gold of *Sunday* and *Daily Sport* and the

Ann Summers's sex chain respectively. Others, including two prominent north London families, also invested heavily.[5]

Some streets have been slow to change and for a time Green's Court was the biggest no-go area in Soho. In one week in 1998 there was a siege at a club, categorised as a juice bar, a police raid, a shooting and a stabbing.[6]

Although the importation of women for sex has continued, there has been no such tradition of importing young men for brothel work. From time to time there have been instances of male brothels in Soho but these have been relatively rare. In the late 1990s there was a sort of male brothel in Great Windmill Street disguised as a life-drawing class:

> Drinks were sold illegally and there were little rooms at the back where customers could take the models. Drinks were at an exorbitantly high price and customers who were issued with pads and a pencil bought counters to pay for the drinks and boys. At the end of the evening the boys cashed in their counters and the management kept twenty per cent. There were raids but by the time the door was opened there would be men drawing a life model.[7]

At the upper end of Berwick Street around the same time there was a gay peep show operated by an 18-year-old called Tommy on behalf of its Maltese owner. The young man propositioned one of the Soho children coming back from school, offering him a job dancing and the opportunity to go with the clients. The police were informed and the club had a visit. Later Tommy spoke to David Avery of the Soho Society, saying that he hadn't known the boy was so young, something Avery did not believe. Nevertheless, Tommy was having a hard time:

> Well it's killing me at the moment because I'm not only running the place but I'm having to do the dancing and getting fucked every night. Mr G. makes me open at 10 am and I can't close until two in the morning. I'm getting fucked about forty times a day and it's killing me. I gotta have some help, I gotta have some help.[8]

While most of the importers of women are East European and Triads, in the middle 1990s Carlos Pires, a balding pimp from Brazil, persuaded around 100 girls to come to London to work as nannies, maids, dancers and escorts and, of course, all ended in prostitution working 12-hour shifts six or seven days a week. In his case the girls were sent, often dressed only in a fur coat and shoes, to hotels. Of the little English they knew one phrase was among the first learned, 'Where is my present?'

The clients were charged a minimum of £250, of which the girls could keep £50. They were also charged up to £9,000 for their fare via Lisbon and working papers and another £350 upwards for accommodation, including electricity and television. The girls were kept effectively in bond until the debt was paid off.[9] He received three and a half years.

It had been thought that the next influx of criminals into Soho and London would be the Mafiya (or Russian Mafia), but instead came Albanians. Despite fears of a turf war, the Maltese left in a peaceful and businesslike takeover and, at the turn of the century, as much as 70 per cent of Soho vice was thought to be under the control of Albanian criminals. 'The Maltese? You see them in the betting shop having ten-pence doubles and trebles. The total bet's two pounds eighty, and they think they're going to win a million,' said the Albanian doorman of one strip club contemptuously.[10] The takeover of sex from the Maltese has been seen as a prelude to a takeover of the heroin trade from the Turkish criminals. As a first step the Albanians have become the minders of the Turkish criminals.

Some, such as Niki Adams of the English Collective of Prostitutes, believe that the women are working independently, often the only breadwinner in the family back home, and are not being exploited. Raids by the police on brothels and the council's scheme of compulsory purchase, such as one in February 2001 when 52 flats in Soho were raided and a number of illegal immigrants were detained, are seen by working girls as being disruptive rather than for their protection. Indeed, they point out that they are in much greater danger if they are once again forced onto the streets.[11]

Nevertheless, one gang of Russians imported 30 girls over a two-year period. It is thought there may be 1,000 small Russian gangs in Britain, of which there are approximately 250 in London with three to five members, often a family unit. They are frequently ethnic Russians who have been here up to ten years and have been active the whole time. One family is that of Guilnara Gadzijeva, her husband Vethsalem Muruganthan, a Sri Lankan national, and Olga Chuckanova who took over former Maltese-owned brothels at Market Mews and Stanhope Mews in Mayfair and at 52 Greek and 2 Lisle Street in Soho.

The women were collected at Victoria Station, passports were confiscated from the workers and they had to work until a bounty of £20,000 was repaid to Gadzijeva. Penalties for misconduct such as making an unauthorised telephone call cost the girls £1,000, increasing the bond debt. The girls had to pay for their food and condoms and part with £40 for luxuries such as tights. A trip to Brighton was added to the bill. The charge was £525. Profits, which were thought to run into several million pounds, were sent to accounts in New York banks.

One girl, Tatiana,[12] who had been working an 11-hour shift until 10 pm, was eventually locked up at premises in High Road, Acton, before being moved to Coopers Court in Church Road in the vicinity. She escaped by jumping from the second-floor window of Coopers Court. She hid out for a year but when Gadzijeva's bullies caught up with her and threatened her then boyfriend she went to the police.

She had been lured by an advertisement to work for a cleaning agency in England. The journey, which took ten days, involved walking across the Czech border into Germany and then on through France, Spain and Ireland, where she was put on a plane to Gatwick. She was one of the ones collected at Victoria and taken to Acton. The first day she earned £200 and was told it was not enough.

On 27 February 2004 at Harrow Crown Court, Guilnara Gadzijeva received six years and six months, Muruganthan three years and six months and Chuckanova three years.

By now, as a general rule, the police were mounting prosecutions only where there was evidence of coercion, trafficking in women and particularly in underage girls and, less commonly, boys.

By November 1999 the cost to the unwary of visiting a strip club had increased exponentially and sometimes reprisals were taken. Disgruntled customers shot the barman and manageress at the Go Go Club, Green's Court, where the charge for an orange squash was £265. Both survived. It was not all punter-fuelled revenge, however. That month the manager of the Bizarre Sex Shop had his fingers severed and posted through the shop owner's letterbox in an extortion attempt.[13]

By 2002 the Golden Club, Rupert Street, had a charge of £295 plus 25 per cent service for a hostess to sit with the client. The Kiosk Live Show in Archer Street charged a similar price.[14] Despite the council's clean-up there were now around 20 illegal clubs in a triangle of Great Windmill, Brewer and Rupert Streets and the next year in an interview in London's *Evening Standard* the 24-year-old Polish-born 'Angela' told how a hostess would entertain four or five customers a night, earning up to £1,000 a week.

The punter would be lured into the club with the promise of a massage or private striptease for £5, but, once he was through the door, prices would increase exponentially. The cost of the striptease, performed by peripatetic girls who took calls for work on their mobiles, escalated to £100 upwards, depending on what the hostess thought the man might pay. American clients were known as 'piggy banks' but the most popular were Japanese and Malaysian businessmen. Drinks might be priced at £250 and a bill of £1,000 could be run up in minutes. Those who did not have sufficient cash on them were taken to a cashpoint by the minders, often Maltese or East European. Refusal entailed a beating. Most customers preferred to pay rather than face the indignity of going to the police and giving evidence at court.[15]

The next month Camille Gordon, a hostess at the Blue Bunny club in Archer Street, was killed in a dispute over a £375 bill seemingly racked up in about ten minutes. The dissatisfied punter left the club and returned half an hour later and stabbed her in the chest as she was sitting in the doorway of the club. Despite a £20,000 reward, no one was charged.

It is still possible for an innocent bystander to be in the wrong place at the wrong time in Soho, as 43-year-old Tony Smith discovered shortly before Christmas in 1997. He was simply one in a line of those who were dealt with by north London enforcer Gilbert Wynter, who allegedly worked for the powerful Adams family, who had interests in Soho clubs. It has been alleged, but never proved, that Wynter – who walked with a limp after being hit by a police car in 1992 and who was an enforcer for the family – killed Claude Moseley, the former junior British high-jump champion. Moseley was stabbed to death with a

Samurai sword, more or less slicing him in half, over a drugs deal in 1994. Whoever was responsible, it was thought that Moseley had been lax in his accounting methods. A 22-year-old received three months for contempt when he refused to testify against Wynter. The man, who was serving a five-year sentence for armed robbery, had originally made a statement claiming he witnessed the murder, which took place in his house while he was on the run from prison. The case against Wynter was dropped.

Wynter also freelanced, running the lucrative doorman trade. In 1998 Paul 'Paddlefoot' Anthony received 18 years for shooting Tony Smith in the crowded Emporium nightclub in Kingley Street off Regent Street.[16] Two weeks before Christmas 1997 the 43-year-old father of two went to the club to join a private party. Anthony, together with another, taller, man who was never arrested, appeared and shot him three times from a range of six feet. The first two shots hit him in the chest, leaving a hole the size of a fist. He collapsed on the floor and instinctively pretended to be dead. Anthony, however, wanted to make sure, and stood over him to fire a third shot. The bullet went through Smith's cheek and out through the palate of his mouth. Amazingly, he survived. Another man was also hit. Anthony fled and, when a bouncer set off in pursuit, the second man opened fire again.

The shooting had all the hallmarks of a drug-gang execution but the police were initially baffled. Mr Smith had absolutely no criminal connections and the case was even presented in court as 'motiveless'. In fact, Wynter had ordered the hit with a figure of £300 as the price quoted and, perhaps ill-advisedly, he chose Anthony, a known drug addict. On the night of the killing Anthony was smoking crack in the Costello Park Hotel in Finsbury Park with a girlfriend.

However, the police believe that Anthony and the 'taller man' deliberately chose to shoot the wrong man when they found out – to their horror – who the real target was intended to be. They dared not shoot this formidable figure for fear of inevitable reprisal. On the other hand, they could not go back to Wynter and his employers having refused to carry out the hit. The only solution was to murder somebody else and they all but succeeded. The suggestion is that the correct target was a member of a powerful west London family who Wynter believed had the better of him in a drug deal.

Two years later there was a great deal of speculation over the death of Solly Nahome, the financial adviser for the Adams family, and the disappearance of Wynter. As is often the case, a number of conflicting theories were advanced. The most likely is that both Wynter and Solly Nahome, shot to death outside his home in Finchley, were thought to have been double-crossing their employers.[17]

There again, it was thought that Wynter might have killed Nahome and staged his own disappearance. They had, it appears, been working on a landfill project in a quarry near Oldham as well as being involved in a fraudulent share deal.[18] Ranged against this is the story that Wynter had died because of his vanity. He had been summoned to Islington, where a van was waiting for him. It was a rainy day and he was wearing an expensive suit, which he did not wish to get wet. Holding an umbrella, he backed into the van and, by not paying proper attention to detail, to his death. In support of this, it appears his aunt, who owned five properties in Jamaica, also disappeared about the same time.[19] There was also the thought that he had been killed in another contract execution ordered by the man who was the original target of the failed Anthony hit. Insiders believe Wynter became part of the foundations of the Millennium Dome.

By no means all profits in the area came from vice. By the end of the century Turkish and Kosovan gangs were running pitches of street traders selling chestnuts and hot dogs. Hot-dog sellers in Charing Cross Road were being used to launder drug profits and were also selling Class A drugs while pickpockets lurked by the stands to steal from the purchasers. That year South American gangs were reportedly back stealing luggage from West End hotels and sending it abroad for resale. The district was averaging a stabbing a week. Small-time Jamaican criminals were being flown in by Yardies to deal in drugs. Very often the penalty on arrest was merely deportation.[20]

There were new wrinkles on the old rackets and members of two prominent north London families were there to exploit them. Up to 20 men were working Leicester Square selling for £5 to £10 the free passes handed out by the big nightclubs. The racket had been going on for up to two years and was strictly controlled, with one family having the north side of the square and the other the south side.[21]

Distributing vice cards in telephone boxes became another

lucrative occupation from which the transient population could make up to £160 for an hour's work. Distributors were assembled in a café in Baker Street at breakfast time and sent off onto their clearly defined patches controlled by one of the families. In 1999 injunctions were obtained by Westminster Council against four of the most prolific distributors of vice cards, each of whom had been prosecuted five or six times.[22] It did not solve the problem. In December 2006 the Westminster City Guardians made 78 interventions in relation to prostitute cards, confiscating more than 3,200 of them. Progress was being made. In the previous July over 6,400 cards had been removed.

But life still goes on. Five years ago, Frank Fraser, who as a child crossed Waterloo Bridge to buy stale bread from a Soho bakery, visited the area in his old age:

> London's changed so much, even in recent years. I was in Old Compton Street a month or so before last Christmas and it was packed, but it wasn't packed with the faces as we know them that you used to find there. We was in an Indian restaurant up the Charing Cross Road end and we had a table in the window looking out. There was cars parked all along and black guys were sitting doing their business with drugs. It was beyond belief. Two or three cars with black guys in them. People jumped in, bought and jumped out. There wasn't a copper in sight. If the police had come up there was no way the dealers could have driven away. It's like the police have give up. If I was wanted I think that's where I'd go in future. A wanted man could stay there all night and not see a copper.[23]

A walk around Berwick Street, Great Windmill Street, Old Compton Street and the adjacent courts still shows the unlicensed drinking clubs, strip clubs, hostess bars and the girls working in one-girl flats. After expenses such as rent, advertising and possibly a maid, a girl can expect to clear £2,000 a week. Estimates are that up to 1,000 girls may work the area. A maid is necessary, not only for protection from punters but for the East European girls who cannot speak English. She is also used to keep the girl under control. The spirit of Billy Hill, who died at the age of 71, and the Messinas lives on.

In August 2007 Westminster City Council was still warning

tourists of the dangers of hostess bars with a message: '£5 to get in: £500 to get out'. There were still three clip joints operating and the council was proposing to use Bluetooth technology, sending a warning message to anyone with a compatible mobile phone or palmtop computer within 30 metres of one of the bars. Perhaps parts of Soho have not changed that much after all.

Notes

Introduction

1 Andrew Rose, *Lethal Witness*; 'The Condemned Cell', in *Thomson's Weekly News*, 8 February 1919.
2 *Times*, 28 July 1822, 8, 10 June 1839.
3 For an account of Martin's career in and out of prison see Norman Parker, *Dangerous People, Dangerous Places*, Chapter 13.

Chapter 1: Early Whores and their Pimps

1 Merlin died aged 68 in 1803. There is a portrait of him, *The Ingenious Mechanick*, in the Iveagh Bequest, Hampstead.
2 Giacomo Casanova, *In Paris and London*; J. Rives Childs, *Casanova: A New Perspective*, Chapter 11. Marie Charpillon later became the mistress of the politician John Wilkes.
3 Theresa Berkley, in *Venus School Mistress*, with an introduction by Mary Wilson; Henry Spencer Ashbee, *Index of Forbidden Books*.
4 *Times*, 15 October 1894.
5 Percy Savage, *Savage of Scotland Yard*, p. 156. It is difficult to say of what period he was writing. His comments follow a paragraph dealing with a case in 1908 but he may be referring to a later period.
6 Nat. Arch. MEPO 2 558.
7 G.R. Sims, *Watches of the Night*, pp. 49–50.
8 Quoted by Judith Summers, *Soho*, p. 156.
9 Nat. Arch. MEPO 3 197.

10 Nat. Arch. MEPO 3 197.
11 Nat. Arch. MEPO 3 197.
12 Nat. Arch. MEPO 3 184.
13 *Times*, 2 November 1912.
14 *Morning Advertiser*, 17–21 June 1913.
15 Nat. Arch. HO 45 24649.

Chapter 2: A Crooked Lawyer and his American Clients

1 For accounts of their lives see Ben MacIntyre, *The Napoleon of Crime*; Sophie Lyons, *Why Crime Does Not Pay*; May Churchill Sharpe, *Chicago May, Her Story*. There are also extensive accounts of their misdeeds in the Pinkerton Files in the Library of Congress, Washington.
2 May Churchill Sharpe, *Chicago May*, p. 132.
3 There have been any number of detailed accounts of the case, including H. Montgomery Hyde, *The Cleveland Street Scandal*, and Theo Aronson, *Prince Eddy and the Homosexual Underworld*.
4 Nat. Arch. CLAS, 12 May 1890.
5 *Times*, 21 May 1890.
6 May Churchill Sharpe, *Chicago May*, p. 116.
7 Nat. Arch. Crim. 1 108/2. See also James Morton, *Gangland*.
8 In fact, Guerin remained in England for the next 30 years, drifting into petty crime. In his later years he repeatedly appeared before magistrates up and down the country, usually on charges relating to shoplifting, pickpocketing and small hotel thefts. He died in hospital on 5 December 1940, in Bury, Lancashire where he had been sent as a war refugee. See Eddie Guerin, *The Man from Devil's Island*.
9 Nat. Arch. MEPO 2 10108.
10 *Illustrated Police News*, 29 April 1915.
11 Nat. Arch. PCom 6 28.
12 *Times*, 24 July 1913.

Chapter 3: The Great War

1 *Times*, 11 December 1914.
2 Chartres Biron, *Without Prejudice*, p. 285.
3 George Cornish, *Cornish of the 'Yard'*, p. 67.
4 Nat. Arch. HO 45 24649.
5 'The Cocaine Curse' in *Evening News*, 14 June 1916. The writer Edgar Wallace believed cocaine had first been brought over prewar by American showgirls. *John Bull*, 26 May 1922.

6 'The Cocaine Craze' in *Evening News*, 13 June 1916.
7 Nat. Arch. HO 45 1081 312966.
8 Nat. Arch. MEPO 3 2434.
9 *Daily Chronicle*, 19 July 1916.
10 Michael MacDonagh, *In London During the Great War*, pp. 85–6.
11 *Times*, 7, 9 June 1919; 'Black Pages in the Life of Captain Schiff' in *Empire News*, 15 June 1919.
12 Nat. Arch. MEPO 3 2434.

Chapter 4: Some Dope Dealers

1 *Daily Express*, 11 April 1924.
2 *Sunday Pictorial*, 1 December 1918.
3 *Times*, 13 December 1918; *News of the World*, 15 December 1918.
4 *News of the World*, 30 April 1922. Other demi-mondaines of the period who died through drugs included Audrey Harrison and Vacera Steane. In April 1926 Violet Kempton alleged that her sister had been deliberately poisoned. 'Queer disclosures in Drug Tragedy' in *Empire News*, 4 April 1926.
5 'The White Girl and the Chinaman' in *Empire News*, 30 April 1922.
6 *News of the World*, 30 April 1922.
7 *Empire News*, 29 July 1923. This was fairly typical racist reporting of the time. Girls were forever telling of their ordeals at the hands of the Celestials let alone black men. Even when the girls did not tell their stories but merely appeared in court to support their husbands and lovers, they were described in terms such as 'Vice was written plainly in their dimming eyes and whitened cheeks' in 'Menace of Darkness' in *Empire News*, 12 September 1920.
8 Nat. Arch. MEPO 3 424. The file gives details of his three drug cases. Trevor Allen, *Underworld, The Biography of Charles Brooks, Criminal.*
9 'The Dark Tempter of Chorus Girls', in *Empire News*, 22 July 1923.
10 *News of the World*, 15 October 1922; *Times*, 24 March 1923.
11 *News of the World*, 1 April 1923.
12 'Black Dope King's Spell over White Women' in *Empire News*, 15 September 1929; Val Davis, *Phenomena in Crime*, p. 90.
13 Nat. Arch. HO 45 24778.

Chapter 5: The Club Scene

1 'Return of the Bad Night Clubs' in *Empire News*, 13 September 1925; Jean Stewart, 'Secrets of a Scottish Dancing Girl' in *Thomson's Weekly News*, 6 August 1927. In the article she writes of scams run by the proprietress of

one club, Mrs J., modelled on the infamous Kate Meyrick and her daughter.
2 Netley Lucas, *London and its Criminals*, pp. 65–6.
3 Nat. Arch. HO 144/22301–83693.
4 *John Bull*, 11 July 1925.
5 *John Bull*, 5 December 1925.
6 *John Bull*, 16 October 1926.
7 A popular figure in and around Soho, the racing tipster Peter McKay, Prince Monolulu, was well known on the race tracks. Dressed in African tribal outfit with a feathered headdress, he claimed to be an Abyssinian prince but, in fact, was born in the Virgin Islands around 1870. His cry, 'I gotta horse' was said to have come about when the revivalist preacher Gipsy Smith, vying for the attention of the race crowds called, 'I got religion' and Monolulu replied, 'And I gotta horse.' An amateur dentist and, so he said, lion tamer, he was reputed to have won £35,000 on the 1935 Derby and certainly lost it all. He died in London in February 1965.
8 *Times*, 9, 10 February 1927.
9 Nat. Arch. MEPO 3 386; *John Bull*, 23 February 1923. The *Sunday Express* ran a similar story in 1931 and again the police were dismissive, suggesting the films existed solely in the imagination of a young and overambitious reporter. '2 Guinea Seats at Private Cinema Film' in *Sunday Express*, 11 January 1931.
10 Nat. Arch. MEPO 2 4492. Years later, all forgiven, Isow ran a very successful and fashionable restaurant in Brewer Street.
11 Mark Benney, *Low Company*, p. 182.
12 Robert Fabian, *London After Dark*, p.16.
13 'Freddy Ford, King of Crooks' in *Empire News*, 13 February 1927.
14 The bottle party was a device to get around the licensing laws, which caused no end of trouble to the police and operators alike. Hoey came up with the idea that a client who ordered drink during licensing hours from the wine shop could have it delivered to the table of the club he was in after hours. He retired, another rich man, after a change in the licensing laws put an end to the device.
15 Kate Meyrick, *Secrets of the 43*, p. 101.
16 *Daily Mail*, 25 January 1933.
17 *News of the World*, 28 December 1919. The handsome 26-year-old Lionel or Leon Belcher, an actor who had appeared with the celebrated Mrs Patrick Campbell in *The Thirteenth Chair*, was a drug dealer who bought from Wooldridges in Lisle Street. Belcher narrowly escaped prosecution following the death of the actress Billie Carleton, principally by cutting a deal under which he became a prosecution witness. He appeared in a number of films, the last of which was *Bonnie Mary*, in which his performance was

described by *Kinematograph & Lantern Weekly* on 12 December 1918 as displaying 'remarkable powers as an emotional'. He lived in Great Portland Street with his girlfriend Olive Richardson. After Carleton's death he dropped out of sight. See also *Times*, 8 March 1919.

18 *Empire News*, 30 April 1922; *Sunday Express*, 7 May 1922.

19 Chartres Biron, *Without Prejudice*, p. 334.

20 Nat, Arch. HO 144 17667.

21 *Daily Express*, *Daily Mail*, 16 June 1928.

22 *Daily Express*, 1 June 1928.

23 *Daily Express*, 23 June 1928.

24 Nat. Arch. HO 144 17667.

25 *Times*, 11 December 1928.

26 The police could not say they had not been warned about Goddard. As early as 1922 a young officer, Josling, who had arrested a bookmaker, had been advised by Goddard to 'leave the betting boys alone'. In return Goddard would 'see him all right'. The young officer reported the matter to his seniors, who promptly charged him with making false statements about Goddard and dismissed him from the force.

27 *Evening News*, 27 January 1930.

28 *Daily Mail*, 12 May 1932.

29 *Daily Mail*, 12 May 1932.

30 *Daily Mail*, 20 January 1933.

31 In one of the great unsolved aviation mysteries, Lowenstein vanished from his private plane flying to France. Various theories have been advanced, including that he absent-mindedly opened the rear door, that he committed suicide and that he was murdered by the pilot on the instructions of his wife. His businesses were highly leveraged and his death caused shares to plummet. For an account of his life and an examination of the theories of his death see William Norris, *The Man Who Fell From the Sky*.

32 *Times*, 14 June 1940; *Truth* (Melbourne), 30 August 1940. The point of a successful petition for the restoration of conjugal rights was that if, as was likely, the respondent did not comply there were automatic grounds for a divorce.

33 Nat. Arch. MEPO 3 629. Her other children remained in the background until, in 1943, 34-year-old Gordon Meyrick, who had written some thrillers for the West End stage, committed suicide. *Evening News*, 19 January 1933.

34 Nat. Arch. Crim. 1 735; MEPO 3 758; *Times*, 29 August, 27 October 1934; Daniel Farson, *Soho in the Fifties*, p. 93; Mark Binney, *A Rough Beast*.

35 Nat. Arch. Crim. 1 903.

Chapter 6: The Gangs Are All Here

1 Nat. Arch. MEPO 2 514.
2 Billy Hill, *Boss of Britain's Underworld*, p. 4.
3 *Ibid.*, pp. 4–5.
4 Nat. Arch. HO 45 25720.
5 There is no trace in Sabini's boxing records of the Sutton bout. It is, however, possible that the contest took place at a fairground booth. Until the 1960s, when it was banned by the British Boxing Board of Control, it was common for licensed boxers to take on all comers at booths as part of their training. I am grateful to the boxing historian Harold Alderman, who has traced as far as possible Sabini's boxing career.
6 For a full account of the battles at and away from the racecourses see James Morton, *East End Gangland*.
7 Arthur Tietjen, *Soho*, p. 48.
8 *Daily Telegraph*, 6 December 1922.
9 Nat. Arch. MEPO 3 352; MEPO 3 355. Benneworth is something of a shadowy and unsung figure who reappears over the years. On 8 August 1935 he was involved in the beating of a pickpocket, Joseph Flatman, in the Waterloo Road. Flatman had at once time been a close friend.
10 *Times*, 16 December 1925.
11 Reprinted in Peter Cheyney, *Crime Does Pay*. As if anyone thought it didn't.
12 For a full account of the McDonalds and the Elephant Boys, see Brian McDonald, *Elephant Boys*.
13 On 2 July 1926, Mullins had received four years and his friend Timmy Hayes nine at the Old Bailey after being found guilty of blackmail and assault. Mullins said he could prove the case had been got up by the Sabinis and 'some of the Yiddisher people' in order to get him and Hayes out of the way. For a full account of Mullins's life see James Morton, *East End Gangland*.
14 Another version of the cause of the fight is that John Phillips was trying to persuade Sewell to leave the Italians and join up with Mullins. Brian McDonald, *Elephant Boys*, p. 136. In 1941 Sewell gave evidence against James O'Connor, accused of the robbery-murder of a Kilburn coal merchant. Sewell said O'Connor had sold him some of the jewellery stolen. O'Connor was condemned to death but reprieved. After his release he married the barrister Nemone Lethbridge and wrote a number of plays.
15 *Times*, 24 January, 4 February 1931. In 1938 Reginsky was sued by Philip Meader, a referee whom he beat up in the dressing room after a match at the Seymour Baths. The referee never received the £150 he was awarded because Reginsky was made bankrupt for failing to pay income tax. *Times*, 3, 4 March 1938.

16 Nat. Arch. MEPO 3 910.
17 *Hackney Gazette*, 30 March, 6 April, 27 July 1938; *Times*, 30 May 1938.
18 *Times*, 18 February 1937.
19 Robert Murphy (see Bibliography) dates this as 1938 and places it in 'Foxy's' with Spot's revenge taking place in 1946. Frank Fraser places it in 1943. The correct name of the club was Fox's. Wooder, along with his brother Charles, was a member of the Islington Mob. Charles, who described himself as a boxing promoter, was an expert pickpocket. *Times*, 1 July 1935.
20 They included a sentence of one month passed at Ashford Magistrates' Court on 13 October 1924 for assault on a bookmaker at Wye races. Harry Sabini was acquitted but Bert Marsh and another long-time Sabini supporter, Thomas Mack, were also convicted. *Times*, 15 October 1924.

Chapter 7: The Roaring Twenties and Thirties

1 *John Bull*, 10 July 1926.
2 Ed Glinert, *West End Chronicles*, p. 196.
3 Nat. Arch. MEPO 3 364.
4 J. Henry, *Detective-Inspector Henry's Famous Cases*, pp. 91–2.
5 Nat. Arch. MEPO 3 1606.
6 *Times*, 3 October 1925. Curiously, Periglioni had toured on music halls as Nello in Nello and Mello, a balancing act. Before he became a wrestler, Bert Assirati, later doorman for a number of Soho clubs in the 1960s and 1970s and Rachman enforcer, was Mello.
7 Nat. Arch. MEPO 3 1622; Robert Fabian, *Fabian of the Yard*, Ch. 2. Fabian gives the name of the club as the Cochon.
8 Nat. Arch. MEPO 3 1702.
9 For the file on Sharpe, who was suspected of being involved with the protection of bookmakers, see Nat. Arch. MEPO 3 759.
10 Nat. Arch. MEPO 3 795.
11 Fred Cherrill, *Cherrill of the Yard*, Ch. XIII.
12 *Reynolds News*, 13 March 1927. In fact £1 a night was not as bad as it reads. 'From personal experience I can vouch that on a steady thirty shillings [£1.50] a week a single man lived like a fighting cock in pre-War London . . .' wrote Rayner Heppenstall, *Four Absentees*, p. 14.
13 *News of the World*, 5 August 1923.
14 *News of the World*, 25 July 1926; Nat. Arch. MEPO 3 1352.
15 See Marthe Watts, *The Men in my Life*.

Chapter 8: Violence Has Nothing to Do With It

1 'Five Guineas to be Fleeced' in *Empire News*, 5 January 1919.
2 *Reynolds News*, 29 May, 12 June 1927; *Thomson's Weekly News*, 4 June 1927.
3 Nat. Arch. MEPO 3 372. The file contains accounts of the blackmailing of other men, including one civil servant, who left the country.
4 *Times*, 23 October 1937; Nat. Arch. MEPO 3 923.
5 Nat. Arch. MEPO 3 923; there are a number of accounts of Raymond's activities including Arthur Thorp, *Calling Scotland Yard*, pp. 94–100.
6 *News of the World*, 18 March 1923.
7 *R v Levy*, *Times*, 14 July, 19 August 1926.
8 Sir Ernest Wild sentencing a blackmailer, Piggin, *The Times*, 16 March 1927.
9 *Times*, 24 May 1927; *Reynolds News*, 29 May 1927.
10 The urinal had featured in *Holton v Mead* (1913), the leading case on gay soliciting in which evidence was adduced to show that the carrying of a powder puff by a young Welsh visitor to London could be used to establish his homosexual tendencies and so show his propensities to homosexual soliciting. Matt Houlbrook, ' "The Man with the Powder Puff" in Inter-war London' in *The Historical Journal*, Vol 50 (1) (2007) pp. 146 ff.
11 William Charles Crocker, *Far from Humdrum*, p. 178.
12 For an account of Hobbs's career and the successful blackmailing of 'Mr A' Sir Hari Singh, the nephew of the Maharajah of Kashmir, to the tune of £300,000, see James Morton, *Gangland: The Lawyers*.
13 Bernard O'Donnell, 'Hobbs and O'Connor' in *Empire News*, 3 April 1925.
14 On 27 September 1927 PC Gutteridge was found shot dead on a road between Romford and Ongar. A particular feature of the case was that he had been shot through both eyes, the belief in some circles being that the pupils reflect the last thing a dying person sees and the imprint would have been of his murderer. For one of many accounts of the case, see Gordon Honeycombe, *The Murders of the Black Museum 1870–1970*.
15 *Times*, 10 March, 14 November 1905; S.T. Felstead and Lady Muir, *Sir Richard Muir*, pp. 64–72.
16 Nat. Arch. MEPO 3 441. Josephine O'Dare, 'My Life and My Loves' in *Reynolds News*, 5 June 1927 *et seq.*
17 *News of the World*, 5 February 1928; *Times*, 14 March 1935.
18 We unmask another gang' in *John Bull*, 17 October 1925; Alice Smith, 'Secret Part I Played in Famous Jewel Robberies' in *Thomson's Weekly*, 29 May 1926.
19 *Times*, 13 April 1919, 27 March 1920, 29 July 1920; 'Clara Whiteley's Romance' in *Empire News*, 26 July 1925.
20 Val Davies, *Phenomena in Crime*, pp. 139–40.

Chapter 9: Soho in World War Two

1 *Times*, 10 June 1940.
2 *Daily Express*, 8 July 1940.
3 For an account of the robbery see James Morton, *East End Gangland*. In 1936 Bert Marsh was acquitted of the murder of Massimino Monte Columbo at Wandsworth Greyhound track in a quarrel over the pitches. He was convicted of manslaughter and sentenced to 12 months' imprisonment.
4 There is a full and highly critical account of the regulation 18B process, under which the Sabinis and many others were detained, in A.W. Brian Simpson's *In the Highest Degree Odious*, Chapters 13 and 14. Nat. Arch. HO TS27/496A.
5 'Big Hubby' Distleman ran a string of brothels in the West End, as did his prematurely deceased brother. He died in the 1980s, reputedly leaving £4 million in safety deposit boxes.
6 See Arthur Thorp, *Calling Scotland Yard*, pp. 111–13.
7 The last prior to Mancini was Joseph Jones, a man with a long record of violence who along with two Australian deserters preyed on soldiers on leave in London towards the end of World War One. Under the pretext of taking a man to a gambling club or brothel he would be lured into an alley and beaten and robbed. On 8 November 1917 Gilbert Imlay was attacked on leaving a drinking club in the Waterloo area and died from his injuries. One of the Australians, Ernest Sharp, turned King's Evidence and received seven years. The other, Thomas Maguire, was sentenced to ten years. Jones was hanged at Wandsworth on 21 February 1918.
8 Michael Connor, *The Soho Don*, p. 44. Critics doubt this story and point out that Howard was much more a south London man who after the war ran the very successful Beehive Club in Brixton.
9 Nat. Arch. MEPO 2 308.
10 Lester Powell, 'The Spider's Web of VICE!' in *Sunday Pictorial*, 23 August 1942.
11 Nat. Arch. MEPO 3 2138.
12 For an account of the case see Edward Greeno, *War on the Underworld*.
13 Andrew Rose, *Lethal Witness*, pp. 258–9; Keith Simpson, *Forty Years of Murder*, pp. 94–5.
14 Frank Fraser, *Mad Frank's London*, p. 182.
15 *News of the World*, 7 July 1946. In 1975 in a statement to the police he claimed his birth date was in 1914.
16 *News of the World*, 9 March 1947. Kostanda was not recaptured until he was found at Donnah Aberg's nursing agency in Rosslyn Hill, Hampstead on 7 November 1947. Aberg received 18 months' imprisonment for harbouring

an escapee. Kostanda had been posing as Dr Canning, his middle name. *Times*, 22 January 1948.

17 Frank Fraser, *Mad Frank*, pp. 18–19.
18 Bryan had previously been convicted in the celebrated 1936 Clerkenwell bullion robbery when £2,000 of gold ingots were stolen in a snatch from a lorry. *Times*, 25 September 1936.
19 Billy Hill, *Boss of Britain's Underworld*, p. 73.
20 *Daily Express*, 21 December 1945.
21 'Thousands of Police comb the West End' in *Daily Express*, 15 December 1945; Donald Thomas, *An Underworld at War*, p. 309.
22 Marthe Watts, *The Men in My Life*, p. 194.

Chapter 10: After the War was Over, Didn't We Have Such Fun!

1 Frank Fraser, *Mad Frank*, pp. 46–7.
2 Conversation with author, 12 April 2006.
3 Harry White's version is in *Daily Herald*, 3 October 1955.
4 Billy Hill, *Boss of Britain's Underworld*, p. 7.
5 Jack Spot in *Daily Sketch*, 3 October 1955.
6 Gerald Byrne, 'Frightened men all over Britain' in *Empire News*, 2 October 1955.
7 Billy Hill, *Boss of Britain's Underworld*, p. 155.
8 Quoted in James Morton, *Gangland*, p. 301 of paperback version.
9 Conversation with author, 22 August 2007.
10 Daniel Farson, *Soho in the Fifties*, p. 68.
11 Conversation with author, 11 February 1991.
12 Michael Connor, *The Soho Don*, pp. 60–2.
13 *Daily Mail*, 17 November 1950.
14 Undated letter from Sonny Sullivan to author received in 1994.
15 Conversations with author, various dates.
16 In his book Hill calls Smithson by the name Brownson and claims that the cutting was over a girl whom Smithson fancied. Billy Hill, *Boss of Britain's Underworld*, p. 177.
17 A spinner was a type of crooked roulette wheel that was operated by a wire.
18 Billy Hill, *Boss of Britain's Underworld*, pp. 27–8.
19 *People*, 13 October 1951.
20 Quoted by Robert Murphy, *Smash and Grab*, p. 88.
21 Israel Jacob Solomons was born on 10 December 1900, fourth of seven children of Polish parents in a basement below a fish-and-chip shop in the East End. He had five fingers and a thumb on each hand and already had two teeth. He boxed professionally himself and promoted at the Devonshire

Club in the East End. By the end of the war after the Bruce Woodcock–Jack London fight he became Britain's foremost promoter.

Chapter 11: Goodbye to the Messinas

1 Nat. Arch. MEPO 3 3014; *News of the World*, 6 July 1948.
2 Marthe Watts, *The Men in My Life*, p. 207.
3 Peter Mario's has now become the Chinese restaurant, Harbour City.
4 *People*, 22 July 1955.
5 Nat. Arch. MEPO 4 3037.
6 *People*, 3 September 1950; Robert Murphy, *Smash and Grab*, p. 111.
7 *People*, 10 September 1950. In May 1950 Johnny Bendon slashed Wilfred Bryan in a Shaftesbury Avenue bar in mistake for Arthur Helliwell who wrote a column for the *People*. Bryan had explained that he was not the journalist but it did him no good and he was cut as he left the bar. The resemblance seems to have been that they both wore trilby hats. He received nine stitches in the mouth while Bendon received three years at the Old Bailey. *People*, 21 May, 25 June 1950.
8 Nat. Arch. MEPO 3 3037.
9 Letter to author, 11 September 1998.
10 *Daily Mail*, 17, 18, 19, 24 November 1955.
11 Conversation with author, 24 September 2007.
12 Conversation with author, 11 February 1991.

Chapter 12: Out, Damned Spot!

1 *Middlesex Independent*, 13 March 1953.
2 Conversation with author, 11 February 1991.
3 James Morton and Gerry Parker, *Gangland Bosses*, p. 132.
4 Charles Sidney Careless was another curious officer whose career ended in tatters after his involvement with a former Messina girl for whom he arranged a false passport application. Claiming the underworld had put out a contract of £50,000 on his head, he later sold his story to the *News of the World*.
5 *Middlesex Independent*, 13 March, 25 September 1953.
6 *Times*, 6 March 1956.
7 A suitably immodest account can be found in Billy Hill, *Boss of Britain's Underworld*, Chapter 16. For an admiring but slightly more dispassionate one, see Duncan Webb, *Line up for Crime*, Chapter 7.
8 For differing accounts of the robbery see Billy Hill, *Boss of Britain's Underworld*; James Morton and Gerry Parker, *Gangland Bosses*.

9 Conversation with author, 28 August 2007.
10 *Sunday Chronicle*, 14 August 1955.
11 *Times*, 31 August 1955.
12 Arthur Tietjen, *Soho*, p. 40.
13 Allen Andrews, 'An Empty throne in Gangland' in *Daily Herald*, 1 October 1955.
14 'Spot The Last Gangster' in *Sunday Chronicle*, 2 October 1955.
15 Sidney Williams, 'The Case of the Frightened Bookmaker' in *Daily Herald*, 8 October 1995.
16 *Daily Sketch*, 1 October 1955.
17 Duncan Webb, 'Tinpot Tyrant Jack Spot was "tried" by his own Mob' in the *People*, 25 September 1955.
18 *People*, 2 October 1955; 'The Strange Life of the "Jack Spot" Parson' in *Sunday Dispatch*, 2 October 1955.
19 Rita Comer, 'They call me a Gangster's Moll' in *Sunday Pictorial*, 11 December 1955.
20 *Daily Mail*, 8 December 1955.
21 For a full account of the Spot–Hill relationship and its breakdown see James Morton and Gerry Parker, *Gangland Bosses*.
22 Edward Hart in *True Detective*, September 1993.
23 *Daily Express*, 13, 14 March 1959.
24 Frankie Fraser, *Mad Frank*, p. 90.
25 Quoted in 'That ex-Gangster Party' in *Picture Post*, 3 December 1955.
26 It was an entirely accurate description. Anthony Corallo, for a short period of time head of the Lucchese Family, obtained his nickname 'Ducks' through ducking sentences, and finally received 100 years for his part in conducting the affairs of 'the commission of la Cosa Nostra'. He died in prison.
27 On 21 March 1980, Angelo Bruno left the Cous restaurant in Philadelphia and was shot behind the right ear in his car along with his bodyguard John Stanfa. His death has led to a 25-year power struggle between the rival clans in South Philadelphia.
28 *Times*, 20 July 1971, 24 March 1972.
29 *Daily Telegraph*, 21 November 1971. For accounts of Baker's involvement in the underworld, see Frank Fraser, *Mad Frank*, pp. 150–1.
30 Conversation with author, 23 May 1991.
31 Conversation with author, 29 July 1991.
32 *Mail on Sunday*, 22 January 1984.

Chapter 13: Postwar Clubbing

1 Victor Cooney, who had a conviction for living off immoral earnings, was convicted with her. *News of the World*, 2, 9 July 1950; *Times*, 4 July 1950. Stanley Firmin, *Men in the Shadows*, pp. 82–91.
2 Unpublished manuscript by Peta Fordham.
3 Immediately after the war the big coloured club was the Caribbean in Denman Street, opened in May 1944 and said to have 3,000 members.
4 Conversation with author, 14 March 2005.
5 Conversation with author, 11 August 2006.
6 Conversation with author, 12 July 2007.
7 Conversation with author, 1 March 2006.
8 Conversations with author, 17 January 2007.
9 *Daily Telegraph*, 30 December 2005; Sandy Fawkes, *Killing Time*, republished as *Natural Born Killer: In Love and on the Road with a Serial Killer.*
10 Marilyn Wisbey, *Gangster's Moll*, p. 211. Essex was charged with murder and convicted of manslaughter after a man died in a fight at a South London coffee stall. He was charged a second time following a fight in Leeds prison. He was again convicted of manslaughter and this time received ten years.
11 Duncan Campbell, *The Underworld*, p. 172.
12 Deirdre Fernand, 'Prisoner calls for right to father a child' in *Sunday Times*, 5 March 1989.
13 Billy Hill, *Boss of the Underworld*, pp. 149–52; Michael Connor, *The Soho Don*, pp. 59–61. The book claims that it was Billy Howard who found the premises for the club and put together a syndicate.
14 Christine Keeler, *Sex Scandals*, pp. 17 ff.
15 Conversation with author, 11 June 2002.
16 Conversation with author, 16 August 2007.
17 Nat. Arch. MEPO 26 160.
18 It is much more likely Smith had two men hold Mella down when he did the striping. George Tremlett, *Little Legs*, p. 104.
19 *Rondel v Worsley* [1929], 1 AC 191.
20 Mary Grigg, *The Challenor Case*, p. 16.
21 H. Challenor with A. Draper, *Tanky Challenor*, p. 3; A.E. James, *Report of Inquiry*. For a full account of the affair see Mary Grigg, *The Challenor Case*.
22 *Sunday Mirror*, 14, 21 June 1964.

Chapter 14: Those Were the Krays

1 John Pearson, *The Profession of Violence*, p. 87.
2 Reg Kray, *Villains We Have Known*, p. 14.

3 *Ibid.*, p. 17.

4 'Clubs: Drugs: Thugs' in *Sunday Mirror*, 21 June 1964. To everyone's surprise Rachman left an estate of just £8,000. There were suggestions that those who had held properties as his nominee simply converted their trusteeship to their own benefit. In October 1965 Nash was fined £23,760 and ordered to serve 18 months' hard labour in default in a Tokyo Court over smuggled gold. As a result he was refused re-entry to Britain. He went to live on the Costa del Crime with his new wife, a Korean opera singer, Princess Kimera. It was not a happy time. In November 1987 their daughter Melanie was snatched outside the school she attended in Mijas and an £8 million ransom was demanded. The gang was broken when a man dropped his wallet with the ransom note and a woman who found it handed it to the police. In the ensuing arrests a Frenchman was shot in the throat. Melanie was released unharmed

5 Conversation with author, 16 August 2007.

6 *Ibid.*

7 Frank Fraser, *Mad Frank and Friends*, pp. 49–50. In 1933 Leopold Harris received 14 years for arson. He had been financing a number of agents who were set up in business with highly combustible stock. Fraser's story is not as fanciful as it sounds. While he was in prison Harris was still advising insurance companies from his cell. He was released in 1940. For an account of Harris's career, see Harold Dearden, *The Fire Raisers*.

8 For a full account of the case see Leonard Read, *The Man who Nicked the Krays*, pp. 138–52.

9 Leslie Payne, *The Brotherhood*, p. 116; Nosher Powell, conversation with author, 14 October 2002.

10 *Times*, 3 August 1965.

11 Letter to author, 25 February 2003.

12 Peter Forbes, 'It's time you cleaned up your club, Mr Mills', *People*, 5 July 1964.

13 The last time I heard this from an ex-officer was in July 2007. Sometimes the officer telling the story has seen the note himself but, as in this case, very often he knows another who has seen it.

14 Tony Van den Bergh, *Who killed Freddie Mills?*, p. 68; Jack Birtley, *Freddie Mills*, p. 122. In 1948 McCorkindale brought a petition for the restitution of conjugal rights and of malicious desertion in Johannesburg. Chrissie Mills cross-petitioned. *Evening News*, 12 May 1948.

15 Bill Bavin, *The Strange Death of Freddie Mills*, p. 75.

16 Conversation with author, 24 October 2002. The story also appears in Dan Slater, 'Kray Gay-Love Secret of Freddie Mills Death' in *News of the World*, 5 April 1992. There he gives the lavatory as Chandos Place. He also says that a

Superintendent Cooper and a Sergeant Smith often talked to him about it with Cooper, saying, 'If only Mills's old woman would keep her trap shut. We're trying to protect the man's reputation but the way she's going on we'll have to divulge the lot.'

17 Dan Slater, *ibid.*; Kate Kray and Ronnie Kray, *Murder, Madness and Marriage.*
18 Ed Glinert, *West End Chronicles*, p. 207.
19 Michael Connor, *The Soho Don*, pp. 92–4. Billy Howard's former wife Jan (who was with him at the time of Mills's death) is convinced that her son is wrong and that Mills was not paying protection to him. Conversation with author.
20 Conversation with author, 1 August 2002.
21 Douglas Sutherland, *Portrait of a Decade*, p. 129.
22 *News of the World*, 19 July 1964.
23 Conversation with Bill Sheeran, former member of the British Boxing Board of Control, 13 February 2003.
24 Jack Birtley, *Freddie Mills*, pp. 175–6.
25 Bob Monkhouse, *Crying with Laughter*, p. 133.
26 Leonard Read, *Nipper Read: The Man Who Nicked The Krays*, p. 258.
27 Interview with author, 4 August 2002.
28 Tony Van den Bergh, *Who Killed Freddie Mills?*, p. 188.
29 Peter McInnes, *Freddie my Friend*, pp. 227–8. For other theories on the death of Mills and where his money went see Bill Bavin, *The Strange Death of Freddie Mills*; James Morton, *Fighters*; David Seabrook, *Jack of Jumps.*

Chapter 15: Some Murders

1 Nat. Arch. MEPO 3 2309.
2 *John Bull*, 6 November 1948.
3 Machin was shot and killed in a family dispute while out walking in Forest Gate on 23 May 1973. A man was charged with murder but received five years for manslaughter after a retrial. There is no doubt that Machin was a hard and extremely unpleasant man. He is credited with taking an axe to Jimmy Wooder at Ascot races as well as shooting the bookmaker Harry Barham, but, since his death, there has been a tendency to credit him with any unsolved crime of the period. See James Morton, *East End Gangland.* For the lives and deaths of Fennick and others see Nat. Arch. MEPO 3 3027; Robert Higgins, *In the Name of the Law*, Ch. 9; Sammy Samuels, *Among the Soho Sinners;* George Tremlett, *Little Legs, Muscleman of Soho.* For Machin and his death see James Morton, *East End Gangland.*
4 Frank Fraser, *Mad Frank's Friends*, p. 144. For accounts of the case see Paul Willetts, *North Soho 999*; Robert Fabian, *Fabian of the Yard; Murder Casebook* No. 125.

5 Frank Fraser, *Mad Frank's London*, pp. 108–109.
6 Nat. Arch. MEPO 3 3144; Murder Casebook, No. 119.
7 Bradshaw, who had been lined up to give evidence against a number of his former colleagues, was returned to prison to complete his sentence. Nicky Gerard was shot and killed as he left his daughter's birthday party on 27 June 1982. His cousin Tommy Hole was acquitted of his murder. In turn Hole and his friend Jimmy 'The Crow' Evans were shot dead in the Beckton Arms, Beckton, as they watched television on 5 December 1999. See Duncan Campbell, *The Underworld*; Gilbert Kelland, *Crime in London*; James Morton, *Gangland*.
8 Castigador, 1985, *Guardian*, 31 January 2001.

Chapter 16: Bernie Silver Meets the Maltese

1 Conversation with author, 14 October 2002; Gilbert Kelland, *Crime in London*, pp. 41–5; Robert Murphy, *Smash and Grab*.
2 *The Times*, 10 February 1956.
3 Polly Hepburn, 'Was this suicide really murder?' in *News of the World*, 16 September 1979.
4 Nipper Read, *The Man Who Nicked the Krays*, p. 163.
5 *Daily Telegraph*, 19 October 1976.
6 'Godfather Bernie is back in business' in *Sunday People*, 19 August 1979.
7 *The Sun*, 9 November 1977.
8 In the 1990s the premises of the 400/800 became a large Chinese restaurant.
9 Nat. Arch. MEPO 26 173.
10 *Private Eye*, 8 August 2003.
11 Peter Popham, 'The Maltese Legacy', in *Independent Magazine*, 2 February 1991.

Chapter 17: Beautiful Friendships

1 Cecil Bishop, *Women and Crime*, pp, 194–5.
2 Cr. App R. (1932) 182. During the war Potocki published the Katyn Manifesto, a commentary on the slaughter of Polish officers, an atrocity that the British government had been endeavouring to keep quiet. As a result he was interned. In 1949 he went to live in France, where in 1997 he died in Brignoles.
3 Nat. Arch. MEPO 3 938.
4 Peter Forbes, 'Vice Touts on Wheels' in the *People*, 12 July 1964.
5 For a highly entertaining account of these pioneers see Martin Tomkinson,

The Pornbrokers, p. 36.

6 Philip Jacobson, 'Messrs Mason & Moody, corruption a speciality' in *Sunday Times*, 15 May 1977.

7 *Sunday People*, 6 February 1972; *Sunday Mirror*, 15 May 1975.

8 *Sunday People*, 27 February 1972.

9 *Sunday People*, 6 February 1972.

10 For an account of the coterie of police and criminals at the hotel see Lilian Pizzichini, *Dead Men's Wages*.

11 For an account of his investigation and the resulting trials see Gilbert Kelland, *Crime in London*.

12 *Sunday Mirror*, 18 May 1975. One of the problems for the police is indeed keeping witnesses safe and healthy. In 1969 the 26-year-old Irish-born call girl Sonya Jordan alleged John Stuart had demanded money from her and was living off her immoral earnings, something he denied. He was committed for trial at the Old Bailey but failed to appear. She was found dead on 22 May that year after taking an overdose of barbiturates. The case against him collapsed. It was not until 1985 that he was found guilty of living off the immoral earnings of other prostitutes and sentenced to seven years as well as being fined £75,000 with £30,000 costs. *The Times*, 15 June 1985.

13 Some years later Citron was found selling Rolls-Royce cars in Los Angeles. He was deported and, back in England, promptly disappeared again. Ten years later the fine remained unpaid. Another potential witness, the mail-order pornographer Bernard Mansfield, died following a heart attack. See Gilbert Kelland, *Crime in London*, Chapter 9.

14 *The Times*, 15 August 1978.

15 *Guardian*, 2 July 1994.

Chapter 18: Chinatown, My Chinatown

1 *Police Review*, 21 June 1991; Peter Wilson and Fiona Lafferty, 'Not Sweet, Just Sour' in *Evening Standard*, 1 April 1989.

2 It was a time generally when Irish girls were being exploited by the denizens of Soho, who were enticing them to England with prospects of working as waitresses and then turning them on the streets. Stanley Jackson, *An Indiscreet Guide to Soho*, p. 117.

3 Conversation with author, 12 August 2007.

4 *West End Extra*, 7 March 2003.

5 In the late 1970s he was running a fish-and-chip shop in the Midlands. In September 1984 he was alleged to have been involved in an attempt to extort £2,000 from a Soho waiter but was again acquitted. Fenton Bresler,

The Trail of the Triads.

6 *Daily Mail*, 12 January 1977. Michael Argyle, who during the luncheon adjournment at the Old Bailey could often be found in the local betting shop, was said by the underworld to have his gambling debts paid by some members of the Flying Squad. Argyle, a curious man who had once thrown a child's bicycle into a river, came to fame as the Recorder of Birmingham. There had been a spate of thefts of money from telephone coin boxes and, contrary to the belief that the jailing of offenders does not prevent crime, almost single-handedly put a stop to the thefts by imposing substantial terms of imprisonment. He could not understand why the racing colours of his wife, 'Nigger Brown and Black Cap', might cause offence. He died in 1999.

7 David Black, *Triad Takeover*, pp. 105–7.

8 *Guardian*, 4 December 1992.

9 *The Times*, 7 May 1999.

10 *West End Extra*, 28 February 2003.

11 Jing Ping Chen should not be confused with New York's equally sinister Sister Ping.

12 Tony Thompson, 'Snakehead Empress who made millions trafficking in Misery' in *Observer*, 6 July 2003.

13 Tony Thompson, 'Triads infiltrate Soho Casino' in *Observer*, 10 April 2005.

Chapter 19: Farewell, Old Compton Street

1 Nigel Rosser 'Fall of Vice King 'in *Evening Standard*, 20 August 2002; Keith Dovkants and Nigel Rosser, 'Is it all over for Mr Soho?' in *Evening Standard*, 6 January 2004.

2 Originally a Great Windmill Street cinema, the Palais de Luxe, it opened at noon every weekday and it was so popular that soon there were half a dozen or more rivals. In the week of 7 September 1940 there was 42 shows in the West End and the next week there was only the Windmill left open. As a result it billed itself as 'We Never Closed'. At the end of one show punters would climb over the seats to get nearer to the stage for the next.

3 *Evening Standard*, 6 January 2004.

4 Haydon Bridge, 'West End Boys' in *QX*.

5 Giles Barrie, 'Sex and the kings of Soho' in *Sunday Business*, 12 November 2000.

6 *West End Extra*, 15 January 1999.

7 David Avery talking to Adrian Gatton, 27 January 1999.

8 *Ibid.*

9 Jason Bennetto, 'The Vice Invasion' in *Independent*, 11 August 1997; Michael Hoskins, 'Trafficking in Women for Sexual Exploitation:

Assessment of the Current Threat Within Central London', Metropolitan Police Service, June 1996.

10 Conversation with author, 13 July 2007.

11 Diane Taylor, 'Foreign Bodies' in *Guardian*, 20 February 2001; Ian Burrell, 'Albanian mafia takes control of Soho vice scene' in *Independent*, 18 June 2001.

12 A pseudonym. Rosa Prince, 'I came to London to be a cleaner' in the *Mirror*, 22 March 2004.

13 *West End Extra*, 5, 26 November 1999.

14 *Evening Standard*, 13 December 2002.

15 Alison Roberts, 'Soho hostess reveals all', in *Evening Standard*, 27 October 2003.

16 Paul Cheston and Justin Davenport, 'The hitman, the innocent victim and a world where life is worth £300' in *Evening Standard*, 27 November 1998.

17 John McVicar in *Punch*, 31 July 1999.

18 *Evening Standard*, 29 November 2000.

19 *Guardian*, 19 April 1999.

20 *West End Extra*, 21 May 1999, 19 November 1999, 10 December 1999; *Evening Standard*, 26 September 2000.

21 *West End Extra*, 16 April 1999.

22 *West End Extra*, 29 January 1999.

23 Frank Fraser, *Mad Frank's Britain*.

Bibliography

Allen, T., *Underworld, The Biography of Charles Brooks, Criminal*, Newnes, 1931
Anon., *The Story of Soho*, British Publishing Company, n.d.
Anon., *Venus School Mistress*, Blue Moon Books 1917 (reprinted 1987)
Aronson, T., *Prince Eddy and the Homosexual Underworld*, John Murray, 1994
Ashby, H. S., *Index of Forbidden Books*, Sphere, 1969
Barker, F., and Silvester-Carr, D., *The Black Plaque Guide to London*, Constable, 1987
Bavin, B., *The Strange Death of Freddie Mills*, Howard Baker, 1975
Benney, M., *Low Company*, Peter Davies, 1936
— *What Rough Beast?*, Peter Davies, 1939
Biron, Sir C., *Without Prejudice*, Faber and Faber, 1936
Birtley, J., *Freddie Mills, His Life and Death*, New English Library, 1977
Bishop, C., *Women and Crime*, Chatto & Windus, 1931
Black, D., *Triad Takeover*, Sidgwick & Jackson, 1991
Bleakley, H., *Hangmen of England*, Chapman & Hall, 1929
Booth, N., *ZigZag*, Portrait, 2007
Bradley, J., *Dancing Through Life*, Hollis & Carter, 1947
Bresler, F., *The Trail of the Triads*, Weidenfeld & Nicholson, 1980
Burt, L.J., *Commander Burt of Scotland Yard*, Pan Books, 1959
Campbell, D., *The Underworld*, BBC Books, 1994
Cardwell J. (ed.), *Twenty Years in Soho*, Truslove and Hanson, 1911

Casanova, G. (tr. A. Machen), *The Memoirs of Casanova, In Paris and London*, Elek Books, 1958
Challenor, H., *Tanky Challenor*, Leo Cooper, 1990
Chancellor, E.B., *The Romance of Soho*, Country Life, 1931
Cherrill, F., *Cherrill of the Yard*, Harrap, 1954
Cheyney, P., *Making Crime Pay*, Faber & Faber, 1946
Chilton, J., *Sidney Bechet*, Da Capo Press, 1996
Clayton, A., *Decadent London*, Bloomsbury, 2005
Connor, M., *The Soho Don*, Mainstream, 2002
Cornish, G., *Cornish of the Yard*, Bodley Head, 1934
Cox, B., Shirley, J., and Short, M., *The Fall of Scotland Yard*, Penguin, 1997
Crocker, W.C., *Far From Humdrum*, Hutchinson, 1967
Cullen, T., *The Prostitutes' Padre*, Bodley Head, 1976
Davis, V., *Phenomena in Crime*, John Long, n.d.
Dearden, H., *The Fire Raisers*, Cedric Chivers, 1972
De Montalk, S., *Unquiet World: The Life of Count Geoffrey Potocki de Montalk*, Victoria (NZ) University Press, 2001
de Villeneuve, J, *An Affectionate Punch*, Sidgwick & Jackson, 1986
Duncan, A., *Walking Notorious London*, New Holland, 2004
du Rose, J., *Murder was my Business*, W.H. Allen, 1971
Edmonds, M., *Inside Soho*, Robert Nicholson, 1988
Fabian, R., *London after Dark*, Naldrett Press, 1954
— *Fabian of the Yard*, Cedar Books, 1956
Farson, D., *Soho in the Fifties*, Michael Joseph, 1987
— *Never a Normal Man*, HarperCollins, 1997
— *The Gilded Gutter Life of Francis Bacon*, Century, 1993
Fawkes, S., *Killing Time*, Peter Owen, 1977; republished as *Natural Born Killer: In Love and on the Road with a Serial Killer*, 2004
Felstead, S.T., *The Underworld of London*, John Murray, 1923
Felstead, S.T., and Muir, Lady, *Sir Richard Muir*, John Lane, 1927
Firmin, S., *Men in the Shadows*, Hutchinson, 1953
Fraser, F., *Mad Frank*, Warner Books, 1995
— *Mad Frank and Friends*, Warner Books, 1999
— *Mad Frank's London*, Virgin Books, 2002
— *Mad Frank's Britain*, Virgin Books, 2005
Gay, A., *Crime and Criminals of Victorian London*, Philimore Publications, 2006

Gibson, P., *Capital Companion*, Exeter, Webb & Bowyer, 1985
Glinert, E., *West End Chronicles*, Allen Lane, 2007
Green, S., *Rachman*, Michael Joseph, 1979
Greeno, E., *War on the Underworld*, John Long, 1960
Grigg, M., *The Challenor Case*, Penguin, 1965
Guerin, E., *The Man From Devil's Island*, John Murray, 1928
Henry, J., *Detective Inspector Henry's Famous Cases*, Hutchinson, 1942
Higgins, R., *In the Name of the Law*, John Long, 1958
Hill, B., *Boss of Britain's Underworld*, Naldrett Press, 1955
Hollis, H., *Farewell Leicester Square*, Wm MacLellan (Ebryo), 1983
Horler, S., *London's Underworld*, Hutchinson 1934
Houlbrook, M., *Queer London*, University of Chicago Press, 2005
Hyde, M., *Crime has its Heroes*, Constable, 1976
— *The Cleveland Scandal*, New York, Coward, McCann, 1976
Jackson, S., *An Indiscreet Guide to Soho*, Muse Arts, 1947
Jansen, H., *Jack Spot: Man of a Thousand Cuts*, Alexander Moring, 1958
Keeler, C., and Meadley, R., *Sex Scandals*, Xanadu, 1985
Kelland, G., *Crime in London*, Bodley Head, 1986
Knight, R., and Tracey, B., *Black Knight*, Century, 1990
Kohn, M., *Dope Girls: The Birth of the British Drug Underground*, Granta, 1992
Kray, K., *Murder, Madness and Marriage*, John Blake, 1993
Kray, Reg, *Villains We Have Known*, NK Publications, 1993
Lane, B., and Gregg, W., *The New Encyclopedia of Serial Killers*, Headline, 1992
Lewis, M., *Ted 'Kid' Lewis*, Robson, 1990
Lock, J., *Marlborough Street*, Robert Hale, 1980
Lucas, N., *London and its Criminals*, Williams & Norgate, 1926
Lyons, S., *Why Crime Does Not Pay*, J.S. Ogilvie, 1913
MacDonagh, M., *In London During the Great War*, Eyre & Spottiswood, 1935
McDonald, B., *Elephant Boys*, Edinburgh, Mainstream, 2000
McInnes, P., *Freddie My Friend*, Bournemouth, Caestus Books, 1995
MacIntyre, B., *The Napoleon of Crime*, HarperCollins, 1997
Mackay C., *Through the Long Day*, W.H. Allen, 1887
Maclaren-Ross, J., *Collected Memoirs*, Black Spring Press, 2004

Meyrick, K.E., *Secrets of the 43*, John Long, 1933
Monkhouse, B., *Crying with Laughter*, Century, 1993
Monsarrat, N., *Life is a Four Letter Word*, Cassell, 1970
Morton, J., *Gangland*, Macdonald, 1992
— *East End Gangland*, Warner Books, 2000
— *Gangland: The Lawyers*, Virgin Books, 2003
— *Fighters*, Time Warner, 2005
— and Parker, G., *Gangland Bosses*, Time Warner, 2005
Moseley, S., *The Night Haunts of London*, Stanley Paul, 1920
Murphy, R., *Smash and Grab*, Faber and Faber, 1993
Norris, W., *The Man who Fell From the Sky*, Viking, 1987
Parker, N., *Dangerous People, Dangerous Places*, John Blake, 2007
Payne, G., *My Life with Noël Coward*, Applause, 1994
Payne, L., *The Brotherhood*, Michael Joseph, 1973
Pearl, C., *The Girl with the Swansdown Seat*, Frederick Muller, 1955
Pearson, J., *The Profession of Violence*, Weidenfeld & Nicholson, 1972
Pentelow, M., and Rowe, M., *Characters of Fitzrovia*, Chatto & Windus, 2001
Pizzichini, L., *Dead Men's Wages*, Picador, 2002
Progl, Z., *Woman of the Underworld*, Four Square, 1964
Purcell, E.D., *Forty Years at the Criminal Bar*, T. Fisher Unwin, 1916
Raymond, D., *The Hidden Files*, Little, Brown, 1992
Read, L., *Nipper: The Man who Nicked the Krays*, Time Warner, 2002
Rives Childs, J., *Casanova*, George Allen & Unwin, 1961
— *Casanova: A New Perspective*, Constable, 1989
Roberts, N., *Whores in History*, HarperCollins, 1992
Robey, E., *The Jester and the Court*, William Kimber, 1976
Rose, A., *Lethal Witness*, Sutton Publishing, 2007
Samuels, S., with David, L., *Among the Soho Sinners*, Robert Hale, 1970
Savage, P., *Savage of Scotland Yard*, Hutchinson, n.d.
Seabrook, D., *Jack of Jumps*, Granta Books, 2007
Sharpe, M.C., *Chicago May: Her Story*, Macaulay, 1928
Simpson. A.W.B., *In the Highest Degree Odious*, Clarendon Press, 1992
Simpson, K., *Forty Years of Murder*, Granada, 1980
Sims, G.R., *Watches of the Night*, Greening, 1907
Summers, J., *Soho: A History of London's Colourful Neighbourhood*, Bloomsbury, 1989

— *Empress of Pleasure*, Penguin Books, 2004
Sutherland, D., *Portrait of a Decade: London Life 1945–1955*, Harrap, 1988
Thomas, D., *The Victorian Underworld*, John Murray, 1998
— *An Underworld at War*, John Murray, 2003
Thorp, A., *Calling Scotland Yard*, Allan Wingate, 1954
Tietjen, A., *Soho*, Allan Wingate, 1956
Tomkinson, M., *The Pawnbrokers*, Virgin Books, 1982
Tremlett, G., *Little Legs: Muscleman of Soho*, Unwin Hyman, 1989
Van den Bergh, T., *Who Killed Freddie Mills?*, Constable, 1991
Ward, H., and Gray, T., *Buller*, Hodder & Stoughton, 1974
Watts, M., *The Men in My Life*, Christopher Johnson, 1960
Webb, D., *Deadline for Crime*, Frederick Muller, 1955
— *Line-up for Crime*, Frederick Muller, 1956
Wickstead, B., *Gangbuster*, Macdonald, 1985
Willets, P., *Fear and Loathing in Fitzrovia*, Dewi Lewis, 2003
— *North Soho 999*, Dewi Lewis, 2007
Willis, W.N., *White Slaves in a Piccadilly Flat*, Camden Publishing, 1949
Wisbey, M., *Gangster's Moll*, Warner Books, 2002

Selected articles, reports etc.

Andrews, Allen, 'An Empty throne in Gangland', *Daily Herald* (1 October 1955)
Byrne, Gerald, 'Frightened men all over Britain', *Empire News* (2 October 1955)
'Cocaine in cigarettes – How Thousands of Men are "Doped" and Robbed', *Daily Express* (18 December 1918)
Denning, Lord, *John Profumo and Christine Keeler /1963*, HMSO (1963)
Davenport-Hines, Richard, 'Meyrick, Kate Evelyn', *Oxford Dictionary of National Biography*, Oxford University Press (2004)
Dovkants, Keith, and Rosser, Nigel, 'Is it all over for Mr Soho?', *Evening Standard* (6 January 2004)
'Doped Cigarettes – Used as an Aid to Rob our Soldier-Heroes', *News of the World* (22 December 1918)
Hepburn, Polly, 'Was this suicide really murder?', *News of the World* (16 September 1979)

Hoskins, Michael, 'Trafficking in Women for Sexual Exploitation: Assessment of the Current Threat Within Central London', Metropolitan Police Service (June 1996)

Houlbrook, Matt, ' "The Man with the Powder Puff" in Inter-war London', *Historical Journal*, Vol. 50 (1) (2007)

Jacobson, Philip, 'Messrs Mason & Moody, corruption a speciality', *Sunday Times* (15 May 1977)

James, A.E., *Report of Inquiry into the circumstances in which it was possible for Detective Sergeant Harold Challenor of the Metropolitan Police to continue on duty*, HMSO (1965)

May, Tiggy, Harcopos, Alex, and Turnbull, Paul J., *For Love or Money: Pimps and Management of Sex Work*, Home Office (2000)

Selling Sex in the City, South Bank University Faculty of Humanities and Social Study (June 2001)

O'Dare, Josephine, 'My Life and my Loves', *Reynolds News* (5 June 1927 etc.)

Powell, Lester, 'The Spider's Web of VICE!', *Sunday Pictorial* (23 August 1942)

Prince Rosa, 'I came to London to be a cleaner', *Mirror* (22 March 2004)

Rae, Norman, 'Death waited upstairs for a crook on the run', *News of the World* (9 January 1955)

Roberts, Alison, 'Soho hostess reveals all', *Evening Standard* (27 October 2003)

Rosser, Nigel, 'Fall of Vice King', *Evening Standard* (20 August 2002)

Shore, Heather, 'Kings, Gangsters and Greenhorns: Kate Meyrick and the Gendering of Clubland in inter-war London', unpublished manuscript, University of Portsmouth

Forbes, Peter, 'It's time you cleaned up your club, Mr Mills', *People* (5 July 1964)

Stewart, Jean, 'Secrets of a Scottish Dancing Girl', *Thomson's Weekly News* (6 August 1927)

Smith, Alice, 'Secret Part I played in Famous Jewel Robberies', *Thomson's Weekly* (29 May 1926)

Thompson, Tony, 'Snakehead Empress who made millions trafficking in misery', *Observer* (6 July 2003)

'Triads infiltrate Soho Casino', *Observer* (10 April 2005)

Webb, Duncan, 'Tinpot Tyrant Jack Spot was "tried" by his own Mob', *People* (25 September 1955)

Wilson, Peter, and Lafferty, Fiona, 'Not Sweet, Just Sour', *Evening Standard* (1 April 1989)

Picture Credits

P. 2 All pictures courtesy of Mike Hallinan; P. 3 *(top left)* © popperfoto.com *(top right)* © Topham/PA Archive/PA Photos; *(bottom left)* © Barratts/PA Photos; *(bottom right)* PA Photos/PA Archive; P. 4 *(top left)* © popperfoto.com *(top right)* © TopFoto *(middle)* © popperfoto.com *(bottom)* © AP/TopFoto; P. 5 © *(top)* Getty Images; P. 6 *(top)* © PA/PA Archive/PA Photos; P. 7 *(top left)* © popperfoto.com *(top right)* © Topham Picturepoint *(bottom left)* TopFoto *(bottom right)* © Hulton-Deutsch; P. 8 *(top right)* © Topham/Picturepoint *(bottom)* © Hulton-Deutsch Collection/Corbis

Index